W9-BLW-147

Haunted Moon

An Otherworld Novel

YASMINE GALENORN

JOVE BOOKS, NEW YORK

THE BERKLEY PUBLISHING GROUP
Published by the Penguin Group
Penguin Group (USA) Inc.
375 Hudson Street, New York, New York 10014, USA
Penguin Group (Canada), 90 Eglinton Avenue East, Suite 700, Toronto, Ontario M4P 2Y3, Canada
(a division of Pearson Penguin Canada Inc.) • Penguin Books Ltd, 80 Strand, London WC2R 0RL,
England • Penguin Ireland, 25 St Stephen's Green, Dublin 2, Ireland (a division of Penguin
Books Ltd) • Penguin Group (Australia), 707 Collins Street, Melbourne, Victoria 3008, Australia
(a division of Pearson Australia Group Pty Ltd) • Penguin Books India Pvt Ltd, 11 Community
Centre, Panchsheel Park, New Delhi–110 017, India • Penguin Group (NZ), 67 Apollo Drive,
Rosedale, Auckland 0632, New Zealand (a division of Pearson New Zealand Ltd) • Penguin Books,
Rosebank Office Park, 181 Jan Smuts Avenue, Parktown North 2193, South Africa • Penguin China,
B7 Jiaming Center, 27 East Third Ring Road North, Chaoyang District, Beijing 100020, China

Penguin Books Ltd., Registered Offices: 80 Strand, London WC2R 0RL, England

This is a work of fiction. Names, characters, places, and incidents either are the product of the author's
imagination or are used fictitiously, and any resemblance to actual persons, living or dead, business
establishments, events, or locales is entirely coincidental. The publisher does not have control over
and does not have any responsibility for author or third-party websites or their content.

HAUNTED MOON

A Jove Book / published by arrangement with the author

PUBLISHING HISTORY
Jove mass-market edition / February 2013

Copyright © 2013 by Yasmine Galenorn.
Excerpt from *Night Vision* copyright © 2013 by Yasmine Galenorn.
Cover design by Rita Frangie.
Cover art by Tony Mauro.
Map by Andrew Marshall, copyright © 2012 by Yasmine Galenorn.

ISBN: 978-0-515-15281-4

JOVE®
Jove Books are published by The Berkley Publishing Group,
a division of Penguin Group (USA) Inc.,
375 Hudson Street, New York, New York 10014.
JOVE® is a registered trademark of Penguin Group (USA) Inc.
The "J" design is a trademark of Penguin Group (USA) Inc.

PRINTED IN THE UNITED STATES OF AMERICA

10 9 8 7 6 5 4 3 2 1

ALWAYS LEARNING   **PEARSON**

Dedicated to the memory of Ray Bradbury,
who died while I was writing this book.

Mr. Bradbury,
you were my favorite author, my greatest literary influence,
and a light went out in the world when you left it.

ACKNOWLEDGMENTS

Thank you to all my usual suspects: Samwise—my number one fan and the best husband I could hope for; my agent, Meredith Bernstein; my editor, Kate Seaver; Tony Mauro, my cover artist; my assistant, Andria Holley, and wiki assistant, Scotty Talley; Jenn Price, my moderator. To my furry "Galenorn Gurlz." Most reverent devotion to Ukko, Rauni, Mielikki, and Tapio, my spiritual guardians.

As always, the biggest thank-you goes to my readers. Your support helps keep the series going. You can find me on the Internet at Galenorn En/Visions: www.galenorn.com. For links to social networking sites where you can find me, see my website. You can also find an Otherworld Wikipedia on my website.

If you write to me via snail mail (see my website for the address or write via my publisher), please enclose a self-addressed stamped envelope with your letter if you would like a reply. Lots of promo goodies are available. See my site for info.

The Painted Panther
Yasmine Galenorn
July 2012

Faerie is a perilous land, and in it are pitfalls for the unwary and dungeons for the overbold.

J.R.R. TOLKIEN, *ON FAIRY STORIES*

Goddess, is no myth inane,
You will say of those who walk
In the woods of Westermain.

GEORGE MEREDITH, *THE WOODS OF WESTERMAIN*

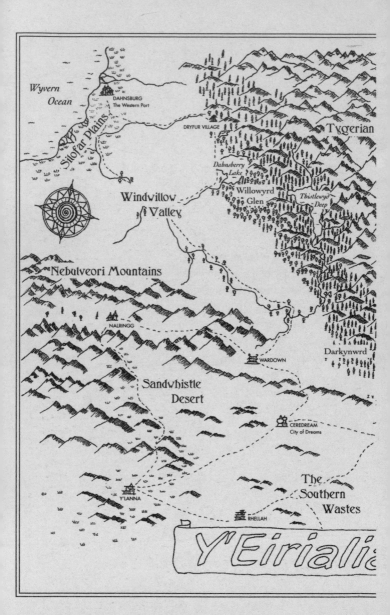

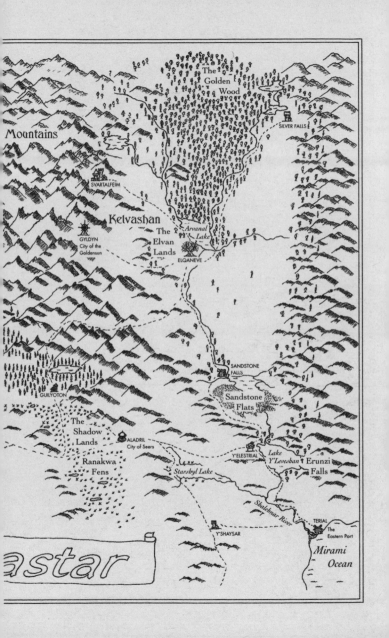

Chapter 1

❧❧❧

"Inhale. Slowly . . . That's it. Now . . . exhale in one, two, three." Morio's voice was low in my ear as he knelt behind me, leaning down, his hands on my shoulders, magic tingling through his fingers, into my body.

I sat cross-legged on the floor, wearing a filmy black dress, my arms extended to the sides. In my left hand, I balanced an orb of obsidian. In my right, I grasped a yew wand, carved with intricate symbols etched in silver.

"Focus on the spirit. Keep your gaze on it." Again, his soft whispers caressed my ear. We were in tune, my youkai and I, as we sat in a flaming Circle under the night sky, in the hidden shadows of a long-forgotten graveyard. The borders of the Circle were ablaze with magical fire—the purple crackle of death magic—and I was doing my best to control it, struggling to multitask the spells we were working on.

We were in a small cemetery, one shrouded with disuse and neglect. The smell of earth hung pungent in my nose, and a scuttling of bugs across the ground made me shiver, but I forced myself to ignore them, doing my best to forget they were there as I stared at the spirit hovering in front of me.

The ghost was luminous in the night, rising above us, spiraling up from the skull that rested on the ground by my feet. I had no idea who the spirit had been, or why it was here. My task was to break through its barriers and destroy it, setting it free to rest, or—if it would not go willingly—sending it into oblivion.

I gathered the rush of energy Morio was feeding me into a focused beam. The rumbling power twisted through my body, a radiant heat, a purple flame. The tingles sparked, crackling through muscle and sinew as the power grew, buoying me up until I spiraled out of my body.

Looming large before the spirit, I struggled to keep control—both of the flames forming the Circle and of those bucking through me like a horse unwilling to take a master. Morio was forcing the power through me faster than I'd ever been able to take it before, and I struggled to keep atop of it. I lowered my head, searching for the key. And there . . . hiding behind a wayward spark, *there it was*.

All magic—all energy—had a key, a signature. *Control the key, control the force.*

Reaching out, I latched onto the signature and the flames flared up. At first they resisted my control, but I wouldn't let go. After a struggle, they surrendered and quit fighting me. As they gave in to my will, I shaped them, smoothing them into a sheet of fire, a backwash of flame, ready to surge forth at my command.

The spirit seemed to sense my intent and shrank back, wailing.

I raised my palms to it. "Go, go now or I will destroy you."

The spirit refused to move but instead shrieked and aimed for me, its lifeless sockets staring intently.

I tried once more. "I command you to depart this realm."

Again, nothing, but it was obvious the ghost was planning something nasty. I sucked in a deep breath and flipped my hands up, my palms facing forward.

"Death took you once; let death take you again." And then, I summoned the release word. *"Atataq!"*

The sound of the fire roared through me as it poured from my hands, soaring with the pulse of my blood. The flame carried me with it, rising like a purple phoenix to blot out the moon. I swung astride its back, riding it like I might ride a lover, the rush of orgasm building within me as the flame dove and turned, aiming for the spirit. As the fiery arrow barreled down to knife through the ghost, exploding the spirit into vapor, I came hard and sharp, letting out a sharp, short scream.

The spirit vanished as I struggled to shake out of my sudden passion-filled daze.

Still astride the phoenix, I realized the magical bird was beginning to turn its head. *Oh shit.* The gleam in its eye told me I was its next target.

Slightly rattled, I heard Morio shout, "Control it! Take control or the fire will go after you next!"

Quickly, I brought my attention back to the key, struggling to regain my hold on it. The phoenix paused.

"Bring it back now. Damn it, do what I say! Roll the power back *now*—there . . . you've almost got it." Morio's voice was abrupt, as a good teacher's should be.

I shook my head to clear my thoughts and reined in the power, reeling it back. I worked it, coaxing it, stroking it. As it began to submit, I demanded that it retreat. Another brief struggle and the fire finally obeyed, receding like a tide, rolling back to the Elemental plane from which it had come. The phoenix turned to face the silent night and then vanished in a bright flash.

I felt as if a fine dust of ash coated every nerve. I was vibrating, polished and cleansed from the inside out. As the wave of fiery death magic reached my crown chakra, I let go, and Morio took over, siphoning it back out of me into the sky, releasing it to the night, back to the haunted moon overhead.

Exhausted, I collapsed. Morio leaned over me, his eyes gleaming. His long black hair hung straight, and I longed to run my hands through it, to feel the silken strands between my fingers. I wanted to pull my Japanese lover, my husband, between my legs, and quench the fire that had built within *me*.

"Do you know how much I want you?" he whispered.

"Do you know how hungry for you I am? Our magic makes me want to fuck you senseless."

"Bring it on. I'll take whatever you have to give me, my love." I was ready to take him right there inside the Circle of flames. But before we could act, my cell phone rang. It was in my purse, which was sitting on the grass, outside of the magical circle. The ring tone played out "Demon Days" by the Gorillaz, which meant it was Chase. Which meant it was probably important.

"Fuck." I pushed myself up to a sitting position. "Get that, would you?"

Morio opened the Circle, stepping over the flames as he did so. He grabbed my phone out of the purse and answered. "Hello? . . . Morio." After a moment, he motioned to me, his expression shifting from lusty to solemn. "Here, you need to take this. I'll start gathering our things."

"Bad?" I didn't want to hear. I really didn't.

He nodded. "Bad." And with that, we were out of the Circle, back to a reality I didn't want to face. But the fact was, reality was growing more and more deadly with each week that passed.

"Camille?" Chase sounded out of breath. The detective was physically fit, so the fact that he was panting worried me.

"What's going down? Where? And how bad?" I didn't spare any words. Phone calls like this were always terse.

"Robbery at one of the graveyards. And we have a handful of bone-walkers running around."

"Robbery? What the fuck are they stealing—and are the bone-walkers the ones doing the looting?"

Chase growled. "*No.* There's more to it—I can't explain now . . ." He paused and sucked in a lungful of air with a grunt. *So* not a good sign. Chase was in great shape for an FBH—full-blooded human. Or rather, an FBH with a tiny hint of elf in his long-distance background.

"Dude, are you okay? Talk to me." Collateral damage in this demonic war had hit us hard, and all too often, as of late. I found myself panicking over late-night calls.

"I'd be fine if I weren't hiding out from a fucking bone-walker who wants to break my neck. Or anything else it can latch onto. I'm playing hide-and-seek with it in Wyvers Point Cemetery, and unfortunately, I'm not the one doing the chasing."

"Let me guess . . . the cemetery is in the Greenbelt Park District?" If I never heard of that area of Seattle again, it would still be too soon.

"Yeah . . . Fourth and Hyland Streets. Get over here as soon as you can. And can you call the others?" He was whispering now. "I'm worried, Camille. Two of my men are lost somewhere in the graveyard, but I don't know where. We're all on the run. Tell you more after you get here and help me get the fuck out of this situation. And Camille . . . I'm hurt. I can't run."

"How bad?" I held my breath, waiting.

"Well, I'm not going to die from the injury, but I might from the bone-walkers because I can't run away from them."

"We'll be there as soon as we can. Just hold on, dude."

I punched the End Call button and turned to Morio, who had been gathering our things. "We've got another grave-yard to pay a call on and we'd better hurry or Chase is going to be on the dinner menu. Bone-walkers on the loose, two of his men are missing, and he's hurt."

As Morio tossed our ritual gear into the back of my Lexus, I called home. We were closer to Wyvers than my sisters, so we'd get there ahead of time. But we'd also expended a lot of energy tonight on our magical practice, and we couldn't take on a full force of undead miscreants without help.

I quickly filled Delilah in on what was going down. "Get over there, now. Chase is hurt, two cops are missing. Gear up for a bone-walker fight. And who knows what the hell else."

"Menolly's at the Wayfarer. We can call her if we need her once we're there. I'll bring Smoky, Shade, and Vanzir. We're booking it out of here now." Delilah punched off and I texted her the location.

Sliding into the driver's seat, I clicked my seat belt shut. While I waited for Morio, I grabbed a candy bar out of the glove compartment and scarfed it down. I desperately needed the energy, so I polished off the chocolate caramel and then went for a protein bar. By then, Morio was swinging into the car and I took off as he slammed the door.

"We couldn't expect the quiet to last for long." Morio pulled his hair back into a ponytail, then yanked off his short kimono. Beneath it, he was wearing a pair of tight black jeans that curved around his butt in an oh-so-flattering way. As he fished a deep blue turtleneck out of a backpack, I managed a glance at his glistening chest.

Morio was buff—not a muscle man, but definitely buff—and I got wet just looking at him. One of my three husbands, he was Japanese, a youkai-kitsune—or loosely translated, a fox-demon, though he wasn't the kind of demon that we were fighting. Together with Smoky, my dragon, and Trillian, my alpha lover and Svartan—the dark and charming Fae—we made quite the quartet.

We'd been in a refreshing lull over the past five weeks, since Menolly and Nerissa got married, and we'd savored every minute. We'd used the time to bone up on our fighting techniques and magical skills, to stockpile weapons, and to hunt down as much information as we could on Gulakah, the Lord of Ghosts. Unfortunately, so far, we'd accumulated a whole lot of nothing in that regard.

We'd also done our best to keep tabs on what was going down with the impending war in Otherworld. When I thought about it, we actually *hadn't* had any downtime, per se. Just a short break from the continual fighting we'd been embroiled in for months now. But even a few days here and there meant the difference between being run ragged and regaining our equilibrium.

Morio finished changing into the turtleneck and fastened his seat belt as I took a turn a little too sharply.

"Try to keep at least two wheels on the road, babe." His eyes twinkled as he dove into our hoard of candy and protein bars. "We're probably going to arrive about ten minutes before the others. So let's take stock of what we've got for a fight, other than magic."

"I have a short dagger. I've started carrying it with me wherever I go. It's strapped to my thigh. But that won't be much help against bone-walkers." I felt better carrying a weapon now, even if it was more of a pacifier than anything that would cause some real damage. "I left the Black Unicorn horn at home, of course."

About a year ago, I'd received a gift—the horn of the Black Unicorn—along with a cloak made from his hide.

The Black Unicorn was the father of the Dahns unicorns, and like the phoenix, he reincarnated every few thousand years, shedding his old body. Eight or nine horns and hides were rumored to exist, and I possessed one set. I was careful to keep that information under wraps, because any number of sorcerers and havoc-mongers would have torn me limb from limb to get them. The artifacts were incredibly powerful, so I was cautious where I took them.

"Yeah, I don't think you want to expend the power of it on walking plant food." Morio sorted through his pack again. "I can take my demonic form, of course. They can't do much against me then, unless there are a lot of them ganging up on me all at once." He held up a curved dagger that looked wickedly sharp. "How are you on magical energy? Did our practice wear you out?"

I gauged my energy level. I was tired; we'd been practicing a spell to destroy or dispel spirits. Ghostbusting, if you will, through magical means. I'd never before successfully cast it, and while I still felt amped up from the energy that had poured through my veins, I couldn't guarantee my accuracy if I had to actually start slinging around energy bolts.

"I can manage a few things, magically, I think, but seriously—don't count on my spells. I think 'backfire' could easily be my go-to game tonight."

He nodded. "Right."

"Speaking of the night, why the fuck do these things always happen when we're ready for bed? Why not in the morning, when we've gotten some sleep, had breakfast, and are good to go?" I swung the car left, onto Wyvers Avenue

NW. The Greenbelt Park District wasn't all that far from the Belles-Faire area, where we lived. Wyvers Point Cemetery was on the border between the two.

"I think ghosts prefer the night. Just like vampires. Or maybe there's just so much activity during the day that they don't peek out of the woodwork as much. Whatever the case, I suggest we concentrate on physical attack tonight. And you be careful. With only a dagger, you're set up as the perfect target." He picked up my bag. "Are you sure you didn't swipe anything good from Roz last time you were poking around in his duster? No firebombs or anything?"

I grinned. Morio knew me, all right. Rozurial, an incubus who lived on our land and who had become enmeshed with our family, wore a long duster à la Neo from *The Matrix*. His coat was filled with everything from wooden stakes to magical bombs to a mini-Uzi. Although, now that I thought about it, last time I looked, the Uzi had been replaced by a magical stun gun we'd managed to liberate from a sorcerer's bar. After we got through with it, the bar had bit the dust. *Literally*. There was nothing left of the building except a pile of toothpicks.

"Nah. I tried to snag some stuff from him yesterday, but he caught me with my hands in the cookie jar and threatened to tell Smoky I was prowling through his pockets. You know what Smoky would think of that."

Smoky was possessive and, being dragon, he didn't always get the joke. He shared me with Morio and Trillian because that was the way things were, and by now he had grown comfortable with the situation. But that was the limit of his generosity, and he'd already thrashed Roz once for a misplaced hand on my butt.

Morio snorted. "He's always and forever going to be a big galoot. You know it, and I know it, and we just have to love him for who he is." He laughed, then sobered. "So, we have two daggers and my bad-assed demon self. Sounds about right. I'll engage the creeps while you rescue Chase."

"Sounds good to me. Just don't send me off on a track-and-field exercise. Not in these shoes." I had worn a pair of my granny boots. They were stilettos, definitely not made for running, but I'd had plenty of practice. On the concrete, I could run in them, but I hadn't expected to be out in the field tonight.

As we came to Atlas Drive, a small side street, I veered onto the darkened road and slowed down. We were no longer fully in the suburbs. Here, the foliage was a little more tangled, the surroundings a little more rural. It was harder to see because the night was dark, the streetlights were few and far between, and the moon had gone into hiding behind a patch of clouds. In the Seattle area, we only had sixty-some days a year that were totally cloud-free, and today—this evening— wasn't one of them.

As I slowed the car, edging along the street, the tangle of branches blossoming out overhead reminded me of our forests back in Otherworld. We were nearing Beltane, the festival celebrating sexuality, fertility, the gods, and the rut of the King Stag, and the plant world was responding to the energy.

The leaves burgeoned out on the tree boughs as the flowers and vegetables sprang to life, all urged on by the growing length of the days and the warming of the soil. My core felt the push as the roots buried themselves deep in the ground, and my body wanted to stretch as the leaves reached for the sun. The ferns were lush, and the grass green, and the days were hovering mostly in the low sixties.

We arrived at Wyvers Point Cemetery, and I eased into the parking lot, into one of the slots near the wrought-iron gates. Why did cemeteries always come outfitted with cast and wrought iron? It burned all of us who had any significant amount of Fae blood in our veins. Steel, we could handle—its makeup was different. Iron—not so much.

I parked the car and turned off the ignition, zipping my keys into the special pouch I kept around my neck when I needed to leave my purse in the car. It also held my cell phone.

Glancing at Morio, I leaned over and pressed my lips to his. "We'd better get out there and find Chase and his men before they get pummeled."

He stroked my face, stirring the heat in my body. "Be careful, babe." His eyes glimmered with brown and topaz. "Keep your eyes open."

"You do the same. The ghosts almost took you from me once. I won't let them do that again." I ran my finger over his thin mustache and goatee, then lightly tapped his lips.

With that, we locked the car behind us and headed to the sidewalk, on alert for the ghosts, and who knew what else.

Wyvers Point Cemetery had been let go to ruin. I doubted if there were any graves newer than fifty years old, and while the grass had been mowed, the weeds tangled thickly along the walkway, and the trees needed a good trimming. Some of the cedar branches were sweeping the ground, and here and there, limbs had been bowed and snapped by the force of the winter snows and winds. Whoever the landscaper was, he needed a quick kick in the ass. But it seemed that regular maintenance was low on the priority list for the grounds-keepers who worked here.

The path was open to the sky until we approached the gates, but, directly through the wrought-iron bars, the trees closed in, shading the sidewalk. With no lights to illuminate the way, an incredible sense of isolation and loneliness emanated from the land.

As my studies of death magic grew deeper, and my training with Aeval and Morgaine became more intense, I was becoming accustomed to the shadowed nature of the woodlands and the secretive feel that permeated the Earthside wild places. Otherworld might be more upfront with the magic, but here, roots ran deep, and so did grudges and longings and long-remembered animosities. The sacred places of this world held on to their anger at being desecrated by concrete and deforestation. The ley lines were very active, and very powerful.

"This is one of the forgotten places." Morio glanced around, a solemn look on his face. He pinpointed what I'd been feeling but unable to put into words. "The graves and their occupants have long been left to brood over their deaths without anyone to grieve for them."

"You feel it, too? I sense betrayal coming from the cemetery."

As I walked through the open gates, I shivered. Death and spirits were becoming common fare, but something about this place unsettled me, and I didn't trust it. Didn't trust anything within the boundaries of this graveyard. It wasn't so much anger, but cunning and the sense of being watched, and stalked.

"Something's been watching us since we stepped out of the car."

"I know. I sense it, too." Morio's voice was light and low, but beneath the gentle tone, I could hear a warning. "On second thought, I don't think we should split up—"

A hoarse shout to our left, through a copse of cedar, cut him off.

"That's Chase!" I headed toward the voice, even as a pair of bone-walkers—living skeletons—broke out from behind a large patch of wild brambles to the left. "You deal with *them*. I'll go find Chase."

Morio quickly transformed into his full demon form. Eight feet tall, with a muzzle and glowing topaz eyes, his hands and feet were still human, though matching the rest of his size. His clothes transformed with him—I wasn't sure on the how or why of it—but he'd never gone all *Incredible Hulk* and ripped out of his shirt and pants. He had one hell of a tail, and he used it to balance himself as he lunged for the undead.

I wasn't too worried about him. Morio could be ruthless when necessary. I headed in the direction from which I'd heard Chase calling. As I ran across the lawn, praying I didn't hit a gopher hole with my heels, I happened to glance up at the moon shining down. She was waxing overhead, and the Moon Mother's light pierced the veil of clouds to hit me full on, charging me with a surge of energy as she bathed me in her magic.

"Chase? Chase?" I slowed, calling his name lightly as I approached the thicket of cedar. My senses on full alert, I reached out, seeking his signature. Chase and I had formed some sort of magical connection, though what it was neither one of us yet understood, but our energies had meshed. We were able to find each other when we needed help. He'd found me from the astral plane when Hyto had captured me, and now . . . I could sense where he was hiding.

I paused, holding out my hands. A tingle guided me to the left, and I followed it, ducking beneath the low limb of a vine maple growing in the shadow of one of the cedars. I'd just pushed my way through the foliage when I heard a noise. A snuffling, like some beast or pig hunting for truffles. Stopping, I tried to sense whether it was friend or foe.

A whisper echoed on the wind.

"She comes, the moon's mistress comes . . . she will not harm, she can help. She can make our home safe again as we tend the spirits in the garden . . ."

"But will she help us? And who is the human-not-so-human? He is frightened. The wayward ones seek him."

Taking a deep breath, I slowly broke through the undergrowth. "Who are you? I can hear you."

There was a shift, and a blur raced by, then—hesitating—turned back. "Priestess?" The voice was wary.

"I am a priestess, yes. Of the Moon Mother." I glanced around, looking for Chase, but could not see him. He was near, though. My senses told me that much. And he needed my help. "I'm looking for my friend—the human-not-so-human. Can you tell me where he is?" I wasn't even sure if we were speaking aloud, but the words were there, hanging in the air.

"Priestess . . . you are from the other side?"

At first, I thought that the creature—whom I still could not see—was asking if I was a spirit, but then I realized what it meant. "Yes, I'm from Otherworld. Who are you? Show yourself to me."

Slowly, as if shedding layers of an invisible cloak, a being appeared before me, emerging from the shadows. About four feet tall, he was formed of leaves and branches, vines and twigs. He reminded me of the walking sticks that inhabited the insect world, only his face was long and his chin pointed, and his eyes were slanted ovals, and on his face, a mere hint of nostrils. A crown of ivy wove around his forehead, and he wore a cape of moss and lichen.

"Are you Elder Fae?" I had never seen a creature like him, not even back in Otherworld, and he fascinated me. The closest I could think of would be Wisteria, the floraed who'd joined forces with the demons, caught in a frenzy of hatred toward humans.

He cocked his head to the right. "No, I be not Elder Fae."

And then I knew what he was. "You're an Earth Elemental!"

Slowly, he nodded. "I am. I am a part of the land itself. I am the guardian of this boneyard. And now, the bones are walking, where they should not be walking. Unnatural magic is afoot and has evil intent." He glanced around and motioned, and another of his kind appeared from the shadows. They moved like leaves on the wind, like walking trees.

Honored—Elementals didn't appear to just anybody, especially since a number of witches tried to summon them up in order to control their movements—I curtsied.

"I know. My friends and I are here to help put the bone-walkers and the wayward dead back in their graves. But I must find my friend—the not-so-human—before they harm him. Can you take me to him?"

I waited, forcing myself to be patient, so *not* one of my virtues. But when dealing with Elementals, patience was key. Especially Earth Elementals, who moved cautiously until they were certain of their course, at which point they could surge forth like an earthquake or landslide.

After a moment, during which they exchanged chattering noises that sounded like sticks rattling, he turned toward me again. "Your friend is in the clearing directly beyond this thicket. He is hurt. If you will clear the wayward ones, we will not forget your help. We guard the bones of this space, and they should not be abroad. Bones are for memories. Bones are to feed the earth and the worms. Bones are not meant to be walking above the ground without flesh and soul attached."

"You're right about that," I whispered, as I started past them.

As I passed by, the Earth Elemental caught my wrist in his hand. A heavy, laden sense of gravity sank me to my knees. "You are young in the world, still. There are ancient powers waking from their slumber. Some are beneficial. Others hunger from the depths. Be wary, Priestess: Not everything that answers to the moon will understand the changes wrought in this world. The Mother is ancient, and some of her children nearly as old."

And with that, he let go and I stumbled forward. I tried to get his warning out of my head, but the words rang in my ears as I pushed my way through the cedars to yet another clearing—the graveyard itself.

And there was Chase, propped up on a tombstone, looking petrified as a bone-walker made its way toward him. Unlike zombies, who moved slowly, bone-walkers could shuffle along at a pretty good clip. And once they reached you, if you couldn't get out of their way, you were toast unless you could totally demolish them. Given an open space and no obligation to destroy them, running away was usually the safest option.

Ghouls were different from both bone-walkers and zombies. They were faster than zombies, even though they were also animated corpses. And far worse, they absorbed life energy as well as eating flesh, and so were doubly dangerous.

A glance at Chase told me he wasn't going anywhere soon. He was leaning against the tombstone, one foot raised. In one hand, he held his Glock 40, even though bullets were no real use against the undead, especially skeletons. Chase was good with a gun—deadly accurate—but the bullets wouldn't stop what was coming our way, and he knew it.

He glanced at me as I headed toward him. Six two, with dark hair cut in a slight shag, he was swarthy with olive skin, brown eyes, and a suave manner. He was muscled and lean, but right now, he mostly looked like he was in pain.

I hurried over to him, eyeing the bone-walkers as I crossed the open swath of grass, past dilapidated headstones that were so old and weathered they were breaking apart. The bone-walker was near enough to worry about, but we still had a few minutes before it reached us.

We didn't have time for small talk. "Can you walk?"

"I stepped in a pothole and twisted my ankle. I managed to hobble over here, but I think I'll seriously fuck my foot up if I put my weight on it." He winced but pushed the pain aside and nodded to the oncoming undead. "What about them? You can't carry me, woman."

"You'd be surprised what I can do. I'm half-Fae, remember?" But the truth was, I *didn't* think I could manage to carry him. I could outrun him, outwalk him, and probably fight him down to the ground, but I wasn't Delilah with her athletic frame, and I wasn't Menolly with her vampiric strength. "Put away the gun; that's not going to do any good, and one of us will end up getting shot."

He tucked it back in the holster. "I didn't think it would help, but I was feeling vulnerable, you know? From now on, I'm carrying an armory, like Roz."

"Wouldn't fit in your suit jacket, babe." I began to edge away from the gravestone. The bone-walker was getting too close for comfort, and still no sign of Morio or the others.

I had to do something. "Hide behind the tombstone. I don't want you getting hit by any backfire if this goes wrong."

Chase knew well enough by now that when I said duck, he'd better move. *Fast.* And duck he did—crouching down behind the marker as I called down the energy of the Moon Mother. There were enough clouds that I was able to find the key for lightning. As I summoned it, I prayed that I'd have the ability to direct the energy without causing massive damage to either Chase or myself.

The familiar tingle ran down through my crown chakra, into my arms and through my fingers. My muscles and aura felt like they'd just been infused with a huge jolt of caffeine. I began to shake. Yeah, I was too tired for this, but we had no choice. I could run, but Chase couldn't, and I wasn't going to leave him alone to get attacked by the bone-walker.

As I took aim, focusing the best I could, I let loose with

the energy bolt. The blast ricocheted out of my body, flaring out into the darkening sky. It wasn't a fork of lightning. Instead, the spell spread out, blanketing a wide swath of grass and gravestones instead of just pinpointing the walking dead. Like a floodlight, my spell lit up the night.

But the energy caught the bone-walker and knocked it on its ass. The creature went flying back, landing hard, giving us precious time while it tried to struggle to its feet again.

Meanwhile, I heard something coming at us from the left. I swung around in time to see a goblin, wearing full leather armor, headed full tilt toward us. He was leading a band of at least twenty other goblins.

"What the fuck? *Goblins?* You didn't say anything about goblins!"

"I didn't know there were any here!" He looked as startled as I was.

"Get that gun back out. Bullets might do some good against them."

Exhausted from casting the energy bolt, on top of everything else Morio and I had done earlier, I fumbled for my cell phone. We needed reinforcements and fast, or Chase and I were going to be mincemeat.

But before I could extract it from the zippered pouch that also held my keys, the goblins were on us. I yanked out my dagger and engaged the leader. As I swiped, desperately trying to focus, Chase let off a volley of bullets and two of the goblins went down, though they weren't dead.

Panicking, I lunged for the goblin's head and my blade connected with the flesh, plunging through to bounce off the bone. I didn't have the strength to drive the blade through his skull. As he lurched back, taking my blade with him, I scrambled to summon up as much energy as I could. I might be able to manage one more energy bolt. But as I dodged, trying to evade my attacker, a blur roared past me, and the goblin went flying. I squinted, trying to see what the hell had just happened.

And there, standing between me and the goblin horde, was Smoky. And he was *pissed*.

Chapter 2

I didn't interrupt, just pulled back and let my dragon do his thing. I turned as Shade and Vanzir swept past me, joining the fight. Delilah was right behind them, holding an extra dagger. She tossed it to mc. I caught the hilt, grinning at her. Six months ago, I would have dropped it, but I'd been learning a lot of tricks during my workouts.

"Thanks! Mine's stuck in a goblin's skull."

"Help Chase while I take your place." She pushed past me and I willingly gave way. My sister was six one, athletic as all hell, and with her short golden shag and sentient silver dagger, she was a deadly opponent. She winked as she passed by. "I actually think I've missed this."

Chase was reloading and took aim at another goblin coming at us. He fired, but the bullet—though it met its mark—ricocheted off the metal epaulettes on the goblin's shoulder. The crack of the gun ripped through the air as the smell of burned powder singed my nose.

"Fuck, I'm out of ammo." He growled, putting the safety on. He slid his gun back into the holster. I glanced around, looking for something that he could use as a weapon. Then I saw it—one of the dead goblins had a sword and it was near enough for me to grab. No doubt the blade was poisoned, but if Chase was cautious, he should be able to use it with no problem.

I darted into the fray—which was now a mishmash of movement in the twilight—and picked up the sword, careful to touch only the hilt. "You have gloves, Chase?"

He nodded, pulling out a pair of latex gloves. "I always carry a pair just in case we run into evidence."

"Here, don't touch the blade—ten to one, it's poisoned and goblin poisons can absorb through your skin. But it will give you something to keep the bogies at bay." As I handed him the sword, hilt first, he hefted it and nodded at me. I quickly turned my back to his, so we weren't caught unawares from either side.

The battle was fully under way. Delilah had engaged two of the goblins, spinning and ducking as she darted in and out of the fray, Lysanthra—her dagger—shimmering in the dim light. Like a cat on her feet—no surprise since she *was* a werecat—Delilah was sturdy and steady in her movements. I envied her that, but our bodies weren't the same shape, and I would never have her abilities. But then again, she didn't wield magic. We each had our own talents.

She kicked one of the goblins in the stomach as she thrust her dagger under the chin of the other and with one smooth movement ratcheted the tip up through his jaw. As he fell, she neatly withdrew her blade, keeping it in hand. The other goblin landed a nasty blow on her knee, and she wavered for a moment before launching a renewed assault on him. Within minutes, he was on his back, against one of the graves, and she landed a clean, quick jab, impaling him through the heart.

As another came at her, I glanced over at Smoky, who was racing—a blur of motion, his nails grown into talons. He never got dirty, never got muddied or bloodied on his clothes, even if he took a hit that cut his skin. My mother-in-law had told me it was a dragon thing, and if I could have bottled the ability, we could have made a fortune and put the laundry detergent companies out of business.

Smoky barreled through the line of goblins as they spilled to the sides, diving for cover when they saw the fury in his eyes and the blood flying in his wake. Vanzir was also embroiled in a fight and doing a damned good job. He had taken on one of the bone-walkers and was smashing it to bits. The skeletal limbs would continue to twitch until the animation spell wore off, but they couldn't do any harm.

As for Shade, he had engaged a pair of bone-walkers. As a purple flame began to emanate from his body, a roar made me turn. Out of the bushes, came Morio. He leaped, rolling onto the ground as he caught hold of a bloatworgle, who was making a run directly for Chase and me. Fuck—a *bloatworgle*, too? They were nasty-assed demons.

Morio, in his full youkai form, was a formidable sight and always took my breath away when I saw him. He landed a nasty swipe across the bloatworgle's back, slowing the demon down.

The bloatworgle was gangly, with a distended belly, and his skin was tough as leather hide. He opened his mouth and a belching gust of fire came shooting out to engulf Morio, who yelped and jumped back. But Smoky had noticed, and he thrust himself between Morio and the bloatworgle, slashing at the demon's face. He landed a direct hit, ripping through the eyes and lips, leaving the creature shredded and bleeding.

Morio did the stop-drop-and-roll move and put out the stray sparks that were threatening to ignite against his fur. By the time he'd leaped to his feet again, Smoky had the bloatworgle down on the ground and was pummeling him. One last punch and the demon bit the dust.

Shade managed to do something to the bone-walkers—I wasn't sure what because my attention had been on Smoky and Morio, but they turned to dust, crumbling to the ground. As I turned to Chase to ask how he was doing, a shriek shattered the air and a spirit—fully visible—went speeding past, looking like it was being dragged by its hair.

What the—

Before any of us could do anything, the spirit vanished from sight, and then a rumbling sound filled the air and the soil of the graveyard moaned—as tombstones toppled over and shattered into pieces.

Chase went down as the headstone he was leaning on crumbled beneath him. I tried to help him, but the ground roiled beneath my feet, and I fell to my knees, the rumbling so loud that I couldn't hear myself think. Shade and Morio were on the ground, too, clasping their hands to their ears.

Moaning softly, I winced as the sound grew louder. It sounded like a freight train, or a vast army on the run, thundering through the cemetery. As I bent over, pressing my hands to my ears to muffle the noise, a sucking sound joined the mix and I looked up in time to see spirits rising from a number of the nearby graves. Some looked surprised, as if they had been slumbering and were now just wakened. Others looked angry and were resisting, and still others, confused.

"What's going on?" I screamed over the noise, trying to be heard.

Smoky and Delilah looked perplexed. Chase looked about ready to pass out. He was either dead tired or in massive pain.

"What's happening? Why are you shouting?" Delilah started to ask, and then she, too, bent over, head to knees. "Oh, hell! My ears!"

The spirits hovered in the air above their graves and then—with a collective wail—were sucked away by some invisible vacuum, into a shimmering vortex that formed in the middle of the air. With one last piercing shriek that almost sent me into a coma, they disappeared, and with them vanished the glowing light. The graveyard fell unnaturally silent, and we were alone in the darkness.

Perhaps this is as good a place as any to introduce myself. I'm Camille D'Artigo, and I'm half-Fae, half human. With my two sisters, I came from Otherworld. We belong to the Otherworld Intelligence Agency—well, actually, now we *run* the Earthside division of the OIA. We were originally shunted over here ostensibly because our half-human heritage skews our powers at times, but I suspect there was another reason—a matter of revenge aimed directly at me. I'm the eldest, and I'm a witch and priestess of the Moon Mother.

I have three husbands—yes, three gorgeous, sexy hunks— and we're as happy as four peas in a pod. Or we would be if it weren't for the demonic war we're facing. Smoky is half white dragon, half silver dragon; Trillian's one of the dark and charming Fae known as Svartans; and Morio's a youkai-kitsune.

Delilah, my middle sister, is a two-faced Were. She resembles our mother, who died when we were still very young. Delilah turns into a golden tabby when stressed, and at the call of the full moon. And she turns into a black panther when duty calls or she gets too angry. She's a Death Maiden, serving under the Autumn Lord, and Shade is her fiancé.

And Menolly, a *jian-tu*-turned-vampire, is the youngest. Married to her werepuma wife, Nerissa, she's also the official consort for Roman, the son of Blood Wyne, the Vampire Queen, as well as his heir. He re-sired her, and it's created an odd blip in their relationship, but they'll work it through. They have to.

When we were first sent over Earthside, we expected to be on an enforced sabbatical—a vacation in Siberia, if you will. What actually happened was that we found ourselves planted squarely on the front lines of a demonic war. And we also discovered that we love our mother's home world as much as we love our father's and our own home.

As I said—we're caught in a demonic war. Shadow Wing, the current ruler in the Subterranean Realms, is doing his best to break through the portals that keep the demons from invading Earthside and Otherworld. He aims to ravage through the land and exert his control over all three realms. He's also wacked—and has been called the Unraveller. If the Demon Lord succeeds, billions of people will die or be enslaved: Fae, human, and Crypto alike. Shadow Wing has managed to establish fronts in both OW and ES—overtly in Other-world where war is brewing, and covertly here Earthside, where his operatives are working behind the scenes to open up the portals.

Here, Earthside, we've gathered a huge assortment of friends and extended family who now know about Shadow Wing. To the last, they've pledged to fight him. And back in Otherworld, we're working with the elves, the unicorns, and some of the Fae.

We need to find the last two spirit seals—we've found seven so far, and lost two of them, so we have only five. The spirit seals, gems that once were joined together to form an ancient artifact, can—when reunited—rip open the portals and allow Shadow Wing full entrance into both of our worlds.

Now that he has two of them, Shadow Wing's starting to make ripples in the fabric of space and time that keep the worlds separated. If he gains any more, the tide may turn in his favor, since his armies are united, and ours are still scrambling to figure out the best defense.

To be honest, we don't know if we can stop him. But as long as we have the breath to fight, we'll keep up the battle. Because if Shadow Wing wins, we *all* lose. And the thought of both of our beloved worlds going down in flames, well, that thought is more than we can bear.

"What the fuck just happened?" Delilah stared at the top-pled gravestones before hurrying over to Chase's side.

I joined her, just as confused as she was. "I think . . . something just sucked the spirits out of this cemetery. Kind of like a giant vacuum cleaner."

"What would do that? And why?" She reached down to give Chase her hand, and I took his other side. We lifted him to his feet, and he draped his arms around our shoulders. "You okay? What's wrong with your leg?"

"I caught my foot in a hole when I was running from a bone-walker. I don't know if it's broken, but it hurts like hell." He sighed. "I'm not even going to pretend I can walk

on my own. But can you find my men? Two officers were out
here with me. I lost track of them when we split up. They
went down a different path to check out a noise we heard,
and I haven't heard from them since."

Morio motioned to Smoky. "You and the girls go look for
his men. I'll carry him back to the parking lot. Shade, come
with me, in case we meet any stragglers."

Shade nodded. Chase let out a *"Huh?"* as Morio, still in
his demonic form, lifted the detective into his arms.

Morio shrugged. "Dude, it's going to be quicker if I carry
you."

"Fine, but hurry. You've got some pretty funky B.O.
going on in this form." Chase gave me a wry what-can-you-
do shrug. Over the past few months, he'd managed to rein in
his ego and had fallen into his place in the group. He was a
vital member, and now he knew we thought of him that way.
So he'd started accepting his physical limitations even as his
psychic powers burgeoned out.

Morio set off with Shade behind him. Smoky, Delilah,
and I turned back to the graveyard. The night was growing
darker, and the clouds now covered the moon. I was tired,
both magically and physically. The sugar and adrenaline
rushes had worn off, and I just wanted to drop into bed.

"Come on, let's get this over with." I hoped, really hoped,
that Chase's men had found a place to hide, or that somehow
they'd made their way back to the parking lot, but the cynic
in me wasn't betting on it. Zombies and bone-walkers might
be slow, but they never tired, and fear made for clumsiness.

We headed for the nearest sidewalk—probably fifty yards
away—in silence. The scattered remnants of the bone-
walkers still twitched, fingers inching along the ground, toes
struggling to move on their own. I passed an arm bone that
still had a hand attached to it, and the fingers were pulling it
along the ground, grasping at blades of grass as it inched
toward us. Smoky gazed at it silently for a moment, then
walked over and stomped on it, crushing it beneath his foot.
That took care of that. He looked back at us.

"Once we find Chase's men, we should bury this flotsam.

These were once living, breathing people. Their remains deserve respect, not this desecration." He rejoined us.

"That they do." I led the way off the grass onto the sidewalk. The path wound through another thicket of trees, this time birch and maple, out into another section of the cemetery. The gravestones here had been toppled, too.

Everything felt empty, eerily so. Though I knew most of the dead were still in the ground, the spirits were gone. Shortly after death, the majority of spirits went on to their next phase in life, or to be with their ancestors, but every graveyard held at least a handful who could not let go. I'd never encountered a completely clear and empty boneyard before, and the feeling unsettled me. It wasn't normal.

"There's nothing left. Whatever sucked up the spirits got them all. Who could do such a thing?" I shivered, drawing my jacket tighter around me.

"Ivana Krask?" Delilah grimaced.

I thought about it for a moment. Ivana Krask, the Maiden of Karask, was one of the Elder Fae—and a definite freak show. She kept a garden of spirits, where she would torment them. For the most part, she took only the angry and dangerous ones. But even though Ivana had a staff that could clear out the ghosts in a limited area, this sort of wholesale pillaging was beyond even her. At least I *thought* it was.

"We'll ask her, but I don't think she was responsible. Never hurts to check, though." As I pushed aside a low-hanging branch overshadowing the sidewalk, I stopped cold. Up ahead, just off the path to the left, was a man, in uniform. Or what was left of a man. And over the body hunkered a pair of zombies, feeding. Great, first bone-walkers, a bloat-worgle, goblins, and now walking meat-bags.

I grimaced as I noticed they'd ripped open his torso and were dipping into the organs. One of the zombies was feasting on intestines, and the slick tubes of viscera hung limply out of the creature's mouth. The zombie had been a young woman, and the sight of her shoveling the offal through her bloodstained lips made me want to retch. I sucked it up—I'd seen a lot of sick things in my time and this was no worse than some of the others—and looked around for the other officer.

A ways up the path, we caught sight of the second body. Again, a zombie was hovering over it, gnawing on an arm. It glanced up at us, a wary gleam in its eye.

Unlike ghouls, who had some sense of sentience and who also fed on energy as well as flesh, zombies and bone-walkers were mere automatons and did not think or reason. All of them ran on magic until they were stopped or until the spell ran out. And all three types of the undead continued on until torn to pieces, and once that happened, they were help-less until the magic fueling the cells leached out or was cut off by the spellcaster.

Smoky silently went into action. He bore down like a bat-tering ram, slamming the zombies off the first body. With one swift blow, he broke the neck of the dead girl, the bloody feast splattering out of her mouth. She came at him, her head drooping to one side. The other zombie went into attack mode, too, intent on defending his meal.

Delilah and I took on the one squatting over the other cop. We had a head start, and it ignored us until we were near enough to be a threat. Then, using the arm as a weapon, the zombie stumbled forward. I pulled out my blade and cir-cled around back of it while Delilah engaged it face-on. With a shout, she spun, one booted foot catching it on the chin.

The zombie's head whipped to the side, the sound of bones cracking. Taking advantage of Delilah's attack, I plunged the dagger into it, shoving forward with all my weight. The zom-bie went down with me on top of it.

"Hurry, while I'm on its back, carve it up!" I tried a choke hold while Delilah got to work. Apparently, I was better at clutching than fighting, because I managed to hold the zom-bie steady while Delilah started sawing through the arm joint with her dagger.

Surprised, I noticed there was no blood splatter. Whoever this had been, he'd been embalmed. The question of how zombies ate—or if they even digested their food—ran through my mind, and I made a mental note to follow up.

Disgusting, yes, but maybe the answer would help us in the future.

Delilah glanced at me as I perched on the back of the zombie. "This was an older body—it was falling apart when the necromancer raised it. In fact, I think the only thing holding it together is the magic."

She whipped through the arm, then cut the hand and fingers from the limb, then tackled the other side. It was kind of like cutting up a side of beef. Except we weren't about to fry up steaks for dinner.

Smoky joined us. "I dispatched the other two," he said, watching as we finished detaching the arms and legs. "Here, I can make quick work of the rest of it. Get back."

"Gladly." I gingerly got up off its back, feeling grubby and hoping there were no parasites clinging to me from the corpse. In a blur of motion, Smoky ripped the thing to shreds.

Meanwhile, Delilah and I returned to the bodies of the fallen officers. "Tom and Markus. Both were fairly new." She hung her head. "I didn't know them all that well, but they seemed nice. I think Markus has a family."

I leaned closer. It was hard to tell what race they'd been, after the zombies had gotten through with them. "Fae? FBH? Elf?"

"Tom was an FBH. Markus was an elf." She pressed her lips together as Smoky returned. The bodies were a mess and it would be hard to get them out of there without making things worse.

"Should we call in a forensics team?"

Delilah shrugged. "Chase has to follow certain procedures but we know what killed these men. We do need the FH-CSI coroner so they can gather . . . everything that's left."

I gazed at the dead men. So much damage. But then, again, even in the FBH community, there were a lot of murders that made just as little sense. I shook my head. "Tomorrow, we pay a visit to Ivana, though I doubt this is her doing. The Elder Fae have no keep with zombies. They aren't buddy-buddy with any of the undead, really, except for a few like the Black Annis, and Kelpie-Woman."

Not wanting to leave the bodies alone, I put through a call to Yugi, Chase's right-hand man at headquarters. "Yugi, get a recovery team out here. We've got two dead officers. We know what killed them—zombies. Don't know who is responsible yet, but we'll find out. Chase is hurt; he sprained his ankle pretty bad, it looks like, but he'll be okay otherwise. Don't think we need forensics, unless you bring out a magical team. We put the zombies back in the grave."

"Right. Where are you?"

"Wyvers Point Cemetery. We're in . . ." I glanced around, but there was no telltale sign of what part of the graveyard we were in. Then I caught sight of a faded sign that read BEL-MONT LANE. "We're on Belmont Lane, one of the paths that runs through the cemetery."

"Hold on . . . calling up a schematic right now." Yugi paused. He was Swedish by birth, a naturalized citizen, and he was an empath. We'd never seen a good demonstration of his abilities, but he'd been with Chase since the formation of the Faerie-Human Crime Scene Investigation unit, since the portals first opened. Now, he was second in charge of the FH-CSI.

"Got it. Okay, sending a team out right now. Can you wait till we get there?"

"Will do. Delilah and I will be in the parking lot." I hung up, then glanced over at Smoky. "Love, can you wait with the bodies? I can't stand the thought of anything else coming along to destroy them."

"Of course, my sweet." He leaned down, his ankle-length silver hair lifting to coil around me. Smoky could do wondrous and sensuous things with his hair in the bedroom. He was six four, pale as cream, and young as dragons went, though he had seen centuries come and go.

He pressed his lips to my forehead, then nodded to Delilah and me. "Be careful on your way back to the parking lot."

We followed the sidewalk, not veering off into the grass

or the undergrowth just in case we'd missed any of the goblins or the zombies. *The goblins . . .* wait a minute.

"*Goblins.* Delilah, the goblins wouldn't be in league with Ivana. Do you think Gulakah, the Lord of Ghosts, is utilizing them now? Maybe Telazhar is sending them over from Otherworld via one of the portals. He would have access to them now, and sending us groups of the buggers is a great way to wreak havoc."

Telazhar, an ancient necromancer from Otherworld, had long ago been banished to the Sub-Realms. He'd led the Scorching Wars, laying waste to a vast region of land now known as the Southern Wastes. Rogue magic rode the sand dunes there, waiting for unwary travelers. And there, sorcerers and necromancers gathered, biding their time and practicing their dark arts.

While Shadow Wing couldn't use the portals yet to send demons through from the Sub-Realms, Telazhar could easily use the portals to send goblins through to Earthside.

"Ten to one you're right. Which means we need to find out which portal he's using and close it down. *If* we can. Or at least post guards on it." She brushed her hand across her eyes as we jogged along the trail. "Sometimes I wish the freaking war would just build to a head so we could get it over with."

"Unfortunately, if that happened now, we'd lose. We still aren't organized enough, and the gods only know what kind of force we need in order to go up against Shadow Wing's armies. Hell, we have enough trouble dealing with just one demon general, let alone a brigade of demons." I shook my head. "I'm as tired as you are, but don't invite hell to rain down on us yet. We aren't ready. *So. Not. Ready.* Remember: Shadow Wing is the Big Bad Wolf. And we're holding Red's basket of goodies, as far as he's concerned."

We reached the parking lot to find Chase on a bench, his leg propped up. Morio and Shade were keeping watch.

Chase looked up expectantly. I hung my head, not wanting to tell him the bad news. Delilah must have sensed my reluctance because she sat down beside him and gave him a sad smile.

He read her expression loud and clear. "They didn't make it, did they?"

She shook her head. "I'm sorry. No. We called Yugi, and he's got a recovery team on the way here. Zombies. We killed them."

Not that it made anything better, really. It would be one thing if we'd caught whoever it was doing the reanimating, but the zombies were simply weapons. They weren't the masterminds.

Chase let out a long sigh. "I just took both of them onto the force. Promised them plenty of adventure and action. I guess they got more than they could handle. I should never have sent them out here. Not knowing what we're facing."

"It wasn't your fault, Chase. They were both experienced, weren't they? They had several years on the job, right?"

I didn't want him to feel guilty. We'd suffered collateral damage before, and the bodies were stacking up. But regardless of how careful we were, there were going to be casualties. We just had to do our best to mitigate how high the body count went.

He gave me a long look. "Tom was a twelve-year veteran on the force. And Markus, he served five years in Queen Asteria's guard. I guess . . . they went in prepared. We just weren't expecting to find zombies."

"What *did* you expect?"

"Someone called in, said they thought they saw grave robbers. Thought teenagers were pulling some prank, or maybe it was a fraternity stunt. With things as quiet as they've been the past few weeks, I guess we got careless." He rubbed his forehead. "I hate this. Tom was single. His family's back in Maine. But Markus, he has three kids and a wife back in Elqaneve. And now, I have to tell them he's dead."

"That's always the hardest part." I hung my head. "Chase, it's going to get worse before it gets better. We just have to do what we can to keep our losses to a minimum. Did you know there were also goblins out here when you went in?"

He frowned. "No. I had no idea there were any until that scene back there in the graveyard." After a pause, he added,

"Dare I ask if you know who's behind this? Or should I just assume we're facing Gulakah's cronies?"

I shrugged. "We aren't positive, but ten to one, yeah, Gulakah and Telazhar are working together. The goblins came from OW, there's little doubt of that. With Telazhar over there, ratcheting it up, I think we should assume he's in close communication with Gulakah."

"Like we are, with Darynal's team." Delilah draped her arm around Chase and hugged him. They'd been an item for a while, until they realized they were better off as friends than lovers. Now they seldom argued.

Darynal was Trillian's blood-oath brother, a mercenary. Together with Taath, a sorcerer, and Quall, an assassin, he and his team were scouting out info for Queen Asteria, spying on Telazhar's growing threat in Otherworld.

"Yeah, only Darynal only has two other members on his team. Telazhar has a freaking army under—" I stopped as my phone rang. As I pulled it out of the pouch and punched the Talk button, a couple of cruisers and a van pulled into the cemetery. Yugi's recovery team was here.

I answered my phone. "Hello?"

"Camille? It's me, Iris. I'm just checking up on you." She sounded a little frantic. Pregnancy hormones were running rampant in her system, and we'd quickly learned that a Finnish house sprite carrying twins was a force of nature. Only a fool would try to cross her.

She was showing now, and so were her moods. We were beginning to see why the Finns revered motherhood so much—the Finnish mothers were the bears of the maternal world, including their extended family. They'd take on an army if that was what it took to protect their loved ones. Iris was having a boy and a girl, and they'd have the fiercest, most loyal mother in the world.

"We're okay. We're about to head home for the evening. Chase has a sprained ankle, but we're fine." We could tell her about everything when we arrived home. No sense worrying her now. "Did you need us to pick anything up on our way back?"

She paused, then laughed. "Yes, please. I'm really craving ice cream right now."

"With pickles?" I was joking, but she made a *tsking* sound.

"Don't stereotype me, missy. I've never been a fan of pickles before, and I'm not a fan of them now. But . . . some bacon would be good. I think we're out. So, bacon and chocolate cherry ice cream, and smoked salmon. We have crackers and plenty of cheese." And with that, she hung up.

I grinned at the phone. "Iris," I said, in answer to Delilah's questioning look.

She laughed. "Ice cream?"

"Oh yeah." I snorted. "And a harangue over stereotyping her cravings. She's a firecracker, all right."

"That's putting it mildly. And I'll bet she asked for chocolate cherry," Morio broke in.

"Right again. Along with bacon and smoked salmon."

As Mallen, the elfin medic who worked most of the middle-of-the-night calls, knelt to examine Chase's ankle, a group of six others—two medics with four armed Fae guards—headed in the direction of the officers' corpses. Shade went with them to stand guard.

Mallen motioned for his assistant to hand him a splint. "I think it's broken. You're going to have to have this x-rayed once we get back to headquarters."

"Fuck." Chase slammed his hand against the bench. "I don't need this right now."

"Better a break than a nasty sprain. Breaks will heal faster, especially since you have the Nectar of Life in you." Mallen strapped the ankle up. "Any cuts or abrasions from the zombies, or the goblins? On any of you? With the zombies, you run the risk of infection. The goblins—poison."

We all examined ourselves. I had a skinned knee, but that was from scraping against a broken piece of tombstone. But Mallen insisted on dousing it with an antibiotic. The brown liquid stung, but I said nothing. *Better safe than sorry.*

I leaned my head wearily against Smoky's shoulder, and he wrapped his arm around me. "I'm tired and worn out. I don't think I can face any more monsters tonight."

He rubbed my temples gently, kissing me softly. "Then you'd better make sure to take home that ice cream, or you'll never get any sleep."

Laughing, I pulled out my keys. Mallen was helping Chase into his squad car. Another officer would drive him back. The men returned, carrying the body bags. We waited until they had all pulled out before getting ready to go. We weren't needed at headquarters tonight. Chase knew everything that we did.

"I'll drive Shade, and we'll stop for the food." Delilah kissed me on the cheek. "You just go home and have a long, hot bath."

"Thanks, Kitten." I was weary, and the promise of a bubble bath made the drive home seem tolerable. As we headed out, Smoky riding shotgun and Morio resting in the back, I was relieved that we weren't far from home, because once I walked through the front door, I was going to be toast for the evening.

Chapter 3

By the time we arrived home, I was the physical and emotional equivalent of a ramen noodle: limp, tasteless, and with no nutritional value whatsoever.

Iris was sitting in the rocking chair, eyeing the door.

I forestalled the question with a raised hand. "Delilah's getting the food."

The glare quickly turned to concern. "Oh, you poor dear. You look done in. Are you hurt, girl?" She started to push herself out of the chair, but Trillian, who was fixing some tea, stopped her.

"Let us worry about Camille. You just rest. You've had a hard evening." He glanced over at me and tipped his head, motioning for me to follow him into the living room.

Hanna, our new house helper, was sitting on the sofa, folding clothes. Maggie, our baby calico gargoyle, was playing on the floor next to her.

"What happened? Is Iris okay?" I dropped into the recliner and leaned back, not daring to close my eyes. If I did, I'd be asleep in a minute.

Hanna glanced up. "She will be fine, but Maggie, she accidentally tripped Iris, and we had to send for the midwife to make certain everything is all right."

"Oh, no! Is she—"

Hanna stopped me before I could continue. "Iris is fine, but the midwife, she tell her, 'Don't you do any heavy lifting for a while.' So, I will do the heavy work, and she can do whatever she feels capable of."

Trillian knelt down and began unlacing my boots for me. "Let me get these off you. The midwife also feels it might be best if Iris stops looking after Maggie until she's given birth. Playing with her is no problem, but to actually attend to her feedings and so forth . . . not such a good idea. Maggie didn't mean to trip Iris, but baby or not, she's still a gargoyle and she can be dangerous. More so, since she doesn't understand what's going on."

I sighed. We knew the time would come when Iris would have to turn over primary care of Maggie, but we'd all hoped it would be later on.

"Hanna, it looks like you're going to be taking care of Maggie more. We'll all pitch in as much as we can. We can make sure her cream drinks are mixed up in the proper proportion and in the fridge, and that her lamb and beef are ground to the right texture. Meanwhile, do you need someone to help with the housework? We can hire someone."

There was a lot to do, looking after everyone who was living here. Iris had managed it without complaint, but she was a house sprite and it was in her nature to look after others.

But Hanna reassured me. "I can do this work. If I need help, I will tell you. Remember where you found me . . . the work here is easy and fulfilling. Working for Hyto, that was a nightmare."

As she said his name, she glanced into my eyes. A look passed between us. Hanna and I had a connection—one forged from bearing the brunt of cruelty and fear. I'd been there; I knew what she'd faced. And Hanna had watched me endure Hyto's brutality and helped me pick up the pieces afterward. In different ways, we'd both faced the long night of the dragon and come through alive, and there was no need for words.

"Whatever you need to make your job easier, just ask." I let out a little sigh of satisfaction as Trillian slipped off my boots. My feet were tired. I loved my heels, but after a full day and then a graveyard fight in them, I was ready to let my feet breathe.

I leaned forward, resting my elbows on my knees as my skirt draped between my legs. Hanna went back to folding clothes. Maggie toddled up to me and I swept her into my arms, hugging her tightly.

"You okay?" Trillian slipped into the oversized chair beside me.

I shook my head. "Two dead cops. Zombies got them. We found goblins out there. And bone-walkers. And a bloatworgle. And if that's not enough, something sucked away every spirit in that graveyard. It felt so good to have a break from fighting. I guess, even though I knew it was a pipe dream, I was hoping maybe we'd lucked out. Maybe Shadow Wing called Gulakah back to the Sub-Realms. But that isn't going to happen, is it?"

Trillian shook his head. "No. It's not going to happen. You know it, in your heart. We're in this war for the long haul, and there's no walking away. A year ago I would have said, let's get the fuck out. But now, I guess I'm as invested as you are."

I gazed into his eyes and reached up to stroke his cheek. Trillian's jet black skin gleamed against my pale hand. His eyes, a piercing blue, stood out like snow against a forest, and his silver hair tumbled down his back in a neat ponytail, the cerulean highlights glimmering in the warm light of our living room.

"I love you more each day. You've always been my alpha, and I've always loved you, but now . . . thank you for coming back into my life, for not letting me walk away. Thank you for reminding me of why we came together."

I'd met Trillian almost fourteen years ago, shortly before Menolly was turned into a vampire. We'd been pulled together as if we were magnets and bound ourselves in a sexual, magical ritual.

And then, six years later, fear had won out. Svartans—the dark and charming Fae, although they were actually cousins to the elves—weren't known for their loyalty. They were heartbreakers, users, and manipulators. At least, that had been the stereotype, and my fear that Trillian would cast me aside grew as the years wore on. Insecure, afraid he'd leave me, I had backed off, even though he insisted that we were mated for life. I had refused to answer his summons, refused to answer his letters, and in the end, I cast a spell to ward him away from my father's house. Trillian disappeared, and I thought he was gone for good.

But I couldn't forget him. The Eleshinar Ritual saw to that. We were forever bound, and it ripped my heart apart to walk away. Other men just didn't interest me, even though my libido was high. What encounters I had were one-nighters, and I had no desire to form a relationship with anybody.

And then, like a thunderbolt, a year and a half ago Trillian had shown up here, Earthside, with a message from my father. One look at him, and I knew that I'd never walk away again. Just like that, he was back in my life. He was my alpha husband, my lover, and we would be together forever.

Now he pulled me to my feet. "Come on, let's get you upstairs."

"I should tell everyone what went down out there—"

"Delilah can do that. There's nothing more that can be done tonight. Chase isn't in danger. The officers who died can't be brought back to life. Let it go. Come upstairs, and we'll take care of you, and help you relax, and then, you can sleep." His lip twitched, and I felt a delicious shiver run through me.

"I'm so tired . . . I don't know how much fun I'll be." I loved my men, I loved sex, but tonight I had very little left to give.

"Shush, and let us worry about the giving." And with that, Trillian swept me up in his arms and carried me up the stairs to the second floor, which housed our rooms.

Home was a three-story Victorian, with a full basement. Delilah and Shade had the third floor. Smoky, Trillian, Morio, and I shared the second floor. Hanna's room was on the main level, along with the main living area.

And Menolly and Nerissa had the basement, where Menolly could be protected during the day when she slept. For a long time, the entrance had remained secret, but with so many people living at our place, we finally just let it go and installed a steel door leading down to her suite. It was still behind the bookshelves, and only the three of us, along with Iris and Nerissa, had keys to get through the imposing barrier, but everybody in the house knew where it was.

Iris, who had made her home in Hanna's room until a few months ago, now lived with Bruce in a cute little trailer out back, while the guys were building their house. It was about half-finished, and they expected to be able to move in by Litha, the summer solstice. And Vanzir, Shamas, and Rozurial slept in a shed-cum-studio apartment down the drive a ways.

We originally owned the house and five acres, but Smoky had recently bought the ten acres that buttressed our land, including Birchwater Pond and a patch of wetlands. Now we had fifteen acres in which to prowl, explore, and expand. We couldn't build on four of the acres—the wetlands themselves—but that just made things more comfortable. The wetlands would be protected.

Instead of carrying me to the bedroom, Trillian swept me into the bathroom and set me down. As he flipped a switch, music began to filter into the room. Morio had wired our suite for sound. A pounding, sensuous beat came on as Lindstrøm and Christabelle's "Lovesick" echoed through the speakers.

I stared at the tub. It was piled high with bubbles and rose petals, while candles lit the room. Sighing, I inhaled the deep spicy scents of Twilight Dream Song, the newest body wash and perfume I'd discovered. With an overtone of vanilla and notes of cinnamon, amber, and peach, it reminded me of the deep woods in Otherworld, of the sparkling lights of the eye catchers, and the vast canopy of stars overhead.

Starting to relax, I held out my arms. Trillian liked undressing me, and on nights like tonight, I was only too happy to let him have his way. He reached out and began unfastening the busks on my corset. As the molded leather loosened, I let out a long breath. Corsets and bustiers gave my double-Ds more support than any bra could, but at the end of the day, it was nice to get out of the boots and the leather.

He pressed against my back, reaching around to gently cup my breasts, his breath warm on my neck. I let out a soft sound and leaned back into his embrace as he fingered my nipples. He ran his thumb along the curve of my breast, sliding it up to the point between them, then slowly traced a line down to the waistband of my skirt.

Reaching around my waist, he held the material with one hand, while he unzipped the skirt with the other. Then he let the skirt go, and it puddled at my feet.

I shivered, even though the room was warm. The combination of his touch with how tired I was made me dizzy, sending me spinning as he slid his fingers beneath the sides of my panties and slowly drew them down.

As I stepped out of the silky material, he kissed my tailbone, then trailed kisses down over the curve of my ass, igniting a spark within me. I wavered, and he held me steady, moving around front, where he slipped his hand between my legs, moving them ever so slightly apart. My stomach quaked, and I reached down to run my hands over his hair as he pressed his lips to my clit, gently stroking with his tongue.

Arching my back, I let out a throaty moan as he settled in, nibbling, tasting me, licking me. As I melted into the sensation, he trailed a hand up my thigh, his skin molten against mine. I came, sharply, quickly, and without warning.

A satisfied smile on his face, Trillian motioned for me to get in the bathtub. My stomach still fluttering, I obeyed, sinking into the flurry of bubbles. As I leaned my head gratefully against the warm porcelain of the tub, the scent of the bath wash rose to tickle my nose, and the rose petals felt like velvet against my skin as they floated atop the mass of bubbles.

I was tired, oh so tired, and with the release of orgasm, my body had gone limp. The candlelight flickered softly as the hot water eased the strain out of my muscles and loosened the grime that had caked on me.

Ever meticulous, Trillian carefully hung up my clothes.

Then he settled down on the floor next to the tub. I draped my hand out, and he took it, stroking my fingers lightly.

"Was it rough tonight?" He kissed the palm of my hand and then let go, and I slid my arm back under the water.

"The spells . . . Morio and I are meshing more and more with the magic. The more I touch his soul during our rituals, the more I realize how deeply he's entwined with the dark moon mysteries. He has incredible potential, Trillian, and I think he's just been waiting for the right partner in order to tap into it. It almost frightens me how strong I feel working with him." I pulled myself up and crossed my arms on the side of the tub, resting my chin on them.

Trillian folded his arms behind his head and stretched out his legs, crossing his feet at the ankles. "As much grief as I give Fox-Boy, I would never underestimate him. So, what do Aeval and Morgaine say about your working with him? Does it interfere with your training?"

I shook my head. "Actually, they are encouraging it. Something is up, Trillian. They've been preparing me for something—something to happen on Beltane, but they won't tell me what. I know Morio will be a part of it. I'm nervous, though, because it feels . . . big."

I generally kept quiet about my training. Most of it was private, just like Delilah's training was with Greta, the leader of the Death Maidens. But here, with Trillian, I could admit how I felt.

He gave me a slow, leisurely smile. "I'd be nervous, too. Aeval is a scary-assed bitch." He chuckled. "Don't get me wrong. I appreciate the Triple Threat, but the thought of spending much time with them doesn't appeal to me in the slightest."

"*Really?*" I snorted. "I thought you'd enjoy it. After all, Aeval and Titania are gorgeous. And Morgaine, well, she's no slouch and looks a lot like me. Just . . . a little older. Which isn't surprising, given she's a distant relation."

Trillian shrugged. "What can I say? I like my women a little less . . . *regal*? No, that's not the right word. Powerful women are an aphrodisiac. And I love that you aren't a shrinking violet. But there's a certain *pretentiousness* that comes with the Fae queens and, while I understand it, that doesn't mean I care to keep their company. When I worked for Tanaquar as a mercenary, I had the same reaction. I can't believe your father actually bedded her." He sobered. "But, are you *safe*? Are they forcing you to move too fast in your training?"

I considered his question. No doubt about it, the training had been intense and fast—twice a week when I wasn't embroiled in a fight or battle with the demons.

And tomorrow, at dusk, I was due back out at Talamh Lonrach Oll, the sovereign Earthside Fae nation recently established by the Court of the Three Queens. Over the past few months, I'd been taught basic etiquette of the Priestesshood, new vocabulary and terminology, rules about training acolytes, and now I was ready to begin the actual magic. Next I would learn to lead rituals.

My training as a Moon Witch had been taxing, but I had the feeling it was going to seem like a piece of cake compared to what I was facing.

"Safe? Are we ever safe, anymore?" After a moment, I shook my head. "No, the training isn't too fast. But it's challenging. I think I'll be facing monsters of a different sort than zombies and ghosts over the coming months. Maybe . . ."

I didn't want to think about it, didn't want to say it, but the thought wouldn't leave my mind. "Maybe I'm most afraid of the monsters who lurk inside of me. My inner demons."

He nodded as he stood, grabbing a towel off the rack. "Let's dry you off and get some food inside you. Then, if you're up for anything, we'll go from there." Throwing the towel over his shoulder, he leaned down and took my hand, helping me out of the bathwater.

I carefully stepped out of the tub and accepted the huge fluffy bath sheet. Wrapping it around myself, I padded out of the bathroom, into the bedroom, where the bed flirted with me like a whore in the Broadway district. I debated. *Hunger? Sleep deprivation? Hunger? Sleep deprivation?* Finally, sleep won out.

"I'm too tired to eat," I said after a moment as I crossed to the bed.

"All right, my love. Crawl into bed and let me make sure you're tucked in properly." Trillian gently folded the blankets around my shoulders, and I was asleep before he could kiss me good night. I slept deeply, not even waking when Morio, Smoky, and Trillian joined me during the night.

I'd fallen asleep early, for me, and so woke to the faintest glimpse of dawn glimmering in the east. The sun would rise in an hour. I slid out from the bed, crawling over Smoky, who was snoring up a storm, to pad across the room and stare at the window. Trillian was still asleep, also, but Morio was up, and he silently entered the room, fresh from the shower, his hair wet, trailing against his kimono. He wrapped his arms around me, and we stared outside at the faint light filtering down to splash across the yard.

As he pressed against my back, I felt his cock rise into a thick, hard erection, and I let out a little moan, wanting him. Wanting *all* my men. Rejuvenated from the long sleep, I was hungry. Hungry for sex, and hungry for food. I glanced back at the bed where Trillian and Smoky were both dead to the world. Morio noticed my look, then took my hand and led me silently out of the room, motioning for me to grab my robe and slippers as we left.

I tied the belt, padding down the stairs after him. He peeked into the kitchen, then nodded. The kitchen was still empty at five A.M. and he stopped to open the fridge and dump several items into a wicker basket sitting on the counter. We slipped out the back door, out onto the enclosed porch, then out the door and down to the dewy grass. I shivered, wishing I'd worn something heavier. Late April in the Pacific Northwest tended to be wet and chilly.

Stars still faintly littered the sky, and we raced across the lawn, hand in hand, toward the trail leading to Birchwater Pond. The sound of birdsong echoed through the forest as we set foot on the path. I paused to stare at a handful of trees that had been uprooted, blasted through. Hyto had left a message for the others when he kidnapped me. When Smoky had discovered the charred trees, he'd gone crazy, ripping up a small section of forest at the mouth of the trail before the others had been able to calm him.

Now I gazed at the fallen timber, shattered like toothpicks, and looked back at Morio. He slowly raised my hand to his lips, kissed the top, and then nodded for me to leave the memories behind. With a shuddering breath, I turned away and followed him down the overgrown path.

Spring was in full sway—although that didn't mean hot or clear days. Not here in the Pacific Northwest. Today the weather promised to be warm, in the low to midsixties. But right now it was around forty-nine degrees.

I inhaled deeply, catching the scent of cedar and fern and moss. I'd come to love the smells of the forests here. Over in Otherworld, Darkynwyrd and Thistlewyd Deep reminded me of the temperate rain forests Earthside, but around Y'Elestrial the trees were more deciduous.

The path was covered with needle and leaf mulch, and here and there a snag had fallen to form an impromptu bench, with moss and mushrooms growing atop the logs. A breeze fluttered through the air, picking up the scents of the forest and amplifying them. Morio and I approached a turn leading to a clearing, where we'd set up a picnic table and benches in anticipation of the summer.

He placed the basket on the picnic table and turned to me, a cunning smile on his face. I grinned. I loved it when his youkai nature began to show itself. I slipped off my robe, shivering. My nightgown—black silk with a slit up the side—fell to my ankles, and I was acutely aware of the brush of the silk against my nipples.

Morio pulled out a scroll.

"What are you up to?"

But he only grinned slyly and then whispered the contents, and a sudden drumming filled the air, emanating from the trees themselves, from leaf and branch and twig and trunk. *The rhythm of passion, of bonfires and long nights dancing around the flames.* I closed my eyes, wavering to the music, as a faint chanting took hold in the beating of the drums. As I began to sway, Morio slowly pulled off his kimono, draping it over the table, and stood naked in front of me, gesturing me toward him.

I slid the straps of my gown off my shoulders and let it fall to the ground, stopping long enough to pick it up so it wouldn't get ruined. After draping it over the picnic table, I gave in—gave myself to the music as the air whistled against my bare skin like long fingers caressing me. Turning to the beat, I danced into Morio's embrace. He caught me by the hands and spun me round, careening around the clearing, our feet barely touching the ground.

My hair streaming behind me, I found myself laughing, unable to stop, for the sheer joy of our dance. The moss was soft under our feet, and the grass glistened with dew. As the sun slowly began to rise, it was as if a long shadow began to fall away from us, the light slowly growing, casting golden ribbons through the meadow. I closed my eyes as it fell on my face, still whirling in the dance with Morio, but then the music changed and an ancient melody drew us close as he wrapped his arms around me, pulling me tight.

I gazed at him—we were nearly the same height—and his eyes flashed with topaz in the depths of their coffee brown. My breasts brushed his chest, and I caught my breath as a wave of hunger raced through me. Hunger for him, hunger for his magic. Tears rose to the surface.

"I'm so lucky to have you . . . to have all three of you . . ." I whispered, but he shook his head.

"Shh . . ." He pressed against me and I felt him, hard and ready, his own desire urgent and pressing.

A low laughter raced through the forest, and I turned as a nearby huckleberry bush shook, moving as something crept behind it. And there—the quivering of a limb on a tree. A fern, fronds waving, waited . . . and then, the flutter of wings in a bush as a Steller's jay flew up, followed by its mate. Squirrels raced up a nearby tree trunk, chasing one another in a mating dance.

I turned back to Morio and he laid me down in the grass, his lips fastening against mine, and all I could think of was how good he smelled—dusty, like the warm promise of summer. As I sank into the kiss, every inch of my body felt lit aflame. He lowered his lips to my neck, sucking gently, and I began to ache, craving his touch, longing to have him inside me.

I tried to shift positions so I could wrap my arms around him, but he grasped my wrists, holding me firm. A shiver raced through me as he pushed me back to trail a path of kisses down my chest, to my breasts. He tongued my right nipple, then took it in his mouth and sucked hard, giving me a little nip. I let out a cry, so aroused that I could barely stand it. But I remained silent as the drums continued to guide him on.

He let go, turning so his lips could linger over my stomach, then down farther, and I gently spread my legs as he lowered his head between them, stroking my clit with his tongue, firing me up, bathing me with his love. Shaking, I cried out, but he rose again, grabbing my hands and holding them to my sides as he once again burrowed deep between my thighs. The stroke of his tongue, the feel of his lips, sent me into a spiral, and I couldn't stop, but let out a long shriek as I came hard and swift.

As I came, Morio rose to his knees, his eyes fully topaz, and I could tell he was trying not to shift. When he was in demonic form, our sex was rough, harsh, and powerful—and I loved it—but today he kept control of his urges and, instead, plunged inside me with a dark grunt, grinding to fill me with his cock. He held my hands over my head and I closed my eyes, letting his thrusts carry me away.

His hips swiveling against me, he drove me deep into the soft mulch of the soil, and the pungent scent filled my nostrils even as I thrust up to meet him, to give him the best leverage. The pulse of his cock inside of me mirrored the drumbeats that echoed through the air around us. As he slid in and out of my cunt, each stroke sent me higher into the sex haze that surrounded us.

For a second, I flashed back to our first tryst—under the

spell of a Faerie Queen—but then my mind cleared and the power of our union grew strong as the magic we were building surged between us. Letting out a growl, I broke free and rolled him over, straddling him, his cock so deep in my pussy that I could swear we'd merged into one being.

I rode him, rode him like a stallion, and as I looked up toward the opening to the clearing, there stood Trillian and Smoky. Both were watching us, their eyes lighting with hunger, and I opened my arms to them. Morio smiled craftily as he grabbed my waist, still moving beneath me.

Smoky and Trillian shed their clothes and, Smoky's hair dancing in the breeze, they joined us, Trillian on one side, Smoky on the other. I took their hands in mine, as they began to kiss their way up my arms. Tendrils of Smoky's hair rose to trace gentle patterns against my skin, and Trillian leaned around to gaze into my face, one hand stroking my back.

Morio let out a long yip, his voice echoing through the woodland, and as he came, I merged with his spirit as we rose, winging higher in the mist of passion that stirred from our lovemaking.

A slow cloud, sparkling purple and silver and green, began to filter through the meadow, and as Morio came, it swirled and spun, a dizzying vortex of energy. Even as I still rode the wave, Smoky scooped me up and was now holding me, his hair securing my back as I wrapped my legs around his waist. He used his hands to brace against the picnic table as he thrust himself in me, and I joyfully rode my dragon, pressing against him, rubbing my breasts against his chest. He whispered something so low in my ear that I could barely hear it, but then I nodded. I knew what he'd asked. He put me down and slid his fingers inside me, then began lubing his cock with my juices.

Trillian smiled darkly and lay down in the grass. As I straddled him, sliding down onto his cock, I pressed my breasts against his chest and raised my butt a little. Slowly, gently, Smoky knelt in back of me, guiding himself into my ass, slowly pressing forward, letting me lead the pace. I slowly leaned into him, knowing just how much pressure I could handle, and he used his hands to keep himself from putting his full weight on both Trillian and me.

They fucked me in rhythm, the drums buoying up our movements, driving us on. Feeling so full I could burst, the friction driving me on, I let out a strangled cry. I needed to come again, wanted to come, wanted to fuck the entire world.

Morio began stroking himself as he watched us, his eyes still glittering. He began to transform into his full demonic self, eight feet of gorgeous youkai, and my breath came in ragged pants as Smoky and Trillian drove me higher into the blur of desire and hunger.

As Morio knelt in front of me, I began licking that gigantic youkai cock of his. It was too big for me to take fully in my mouth, but I slid my lips over the tip and flicked my tongue against him as he stroked himself harder. Watching him was all it took then. With a sudden, sharp ache that echoed through my body, I came, pulsing with the waves of orgasm. Smoky and Trillian came, too, letting out groans as they filled me to overflowing.

We broke apart, but the music became more urgent, and I realized I was building up again. I needed more. I fell onto my knees in the soft grass, clutching at the blades, digging into the ground with my fingers, feeling the rich earth crumble under my touch.

And then Morio was behind me, sliding into my pussy with his engorged cock. In demon form he was huge, but at this point I was so aroused I could easily handle the girth and depth, and he howled, rearing back as he began thrusting against me. Panting, I leaned my forehead against the ground, pressing my breasts into the sweet earth, willing the magic to rise, to spin, to carry us up and aloft.

The beat of the drums grew frantic, and I looked up to see Smoky, eyes flashing, and Trillian, both caught in the web we were building. They knelt on either side and reached out, touching my shoulders, as Morio held my waist.

The power began to build into a cone. And then the bond that tied our souls together linked and we were in unison, all focused on the same outcome, and yet I had no clue what we were aiming for. Morio had set this up, though, and I trusted him. We were following instinct, music pouring around us, the driving beats pushing us higher.

And then I saw it—the cone of power that we were building—and I caught hold of it on the astral level, directing it, spinning it, guiding it as it grew taller and began to swirl.

A moment later, I caught a glimpse of the tethers that kept it tied to us. They were almost broken through. All it would take were a few more strokes from Morio, a few more deep breaths from me, and then . . . as Morio picked up the pace, the orgasm hit me—so hard and deep that I went spiraling out of my body, rising astride the cone of magic. Morio and Trillian and Smoky were there with me, connected to the energy, and I dropped my head back and all the joy and hunger and lust and love that I was feeling welled up into one piercing shriek.

The magical vortex we'd created hung in the air between us, and then, with a sudden *swoosh*, went shooting off into the astral, leaving us teetering for a moment before we went careening head over heels back to our bodies, back to the forest.

A moment later, I opened my eyes. The forest was silent. My men were sprawled around me as I pushed myself up to a sitting position. I glanced at the sky. The sun was just breaking over the horizon. We'd greeted the sunrise with a breath of fire, all right. But just where we'd sent the fire—and to whom or for what it was intended—I had no clue.

I let out a long breath as Morio transformed back into his human form and helped me up. Trillian and Smoky pushed themselves to their feet and began unpacking the picnic basket Morio had thrown together. As I brushed the soil and moss off my body and slid my nightgown and robe back on, it occurred to me that some mornings were worth waking up for.

Chapter 4

As we neared the house, it was obvious that either Hanna or Iris was up. The kitchen lights were on and the window over the sink was open. We could hear the sounds of breakfast being prepared.

As we got closer, I realized it must be Hanna, because Iris and Bruce emerged from their trailer as the four of us—in our robes, headed up the steps to the back porch. I rolled my eyes. We were in for it now.

Iris and Bruce stared at us as they joined us on the porch. Iris smirked. Bruce blushed like he'd just eaten a hot pepper.

"So, I take it the four of you've built up an appetite?" Iris slid past me and opened the kitchen door.

"Um . . . that would be an unqualified *yes*." I inhaled deeply. What little we'd eaten for our breakfast picnic had barely touched my hunger, and the smells coming from the kitchen were tantalizing. I hurried in, eager to see what Hanna had cooked for us. She wasn't quite as good as Iris yet, but she was no slouch in the chef's department.

A big pot of oatmeal bubbled on the stove, along with a

large skillet of scrambled eggs. Hanna was taking sausage links off the grill, and Iris quickly tied on her apron and washed her hands. She began to fix a stack of toast, while Roz, who had just wandered into the kitchen, took over mixing up a pitcher of concentrated orange juice.

We left them to work on breakfast and headed for our rooms. I was beginning to itch from the moss and the dirt, and I pulled off my nightgown and robe, dropping them into the hamper. Though I'd taken care with them, they were still covered with stray bits of forest debris.

"Dibs on the shower. Who's joining me? And I do mean for a *shower*."

Trillian jumped in with me and lathered me up thoroughly. I rinsed off the body wash as he washed his hair under the second shower head. We didn't talk much. My thoughts were running between the scene in the forest—wondering what kind of magic we'd released—and the coming day.

"What are you doing today?" I finally asked as we toweled off and dressed.

"Working on Iris's house. We're really making headway, and we want to see how far we can get before the beginning of June. The plumber comes today, and the electrician." He shrugged. "We want to be done in a month, if possible. Iris and Bruce can't stay in that trailer for long, not with her pregnancy."

Trillian's concern for Iris touched me. My alpha lover had gone from arrogant and snarky to arrogant and . . . caring. He still oozed that Svartan charm, and he still had a razor-sharp tongue when he was annoyed, but he always treated Iris with a deferential respect that made me adore him even more.

We hurried down to breakfast to find the oatmeal, a huge stack of toast, several pounds of bacon, a platter of eggs, a platter of sausage, and a giant bowl of fruit salad waiting. I piled my plate high and accepted a stiff cup of coffee from Hanna, who had discovered the joys of caffeine and, within a short few months, had become as bad an addict as I was.

Nerissa hurried up from the basement, where she shared Menolly's lair. Once it had occurred to them that since

Nerissa slept during the night, and Menolly during the day, they realized there wasn't much of a danger if Nerissa shared the same sleeping space, and she'd moved in.

Menolly's wife was gorgeous, a golden Amazon of a woman, and a werepuma. She worked for Chase as a victim's rights counselor, and today she was dressed in tidy jeans and a button-down shirt.

"You don't look like you're dressed for the office," Delilah said, peeking in from the laundry room. The washer rhythmically thumped in the background, and I gathered she was making an attempt to wash clothes. I hoped, for my own sake, that none of them were mine.

Nerissa shrugged, hugging Iris, then grabbed a plate and began to fill it with fruit salad, bacon, and sausage. She didn't care for bread much and tended to follow her more carnivorous side.

"I have to go out to an apartment building that burned down during the night. There were a lot of displaced people there—mostly Supes—and they're going to need someone to help them find temporary quarters. Better I dress like this rather than too fancy, considering most of them have just lost everything they have in the world." She wrinkled her nose. "I hate working fires. The smells are always so strong they make me gag."

"It wasn't an explosion?" I glanced up. Not long ago, Supes had been the target of some pretty nasty hate crime actions. But she eased my mind.

"No, don't sweat it. Faulty wiring. Slumlord stuff, and boy, is he going to pay, both monetarily and with a tidy jail term. He deliberately refused to bring the place up to code. Two people died, so he might even face negligent manslaughter charges, or whatever you call it."

As I slid into a chair and dug into my food, Iris put the last platter of sausage onto the table, then stretched. She looked tired, and I realized that having twins was going to impact her a lot more than if she were carting around just one baby in that womb.

As if reading my mind, Iris eased herself into the rocking

chair, letting Hanna take over. "Twins take it out of you. Oh!
I forgot to mention it yesterday. Bruce got hired on for the
fall semester at the UW. He's going to continue as head of
the Irish Studies Department for another year." She beamed.
Bruce, her leprechaun husband, was a professor, even though
he had never needed to work a day in his life, considering
how wealthy his parents were.

We all cheered. Good news was good news, and every
drop was a reason for celebration.

"Thank you," he said, blushing. "I love the work. But, I'm
going to be late if I don't get moving." Grabbing his briefcase,
he headed for the front door after giving Iris a deep kiss. His
driver showed up every morning at eight A.M. promptly.
Bruce had his own limo. We'd also discovered that he donated
his entire salary to charity—mostly to the food banks and to
the animal shelters—and lived off the family money.

Iris waved him off, then pushed herself out of the rocking
chair. "I'm going out to the trailer for a nap. Hanna, hold
down the fort for me." Blowing a kiss to all of us, she headed
out the back door.

I glanced over at the wards I'd set up on the house to
make certain the crystals were still glowing clear. If they
went off, we'd all know it, but it eased my mind to double-
check, especially after a night like last night. Polishing off
the last bite of toast, I carried my plate over to the sink, then
turned around, leaning against the counter.

"I guess we should talk about what went down last night in
the cemetery," I started, but the phone rang, interrupting me.

Delilah picked up. After a few muffled answers, she hung
up and motioned to me. "Hope you're up for action, because
Chase needs us."

"Oh, crap. What now?"

"Another grave robbery—en masse—and another officer
dead thanks to . . . well . . . something. He also mentioned
concern about some missing witches." She ran into the living room to gather her keys and purse. I was about to ask her
how his ankle was doing, but the phone rang again. Trillian
picked up and, after a moment, handed the receiver to me.

"Hello?" I didn't want any more bad news. The break in our dry spell was not welcome. But more bad news it was.

"Camille, can you come over? We have a problem here." It was Lindsey Cartridge, the FBH director of the Green Goddess Women's Shelter and leader of the most prominent coven in Seattle.

My first thought was that something was wrong with her baby. But when I asked, she put that fear to rest.

"No, Feddrika is thriving. But remember when my coven was having problems a couple of months ago? Looks like it's not over yet."

"More psychic vampires?" I so did not want to deal with more bhouts—ghosts who ate magical energy and transferred it to their controller. Gulakah had really messed with a good share of the witches in the area, as well as a number of the magic-using Fae.

"Not exactly. One of my covener's sons is in trouble. Sean was out hunting for graveyard dirt—don't even say a word about that."

I chuckled. I couldn't very well say much, seeing that I used graveyard dirt myself. "Go on. I'm listening."

"Well, he was out early this morning digging up a little graveyard dirt when he saw grave robbers in the cemetery. He managed to hide before they caught sight of him. When the cops showed up, they got into a fight with the thieves. Sean managed to escape before he was caught, but he's terrified. And he said there were some odd things going on there— the energy was fucked up."

I bit my lip. This was all getting too close for comfort. Thinking for a moment, I finally said, "You, your covener, and Sean meet us at the FH-CSI in an hour or so. You *have* to tell Chase about this. I promise, we'll make sure Sean doesn't get into trouble. At least not more than a dressing-down."

Lindsey agreed and hung up. By that time, Delilah was back and we headed out. We took my car. Delilah's Jeep had been acting up and Jason Binds, our friend Tim's husband, had said he would come out to look at it today. As I tossed my purse into the back and strapped on my seat belt, it occurred to me that vacation was over and we were firmly back in the trenches.

"I need to stop by Mystic Charms before we head to HQ. It's on the way, and I'll only be a few minutes."

The minute Delilah had shut her door, I eased out of the driveway and headed onto the—for once—dry roads. The sun was peeking through wispy clouds, in that perfect union of cool breeze and warming rays that sparked the imagination and cleared the head.

I rolled down my window and inhaled deeply. Someone, somewhere, had recently mowed their lawn. The clean, newly shorn grass smell gave way to rotten eggs as we passed through where a skunk had let loose.

Delilah let out a muffled "Ugh," and I grinned at her. Ever since she'd been skunked, she gave them a wide berth.

And then we were nearing the metropolitan area, and I closed the window and turned on the air. Exhaust wasn't my idea of a good time.

"Marion called last night," Delilah said.

"She and Douglas find a house yet?" Marion was a friend of ours—a coyote shifter—who had been displaced when the Koyanni burned down her house and her café. The café had been restored, but she and her husband had been living with our neighbor Wilbur—our neighborhood necromancer and frootloop—helping him out. He'd also been a victim of collateral damage, only instead of a burned shell of a house, he was missing a leg.

"Yeah, they're closing on it and moving in about three weeks. Marion's sister came to get Snickers, their cat, when they moved in with Wilbur. She's going to keep him for them until they move. They didn't dare take Snickers to Wilbur's, not with Martin around. He might eat him." Delilah grimaced, and I grimaced along with her.

"He's a freak show, that's for sure." I sighed. "But I guess he's *our* freak show, as much as we might not want to claim him. I imagine Wilbur will be glad to have his house back, though."

"Marion thinks he's going to miss them."

"He's such an odd duck. Just when I think I might actually like him, he goes and does something to piss me off. He wanted to borrow Rodney the other night, but Morio told him to fuck off."

"What did he want with Rodney?" Delilah sounded as suspicious as I felt.

"I dunno, but it couldn't be anything good."

Rodney was a bane and a curse, though he'd been given to us as a gift. The bone golem would have made the perfect love child of Howard Stern and Rodney Dangerfield. Toss in a touch of Don Rickles, and he'd be the perfect storm. We couldn't get rid of the little freak, though, because Grandmother Coyote had given him to Morio. I not-so-secretly hoped that one day Rodney would find himself on the business end of a very big sledgehammer.

As we neared the corner of Strand and Oakes, I pulled into a space that opened up even as we drove down the street. *Bingo!* Right in front of Mystic Charms. I had a knack for finding parking whenever I needed it.

"You want to stay here, or come in?" I leaned over the backseat to grab my purse and glanced into my side mirror to see if anybody was coming. Last thing I needed was for someone to take off my door when I opened it.

"Coming with." Delilah hopped out. The sidewalks were cracked, barely above street level, and when the rains flooded the streets, the shops put out sandbags, just in case. But it was a low-rent district, and businesses that skimped by on a shoestring found it easier to survive here.

As we headed into the store, I automatically scanned the room for any sign of trouble. It was second nature now—especially when we were dealing with magical shops and clubs.

Mystic Charms was a homey little shop, but looks were deceiving. The owners were an interracial couple—an FBH witch and her Fae husband. Laslan had come over from Otherworld, met Beth, and fallen in love, much as our father had done with our mother. But instead of going back to Otherworld with him, Beth had persuaded him to give it a go over

Earthside. They were both powerful, each in their own form of magic, and I respected their integrity, so I frequented their shop.

Delilah hovered over some pretty candles, while I checked out the other patrons in the shop. There were two who were obviously Wiccan—which was merely one branch of FBH paganism and witchcraft.

Another woman resonated with a dark, deep, shamanic energy. She felt edgy and powerful, and intriguing.

A fourth was flipping through the how-to books on the shelf, looking frustrated. I wanted to go over and tell him to quit reading and go out and just explore his magic, but that wasn't my place.

Instead, I picked up a basket and glanced around, looking for the herbs and oils, which had been moved from their usual location.

In fact, now that I looked around, I saw that the entire shop had undergone a change in looks. After a moment, I spied the herbs and headed over to a wall that was now lined with cubbyholes.

Within each niche stood a jar filled with herbs. They were in alphabetical order, and as I set down the basket and began moving the mandrake root and wormwood to the counter with scales and plastic sacks, the man slammed the book he was holding back onto the shelf and, with a disgruntled sigh, headed out the door.

Beth, who had been watching him from behind the counter, marched over and tried to smooth the ruffled pages, then sighed and carried the book back to the counter. She turned just in time to catch my eye.

"Camille!" She bustled over to give me a hug.

"Who was Mr. Disappointed?" I nodded to the figure retreating out the door.

"Oh, him. Don't mind him, except, damn it, he ruined another book. I don't like to send them back—it messes up the authors—so I just buy them and add them to the lending library I keep in my home. Then I send Jake an invoice and he pays it without comment."

"What's his problem? He looked disgruntled." In fact, he'd looked downright pissed off.

"Disgruntled? Yeah, that's Jake all right. He's always in here, looking for books to give him power. He doesn't want to actually do the work, and he's always looking in the sections that would burn his fingers, *if* he ever tried casting any of the spells from them. He's not a bad person, per se. Just lazy, whiny, and apathetic. He shouldn't be practicing magic in the first place. But enough about him. What do you need?"

She wrapped an arm around my shoulder as we turned to face the wall of herbs. "Do you like what I've done with the place?"

"I love it."

And I did. Everything was organized and tidy. I glanced up at Beth. She was taller than I was, and larger—the woman was plump, that was for sure, but she wore it well, and her gypsy skirt and halter top suited her, as did the armful of bangle bracelets and the large chunk of smoky quartz hanging around her neck.

"I need herbs. Mandrake, wormwood, and a few others. I'm also looking for several oils—and they *must* be essential. No fragrance oils. Rose, and jasmine." The differences between synthetic oils and essential were myriad—sometimes the scent was what I needed when it came to spell work and a fragrance oil was fine. But in this case, I definitely needed the essence of the plant.

She snorted. "*Pure* jasmine oil? You prepared to pay a hundred bucks for a tiny bottle? Then I have it for you." She nodded me into the back room. I glanced at Delilah, who was sitting at one of the small tables in the corner of the shop, flipping through a magazine. She waved for me to go ahead.

The room into which Beth led me was small, with a desk and two chairs on the other side. She motioned for me to sit down. While I waited, she unlocked a drawer on an apothecary chest behind her desk and pulled out a small bottle.

"Here we go. Jasmine oil. One-eighth of an ounce for forty-five dollars. And the rose absolute is forty."

I picked up the bottle. One-eighth of an ounce was a very

small amount, but for what I was making, I didn't need a great deal. "Two bottles of each, please."

"Good. And what herbs did you need? I can start Kerri on getting them packaged for you."

"I need some cut mandrake root—two ounces—an ounce of sacred tobacco, as well as an ounce each of wormwood, damiana, and kava kava; a big chunk of amber resin; and three ounces of galangal."

She set out my oils, locked the drawer again, and then quickly jotted down what I wanted. "Anything else?"

"Yes, actually. Bone chips. Silver dust. A sweetgrass braid. Two smudge sticks—sage and cedar." I usually made my own, but we'd gone through my entire stash and my herbs weren't mature enough to plunder in order to make more. So, until later in the season, I was working off store-bought ingredients.

As we headed back to the front of the shop, Beth stopped to give Kerri—her older daughter from her first marriage—my list. The girl began to pull herbs and measure them out for me. I wandered over to Delilah.

"Almost done. Anything interesting?"

She was reading an issue of *Supe-R-Natural Weekly*, a small newspaper on a shoestring budget at a regional press started by two Weres and one of the ES Fae. We had a subscription, though there usually wasn't much in it. But we liked supporting our brothers-in-arms.

"Actually, something did catch my eye. Look." She pushed the paper across the table. I picked it up and looked where she pointed. An advertisement that took up about one-eighth of the page, for a meeting coming up in two days. Run by none other than the Aleksais Psychic Network.

"Fuck . . . you have to be kidding."

The Aleksais Psychic Network was the group we suspected of colluding with Gulakah to bring in the bhouts. They'd been accused of luring away Fae and magic-using FBHs, a lot like the Moonies had indoctrinated their cult members. We'd been trying to find some leads on them, and all we would have had to do was check the local magical rags.

"Why didn't we see this in our issue? Did we even *get* this issue?" I glanced at the front of the paper. It had been out for several days.

"We might have accidentally let it lapse."

"This would be the perfect way to check them out." I looked up at my sister, who gave me a slow nod.

"But they'd know who we were. We are pretty visible, you have to agree with me on that." She frowned, thinking.

I leaned back, glancing over my shoulder. Beth had my packages almost ready to go. "You're right. But there are ways around that. I have some ideas. I'll need help implementing them, though."

"Camille—your purchases." Beth called from the counter, and I pushed to my feet and headed over, handing my credit card to Kerri as she rang up the herbs and oils.

I glanced at the woman who'd first caught my attention—the one with shamanic energy. Her energy was stronger than I'd thought, and I found myself staring openly at her. She glanced at me, her dark gaze lingering on my face. It took everything I had to pull my attention away.

As Kerri handed me my package, I turned to Beth. "Who's that?"

Beth glanced over at the woman, who had gone back to hunting through the shelves, then back at me. "Her name is Zinnia. She is one tough cookie, and nobody messes with her. Not nasty, but if you fuck with her, she'll sure as hell fuck with you. And when she means business, heads roll in the magical world."

"Zinnia, huh?" I made a note to remember her name and check her out later, when we had time. It paid to know the stronger witches in the FBH world.

I signed the credit card slip, picked up my package, and—with one last look at Zinnia, who was studiously ignoring me—headed toward the door. Delilah fell in beside me. I'd added the newspaper to my purchases so we'd have the information in the advertisement. Back in the car, I eased into traffic and we were headed to the FH-CSI.

* * *

Chase was sitting at his desk, his leg in a splint propped up on a footstool. When we walked in, he jerked his head up. "About time. Where were you?"

I waved off his question. "Chill, Johnson. We do have other things to do besides hold your hand all the time. We're here now, so let's get on with this." But I flashed him a smile to let him know I was just teasing.

"How's your foot?" Delilah gave him a quick hug, and Chase kissed her on the cheek right about the moment Sharah walked in. I glanced at the elfin medic. Queen Asteria's niece, Sharah was also Chase's current girlfriend, and she was pregnant with his baby.

Her gaze darted from Chase to Delilah, then back to Chase again, and I knew what *that* look meant. But both Chase and Delilah were busy chatting and I wanted to smack them upside the head. Clueless, with a capital *C*.

"Chase, here's the report on your officers." Sharah's voice was abrupt, and I caught the same hint that I heard with Iris—hormones running rampant and affecting her emotions.

I edged over to Delilah and gave her a sharp nod to move out of the way. She glanced at me, then over at Sharah, and as understanding filled her eyes, she quickly moved away from Chase and took a seat.

"Thanks." He glanced over at Delilah, still blissfully unaware of his faux pas. "Broke the ankle. Shouldn't take too long to heal, though. It was a clean fracture. Hurts like an SOB." Chase, still blissfully unaware, picked up the reports. Sharah pulled away, scowling, and left the room. The minute the door closed, I swung around.

"Idiot. Can't you see she was upset?" Hands on my hips, I glared at him, then turned to Delilah. "And you . . . you know better than that."

"What? What did I do? What's wrong now?" Yep. He had that deer-caught-in-the-headlights look. Clueless.

"Use your brain. Sharah's very pregnant, and very volatile. She comes in here, sees you and Delilah exchanging a kiss—albeit a friendly one—but given your history, I imagine she feels a little insecure. And being pregnant isn't going to help. Instead of dropping what you were doing and greeting her like you really love her, you brushed her off with a peck on the cheek."

"But we're at work . . ."

"Dude. *Pregnant woman who loves you?* Work, schmerk. You could have at least given her a smile or something."

Chase groaned, his expression shifting from clueless to *oh-I-am-so-fucked.* "Oh man, nobody warns you about this stuff. Why isn't there a father-to-be manual that gives you the heads-up on everything you should know during your woman's pregnancy?"

Delilah let out a sigh. "I am so stupid. I didn't even think about what she might think. Camille's right. You'd better apologize, but give her time to cool off. And some flowers wouldn't hurt." She rubbed her temples. "She might still think we have feelings for each other—"

"We do." Chase stared at her. "And we always will, but they aren't . . . I'm not . . ."

"I'm not in love with you, either," Delilah said gently, smiling. "But Sharah's the one who needs to know that."

"Fine. Chase is going to buy flowers and eat crow, and you both are going to be careful about the touchy-feely stuff. Let's get on with it. Lindsey Cartridge is on the way down here right now, Chase. She has some information that may be important in your investigation of this morning's events." I quickly outlined what she'd told me. "I promised her that the kid wouldn't get in trouble."

Chase let out an exasperated sigh. "You do know desecration of a grave is a misdemeanor?"

I stared at him. "Uh, yeah. *I* use graveyard dust, too, so you want to lock me up while you're at it?"

After a long pause, Chase shrugged and flipped through the report. "Whatever. We've got more worries than a kid trying to steal some dirt. If he really did see the grave robbers and knows what happened to my officer, then I don't care what he was doing . . . within reason."

"What cemetery did they hit this time?"

"The Wedgewood. So, really, is there any way to find out if they drained off the souls or spirits or whatever spooks were hanging around there?" He frowned, pausing over the papers Sharah had given him. "Zombie attack probably killed this officer, too. His neck was broken and his arm was . . . gnawed on. Hell of a thing to tell his wife."

"Can you tell her it was a dog?" Delilah asked.

"And that would be better, how? Might turn her against dogs the rest of her life." Pursing his lips, he closed the file and tossed it back on the desk. "I won't tell her it was zombies, but I have to tell her he was mauled. Maybe I'll just leave it at that."

Just then, Yugi knocked on the door and peeked in. "Lindsey Cartridge to see you. She's with another woman, and a teenage boy."

Chase glanced around his office. It wasn't the most spacious cubicle. He reached for his crutches, wobbled to his feet, and motioned for us to follow him. "Is anybody using conference room B right now?"

Yugi shook his head. "Nope, it's free."

"Have them meet us there, then."

"Sure thing, Chief." Yugi saluted and headed back the way he'd come.

Delilah and I followed Chase into the empty conference room, careful not to trip him up. He was strong, but crutches are never anybody's best friend.

The room looked like it got quite a bit of use. Several empty steno pads were scattered around the table, and a couple of gory case pictures hung on one bulletin board, apparently forgotten from the last meeting. I stared at the mangled bodies, slightly queasy.

Following my gaze, Chase asked me to take them down before Lindsey and her friends were escorted in. I grimaced but moved over to the photos. I'd no more than unpinned them from the corkboard and tucked them in a drawer on one of the built-in counters when Lindsey walked in.

A little shorter than me, she had long wheat-colored hair pulled back in a ponytail, and she was athletic as hell. For an FBH, she could give Delilah a run for her money. Even though she'd had a baby only a few months before, the woman was built like a freight train, and I had no doubt she could bash in a few heads.

Behind her was a woman as petite as Menolly, with curly brown hair, and a boy who resembled her, except for his height. He towered over her, looking like a frightened rabbit.

As they silently sat down at the table, Chase motioned to the coffee urn. "If you want, we have fresh coffee, and there's also hot water for tea. Would you like a soda?" He glanced at the boy.

"Um . . . sure. Coke, please." The kid's voice was shaky, and he sounded surprised. I had the feeling he was waiting for the iron to drop in the fire.

Chase gave Delilah a dollar, who plugged it into the vending machine. She handed the kid a Coke. Lindsey fixed coffee for herself and her friend. When she glanced over at us, Delilah and I shook our heads. Delilah didn't like coffee, and I'd tasted the coffee at HQ before. I knew better.

Chase motioned for us to gather round. He sat across from the boy but leaned back in his chair and stuck his hands in his pockets. I knew what he was up to with his casual stance. He was trying to diminish some of the authoritarian scare that cops held over kids.

"Why don't you introduce me to your friends, Lindsey?" He nodded to her.

Lindsey gave him a nod in return. "Sure thing. This is Tracy Smyth and her son, Sean. Tracy, Sean, this is Detective Johnson—he's the director of the Faerie-Human Crime Scene Investigation unit. Tracy is part of my coven, Detective. And Sean is in my training coven for teens."

Chase leaned forward, shook Tracy's hand, and gave Sean a friendly nod. "Thank you both for coming down. Lindsey said that you may have seen something this morning, Sean? Something frightening?"

Sean glanced at his mother, who tried to reassure him.

"It's okay. Go on. Tell him what you saw, honey." She patted his arm and he pulled away.

"*Mommmm*, don't call me that in public." He blushed. Ah yes, the teen years. FBHs had it hard when it came to hormones and puberty. The Fae were born with them already active. We grew up used to them raging through our systems. But that didn't necessarily help us control them.

"Your mother is just concerned, son. Maybe cut her a little slack?" Chase flashed a smile at Sean, who shrugged, then cracked a smile of his own.

"Yeah, okay. Sorry, Mom."

"Now, suppose you tell me what you saw." Chase leaned forward and pulled a steno pad toward him as he took out a pen from his jacket. "And don't worry. If what Ms. Cartridge has told me is true, you're not going to get in trouble. You could help us a great deal if you'd tell us everything you witnessed. One of my officers was killed early this morning. He left a wife, and a daughter just about your age. If you noticed anything, you could make a great difference by helping us catch whoever did this."

Sean worried his lip for a moment, then let out a long sigh. "I was out in the graveyard—"

"Which one?"

"The Wedgewood Cemetery. Part of our magical training is to learn how to use graveyard dirt. Usually we have some around the house, but we were out and I have Circle tonight and needed to finish my homework for it." Sean's voice started to even out a little as he spoke. He stopped to take a swig of the soda, then wiped his mouth.

"Homework. Gets you every time, doesn't it, whether it's school or magic?" Chase raised his eyebrows, and the kid visibly relaxed.

"Yeah, sure does. And Lindsey—Ms. Cartridge—works us hard. She's tough—" He gulped and flashed Lindsey a sheepish smile. "Sorry, Ms. Cartridge, but you know you make us work hard. But you're fair. Anyway, I was working by the hours, so I had to get up really early in the morning to do this."

"What's that mean?" Chase asked, glancing up. I couldn't

tell if he really wanted to know or was just trying to draw out Sean, but whatever the case, it worked.

Sean warmed up, leaning forward. "See, there are specific parts of the day that relate to some spells, and you have to do the work within that time period or you mess it up. I was supposed to do an early morning meditation on the ancestors, and the main spell component is graveyard dirt. That's when I realized we were out of it. We live near the cemetery, so I thought I'd just run over there and grab a handful."

"You know that dirt wouldn't be consecrated and cleansed, Sean." Lindsey frowned at him.

"I know, but what else was I gonna do? You'd think I was shirking if I didn't do my best to gather what I needed. And you always know when we're fudging our answers about homework." Sean scowled, staring at the table.

"Yes, but you can always use a substitute. Remember, I told you that mixing valerian, mandrake, belladonna, and garden soil will work in a pinch." She tapped the table with her fingernails. "Just remember that next time, okay?"

Sean ducked his head. "Sorry, Ms. C."

Chase cleared his throat. "If we could leave the teaching till later?"

Lindsey blushed. "Oh, geez, I'm sorry!"

With a chuckle, Chase waved off her apology. "Not a problem. Okay, Sean, how about you continue? You decided to go over to the cemetery to grab a handful of graveyard dirt?"

Sean nodded. "Yeah. I threw on my jacket and ran over there. There wasn't anybody there, that I could tell at first, so I headed in to find an old grave—I didn't want to disturb anybody who'd recently been buried, and the older the graveyard dirt, the better."

"Really? That's interesting."

As I watched them talk, it occurred to me that Chase was going to make a great father. He had a way with kids that I didn't really understand, but could appreciate. Sharah's baby was going to be well loved, at least over here Earthside. Being half-breed and a member of the royal family would bring its own set of problems back in Otherworld.

Sean leaned forward, cradling his Coke between his hands. "Yeah, the age of the dirt matters. You wouldn't think so, but it does. New graves? Too chaotic. Old graveyard dirt is more powerful and focused. Anyway, I was wandering through the cemetery and I heard some noises. The sidewalk curved next to a really old cedar tree, and I heard some yelling—it was coming from around the tree. I sneaked up behind the cedar. I didn't know what was going on, and it seemed smart to stay out of sight until I knew."

"Good thinking." I gave him a firm nod.

He looked at me and blushed. His eyes lingered over my breasts, and then he blushed again and looked away quickly. Yep. Hormones.

"Thanks. Well, I peeked around the tree trunk, and I saw . . ." Here, Sean paled again, the ease fading out of his expression. Frightened Rabbit was back.

"Go on, tell Detective Johnson what you told me." Tracy reached out and put her hand on Sean's arm. He didn't shake her off this time.

"I saw something . . . bodies . . . they looked like they were from that old movie, *Night of the Living Dead*. There were several of them. And they had hold of this cop—I didn't see how they caught him, but they were holding him down and they were . . ." His voice cracked, and tears formed in his eyes. He dashed them away angrily and rested his fists on the table.

"What were they doing, Sean? It's okay to tell us." I leaned across the table and put my hand over his.

"They were tearing him apart. Ripping into him like he was a piece of meat. He was still alive and they tore out his guts! I could hear him screaming."

Chase pressed his lips together and let out a slow sigh. "Breathe, Sean. Take a slow, deep breath."

Sean sniffled and caught his breath. I wished Nerissa was around. This boy was going to need some counseling for sure. But she was out at the scene of the apartment fire. Glancing around, I caught sight of a box of tissues and silently carried it over to Sean, stopping to gently pat him on the shoulder.

After a moment, Sean cleared his throat and wiped his eyes. "I . . . I saw someone else there. Two guys, actually."

"Who? Can you describe them?" Chase was instantly alert again. "Were they being attacked, too?"

With a shake of his head, Sean turned a haunted look at his mother and Lindsey. "We know one of them, and the other . . . I think we saw him at that psychic fair we were at before the weird stuff started happening to the coven. I couldn't believe they both just stood there watching. They didn't do anything to try to help the officer." Then, pausing, he hung his head. "But I didn't try to help, either. I guess I'm just as bad."

"Sean, there wasn't anything you could have done. Please, know that. These creatures are terribly powerful and they would have killed you, too. Now, tell us who you saw and what they were doing." I caught his gaze, unmasking my Fae glamour just enough to give my words a boost. Sean was young and impressionable.

He wiped his eyes again, then blew his nose, all the while staring at me. After a few seconds, he let out another breath. "Yeah, I guess you're right. The guy we know—his name is Jake. Jake Evans. He's a member of our Temple."

"Jake?" Lindsey sounded shocked. "Jake Evans was there?" She turned to us. "Jake is—*was*—a member of our Temple. He belonged to our pagan study group, off which our coven and the training coven hived. Temple is for people who don't want to actively work magic, but want to get together to study our beliefs in a less hands-on way, or for those who just don't have the discipline or calling to attend Circle. They also celebrate the Sabbats—the high holidays—with us. But Jake left Temple last month."

Jake. The name rang a bell. Where had I heard that recently? And then I snapped my fingers. "Does he frequent Mystic Charms?"

Lindsey nodded. "He makes a nuisance of himself there. Drives Beth nuts."

"I think we saw him this morning." I turned to Delilah. "Remember the guy we saw this morning at the shop? The one who seemed pissed he couldn't find what he wanted?" Confused, I turned back to Lindsey. "I didn't sense a lot of power coming from him."

"He has very little of his own. But he's easily manipulated and would make a good conduit." Lindsey frowned. "Remember the mess that went down when we were being drained of energy near the equinox? Jake . . . that's right about when he started to change. And right after that, he left Temple."

"Why?" Delilah twisted her lip. "Did he get kicked out or leave on his own?"

"A little of both." Lindsey glanced over at us. "As I mentioned, he craved power and was dabbling in questionable areas, magic that we don't allow from the Temple members." She paused, then said, "Camille, there's something else about him. He joined the Aleksais Psychic Network and signed over his house to them. It's up for sale now. He gave them all the money he had and moved into their commune. I know because his sister told me."

There it was again. The Aleksais Psychic Network. More than ever, my intuition told me that we had to get in there and see what the hell they were doing. Remembering what else Sean had said, I turned back to the boy. "You said you saw someone else there?"

He nodded. "I don't know his name, but he was standing back a ways, and he had . . . something in his hand. It looked like a scroll, and he was reading from it. He was a little on the short side, and had short hair . . . he wore glasses. He was at the fair, Mom. Ms. C—you remember him? He was talking to you a lot."

Lindsey rubbed the bridge of her nose. "How can I forget? Halcon Davis. He made me nervous."

And once again, we were right back to the Aleksais Psychic Network.

"Lindsey, you said Jake wasn't very powerful on his own, but that he might make a good conduit. You also said he was starting to dabble in questionable areas. Do you mean necromancy or sorcery?"

Lindsey blanched. "Yeah, though I'm not sure which. I wouldn't let him into the coven because when someone's out for power, they can be dangerous even if they don't have the innate abilities. And he wasn't willing to abide by our rules. Several times, I almost kicked him out because he was a disruption. But I never thought . . ."

I mulled over what we knew. "I wonder if he's being possessed. Could Halcon have been controlling him? And we know the Aleksais Psychic Network is tied into . . . a lot of nasty things." I'd almost said *Gulakah* but caught myself before I slipped.

Lindsey closed her eyes. "Crap. You think someone was using him as a conduit to raise zombies?"

Sean let out a strangled cry. "Zombies?"

"Silence, Sean." Lindsey motioned for him to be quiet.

I held her gaze. "Quite possibly. The scrolls for that usually take more than one person unless the spellcaster is advanced," I finally said. "I think Jake is being used in this . . . situation."

"You think Halcon is advanced enough to do it?" Delilah asked, cocking her head.

Pushing my chair back, I stood and crossed to the counter, where I poured myself a cup of the harshest coffee I'd taste all day. I grimaced as I sipped it, but I needed the jolt. "I don't know. Quite possibly." All I really knew was that he was connected with Gulakah.

Of course, we might be wrong. It wasn't like we'd been wrong before—Harold Young had been an FBH out for power, and Dante's Hellions had possessed one of the spirit seals but weren't exactly hooked up with Shadow Wing, even though they thought they were.

But this time, I really believed there was a strong connection between the APN and Gulakah—and, therefore, Shadow Wing. We needed to be sure, though, and we needed to find out soon. And the ad in the *Supe-R-Natural Weekly* was our ticket to find out.

"Okay, here's the deal. Sean, you stay out of the cemetery for now. Use the substitutions Lindsey taught you. *Nobody say anything about this to anybody.*" I looked directly at Sean. "Listen, I know you'll be tempted to tell your friends, because hey—who sees zombies every day? But you *can't.* A lot of people could get hurt if this gets out. Promise?"

He held my gaze for a moment, and then, swallowing, he gave me a single nod. "I get it. I promise."

"Good. We're counting on you." I let out a long sigh. This was going to be a bumpy ride, and I wasn't looking forward to it.

Chapter 5

After Lindsey, Tracy, and Sean left, we went back to Chase's office. Delilah and I settled onto the sofa that was in the corner of the room. Chase must have been tired of sitting in his chair, because he eased onto his desk and sat there facing us, his legs spread apart like his balls were too big for him to close them. Men had that habit, I'd noticed.

"First, that's not good for your foot to hang like that. And secondly . . ." Delilah's expression darkened. "Dude, do you know what that reminds me of?" Her words hung in the air.

Chase looked blank for a moment, then blushed and quickly hobbled to his chair. "Sorry, I didn't even think of that."

"It's water under the bridge, but you know, some visuals you just can't get out of your brain. There's not enough brain bleach in the world. And Erika's lips planted around your cock is one of those images." She grimaced.

Speechless that she actually went there, I stared at the ceiling . . . hard. Best to just let the subject die without resuscitating it.

Flustered, Chase shuffled through some papers, and I decided to take the reins of the conversation and steer it someplace a bit more relevant.

"Let's talk about what Sean told us, shall we? But first, let me put in a quick call to Beth at Mystic Charms. I just want to verify something." I pulled out my cell phone and dialed her number. She answered within two rings. "Beth, it's Camille. You know that guy this morning? Jake? Can you tell me what his last name is?"

After a brief pause, she let out a little huff. "Evans. Jake Evans. I know because he bounced a check in here a few months ago, and I told him from that moment on, it was cash only if he wanted something. That's how I got his address to send him those invoices—off the check. I also have a feeling he's been plundering stuff from the store, though."

"Shoplifting?"

"Well, he's not paying for those books I think he hides under his coat and walks out with—the ones he doesn't trash. But I haven't been quick enough to stop him. I'm considering putting a hex on the section he frequents or something."

I realized we'd forgotten to get the address for the Aleksais Psychic Network from Lindsey, if she even knew where it was. "Do you know where he's currently living? Apparently he's not at his old home, since he packed it up and moved to the Aleksais Psychic Network's commune."

"Just the address that was on the check. I still have it somewhere." After a moment she came back on. "Sorry, PO box in Seattle. No home address. And about the Aleksais Psychic Network . . . they're bad news, Camille. Don't get involved with them." Apparently another customer came into the shop. "Gotta go—customer up front."

As I punched the End Call button, I glanced up. "Well, that confirms it—the guy in Mystic Charms this morning *was* Jake Evans. If he was out at the Wedgewood Cemetery early, and then at Mystic Charms this morning, he probably lives nearby. Which means the APN is somewhere in the area."

"Unless he's just hanging out in the city for the day."

Delilah shrugged. "We don't know that the Aleksais Psychic Network is headquartered in the city. Could be they're a ways out."

"True. At least we know that Jake Evans is connected with them now. We know that he was in the graveyard with Halcon Davis, who was reading a scroll, and there were zombies there. They either instigated a murder or witnessed it and did nothing to stop it or report it."

"So he's a loser who has no power of his own, but he's easily manipulated by others. Great. And now he's digging up graves with a man who sounds like a librarian." Chase let out a disgruntled snort. "Can't we ever just get a run-of-the-mill break-and-enter, or maybe a bar brawl?"

"Be careful what you ask for, or you might get it. Want to break up a brawl between a couple of moonstruck werewolves, perhaps?" Delilah snickered, then sobered quickly.

"I was hoping that you guys could figure out if . . . the spirits were sucked out. Like last night?" Chase tossed his pen on the table. "If you told me five years ago I'd be asking questions like that, I would have carted you off to the loony bin."

"We can," I said. "Or at least, we can try. So, what's our next step?"

Chase pulled up his computer. "Before we do anything else, let's look up Jake in the records. See if he's been . . . oh my. Jake Evans, is this him?" He turned the monitor so we could see it.

That was him, short, balding, a little pudgy, and snide looking. I nodded. "What's he been up to?"

"Jake's been a busy boy over the past few years. I wonder if Lindsey knows about his record . . ."

"What did he do?" Delilah asked.

"It seems that our friend Jake has played the con man fast and loose. He tried to pull off several pyramid schemes and managed to plea-bargain his way out of all the charges in return for information on his partners. He's been arrested four times for shoplifting. He's been arrested twice for brawling—in a bar no less, so maybe I will get what I was asking for."

I frowned. What was a petty thug like Jake doing in the Temple to begin with? They usually watched the ethics of their members carefully, and stealing wasn't high on the good-behavior list. "Find anything else?"

"Yeah. Two DUIs, a host of unpaid parking tickets, and he's suspected in an attempt at insurance fraud. Apparently wasn't enough proof to make an arrest on that one." Chase frowned and sat back. "He's a small-time con artist—why the hell is he robbing graves?"

"Because he's easily influenced, and he has the potential to wreak havoc if he's being used as a vessel. Remember, Gulakah was trying to control those with magical power using bhouts. Now that the bhouts have been scattered and his Demon Gate shattered, he's looking for other ways to extend his influence. Halcon must have found him."

"But wouldn't it make more sense if Jake had power or influence?" Chase looked confused.

"Not necessarily. If Jake has the potential to be a good vessel, then it's actually better for Gulakah that the guy's a loser. He won't have that much confidence, and that will make it easier to control him."

"But why the grave robbing?" Chase looked confused.

"Well, they were sucking up spirits last night. Maybe they're trying to find a way to replace the bhouts? Maybe the spirits are dislodged when the bodies are reanimated? Maybe the zombies are for some freakshow army and the spirits are for something else. I don't know. But maybe Ivana can tell us what uses spirits have, seeing how she loves her garden of ghosts so dearly?" I glanced over at Delilah. "Menolly's asleep. Tonight, I won't be able to go with her if she visits Ivana because I'm due at Talamh Lonrach Oll for training. So I think we should pay a visit to the Maiden of Karask now."

Delilah's eyes grew wide. "Shit. You're serious, aren't you?"

"Hell, yes. Menolly might be Ivana's special buddy, but we need to talk to her *today*." I punched in Ivana's number— we'd gotten it from Menolly, just in case we ever needed the wingnut army on our side.

One ring . . . five rings . . . and then on the sixth, she picked up.

"What do you want, Witch Girl?"

"How'd you know it was me?" I wasn't surprised she knew. Given that it was Ivana, anything was possible. Especially things I *really* didn't want to think about.

"How do you think? I have Caller ID, Witch. Now, what do you want?" Ivana sounded pissed, but I had the feeling it wasn't at me. No, she sounded *preoccupied* and pissed.

"Ivana, I have a question. If you might answer, it would be considered . . ." I paused. When dealing with the Elder Fae, *never, ever* use the word *favor* or you'll forever be in their debt. "I'm going to ask you a question. Answer if you like."

"*Not* so dim, then? I was waiting for you to slip. But you remember your lessons, correct? Well, then, ask your question. The morning's a loss anyway, and my beautiful garden stands in ruins."

To my horror, huge sobs echoed through the line. What the fuck was I supposed to say to her now? *There, there, I'm sorry your dungeon of horrors got trampled?* Or whatever the hell had happened to it. And by the way . . . what *had* happened to it?

"Ivana, were you out in the graveyards gathering spirits last night and this morning?" I knew it wasn't the appropriate way to phrase it—there was a whole song-and-dance the Elder Fae went through, but right now we just needed information, and I wasn't feeling all that much like waltzing.

A long silence, then . . . "Witch, you are rudeness incarnate. But since I like your sister—the Dead Girl—I will answer you. No, I was not out *rummaging through the boneyards*. I was fighting off some unseen force that emptied my garden of ghosts."

I stared at my phone. *What the fuck?* "Ivana, you said your garden of ghosts was . . ."

"Gutted. Sucked dry. Gone, just like the days when bright meat was easy to come by and humans weren't so squeamish about the gifts they offered us to keep our tricks and taunts at bay." She sighed, as if an era of beauty had passed by.

"Give it a break. You know what Menolly told you—*no bright meat!* No babies!" I wasn't squeamish about much, but Ivana wasn't joking and neither was I. There were plenty of creatures who relished young flesh, with a side of steak sauce. Trying to wipe away the mental image that conjured up, I continued before she could protest. "Ivana, I want to come look at your garden. I'm trying to figure out what's stealing the spirits around Seattle—and why."

Delilah motioned to me frantically. *No!* she mouthed, but I turned away and pretended not to see her.

Ivana hesitated, then cackled. "It has been a long day since I had a visitor, but yes, child. Come visit me, by all means. But do not bring an army. Only four others may accompany you."

I mentally raced through who would be the most effective if she turned nasty. "Fine . . . how do we get to your home?"

"The portal in Tangleroot Park? I'll be waiting on the other side. I'll configure it. And from there, we will travel to my home. I will not tell you how to get to my home by the normal route. You half-breed girls, you are from the other side. You are not ancient Fae. At the end of one of your hours, meet me there." And then she hung up. I put my phone away and looked up.

It was obvious Delilah had overheard the conversation.

She erupted like Vesuvius on steroids. "Are you fucking insane? She'll lead us into a trap and eat us. Or worse." Shuddering, she held herself, rocking back and forth. "I'm not that squeamish anymore, but she's a total freak and she scares the hell out of me."

Chase cleared his throat. "I have to agree with Delilah. Not a good plan. Really, just . . . *not.* I'm glad I've got a good excuse not to join you." He pointed to his leg. "Foot. Hurts. Can't walk far. *Really.*"

"Right, and I've got some swampland to sell you." I flashed him a snarky look. "Fine, I'll let you out of this one. But we're going. She's expecting us. I'll put in a call to Morio, Smoky, and Shade. They're most likely to be able to help us corral her if we have to. Meanwhile, Delilah, why don't you run down to the cafeteria and grab us something."

Shaking her head, my sister marched out of the room. She looked pissed. I prayed that she and Chase weren't right, and that this wasn't the biggest mistake of my day. And I really didn't want to listen to a bunch of *I-told-you-so*s.

As I punched the End Call button, my ears were ringing. Smoky had *not* been pleased. I had the feeling he'd be showing his displeasure come the next available chance. Over the months, I'd discovered that my dragon had a fetish for spanking. He never took it into painful territory, but he liked playing the big bad dragon, and whenever I really crossed the line, he gave me a good licking. And then he'd fuck me till I was spinning with orgasms.

Come to think about it, maybe going to see Ivana had its pluses.

Once we arrived at Tangleroot Park, we sat on a bench near where a rogue portal had opened up some time back.

During the Great Divide, the Elder Fae Lords had ripped the worlds apart. For thousands of years, the division had been sealed by the spirit seals. But the separation was unnatural. Now, as the spirit seals made their way to the surface again, the fabric of space and time surrounding the portals was breaking down. Rogue portals, unable to be controlled, were appearing. They were unstable and could lead to disaster.

Aeval had attempted to close the rogue portal, but it refused any attempts, and each time it activated, we never knew where the destination would be. Finally, we'd stationed several Earthside Fae to watch over it, and Aeval cast an illusion spell to keep the FBHs from seeing it.

"I can't believe it's not even eleven A.M. and we're going to portal-hop over to Ivana's for tea and a stroll through her ghost garden. Damned Chase and his broken ankle." Delilah snorted. "He got off easy."

Smoky leaned down on my left side and whispered into my ear. "Your sister is right. This is truly one of the most reckless ideas you've ever had. And later on, I'll show you just how reckless." His hair tickled my arm, tracing a sensuous line down it. I shivered and he laughed, low and throaty.

Just then, the portal shifted. I stepped in front of it, and Smoky, Morio, and Shade stood beside me.

"Oh brother, here we go." Delilah, rolling her eyes, joined us.

As the flicker of energy grew, opening out into a vortex, I heard Ivana's voice from the other side.

"Witch Girl, hurry up. Don't dawdle." As always, Ivana gave me the creeps. She was so far from human that even the timbre of her voice made me nervous. But she was what she was, and the Elder Fae were part of my heritage.

As I approached the portal, I sucked in a deep breath. Since this had been my idea, I was going first. If there were traps on the other side, I didn't want the others to get hit by them. I glanced at Morio, who gave me a nod, and plunged through the veil of energy.

Unlike the portals set up by the spirit seals, rogue portals were wild and feral, and their energy shifted constantly. I'd been through this one several times, and the first two times, the energy had sucked me in, called to me like a siren song. This time, I found myself passing through a wind tunnel. I shivered, freezing as I struggled to walk against the raging winds. They howled, twisting my hair and buffeting me so much that my ears were beginning to hurt.

Finally, just as I was ready to chuck the whole thing and head back, a light shimmered up ahead, and there was Ivana, peering through the vortex on the other end. Her odd, bird-like face was covered with gnarls and bumps that might have been warts, but I didn't want to get close enough to find out. She reminded me of a demented bag lady, but I also knew that was simply a disguise. The Elder Fae cloaked themselves under layers of illusion, and unless they chose to reveal themselves, it was almost impossible to ferret through to see the real being beneath the masks.

She waved for us to hurry and, with a gulp and a prayer that I hadn't made a serious mistake, I leaped out of the vortex, through the crackling veil of power, to land on solid ground.

As I stepped out of the way to allow the others to come through behind me, I was startled to find that I was standing in a vast garden filled with marigolds and primroses and peonies, as well as numerous tombstones that were weathered and aged. The garden—at least a double lot in size—sat behind a charming cottage.

The house was very Cape Cod, relatively large considering the style, and a white picket fence surrounded the entire lot. Beyond the fence, a ravine led into a patch of woods. Although there were electricity lines hooked up to the house, when I tried to gauge where we were, I had the feeling we'd left Seattle far behind.

"It's lovely." I inhaled deeply. The air here was clean, though I thought I could still sense a hint of city pollution.

"What did you expect? A gingerbread house and a trail of bread crumbs?"

I started to answer but decided that sometimes, silence *was* golden. Shrugging, I looked around at the tombstones, wondering who the hell they belonged to.

Ivana hoisted her staff—a silver branch about three feet long—and jabbed it toward the garden. "My garden. I had collected over a hundred ghosts here yesterday morning. Now . . ." Her voice dropped and a look of sadness veiled her eyes. "Now, they're all gone. All my lovely ghosts, gone."

Not sure of how to respond, I just stood there. Yes, Ivana tortured them and made their spirit lives hell, but considering they were the worst of the worst—the angry ghosts, the hungry ghosts who tormented humans—I found myself conflicted.

Shade glanced around at the yard. "What the hell do you keep them here for, anyway?"

I blinked. One simply did not speak to the Elder Fae like that, but then again, he was half dragon, and dragons generally said whatever they wanted to. Ivana regarded him, a nasty crease in her brow, then chuckled.

"You really want to know, Master Dragon? I milk their anger and hatred, and from that delicious brew, I create magic." She leaned in toward him, and the blur that continually surrounded her form seemed to grow taller. "Do you wish to know what I do with that magic?"

He regarded her quietly, then shook his head. "No, Maiden of Karask. I think none of us wants to know." He knelt down by one of the headstones that had been knocked over. "You had them firmly bound here, didn't you?"

She nodded. "Why? What sayeth you, Prince of Bones?"

He touched the stone, and a faint violet light filtered out from his fingertips, sizzling as it came into contact with the granite. "The ghosts were ripped violently from your garden. Plucked like unripe carrots, not ready to come out of the earth yet." Slowly standing, he dusted his hands on his pants.

"These ghosts . . . they did not go willingly. Whatever harvested them sucked them out without warning. I'm not even sure if they exist anymore, not as the spirits they were. I believe the consciousness of these creatures is gone. Our enemies were after the energy that kept them active."

"You mean, somebody *killed* the ghosts?" I asked, cocking my head.

"Yes, that would be one way to phrase it. Whatever or whoever stole these ghosts harvested them for their essence, and, in doing so, destroyed their conscious selves. They stole the life force that propelled the ghosts."

Delilah let out a gasp. "Like when the Death Maidens have to cast a soul into oblivion."

Shade nodded. "Yes, except for one thing. Death Maidens return the energy to the central pool, to be cleansed and reborn anew. Whatever took the ghosts is keeping the energy for its own use. It fed on them."

Ivana let out an irritated grumble.

As I stared at her garden, the scope of what we were facing started to settle in. Whatever was cleaning out the boneyards was strong enough to destroy a hundred spirits at a time and to harvest their energy and send the souls spiraling into oblivion. We knew Gulakah was huge and powerful, but the fact that he was a *god* was beginning to ramrod itself through my thoughts.

Morio motioned to me. "Let's see if we can get anything off the tombstones."

"Psychometry? I've never been extremely good with that." I wasn't good at just touching an object to find out about its background or the people who owned it. Unless the Demonkin had been in possession of it, and then I could sense their energy.

"No, but with my help, we might be able to strengthen that part of you."

He took my hand, his fingers curling around my own, and the feel of his skin was like smooth satin. I kissed his fingers and closed my eyes, and he moved his hands to rest on my shoulders.

I slowly let out a long breath and quickly sank into trance. As I slid deeper into the whirling darkness, Morio's breathing registered, pacing my own. And then the beating of his heart mirrored mine.

"Can you hear me?" Morio's thoughts came through. Or perhaps he was whispering—I couldn't tell at this point.

"Yes, love. What do you wish me to do now?"

Unless we were working with Moon magic, I let Morio lead. He was my teacher in this dark realm. He knew how to navigate the currents of death magic without letting them sweep him away. I trusted him.

"Kneel down, and with your left hand, touch the tombstone in front of us. Let your mind embrace the form and shape and feel. Open to any impressions that might come through."

I did as he asked, sinking to the ground slowly, making sure Morio stayed connected to me. Physical contact wasn't absolutely necessary, but it made things a lot easier.

The ground was soft and moist beneath my knees, and I felt like I was sinking into the earth. A reverberation of magic ran through Ivana's land and it sang to me. I caught my breath, wanting to unhook my corset, to press my breasts into the soil. At that moment, Morio let out a small sound and I realized he was feeling it, too—through me.

"Ivana, what is this energy . . ." My words drifted off as I opened my eyes and looked over at her. It took everything I had not to reel back, to break the connection and spell.

For there she stood, Ivana, the Maiden of Karask, only she was no longer hideous and gnarled, but tall and brilliant and dark as the evening sky. Her hair flowed now, long and silver, with black streaks running through it. She was taller than Smoky, and her face was angular, pale as the moon's silver light, and her eyes glowed with a dark burgundy—not in the way of vampires, but like hot coals in the middle of a white sea.

Ivana Krask was terrifying in her unnatural beauty—far more than Aeval or Titania. A magnetic pulse resounded from her core, shimmering out in concentric rings, and it captured me with a deep rhythmic vibration. I wanted to run to her, to fall at her feet.

Fighting with my instinct, I forced myself to hold steady. Morio was struggling, too. I could feel longing rise up in Morio—a deep hunger. I reached up, took his hand, and squeezed as hard as I could, driving my nails into his skin to shake him out of his stupor. He moaned softly but then shook his head and glanced at me as he steadied himself.

Shade was holding Delilah as she huddled in his arms, weeping. I didn't know what was going on, but she didn't look hurt, so I returned my attention to Ivana, who slowly crossed to stand beside me.

"What is this?" I stared up at her.

She laughed again, then leaned down. She kissed one finger, then pressed it to my lips. "Witch Girl, never forget, the Elder Fae have many forms and more power than you can ever hope to possess. I am showing you my power."

"Why would you do that?"

"You need to know. For this creature who gobbled up my ghosties, it is stronger than I am. So before you go delving into the grave for its bugaboos and secrets, best you know my own strength. Then, you can decide whether to proceed. You suspected me of raiding the boneyards. I could, if I chose to. But I leave some things be. The ghosties in boneyards, they are home and I do not invade their space. I only go after the spirits who wander, whose fury keeps them from resting. This . . . thing . . . whatever it is, plays by its own rules. It eats its fill and scatters the bones."

I looked around. "I see no bones."

"This is no graveyard, but only a ghostly repository. But the bones . . . the bone-walkers and the ghoulies and the zombinos . . . they travel in the wake of this creature. To create such an army . . . think of the power it takes."

I nodded. I didn't want to tell her that we already knew we were facing a god—it didn't seem a wise choice to spill secrets at this point.

"I hear your words." I would not thank her for her advice—that would be giving her too much power over me—but I wanted her to know I appreciated the attempt.

And then, turning back, I pressed my hand against the tombstone. At first, the energy was slow, seeping up from the soil. There was the residue from the ghost who had been anchored to it—hateful and angry and bitter. And then, as I searched, trying to sort out the blur of sensations and impressions, Morio fed me more energy. Without warning, in one long lash of the whip, the sky split open, and I was catapulted into the heart of Gulakah.

Chapter 6

At first, everything was dark and murky, and then a screaming fear shot through me as I found myself floundering in a
sea of gray, murky liquid ooze. I blinked, shaking my head
as I broke through the water and came up for air. How the
hell had I gotten here? And where was here?

But a crest of waves crashed against me, thick and sloshing, and I pushed all questions out of my mind as I fought to
keep above the surface. It was then that I noticed the snakes.

Fuck.

All around me, snakes writhed through the muddy ocean,
snapping as they came near. I kicked, desperately trying to
tread water—if this liquid murk could be called *water*. Viscous, it reminded me of paint, and was sticky and cold. The
smell of rotting detritus filled my nostrils, like old briny sea-
weed washed up on the shore, and overripe clams.

As the liquid churned, threatening to suck me under, I
noticed something moving just beneath the surface. Great,
what the fuck was next?

In the back of my mind, I was hoping for something to

hold on to, like a piece of wood or maybe, if I was lucky, a life vest. No such luck. As I saw what was rising from the water, I kicked as hard as I could, making a sharp turn. *Exit, stage left.* Or any place that wasn't here.

What looked like a giant matte black eyeball rose out of the water. It rippled with veins, and hundreds of writhing snakes were attached to it, like the tentacles on an octopus. I wasn't sure how much of it remained underwater, but the eye was as big as a boulder and I didn't want to stick around to find out how big the entire creature was.

Terrified, I launched myself through the water, kicking with long strokes. The ooze tried to suck me down, and my skirts were getting caught in my legs. Part of me wanted to ask, *How can this be real?* But the fear in my heart, and the fact that I was swimming away from some freakshow monster, overshadowed the side of me seeking a logical answer.

I struggled against the sloshing waves. The liquid was trickier than the actual ocean. As I fought to remain above the waves, they battered me. I frantically looked for some sign of land. In the distance, I could see what looked like a faint silvery shore, but it was a long way off—and I began to think that maybe, just maybe, I wasn't going to make it out of this one.

I glanced over my shoulder. The creature was rising high out of the water, its body visible, and I realized I'd seen it somewhere before. And then, I knew who it was, only here, he was a giant, and malformed.

As he reared up, I screamed, some of the murky liquid splashing into my mouth. It tasted like mold and mildew and I spit it out, trying not to gag. As I treaded water, trying to keep the roiling waves from crashing over me, the creature continued to rise, deep and dark and from the depths of the Netherworld. It stank of Demonkin, putrid and dripping with hunger and unquenched desire.

Gulakah.
The Lord of Ghosts.
And he senses you.

I let out a strangled cry as the god turned toward me, his eyeball retracting into his head, the snakes now writhing like hair. Medusa's coils. As he leaned down, aiming toward me, I sucked in a deep breath and dove, deep into the water, letting it suck me down. Better to drown in the depths than let him catch hold of me.

My lungs burned as I began to drift downward, floating free, unable to see. There was no question about breaking the surface again. Gulakah was there, and I couldn't fight him. There was no escape.

As my lungs tightened, I steeled myself, preparing for the rush of liquid into my body, for the end. I didn't know how I'd gotten here, and all I could do was pray that they'd find me somehow. Smoky, Morio, and Trillian would feel the Soul Symbiont bond break—they'd know that I was dead. Resigning myself, I gave in, embraced the ocean of gray, and as I began to let out my breath, I tumbled forward, downward, and hit my head on something hard.

What the fuck?

"Ow." I rubbed my head.

First realization: I could hear myself.

Second realization: I wasn't drowning.

Third realization: I was sitting in front of a tombstone, on the ground, and Smoky was reaching down to grab me up in his arms.

"Camille, are you okay? We couldn't snap you out of the trance." He sounded frantic, my dragon did, and he held me tight as I clung to him, my arms around his shoulders. The sensation of drowning still echoed through my body, and I was confused and on the verge of panic.

Morio rubbed my back and said something to Smoky that I couldn't catch. But I could hear Delilah ranting at Ivana— *so* not a good thing. I tried to get Smoky to put me down, but he wouldn't—he just held on and refused to let go, long tendrils of his hair reaching up to give him a better hold on me. Not that he needed it, with his strength.

"What the hell did you do to her?" Delilah was screaming at Ivana.

"Shush the tongue, Puss in Boots. I did nothing to Witch Girl."

Ivana's voice rolled along the ground with a wave of command. She straightened to full height and—still a vision of dizzying beauty—her voice ricocheted through the yard, knocking over the tombstones that were still standing. A high-pitched keen shot straight through my head, stabbing my third eye as a migraine slammed me. Moaning, I slumped against Smoky, trying to hide my eyes from the light.

Ivana began to laugh. "The Witch cannot handle the pitch of my true voice? Then I will play nice for now." Within seconds, Ivana the bag lady was back, and her voice was once again the sarcastic tone that grated but did not send me screaming for a quiet, dark place. The headache began to ease up immediately.

More confused than ever, I persuaded Smoky to set me down, still reeling from everything that had gone on. A little unsteady on my feet, I crossed to one of the fallen tombstones and gingerly sat down.

"So, I didn't actually *go* anywhere? I didn't disappear?"

Smoky shook his head. "No. We couldn't drag you off the tombstone. It was as if it had a suction grip on you and you were gasping for air, like you were being suffocated."

I cast a long look at the grave marker, but it looked perfectly normal. I didn't really want to touch it again but leaned over and placed a light finger on it. Cold stone. Nothing more.

"Fuck me hard."

"Gladly," Morio spit out before he could stop himself. I gave him a faint grin as he backpedaled. "Sorry. Just habit. What happened?"

I glanced up at Ivana. Not sure how much she knew, I was hesitant to talk in front of her. I didn't trust her, even though she had come to our aid several times. Morio caught my hesitation and gave me a tight shake of the head.

"We should go." He reached down to give me a hand.

"But what of my ghosties? Who stole them?" Ivana's crass voice was grating, but after hearing her true voice, it didn't bother me nearly as much. She was far more powerful than even I'd thought, and this was yet another issue we had to rethink.

"They're gone. I'm not sure what took them, but whatever it is, you're right. It's big and it's bad. I suggest you refrain from ghost hunting for a while. Whatever it is might come back and this time might just go after you, too."

The thought of telling her who did it, of seeing her go up against Gulakah, offered an intriguing set of possibilities, but then I decided that might not be such a good idea.

She frowned. "As you will, Witch Girl. But suspicion abounds . . . you are not telling the Maiden of Karask all you know, but soon enough, all will reveal. No doubt about that. No doubt at all. Now go, unless you should wish to come into my house for tea. I've oinker left and it heats to a nice broth." She touched her nose, like Santa Claus, and I shivered. Not quite so jolly and safe, although I'd met the real Santa—the Holly King—and he was far from the happy fat man portrayed in the movies.

Ivana escorted us back to the portal, and we hurried through. We were all eager to get away from her, even Shade, who seemed the least bothered. As soon as we were back in Tangleroot Park, I let down my guard and collapsed on the sidewalk, thoroughly worn out.

Delilah knelt by my side. "Camille, what the hell happened? Do you need to see Sharah or Mallen?"

I shook my head. "I don't think so, but I'm so exhausted. And confused." Smoky gathered me in his arms, this time ignoring my requests to be set down. His long legs made quick work of the path, and he wouldn't let anybody question me till we reached the car. Delilah took my keys—she didn't trust me to drive—and we settled in, with me sitting in the back between Smoky and Morio, and Shade up front with her.

"Okay, now . . . in the safety of the car, tell us, what the fuck happened to you?" Morio was looking decidedly bent out of shape. I knew him well enough to know that he wanted to go attack whatever had hurt me, but I also knew there was no way he could beat up on the enemy I'd faced.

But had I really faced Gulakah? Was it truly him? Or had

something different just put the idea in my head? Shaking off the doubt, I began to tell them what had happened from the moment I touched the tombstone. As I finished, they sat there, staring at me, mouths agape.

"So, I want to know—where the hell was I? No ocean on this planet, that's for sure."

Morio shook his head. "I don't know, but I think you really did land somewhere near Gulakah. You can't fake the power of his fear."

Shade cleared his throat. "I don't think you were in an actual ocean."

I frowned. "That seems obvious, since I'm not covered with gray ooze. But I was in some body of . . . liquid, at least my spirit was."

"No," he interrupted. "I don't think you were. I think . . . what I think is almost too frightening to suggest." He stared at me, unblinking, those gorgeous eyes stark against the warm toffee of his skin.

"Just say it, dude." I was tired of people circumnavigating things.

"I think . . . I think you projected yourself inside Gula-kah's mind."

His words hit me like a brick wall, tumbling down.

"Fuck. No." Reeling at the thought, I shook my head. I couldn't have landed in the mind of a god—especially Gulakah. "No, no . . . no . . ."

Morio took hold of me and held me tight. "It's okay, Camille. It's okay."

I shook him off. "I can't have landed in the mind of a god. That means that . . . the ooze . . . the water and the creature . . ."

"Must be parts of him. I'm not sure about this, but Camille—" Shade held his hand up as I started to protest some more. "Calm down. You may just have netted us some very valuable information. If you did manage to mind-touch Gulakah, we can learn from what you experienced."

Pressing my lips together, I leaned against Smoky, wanting to forget the whole thing. I wasn't sure why the idea bothered me so much. Maybe it was that Gulakah reminded me of Hyto, only worse. Gulakah wanted to be feared and revered. He was terrifying, and his energy was warped and twisted, a lot like Hyto. The gods weren't all that more powerful than some of the ancient dragons.

But Shade was right. If I could remember anything that might give us a clue on how to fight the Lord of Ghosts, it would help us. I strained to recall anything I hadn't already told them, but nothing cropped up.

"I'm sorry . . . I told you everything I remember."

Shade let out a sigh. "If there is any way . . . if we could only go into your mind and see what you saw . . ."

I shuddered. I'd already had someone root around in my head, and I wanted no part of that.

"Maybe you'll remember more later," Morio said, changing the subject.

I tossed a glance at Smoky. He pressed his lips together, saying nothing.

"I'll do my best." I leaned back, closing my eyes. So much had gone on today that all I wanted was a chance to go home, take a long bath, relax, and prepare for the evening ahead. Training under Aeval was difficult at best, and I needed to recharge and calm down before I headed out to Talamh Lonrach Oll.

We arrived home. I asked Delilah to phone Chase and tell him what we'd found out. She nodded, and I headed upstairs, nixing any company. I wanted to be alone, to relax. Smoky and Morio went out to work on Iris's house, while Trillian took over in the kitchen, helping Iris and Hanna fix lunch.

As I filled the bathtub with water and poured in caramel-apple-scented bath gel, the bubbles frothed up. While the tub filled, I went into the bedroom and stepped out of my skirt, unfastened my corset, and shimmied out of my panties.

Misty was wandering around, and she looked up at me with her plume of a tail waving, then padded behind me as I returned to the bath. I sat down on the edge of the tub and petted her, my hand gliding over the silky energy that surrounded her spirit. It wasn't the same as petting a living cat, but it felt softer, and—in some ways—her purr seemed louder, the song reverberating through my aura rather than in through my ears.

"Today freaked me out," I told her.

She purred, leaning into my hand.

"And now I have to go out to Talamh Lonrach Oll and face another challenge. I'm tired."

Gazing up at me with those beautiful green eyes, she let out a *purp*.

"Life is getting more complicated," I continued as she jumped up on the edge of the tub beside me. I stroked her under the chin. "It's been eighteen months since Jocko died and we first found out about the demons and Shadow Wing. Now the war is getting worse. And Menolly and Delilah and I all have our separate paths to which we also have to devote time and energy. The world is getting bigger, Misty. There's more to do. And less time in which to do it. I miss the old days. I miss not being afraid of who's just around the corner, waiting to destroy the world. But I guess . . . there's no going back, is there?"

Misty cocked her head, then rubbed against me again and jumped back onto the floor. The tub was full, so I turned off the water, as—with one last tap on my leg for another head scratch—Misty vanished, disappearing through the door.

It had seemed odd at first, seeing her walk through the walls, but now I was used to it. Lighting several candles, I dimmed the light and dipped one toe in the tub, taking a deep breath as the heat registered through my foot. It was almost too hot, but not quite, and I sank gratefully into the mass of bubbles, leaned back, and closed my eyes.

As the warmth of the water raced through me, loosening my muscles and helping me relax, I tried to let go of my worries and just drift in the comfort and safety of being home.

Images floated through my mind—Smoky's stern but loving embrace, Trillian's cunning smile, Morio's passion when the magic caught both of us up in its grasp . . . Then I flashed on Delilah and how far she'd come over the time we'd been Earthside. Menolly, too . . .

As the images became flashes of light and energy and

sound, I felt myself starting to drift off and, realizing how tired I really felt, I settled deeper in the tub. Breathing deeply, I let myself slip into a light trance.

I was walking on a shore of some alien world—at least it felt alien. The sky was silver, and the water gunmetal gray. As I scanned the horizon, I realized that I knew this place. I was just seeing it from a different perspective. A dark cloud settled over my mood as I realized I was back in Gulakah's mind.

What ties me to you, you freakazoid of a god?

I shivered, wrapping my arms around me, and glanced down. Naked, of course. Because I was naked in the bathtub. It began to register that I wasn't feeling the overwhelming sense of fear I had before.

Am I really here, then? Or am I taking a trip down memory lane?

I prayed it was the latter—I *really* didn't want to play psychic footsie with a god of dreams who had delusions of grandeur. Well, perhaps they weren't *delusions*—he was powerful—but he'd abused his power and that was what got him kicked out of the Netherworld and down into Shadow Wing's territory.

Get real. I have to be strolling through my memories, or I couldn't keep up this sort of rational prattle. By now, if this were real, I'd be back swimming in the ocean. So, going on the theory that I'm safe, let's have a look around.

I had only seen the faint outline of the shore when I'd actually been in Gulakah's mind, but now I was walking on it. Which meant that either I had to know about it somehow or my mind was trying to fill in the details.

Pausing, I turned to the open sea. The gray waves crested against the shore, leaving a sickly foam behind. I knelt down and stared at the lacework residue. Why gray? But I knew the answer. During the times I'd been in the Netherworld, gray mists had roiled through, and the sky was an unending silver.

There was never any change, from what Shade had told us. Since Gulakah had been the Lord of Ghosts there, of course his energy would be filled with the silvery mist. The same as many of the spirits Morio and I dealt with.

Something about that thought registered as important. I tried to reason it out.

Ghosts . . . Ghosts are left over and out of place—spirits who haven't moved on. They're unnatural, out of step with the Eternal Return.

As I knelt on the edge of an ocean of nightmares, it hit me like a brick wall. Gulakah was a god out of step—a god who didn't belong in the natural order. He'd sought to increase his power, which would have put him even more out of sync with the Netherworld, because all realms had their own balance. And when things got out of balance . . .

"Very good, Camille."

Startled, I almost fell forward but caught myself. I turned around.

Standing next to me was a woman as elegant as a diamond necklace. She was a little taller than me, and buxom, wearing a beaded corset in shades of ivory and silver. Her skirt was long and flowed to her ankles—the color of mist. Beneath a headdress—silver and crowned with crystal antlers—her hair flowed to her knees, its color caught between white and ice, and her eyes were deep black, with silver flecks.

In one hand she held a thin wand, in the other a sparkle of glowing light. It twinkled as she held it out, then blew on it. The light flew up from her hand into the air, where it spiraled for a moment, then took a nosedive toward me, exploding as it covered me with light.

"What—who are you?" I stood, still naked. But she didn't even blink.

"Don't you know me, Camille? You should. I'm Pentangle, the Mistress of Magic."

I stumbled back, then fell to my knees and bowed my head.

Pentangle, one of the Hags of Fate. Pentangle, the Mother of Magic.

"My lady, what would you ask of me?" I had no clue how Pentangle had ended up in my thoughts, but I decided to just go with the flow.

"First, you aren't roaming in your memories." She smiled faintly, and the energy flowing off her blasted through me like a surge from a furnace, leaving me a toasty pink.

How had she read my mind? Could she be right?

"Then where the hell am I? If I'm back in Gulakah's mind, shouldn't I be feeling stark, raving terror?"

She gazed beyond me, toward the unending ocean. "You are not in Gulakah's mind, although yes, you were . . . the first time."

Before I could speak, she held up her hand.

"Yes, I know what happened. I am the Mistress of Magic. I guard the strands that manipulate energy. I know much of what goes on in the magical realm, when I choose to direct my focus. And I know what happened to you. I can read you like the books you so love. Don't play shy with me, girl. I could dip into your mind and strip you down to the core, should I choose."

I'd only ever encountered one other Hag of Fate—and that was Grandmother Coyote. And she seemed more human than Pentangle. Grandmother Coyote was firm and solid and lived in the woods near our home. Or at least she had a foothold there.

The Hags of Fate were immortal, like the Elemental Lords and the Harvestmen. Powerful beyond even the gods, they usually intervened in human affairs to right a balance gone wrong. Even if that meant giving evil a nudge now and then. They usually kept to themselves, but when they appeared, you knew something was about to break loose.

"Then where am I?" I glanced around. If I wasn't just roaming through my memories, and I wasn't in Gulakah's mind, I must have been . . . *where?*

"You're standing on the edge of the Ocean of Anger. You're in the Netherworld, and you're looking at one of the strongest forces that keeps ghosts tied to the mortal realm. This body of . . . emotion . . . is created by all the residue anger and fury that ghosts bring with them to the Netherworld. And it was Gulakah's undoing. He began to use it as a personal magical source, and the more he focused on it, the more powerful the angry ghosts became in the mortal world. That's why he was cast out—he disrupted the balance. But the damage has been done. The energy pool is too powerful, thanks to his meddling, and the balance continues to shift. The ocean feeds too many spirits over on the mortal planes. They, in turn, keep feeding the ocean, creating a synergistic effect."

I knelt down and touched the liquid with my fingers. Once again, the feelings of terror and powerlessness ran through me, and I glanced at her over my shoulder. "So, my fear?"

"You are corporeal. Your fear is a normal reaction. The angry ghosts thrive on it. So does Gulakah. The ocean that you were lost in? You slipped into his connection to this primal pool of energy. He has found a way to continue to tap into the Ocean of Anger from where he now resides."

And with that, Pentangle turned and began to walk gently up the shore, the silvery sand shifting as she made her way through it. Her feet were bare, and the edge of her hem trailed along the moist dunes.

"Wait! Why did you show me this?" I started to follow her but found I could not move. My feet were stuck in the sand.

Over her shoulder, without turning around, she said, "Because you needed to know. Do not forget my words. The only way the balance here will be restored is with Gulakah's defeat."

And then she vanished. I turned back to the ocean, folding my arms across my chest. So this was the Netherworld. I'd been here before, but never so far in, and I knew that I had to leave this place soon. The living did not fare well here, whether in spirit or body. As I stared out over the sheen, the wind sprang up and buffeted around me, bringing with it the scent of decay, and old arguments, and long-forgotten furies. I blocked them, putting up a shield to keep them from infecting my mood.

Gulakah had long been banished from the Netherworld, and this ocean had been churning all that time. Perhaps this was why there seemed to be so much ghostly activity over Earthside. How long had the balance been disrupted? For centuries, at least. And how many spirits had been trapped, unable to move on, because they'd been caught up by the primal force of anger that kept them bound to the world of the living?

Too many. The words sprang to my thoughts. Too many, and they would only increase until we stopped the Lord of Ghosts. But could we truly kill him? And were we supposed to? Killing a demon general was one thing. But killing a god . . . that just seemed wrong.

She didn't say Gulakah's death . . . but his defeat.

True, I argued with myself, but what did *defeat* mean? If we sent him back to the Netherworld, would they just evict him again? If we sent him back to the Subterranean Realms, Shadow Wing would just use him again. If we killed him . . . then what?

More confused than ever, I decided it was time to leave this place. I sucked in a deep breath, blinked, and opened my eyes.

The bubbles had dissipated, and the water was cooling. I waited for the water to drain out, then turned on the shower and quickly rinsed off the residue soap. As I toweled off and padded back into my room to dress, the thought crossed my mind that we might have met our match in Gulakah.

And then the unwelcome thought intruded that if Gulakah was this strong and he was working for Shadow Wing, just how the hell strong was the Demon Lord himself? And with that cheerful question playing and replaying in my head, I slipped into a calf-length gauze skirt, fastened a plum-colored bustier over the top, and headed downstairs to eat a late lunch and talk to the others.

Chapter 7

⚘

Downstairs, I was happy to discover that Iris and Hanna had fixed a buffet of sandwich makings and clam chowder. My stomach rumbled as I fixed a ham on sourdough with Monterey Jack and ladled myself out a big bowl of the soup. As I slid into my chair, I looked at the others.

"I know why the ghostly activity is so strong." I bit into my sandwich as the others stopped to stare at me.

"Well, are you going to tell us?" Vanzir asked, leaning back in his chair. A sandwich a mile high towered on his plate. I grinned. Vanzir didn't always eat food—he didn't need to feed in the same way we did—but now and then he got a hankering for something and he'd vacuum up everything in sight.

"I'm getting around to it," I said, around a mouthful of food. After I finished chewing and swallowing, I told them what had happened in the bathtub. "So, yes, Gulakah is responsible for the increase in ghostly activity, but it's not just lately—it's been since before he was banished from the

Netherworld. Which means that it must have been going on a long time here, Earthside."

"And it's increased lately because of his actual presence here," Delilah said. "Pentangle said the only way to restore the balance . . ."

"Is to defeat him. But Gulakah is a *god*. How the fuck do we kill a god?" I motioned to Morio. "Pass the salt, please?"

He handed me the shaker, and I sprinkled it in my chowder.

"The gods are not immortal, though far more so than us. He must have some sort of weakness." Morio leaned back, frowning. "But what is it?"

"His ego?" I shrugged. "He seems to think he's invincible."

"But he can't truly believe that. Charlotine managed to repel him with a spell when we went after him out at the cave. She didn't hurt him, but she did manage to affect him. That had to sting." Shade frowned. "No, he's not stupid—we can't bank on his ego blinding him. We have to find a way into his inner sanctum."

"Well, if he is associated with the Aleksais Psychic Network, Camille can go to their psychic fair that takes place on the thirtieth. We found the advertisement this morning." Delilah slapped the newspaper that we'd gotten at Mystic Charms on the table.

"I'm going to need to disguise myself, though. I can't go in looking this way or they'll know who I am." I frowned. "Iris, do you have any illusion magic that might work on me?"

She frowned. "I think so . . . we could dye your hair platinum!" Even as I started to protest, she grinned at me. "I know, I know. But I think . . . Morio, you have some illusion magic, too?"

An idea hit me. I turned to Trillian, who was working on his second sandwich. "My love, remember the talismans you found for us when we first met?"

His icy eyes twinkled. "I do. And I might know where we could scare up a couple more of those. They're pricey to come by, and I'll have to head back to Y'Elestrial to find them, but I can do that this afternoon."

"Price doesn't matter." Smoky glanced at him. "I have gold should we need it—currency everywhere. Camille's safety is tantamount."

Trillian nodded. "You will come with me, then? I don't know how much they'll be. We shouldn't be gone longer than the night."

My mind flashed to an image of the two of them, skipping down a yellow brick road together, and I coughed, almost choking on my sandwich. Morio slapped me on the back as Iris handed me a glass of water. Wisely, I bit my tongue, but I couldn't suppress a snort.

Trillian gave me a long look. "You have something to say, wife?"

"I don't think she believes we can take a trip together without killing each other." Smoky joined in.

I face-palmed, groaning. "Enough, you two. This is serious."

"Now look—she's been caught and is trying to divert attention." Smoky was enjoying himself. I could see it in his eyes.

Trillian nodded. "We need to teach her better manners."

"Agreed." Smoky pushed back his plate. "So, what are the plans for this afternoon and evening? Trillian and I will be headed to Otherworld."

"I'm due out at Talamh Lonrach Oll tonight, so I'm just going to hang around the house and rest this afternoon." I didn't want to overtax myself before tonight. The Triple Threat were likely to put me through the wringer.

Delilah finished off her potato chips and wiped her hands. "I think I'll head to the office. I haven't been there for a few days, and I need to check messages and see if anybody has any jobs for me. I'll check in with Giselle for you, Camille, and make sure everything is going well at the Indigo Crescent. Then, I guess . . ."

"After that, you can help me research ways to dispatch a god." Roz leaned forward, resting his elbows on the table.

"There has to be some weakness recorded. We can go talk to Carter this evening. He's part Titan. He has to know something about the gods."

"Good idea," Delilah said, carrying her plate to the counter.

"I'll stay home, with Menolly and Vanzir. We can watch over the house this evening since Camille, Smoky, and Trillian will be gone." Shade grinned. "Menolly and I are teaching Nerissa to defend herself, so it will give us time to practice."

I knew that Menolly and Shade had been training Nerissa in hand-to-hand combat. Nerissa could defend herself just fine in werepuma form, but she'd never really learned in human form, and now that she and Menolly were married and she was living here, it stood to reason that she should get in some practice.

I pushed back from the table. "I need to meditate before tonight. I'm going to sit in the yard for a while."

The others nodded. I kissed each of my men before I headed outside. In the hallway, I stopped long enough to grab my ritual staff. Aeval had given it to me right before I'd accompanied Iris on her journey to the Northlands. Nobody had taught me how to use it yet, and I knew better than to ask for details. They would train me when they saw fit.

The staff was a little taller than me. Made of polished yew, a knob of silver atop the staff held a quartz crystal ball almost the size of my fist. A wire network wove over the top to keep it firmly secure. The foot of the staff was silver-clad, and it fit neatly in my hand.

I carried it outside to the front yard, where my herb garden was just starting to make an appearance for the year. The new growth cheered my mood as I headed for the low rock I'd had Smoky bring me from out near Mount Rainier. It was smooth, flat, and comfortable and felt more natural than a bench. I carried the staff over to the rock and settled down on it, staring at the garden.

The lavender was growing, and the thyme bush was looking good. The comfrey was taking up an entire corner in the garden. Sage and rosemary and fennel grew in the kitchen-herbs section.

And then there were the herbs that were not pantry-friendly, but that I needed for spell work. Belladonna and wormwood, rue and mandrake. My mandrake plants were a little over a year old, and they had a ways to go before I could harvest them for the work we needed to do. But all of my dark moon plants were planted safely away from the ones we could eat as well as use in spell work.

As I leaned back, the cool breeze flowed across me. Once again, I tumbled deep into trance. Everything felt heightened, from the hairs on my arms to the air playing across my lips. My nipples stiffened in response—going into trance could be an incredibly sensual experience. Magic and sexuality were intricately entwined, and when one force woke in the body, so did the other.

The staff was still in my hands, and I ran my fingers lightly over it as I drifted gently with the astral currents. The yew branch resonated in my hand, a tingle flowing up my arm.

Yew—the tree of transformation and the Eternal Return—was one of the most sacred and potent trees there was, even more so than oak. The yew was for new moon work, for death magic, and the magic of the Dark Goddesses. It was the tree of renewal, the tree of death and of birth.

I traced over the surface and paused. Something tingled beneath my fingertips—a carving? Runes? But when I looked, I could see nothing but smooth wood. I raised the staff to my nose and inhaled deeply. A faint scent wafted up, one that I felt I should recognize but that eluded me.

Turning my attention to the silver cradle holding the crystal, I gazed into the quartz, rainbows shimmering from the internal fractures—prisms dappling the globe. They whispered to me, but their song was just beyond reach.

After a while, I took three deep breaths and held the last, letting it wash through me as I slowly brought myself out of the trance. Setting the staff aside, I glanced at my phone. Nearly six P.M. Almost time to head out to Talamh Lonrach Oll. I wrapped my arms around my knees until I felt awake

enough to drive, and then stood and put my staff in the car.
My priestess robes were already in there.

As I walked back to the house to let them know I was
leaving, Smoky and Trillian came out.

"Are you headed to Grandmother Coyote's portal now?" I
ran over to them and slid my arms around their waists.

"Yes, we go to Otherworld." Smoky leaned down and
kissed my head.

Not to be outdone, Trillian planted a passionate one on
my lips. "Be safe, wife. Do not make us fret when we return.
We'll be back tomorrow at the latest."

Smoky swept me into his arms. "Trillian is right—be
careful. I still do not trust the Triple Threat. But Aeval will
guard you. She needs you. For what, I do not know, but I
recognize the look on her face." He kissed me again, then set
me down.

I touched his arm. "Want me to drop you off? I'm going
now." They looked at each other, then shrugged and nodded.
I held up one finger. "Wait right here. I just want to let the
others know I'm leaving."

I peeked into the hall and saw my purse and keys where
I'd left them on the hall table. As I grabbed them, I called
out, "Leaving for Talamh Lonrach Oll."

"Be safe!" Iris's voice echoed from the kitchen.

And so we were off. I dropped Smoky and Trillian at the
edge of Grandmother Coyote's land, then headed out to the
freeway. It was going to be a long night, but at least I wasn't
feeling too exhausted. The trance work—both in the bath
and in the garden—had recharged me.

All the way there, my thoughts were filled with a vast
churning of ocean. All that anger and fury and pent-up
rage . . . what a waste of energy.

If Otherworld was the U.N. of Faerieland, so to speak,
Talamh Lonrach Oll was Faerieland over Earthside. Set on a
thousand acres of land, northeast of Seattle and buttressed
against the foothills of the Cascade Mountains, Talamh

Lonrach Oll—the Land of Brilliant Apples—was the Sovereign Nation for the Earthside Fae. Ruled over by Titania, Queen of Light and Morning; Aeval, Queen of Shadow and Night; and lastly, our distant cousin Morgaine, who had been crowned the Queen of Dusk and Twilight, it was a growing, thriving community.

The government had agreed to a treaty with the Fae Queens—the Triple Threat, as I liked to call them. As long as they didn't incite any antigovernment activities, they had permission to buy up to five thousand acres and claim it as a sovereign nation, where they could make their own rules and lead their nation. The rolls were growing quickly and their numbers already rivaled those of the Supe Community Council, at least for this area.

While most of the Fae did not live at Talamh Lonrach Oll, enough did to make it a thriving community, and the TLO Warriors were also a growing strength. Over one hundred strong at this point, the militia trained vigorously. The Triple Threat knew about the demon menace and had promised their support to us, especially since I'd joined Aeval's Court.

I parked outside the silver gates that guarded the land. The land was completely warded, and I knew better than try to enter at a place other than the main gate. As I stepped out of the car, I was instantly hit by the rush of energy. Talamh Lonrach Oll was powerful, and its roots were buried so deep in history that no mortal could ever fathom just how aged the foundations of this land were. Not just the actual land itself, but the powers of Titania, Aeval, and even Morgaine—though our cousin was only half-Fae, like ourselves.

A scent wafted by—the smell of oakmoss and narcissus, of violets and newly mown hay, and a dozen other minor notes feeding into it. This was the fragrance of dark magic, the scent of summer passion, of sparkling lights in the forest at midnight, and it was the scent of my destiny.

The guards at the gate recognized me and swung it open, bowing as I entered. I curtsied to them, out of habit, and they waved me toward the horse and carriage that was waiting.

The carriage was open, but since it wasn't raining and the weather was cool but not cold, I didn't mind.

The driver offered me his hand and I stepped in, carrying my bag of ritual gear and clothing, and then he handed my staff up to me and I balanced it across my lap. I had no idea where we were going; all I knew was that he would take me to where Aeval and Morgaine had bid him drive.

He let out a sound and the horse moved forward. As I leaned back, the evening fell into twilight. The sky was partially overcast, but the last of the sunlight filtered through, glancing off the trees. It was nearing evening.

The cobblestones resounded with the quiet clopping of the horse's hooves as the path swerved and bent through the compound. Houses, all single-story, had gone up here and there, and more were being built as the population of Talamh Lonrach Oll grew. There were no electrical lines—the power for the nation came from the earth, through magic, and via wind, steam, and sun. The paths were lit with eye catchers, and signs marked the streets. The ES Fae Queens had borrowed the magic of the eye catchers from Otherworld, and in return, OW was borrowing some of the concepts of technology from over Earthside, only to create a new blend between magic and science.

A sadness crept into my heart when I realized that my homeworld was changing, but then again, it had originally been a part of Earthside, and it seemed natural that both worlds should integrate back together.

On one level, I secretly hoped the portals would rip, that the division wouldn't hold, and that Otherworld and Earthside would reunite, but I also knew that might entail a great disaster. Even though I liked the thought of unification, I realized it wasn't necessarily best.

We turned down another road, and as the carriage rumbled through a heavily wooded patch, opening out onto a cottage and a grotto beyond, I knew where I was. I'd initiated into Aeval's Court here, during the winter solstice. As the driver helped me down, handing me my staff, my stomach fluttered. Magic was in the wind, magic was in the very land here, imbued with the elements and the energy of the moon and the sun.

The cedars and firs hadn't changed since the winter solstice when I'd been here, except for the bright green of new growth. But the deciduous trees had blossomed out, and their young leaves now crowded the branches, creating a tapestry of shadow and light as the last of the sunlight shimmered through them.

Huckleberries were growing thick, as were ferns and brambles, and wild rhododendrons that had somehow become seeded here. Rowan trees, also known as mountain ash, ringed the grove, and their berries were white, not yet ready to turn the brilliant orange that marked them in the late summer and autumn.

The drone of bees and insects hummed in my ears. Overhead, the fading remnants of the day began to give way, and twilight took hold. Morgaine's time was beginning to fade as Aeval's rule ascended.

Sometimes I wondered why, though Morgaine had been assigned to train me, it was to Aeval's Court that I'd been ordered to pledge myself, and why Aeval so often took over the training. But when I approached the subject, no one would answer, and I had come to the conclusion that the more I pressed, the less likely I was to find out, so I had quit asking. I knew when to back off.

I carried my bag and staff into the cottage, which was used as a preparation area. I had begun to sort out my garb for the evening when an acolyte approached. She looked a little scared, and I grinned as she stumbled over her words.

"Lady Camille? I have word . . . I'm here . . . they wanted me to tell you . . ." The poor girl looked so starstruck that I took pity on her.

"Don't be nervous. What's your name?"

"Tanya."

That surprised me. Tanya was a human name and not one found in most Fae families.

"Well, Tanya, if it's bad news, just tell me." I had the feeling her nerves were a result of the star-factor thing, but I had learned never to assume. That could land you in a whole world of hurt. Or embarrassment.

Turned out, I was right. She blushed, then gave me a little shrug. "I'm sorry. I'm just nervous. I've heard so much about you. Okay, let me start again."

As she took a deep breath, I realized Tanya was an FBH, not Fae at all. That alone was enough to make me blink, but before I could ask about it, she launched in again, and this time the words came out without any problem.

"Mistress Morgaine asked me to take your regalia and staff. She bids you take a ceremonial bath in the hot springs first, and then cross to the other side, where you will be dressed for the ritual. You may leave your clothes here."

That was odd, but I just nodded and entered the cottage.

The living room was lit with dozens of candles that flickered brightly in glass hurricane jars. The little house had four rooms.

The kitchen was the color of pale sunshine. It held a round table with eight chairs and had a wood cookstove, but the stove wasn't made out of cast iron. I wasn't sure just what it was made from, but it worked really well. There was also an old-fashioned icebox that was kept chilled through ice and snow magic. With only cold running water, the stove was used to heat water for washing dishes.

The Fae Queens did believe in plumbing and had hired contractors to install septic systems. The bathroom contained a shower. With the hot springs outside, who needed a warm bath?

The other two rooms were the main gathering room—essentially a living room—and a chamber to the side, the size of a small bedroom. It was used as a ritual locker room.

I hurried to change. Best not to keep Morgaine waiting. Even more so, Aeval, and I had a feeling she would be there tonight as well.

Stripping, I hung up my clothing, then slid into a sheer robe that was hanging on a peg on the wall. I tucked my purse into one of the wooden lockers. I'd already handed my staff and ritual garb to Tanya, who was waiting for me in the living room. With a quick pit stop in the bathroom, I took care of business and washed my hands. As I stared at myself in the mirror, I wondered if I was up to whatever challenge lay ahead. But there was only one way to find out. Exhaling slowly, I rejoined Tanya.

She led me out the back door. The smooth slate path was cool under my bare feet. As we headed down the slight incline, the last glimpses of daylight began to vanish. Menolly would be waking up now, I thought, then brought my focus back to where I was. Magic required absolute concentration, especially when working with the Dark Queens.

A hush settled over the grove, the echo of birdsong reverberating from tree to tree in the cool scent of the evening. The temperature was brisk, a hint of moisture hanging heavy in the air, and I shivered beneath the light fabric of the robe.

Tanya said nothing more—she kept her eyes on the path in front of her, carrying my bag of regalia and my staff. I followed behind her. A flutter rustled in the brushes nearby, and I glanced just in time to see something dart through the foliage. Whatever it was, I knew it was neither human nor animal. Fae, perhaps—but most likely an Elemental, as tied to the earth as I was tied to the moon.

After a few minutes, we reached the shore of the hot springs. It was large—a pond, really—and steam drifted from its surface, creating a fine mist that rolled across to the other side. The scent of warm water and moss and sand rose to greet me, and I let the robe slip from my shoulders, draping it across a bush. Tanya curtsied, then picked up the robe and headed off down the path.

Cautiously, I put one foot into the water.

It was as warm as I remembered it, sending a delicious shiver up my spine. Step by step, I descended into the pool. Gentle waves, stirred by the breeze, lapped steadily around me, parting as I waded through them. The soothing water began to calm my nerves. I paused for a moment when it was hip deep, resting my hands on the glistening surface. As I closed my eyes, the energy began to flow through me, soaking into my skin, washing away stress and worry and fear.

My breathing eased, the knot in my chest dissolving. Once it vanished, I noticed the crick in my neck, the bruise on my leg, the faint ache at the base of my tailbone. Wading deeper into the water until it was chest high, I paused again, my breasts lightly resting on the surface.

A dark eroticism began to creep into my thoughts, my nipples stiffening as I grew aroused. My stomach fluttered as an ache began to build between my legs. I tried to ignore it, tried to brush it away, but the slow burn flickered through my body, and I found myself breathing heavier as the water caressed me.

Not quite sure what to do—nobody had given me instructions on how to handle it if I suddenly found myself horny as hell during my training Circles—I decided to just push through and move on. I breathed through the wave of desire, then waded to the center of the pool, where I ducked under. As I came to the surface, I began the journey out again.

When I reached the shore on the other side, Morgaine was waiting. She motioned for me to stand before her, naked and covered with a sheen of water. Two cloaked figures stepped forward. One moved to the side as the other gestured for me to assume the Priestess Pose.

I stretched out my arms to my sides, and spread my legs, chin tilted toward the sky. The figure knelt and began to towel me off.

This could get tricky. The person holding the towel gently stroked the material down each leg. I did my best not to shudder at the soft material grazing my skin. As the towel reached my pussy, and quietly, softly, dried my pubic hair, it took every fiber I had not to respond, not to let out a moan or even a sigh.

My attendant rose and dried my torso, then stroked the towel up over each breast. Again, I restrained myself, biting my lip as I stared up at the first stars creeping into view. My arousal was strong now and it took everything I had to ignore it, to focus through the desire and lust. For all I knew, this was part of the training, and that thought kept me from breaking my stance.

When I was dry, the robed figures stood back, and Morgaine gave me a brilliant, if slightly terrifying, smile.

Two women stepped out from behind a nearby huckleberry bush, carrying my garb. One held my dress, and I raised my arms as she slid it down my body, making sure the halter was firmly tied behind my neck. She fastened my silver belt around my waist.

The other held my matching kimono. Both dress and kimono were made from spidersilk—the strongest fabric in Otherworld—sheer, warm, yet lightweight. The dress and kimono were woven with the pattern of peacock feathers, in blues and greens and plums.

After I was dressed, the first attendant held up my circlet—a silver band. In the front, a round moon sparkled silver, with a bronze crescent atop it, horns pointing up. She placed it around my head, then handed me my staff.

Morgaine nodded, walking around me. "Very good, very good. You are ready."

Morgaine was our distant cousin, if you counted the crossover of time, and she was shorter than Menolly. Petite, barely four-eleven, she had hair that reached her knees, bound back in an intricate pattern of braids and free flowing locks. A silver crescent had long ago been branded on her forehead. She was pretty, even lovely in a way, and her eyes were dark. When she was working magic, they flashed silver, much like my own. She was old—she'd been alive before the Great Divide, and she had to have taken the Nectar of Life at least once. Half-Fae could not live that long without help.

But Morgaine was greedy, whereas Titania and Aeval had no need for avarice. Morgaine craved power, and we weren't sure exactly to what lengths she'd go to get it. At this point, Aeval and Titania kept her in check.

She motioned to the robed attendants, and they shed their anonymity with their robes. A sick feeling lurched in the bottom of my stomach.

The one who had toweled me off was Mordred, Morgaine's nephew. He hated us—he resented our family connection to her, and like his aunt, he burned for power. He gave me a narrow look, and the leer on his face disturbed me. Hatred and lust were ill-met partners. I'd learned that all too painfully from Hyto.

The other attendant was Arturo, an FBH who also had taken the Nectar of Life. He was in love with Morgaine. He followed her at her will, and she commanded him but seldom showed him anything but the barest of courtesy. Now he nodded slowly to me, smiling faintly.

"Aeval waits for us in the center of the Grove." Morgaine's voice grated over the Dark Queen's name. "She has claimed this night of teaching."

I prepared to follow my cousin, but she stopped, turning to me.

"You may sit in the favor of the Queen of Shadow and Night, but you have much to learn, my girl. I gave you the chance to join my court and you snubbed your nose. But let Aeval snap her fingers and you come dancing like a puppet. I will never forgive the insult. While I will not interfere with your training—I take my duties seriously—at some point, my dear young cousin, we will meet head to head, and I will teach you what it means to truly bear our lineage. For now, however . . . we go to meet the Night."

And with that, she turned abruptly and headed down the path, into the grove. Mordred shot me a sickly smile, and as I passed by him, he let out a soft snicker, and one hand shot out to grab my ass.

I caught him by the wrist and gazed up at him, and said one word. "Smoky."

Mordred pulled away, but the look on his face told me that he was definitely my enemy. And both he and I knew it.

Chapter 8

Morgaine led me down a narrow path, and at my back, Mordred and Arturo followed. I wasn't at all comfortable with Mordred so close behind me, but there was nothing I could do.

We entered the glade in which I'd had my initiation into Aeval's Court. What happened that night would remain secret—as all highly personal rites should. Nobody, except those who were there, knew what I'd done.

As we exited the confines of the path and entered the clearing, the clouds parted to let the crescent moon shine down. We were almost at waxing, and the silver light from the Moon Mother illuminated the glade.

Aeval and Titania stood in the center of a pentagram that was marked in the grass. Between them stood a tall man, and in the light of the crescent moon, he practically glowed. As we approached, Morgaine stepped into the center, standing just outside the inner circle.

Aeval looked beyond me at Arturo and Mordred, and a

faint sneer appeared on her lips. "You are dismissed. Both of you. Return to Morgaine's court and wait for her there."

Mordred stiffened, gave Aeval a short bow, and turned to stride away. Arturo was more courteous and gave her a deep bow before sauntering off. They were trouble, that pair, though Mordred was far more dangerous than Arturo.

Aeval waited for a moment, then turned to Morgaine, and what was said, I could not hear, but something passed between them and Morgaine shot me a venomous look.

Titania cleared her throat and motioned me forward. I approached them, unsure of how they wanted me to enter the sigil in which they stood. The Queen of Light and Morning noticed my hesitation and gestured toward the top point of the star. "You may enter at that gate."

I silently circled the pentagram, then entered the path that would lead to casting the rune in a deosil—or clockwise—manner. As I stepped onto the trampled grass that made up the first line of the symbol, a rush of energy washed over me and I caught my breath in the beauty of the power. It summoned me in. If I hadn't been invited, it would have burned me to cinders.

As I followed the line, stopping at the center where they stood, Aeval broke into a smile and beckoned me in. "Camille, welcome, my child."

I swallowed my caution and joined them, and she draped her arm around my shoulders, drawing me near. Catching my breath, I wondered what was up. The Queen of Shadow and Night was seldom this demonstrative. Something must have her feeling good. Either that, or I was in for hell week and she was cushioning the blow.

The man standing between Aeval and Titania turned to me, a cunning smile playing on his face. Something seemed familiar about him. He was pale as the moonlight, with curly blue-black hair to his shoulders and dark eyes. His lips were ruddy. Not the red of lipstick, but naturally dark. He was around Trillian's height, not extremely tall, and his frame was lean and muscular. He wore a pair of black trousers and a white shirt that was open to the waist, showing a glimpse of thick chest hair. Gold and silver chains hung around his neck. A black vest completed the pseudo-pirate look, but somehow he made it work.

Aeval glanced at him, then at me. "Camille, before your training tonight, we have several things to discuss. Matters best left for here, in the sacred grove where all is protected from spies."

Uh-oh. That didn't bode well. I waited, not sure what to say.

"I want you to meet Bran. Bran, this is Priestess Camille te Maria—Camille D'Artigo."

I held out my hand. Instead of shaking it, he lifted my fingers to his lips, then turned my palm up and pressed his lips to my wrist, and I swear he nipped the skin as he kissed me. A spark of hunger ran through me, and the arousal I'd felt earlier, in the pool, returned full force. I had to catch myself before I gasped. I pulled my hand away as quickly as I could without being rude.

"Pleased to meet you . . ." I still didn't have a clue who he was, though something inside told me that I knew him, that I'd felt his energy before.

Titania caught my eye. "What Aeval has neglected to mention is that Bran is the son of Raven Mother and the Black Unicorn."

Raven Mother. The Black Unicorn . . .

Speechless, I turned to Bran, searching his face. I had killed his father, had sacrificed the Black Unicorn so that he might live again.

Raven Mother, one of the Elemental Queens, was the nemesis of the Moon Mother, constantly seeking to steal my lady's power. Raven Mother was jealous of the silvery moon, coveting the sparkling magic over which the Moon Mother ruled. To say we all had a volatile relationship was an understatement.

Bran held my gaze, his lips pursed. He reached out and took my hand again. I wanted to pull away, unsure of where this was going, but decided against it. Doing so might seem an insult. I glanced at Aeval, hoping she might intervene, but she seemed to have no interest in doing so.

His fingers were like fire against my own. One thing was for sure—Bran had considerable power. The tingling of his touch jarred me, racing up my arm like a thousand needles. His eyes sparkled with cold light.

"So, you are the priestess who sacrificed my father."

And there it was. But I still had no clue of whether he was toying with me, or whether this was just his nature.

"I had no choice. It was my destiny, and your father chose me to fulfill his rebirth." What I wanted to say was, *Look dude, deal with it, and let's not make this any more awkward than it already is,* but there was a time and place for attitude, and this wasn't it. Outspoken or not, I knew when to opt for diplomacy.

He raked his nails along the skin of my hand as he pulled away, almost breaking the skin but not quite. "So I've heard. My mother has much to say about you. She is . . . quite taken with you."

I stared at the marks on my arm—long white scratches but not enough to call him on it. A glance at Aeval told me she was scrutinizing me, waiting for my reaction. Not sure what she wanted—or expected—I drew myself up, straightening my shoulders.

"If you have a problem with me, let's clear the air now. I'm not sure why you're here, but obviously there's some reason. Chances are with the way things are developing, we're going to have to work together on something. So if you have a grievance? If you're pissed at me for doing what your father basically ordered me to do? Tell me now." I stared at him, holding his gaze, unwilling to back down.

One beat. Two beats. And then . . .

"A problem with you? Not at all. My father makes his own choices. You might count me more in my mother's court. I take after her." His voice was smooth, and again—the cunning smile.

Instantly on my guard, I tried to gauge what it was about

him that I didn't like. The jabs he'd made weren't really even jabs, except for scratching my arm, but there was something unsettling about Bran, and I couldn't put my finger on it.

And then it came to me. I couldn't read him, like I could so many other people.

And because I couldn't read him, I didn't know whether to trust him. The man unnerved me. Even then, *man* wasn't the right word. The son of an Elemental Queen who was as chaotic as they come, and the father of the Dahns Unicorns? Trickster energy. Pure, essential trickster.

"Then we are settled?" Aeval nodded to me, a faint smile on her face. "Bran is here to train the warriors of Talamh Lonrach Oll. He is a sorcerer, and an adept hand-to-hand warrior. He will lead the helm if we need him."

I whirled around, staring at her. What the fuck? Had she told Raven Mother what we were facing? Opening my mouth to protest, I stopped cold at the look on her face.

Then again, if Raven Mother and the Black Unicorn didn't already know about Shadow Wing, it would be a miracle. I swallowed my protest and held my breath to a count of five, then let it out slowly. Politics sucked, especially when I wasn't the one making up the rules.

"I see." There wasn't much else I could say.

"And *you* will be the liaison between Bran, the FH-CSI, and the Otherworld Intelligence Agency." Again, the frozen smile, daring me to object.

And again, I sucked it up and nodded as gracefully as I could. "As you will." Crap. I'd have to deal with Bran, like it or not. And right now, I didn't like it one bit. I turned to him. "We should talk in the next few days, get some things straight." *Like the fact that we're running the show from our side and you'd better play along.*

"I look forward to it." Again, the smooth voice covering the glittering eyes. Oh, the man was trouble. Attractive trouble, yes, but he set me on edge and I knew my sisters would feel the same. We were going to have a high old time coordinating this particular little corner of our ever-expanding world.

I glanced at Titania. She didn't look all that comfortable,

either, and Morgaine looked positively furious. What the fuck was she upset about? She was glaring at Bran like he'd usurped her position.

Bingo. It wasn't *her* position she was upset about. Ten to one she'd been wrangling some scheme to install Mordred as leader of the TLO Warriors. And Aeval and Titania were having none of that.

Titania cleared her throat when she noticed me staring at her. "I think, then, introductions are finished. Camille, we have yet one more issue to drop in your lap before you get on with your training for the evening."

This was turning out to be more fun than a barrel of rabid monkeys. My energy for the evening was about ready to fly the coop. I let out a long sigh, and Aeval must have noticed my oh-so-subtle eye roll because she reached over and tipped my chin up.

"Patience."

At Bran's snort, she gave him a sideways glance. "*Enough.* You are in *my* court now, and regardless of your parentage, you *will* behave accordingly."

"Yes, my lady." Bran pressed his lips together, looking none too happy, but he sobered and gave her a half nod. Feeling vindicated, I flashed him a cheery smile.

"As I said, we have a problem, and we want you to investigate. It is not something we are set up for. I believe, from our past discussions, that you have more information available than we do."

"Do you mean me and my sisters, or me in particular?"

"You and your sisters. This quite possibly impacts your own investigations on the matter." Aeval folded her arms across her chest. She glanced over at Bran, then back at me, and for a moment I thought I saw a flutter of doubt wash through her eyes, but then she shook her head. "One of our nobles—Lord Faerman—came to us two days past. His wife has run off, apparently seduced by the cult you call the Aleksais Psychic Network. Faerman wants her back."

The inflection in her voice was clear. *Bring her back. Alive.* "What's her name? What happened?"

Aeval cocked her head to the side, tapping her cheek with one long nail. "Her name is Syringa. She went to a meeting of the APN as a favor to a friend. Faerman says Syringa told him she wasn't interested, but her friend Shirley didn't want to go alone. This was last week. That night, she vanished. Shirley's vanished, too."

Syringa? That was the name of a lilac tree.

"Is she a dryad?" Dryads would never run off with a human group—they barely tolerated humans, just like most of the wood sprites, floraeds, and other woodland spirits. House sprites like Iris actually liked humans and paired up with families. But the Earthside woodland Fae? Not so much.

"Not fully. But yes, her lineage includes the woodland Fae. She's doesn't hold the human world as anathema, if that is what you are asking, but I don't believe she would choose to run off from her home and family. She loves her husband. We would consider it a great favor if you would find her and bring her back where she belongs."

I knew it wasn't a favor she was asking, but a command. "As you will, my lady." But actually, this might work in our favor, since I was going in undercover to check them out anyway. "We'll do our best. I'll need a few days, though."

"I know you will. I will tell Lord Faerman to be patient." And with that, she moved to the center of the pentagram. "And now, Titania, you and Morgaine may escort Bran back to the palace."

Bran bowed to me. "Until later, my lovely priestess."

I held his gaze for a moment. I had his number all right, smooth voice and suave demeanor notwithstanding. "Right. Later."

Morgaine shot me another dirty look, but she and Titania escorted Bran out of the pentagram and began walking back toward the path leading out of the clearing. Aeval waited until they vanished from sight.

I let out a long breath. I liked Titania, though we didn't have much in common, but I could do without the other two.

I was running out of steam, and I still had the ritual ahead of me.

Aeval moved to the center of the pentagram and motioned me to kneel in front of her. I quickly obeyed. One thing I'd learned from childhood on up—when your teacher instructs you to do something, you do it. Yes, you could ask why, but you still obeyed.

As I knelt, she took a small bottle from her pocket and brushed my lips with her fingers. I opened them, and she poured three drops on my tongue.

I swallowed. A streak of fire raced down my throat, burning me through, and I reeled as the energy buoyed me up, recharging my muscles and clearing my mind. I glanced up at the sky and saw that the clouds had parted to reveal the stars, glimmering down from their icy perch.

Caught by their beauty, I raised my arm, reaching up to them. The moon, almost full, watched over the night, the Moon Mother's power always present no matter what phase she was in.

Aeval remained silent, a soft smile replacing her usual serious expression. She wound her fingers through mine, closing them tightly over my hand. Her power, magnetic and sparkling, radiated through me, and once again, I felt a surge of rejuvenation as the weariness of the day fell away.

I laughed then and squeezed her hand. She gave me a quick nod and let go of my hand, stepping back. Motioning for me to stand, Aeval waited till I was on my feet; then she moved to each point of the pentagram, where she lit a candle and called out an invocation.

First came green for the Earth, in a hurricane glass so that it would neither go out in the wind nor start any inadvertent fires. Aeval lit the candle just outside the circle surrounding the pentagram.

"Spirits of Earth, this sovereign night, ground and center this sacred rite."

The earth shifted, deep in the core beneath my feet, as a rush of energy rose through the soil to steady both me and the ritual to come. Aeval waited a moment, then nodded and moved to the next point—outside the circle again—where she lit a white candle for the Air.

"Spirits of Air, this sovereign night, buoy aloft this sacred rite."

The words were simple, but as she spoke, a breeze sprang up to gust around me, and laughter lightly rolled in off the wind. My mind cleared, although the energy from the potion remained, and I could sense everything keenly, clearly, as if a veil had lifted.

Aeval moved to the next point and lit a red candle.

"Spirits of Fire, this sovereign night, burn bright with passion this sacred rite."

Once again, the Elements sprang to her bidding and I responded. As it had when I was in the pool, my body began to ache with the most exquisite desire, and I found myself reeling, my pussy growing wet, my nipples stiffening. The breeze made it feel like a hundred hot fingers were tickling over my skin.

Aeval moved on to the fourth point, where she lit the blue candle.

"Spirits of Water, this sovereign night, wash through and cleanse this sacred rite."

A wave rolled through; I could hear it churning as it engulfed me, an unseen force so strong that I stumbled, reeling. As it washed through my body and soul, any lingering worries and troubles were swept away and I stood stronger, taller, focused only on what was happening.

Aeval lit a black candle at the center point at the top of the pentagram, and whispered, her words faint and distant.

"Spirit of the Universal dance, bring to this rite your sacred trance."

As the invocation echoed on the breeze, I was sucked deep into a long tunnel, swiftly moving inward, toward the core of my being, with everything around me surreal and vivid. The eye catchers glowed deeper, the stars twinkled brighter, and the auras of the trees began to shimmer and glow until the forest was lit up like nature's carnival.

Lastly, Aeval lit a silver candle to one side of the black, and a gold to the other side. She raised her hands to the sky and turned to the crescent moon, her voice echoing through the glade.

"Mother Moon, shining bright, over Earth, Air, Fire, Water, ride your priestess, take her now, Camille, your sacred daughter! Lord of Horns, Father of Earth, Guardian, Provider, Brother, call now, your newborn priest, Our Beloved Lady's Lover."

As the Moon Mother descended to ride my shoulders, I turned to see a figure edge out of the forest. Male, that much I knew; he was glowing with the light of a priest. Of a god. And he was *mine*. I knew he was mine, and I dropped my kimono where I stood. As he began to walk toward me, I shrugged out of my dress. Aeval forgotten, the ritual forgotten, all I could think about was how I needed to rid myself of my clothing, for the chase was on.

Naked, I stood bathed in the moonlight, waiting, edging slightly to the left.

He moved, darting in my direction, and I ran lightly out of the Circle, laughing, turning to beckon him on, to tease him in. I wanted him, but he'd have to earn the right. No one claimed me without proving himself worthy, and whether he be mortal or god, he would have to meet me and match me.

I circled around the outside of the pentagram, the wind nipping my heels. He laughed, throaty and rich, and from someplace deep within me, I recognized the voice but could give no name to it. For he truly had no name, and neither did I. We were male and female, god and goddess, polarities in the great dance of the universe. Like magnets, we were drawn together, but the moment he came too close, I pushed away, running out of reach.

I still could not see him; he was cloaked in shadow, covered by a veil that I could not penetrate. But I did not fear him. He was my match, he was the Chosen One. And I—I was his Sovereign Queen. To be worthy of his status, he must meet me and convince me he was worthy. And then I would allow him in, ride him into the night, and he would emerge sanctified and holy, cleansed in my sacred light and sex.

His laughter faded as he paused, eyeing me. I stopped, shoulders back, hair streaming in the wind. The mood shifted, and intent now—the playfulness vanishing—he began to advance. I stepped back, into the pentagram, into the center.

"You must earn the right to taste my body. You must earn the right to be King Stag of the Forest." My voice echoed into the night, the words coming from deep within me.

"I claim you." Again, the voice resonated with me, even in its quiet ferocity. "Name the challenge."

He must pass three tests, as it was in the days of old. Before I could stop myself, I said, "The challenge of demons."

"So be it." His words echoed with a frightening clarity.

I raised one hand, not sure what I was doing but only knowing that I had to. As I did, the image of a woman appeared—terrifying and beautiful. She was Japanese, and I recognized her as Demonkin. The man cried out and pulled back, his fear tangible in the night. She laughed and held up a spear.

He met her with a katana—where he got it, I could not see—but they fought, spear meeting the sword with deadly precision. Her expression was set; she was out to kill him if possible. She radiated anger and lust, the desire for blood. As she opened her mouth, I saw fangs, pearly white, with blood dripping.

She dove for him, knocking the katana out of his hand, and he let out a shout, but at the last minute, he managed to slip out of her grasp and dart around behind her. He wrestled the spear away from her and, without fanfare, without hesitation, plunged it through her chest. With a scream, she burst into dust and ash and vanished.

I still could not see his face as he turned to me and raised his hand in salute.

"One," he said.

The trance pulled me deeper and I waved my hand again, letting instinct take over. Ritual magic fell where it would, and I just went along for the ride. The Moon Mother was leading the journey tonight. I was merely her vessel.

A whirl of light sparkled in the clearing, and a vague shape rose out of it, taking the form of a large serpent, crimson red with white diamonds patterned along its body. I stumbled back, out of the way. The snake had to be thirty feet long and as thick around as Menolly was. It swayed back and forth in front of him, as if he were a snake charmer. Hissing, its tongue forked out as it loomed over him.

"You. You came back." He raised his hands. "It's been a long time . . ."

The snake coiled to strike. As it launched toward him, he stood there, waiting for it. I wanted to shout *Get out of the way*, but my voice froze and all I could do was watch. It spiraled around him, buoying him up in its embrace. I winced, expecting to hear him cry out as it snapped his bones, but he just wrapped his arms around the snake and held on, pressing his face against the scaled body. The snake twisted, swinging him this way and that, but he held tight, and for a moment, it sounded like he was crying.

"I'm sorry. I'm sorry I left you. I had to run, or we'd both die. I had no choice. But I went back. I promise you, I went back to the field for days on end, looking for you. But by then, you were gone." His voice faded, regret and loss echoing through his words.

And then I understood this challenge. Some demons . . . some demons weren't the ones who had tried to hurt us. Some demons were the people we'd fled from but could never leave behind, memories that would haunt us forever. I backed away. He needed to come to grips with whatever this snake represented—with whomever he'd lost.

Another moment, and the snake stilled its movements, and then, gently, it let go, and the man stumbled to his knees, gasping for breath. The snake reached down and gently touched the top of his head with a flicker of its tongue, then turned and vanished back into the shimmering light.

He raised a hand as it went, holding it out, as he whispered, "Good-bye."

That one word was so filled with sorrow and loss and finality that it made me hang my head. I was an intruder on his memory, and it didn't feel right. I turned away for what seemed like hours.

And then, "Two."

I turned. He was looking at me, his face still cloaked in shadow, his form still a blur.

A prickling at the base of my neck told me that his last challenge would be the biggest. I looked up at the stars and then nodded. With another wave of the hand, I braced myself for whatever might come into the glade.

But nothing appeared.

And then a soft whisper called out my name. My skin prickling, I turned. There, in the moonlight, stood my mother. *Maria D'Artigo*. My mother, my greatest loss.

She was wearing the gown she wore for her death ceremony. My father's people were buried naked beneath the trees, but for the preceding ritual, when we were being consigned to the Land of the Silver Falls, our dead were dressed in ritual garb—gowns of silver, the color of the moon, for women. And for the men, golden trousers and shirts, the color of the sun.

I cocked my head. This was *his* challenge, so why was my mother here? And why would she be here at all?

But as I watched her, the questions vanished from my thoughts and all I could see was how beautiful my mother had been. Waxen and fair, her hair trailed down her shoulders, the same golden shade as Delilah's. But her eyes were closed, and blood ran down her cheek from a large gash in her head.

The challenge forgotten, I ran toward her. "Mother? Mother!"

She opened her eyes. They were white, with no gleaming hazel, no pupils, no warmth or welcome in them. Lifting one hand, she pointed an accusatory finger at me. "You took my place. You stole my memory, and you replaced me."

Stopped cold by the chill of her words, I hesitated. I *had* taken her place, because I was forced to. I'd filled her shoes as best as I could, even though I could never be the woman she was. As I opened my mouth to protest, a well of anger cropped up that I didn't know was there.

"*You left us.* You wouldn't drink the Nectar of Life. *You abandoned us.* You could have lived if you had let Father give you the potion. You could have stayed with us, but you chose to die." The words startled me, even though—in my darkest nights—I knew I'd felt them. *Thought them.* But the guilt had driven them deep inside, and I had never once breathed them aloud.

She dropped her hand and crossed her arms. "I chose to stand by my beliefs. I loved your father, but I was human. I chose to remain human."

"You chose to be a *coward*!" The words reverberated through the night, and I clasped my hand to my mouth, immediately ashamed of what I'd said. How could I call my own mother a coward? She'd given up everything she ever knew to follow Sephreh back to Otherworld. She'd chosen a life alien to her own and had raised us with love. How could I accuse her of being so weak?

"I chose . . . I chose . . ." And then, she paused, and the anger vanished even as she let out a long sigh and slumped her shoulders. "Camille . . . I was more afraid of living a thousand years than I was of dying. I understood what it meant to die. I didn't know if I could live that long and stay sane. I wasn't born to it, like you and your sisters, and your father."

"But we needed you." As if the dam had burst, I let it all out. "We needed you. *I needed you.* I had to grow up too fast. I had to take your place because *somebody* had to, and Delilah and Menolly were too young. I had to become their mother—when I just wanted to be a girl. And Father, he's never recovered from your death. He loved you. He *worshiped* you. I could never do anything right—he never let me forget that you were perfect and I . . . I wasn't."

Tears streaming down my cheeks, I flung my fury at her, not caring if I hurt her, not caring if she hated me. "I needed you so many times, but you weren't there. At least I did what I could for my sisters, but there was *no one* there for me when I needed a mother . . . when I needed someone to hold me and tell me it would all be okay! Father was too busy with the Guard and too busy mourning you to notice that his children needed him. How could you do that to me?"

My mother hung her head, and all the fight vanished. "I can't make it right, Camille. I can't go back and change what was. No one can. I'm sorry. I made the choice I had to. It was my life to keep or let go. But I'm so sorry that I hurt you. I watch over you and your sisters; I keep an eye out on you. I can't intervene, but I never forget you. I'm with you whether or not you realize it."

Weeping, I sank to the ground. "I needed you . . . I need my mother."

She glided forward, her spirit so bright she almost blinded me. As she knelt by my side, her arms slid around my shoulders and she crooned softly.

"Hush, my girl. You had to take on too much. But you can let it go now . . . you can let some of that go. You have so many responsibilities, but your sisters are grown. You don't have to play the role of their mother anymore. You can live for yourself and your lovers. Lean on them, and lean on your friends. And when you need me, remember, I am here. I am listening."

I pressed my face against the soft touch of the spirit, like I did Misty, at home, and cried like I had never cried before. I cried for the years of trying to meet Father's expectations. I cried for having to face Menolly's death and rebirth without Mother's help. I cried for the isolation I'd felt when Hyto kidnapped me. And, after a long while, my tears lessened. It felt like a lump that had been lodged in my throat all these years had shifted and loosened. With a hiccup, it vanished, and I sat back, hanging my head.

"I'm sorry. I'm sorry I said all those things—"

"No," my mother said. "You needed to face the fact that as much as you love me, you're also angry. You squashed those feelings down so hard, they were eating you alive. They were draining you."

Sniffling, I nodded. She rose, and I stood beside her.

"I miss you."

"I miss you, too, honey."

"I love you."

And my mother looked at me, and for a flicker, I saw the lovely hazel eyes that used to watch over me, and they twinkled with tears. "I love you, too. I have to go, now. Please . . . I'm happy. I'm waiting for you—but it will be a long, long wait, I think, and I hope. Which is as it should be."

And then, before I could say another word, she turned, walked back into a misty veil, and vanished.

Spent, I turned back to stare at the figure in the shadows. "Why her? Why me? I thought this was *your* challenge."

"It was. My challenge was to stand back and let you fight your own battle. My challenge was to watch you work through one of the deepest losses you've ever experienced without stepping in to help. And so . . . three."

And then he moved forward, and the moonlight shimmered over him, revealing his face. *Morio*. My magical match. The priest to my priestess. The King Stag of the Woodland, and I was his goddess.

Once again, the moon swept down to gather me up in her frenzy. I opened my arms. He moved into my embrace, sliding out of his kimono. As he held me, naked and erect, the Moon Mother shimmered overhead, and the night-singing birds echoed through the woodland, and then I was off and running and he followed me, into the dance, onto the web, into the arms of the Moon Mother and the Horned One.

Chapter 9

✦⌒◈⌒✦

Beltane was coming, and the energy rode us hard. The King Stag was in rut, ready to mate with the Goddess of Sovereignty in order to claim kingship, and nothing could keep them apart. And the Moon Mother was riding me high.

I kept phasing in and out. I was the goddess, I was myself, then back again. The Moon Mother laughed, and her laughter poured out of my throat, rich and heady.

Morio's youkai side was on the verge of showing, but instead of shifting into demonic form, I could see the auric outline of antlers rising high above his head, and his lusty smile was backed by the power of the god.

As I drew back, leading him to the center of the pentagram, muffled sounds from the woods caught my attention. The night creatures had come out to watch. I scuffed through a scattered handful of leaves, and several pale moths—Pale Beauties—fluttered up around my face, then went winging overhead, glowing luminous white in the moonlight. They circled around, wings flickering in the night breeze, and then, as if raising a silent call, were joined by a kaleidoscope of their kin, swirling, dancing, diving, darting through the air. We watched, hand in hand, as they danced in silent unison, like a murmuration of starlings.

Laughing in wonder and joy, I turned to Morio. He gazed at me, holding my hands.

"When we mate . . ."

"Then I will be fit to be your priest. I will have earned the right."

And then I understood. Tonight was really *his* initiation. He would walk beside me, under the Moon Mother, as my magical consort as well as my husband. I drew him into the center of the pentagram, and the candles at each point sparked, their flames flaring higher. I made him stand back, arms at his sides, naked beneath the moon, and knelt at his feet.

I kissed the tops of his feet softly. "Blessed are thy feet, that walk the path of the gods. May you never stray from the path."

He swayed in the gentle breeze.

I kissed his knees. "Blessed are thy knees, that kneel at the altar of the gods. May they always remind you of those who watch over us."

Morio sucked in a deep breath and then slowly let it out as I remained on my knees.

I leaned forward and placed a gentle kiss on the pubic bone right above his cock and balls. "Blessed are thy loins, that plow the field and furrow and tend to the needs of the goddess. May you always remain virile and embody the god in your passion."

As Morio gave a soft moan, his penis began to rise and I resisted the impulse to give it a long, slow lick. That would come later.

I rose to my feet and leaned forward, kissing his heart. "Blessed is thy heart, may you forever find passion and joy in the service of the gods."

He was in trance, fully now. His eyes were brilliant topaz, and while he showed no signs of shifting, the energy shifted around him like a violet cloak, crackling and sizzling every time our bodies touched. I pressed my lips against his lips and kissed him fully.

"Blessed are thy lips, that voice the words of the gods. May you forever speak the truth of your path."

And then, as I stepped back, I whispered, "May the Horned One bless you and guide you, may the goddess watch over you and dance with you, may the Elements hearken to your call, may the Magic ride you wild and free. May you be forever bound with the powers that embody the Earth. May your path be brilliant and true."

Morio let out a low laugh, and then, with a delighted look on his face, he reached for me. I moved into his embrace and he caught me around the waist, lifting me into the center of the pentagram. I could feel the god looming large over him, his footprints all over Morio's aura. He was riding his shoulders, the fecundity of the forest and the rut merging with my husband, my priest, to amplify his strength and his passion.

Magnetized, desiring him with an ache so deep it seemed to run straight through to my toes, I pulled him to me, fastening my lips to his, pressing my breasts against his chest, my hips against his erection. He was firm, and strong, and vibrant. Alive, in the way that the forest lived. Alive, in the fertile virility of springtime in the forest.

I was hungry for more than just sex. I wanted communion of the body and spirit, the merging of magic with magic, passion with passion, two halves coming together to form a whole.

He lowered his lips to my neck, and I tossed my hair back as he gently licked, then fastened onto my skin—not biting, not nipping—but trailing a path of kisses down my shoulder, then down to my breast.

We fell to our knees, and he leaned me back, his tongue working my nipple. I looked over his shoulder at the night sky, the stars shining down on us, as the rich scent of grass and loam filled my lungs. Nearby, a rustle in the brushes told me we were not alone, but I didn't care. We were uniting in the Great Rite; let all of nature watch if it wanted.

My clit was burning, and I wanted him to thrust my knees

apart, drive himself between them. Morio trailed his lips down the smooth skin of my stomach, down toward the V between my thighs. He glanced up at me, his eyes gleaming, and I groaned and began caressing my breasts as he watched. The light in his eyes flickered and he buried his head between my legs, licking, stroking, eating me out.

I began to laugh as he tickled and teased me and the pressure built. "Oh gods, I can't stand it, hurry up please, let me come!"

Morio sat back on his feet, balancing himself by holding on to my knees. "What do you say, wife?"

"Please, please let me come!" I was so close, but I couldn't stop laughing, and the tension was driving me crazy.

A twinkle in his look, he cocked his head. "I want to watch you touch yourself. Show me how you like it, Camille. Show me what you do."

Mesmerized by his voice, his intoxicating scent, I reached down as he greedily watched, and slid one finger on my clit, gently stroking the fires to a heady flame. With my other hand, I stroked my breast, playing over the nipples. Shifting my hips, I squirmed, panting raggedly as I circled my clit faster and faster, rubbing hard enough to drive away the laughter and bring on that dark need.

His erection thick and pulsing, he wrapped his fist around his cock, rubbing hard as he continued to watch. Drops of pre-cum appeared on the tip of his penis—sex-sweat—and I licked my lips, hungry for him to fill me—to fill my mouth, my ass, my cunt.

Morio read my needs, and he crawled up me until he was able to kneel above me, his cock thrusting into my waiting mouth. I continued to masturbate, harder and faster as he pumped into me, my lips forming a tight seal around the head of his cock. He tasted of salt and brine and forest meadows, and I sucked eagerly, licking and nibbling until I suddenly found myself on the peak, cascading over in a series of waves, the orgasm tumbling me into the waiting rapids below.

Not done yet, Morio pulled out of my mouth and flipped

me over, driving his cock deep into my pussy, the hardness forcing its way through the folds of my vagina. He worked one finger into my ass, slowly, methodically, and I let out another moan as I began to build again, faster this time.

"I want to fuck you, to drive so deep you never, ever forget I've been inside you," he whispered. "Open to me, let me in, never ever turn me away."

"Never . . ." I was building again, as the night seemed to pulse in time to our fucking. The breeze whipped up, faster, lashing against our skin, and as I looked up, the flurry of the Pale Beauty moths blotted out the sky except for the moon.

Morio beat a rapid tattoo against my ass, jarring me as he drove deeper and deeper with each thrust. I could feel the Horned God, riding him, riding me—as if superimposed over him. As the passion of the Horned One flowed from Morio's aura into mine, I reveled in the communion. I was his consort, and he was mine. As I was Morio's wife and he was my husband, I was his priestess and he was my priest. The god was connected to all men, and the goddess to all women, and the divine pair was reenacting their mating dance through us.

Honored and swept up in the cosmic dance—the union of male and female—I spiraled in and out of my body as we built toward the climax, and then Morio let out a great roar, holding tight to my waist, and I tumbled into orgasm again, set off by his pleasure, and the entire forest vibrated with our passion.

Morio pulled away and sat on the ground, looking dazed. I rolled to a sitting position, feeling more than satisfied but also a little dazed. The energy was starting to lift, leaving me a little chilly, too.

"Wow." I stared at him. "I didn't know you were going to be part of the ritual tonight. I expected something more . . . more . . ."

"Traumatizing?" He ducked his head, smiling. "They contacted me and told me that I needed to formally bind myself as your priest. Just working magic together isn't enough. Neither was our Soul Symbiont ritual. I guess Beltane is going to be big, right?"

Slowly nodding, I wrapped my arms around my knees, huddling in the now-chilly darkness. "Aeval told me to be prepared for the Hunt . . . Beltane is on a full moon, and the Wild Hunt on a Sabbat night? I have no clue what to expect."

Morio scooted over to me and wrapped his arms around my shoulders, his body heat warming me.

"I've run with the Hunt ever since I was first initiated into the Moon Mother's service. But . . . this feels big, and cold, and different than anything I've ever done. It reminds me of when the Moon Mother caught me up, when I was held captive by Hyto. She took me on a rampage—I tore through the skies with her." And it had felt good. Cleansing, to destroy, smash, take out my fury on the world.

Morio let out a murmur. "I do understand."

"Tell me . . . what was the demon you fought? And the snake . . . unless, of course, they are private parts of your life you'd rather not share?"

He paused, then let out a long, slow breath. "The demon, I fought when I was younger. I was grown and on my own, but still naïve and still easily swayed. She presented herself as a beautiful woman and seduced me. I had been traveling with a companion—a very devout monk—and she used me to get to him, to make him break his vows. After she corrupted him, she tortured and killed him. I was helpless to intervene. I managed to track her down and kill her, but I've never forgiven myself for being so blind to the danger."

Regret . . . it was in his voice. I knew my men had secrets they kept—just as I did, although Trillian and I were most open with one another. We talked about everything. But Morio had told me little of his past. I knew less about him than I did Smoky and far less than I knew about my alpha lover.

"I'm sorry." There wasn't much else I could say.

"No, it was long ago, and over. But I think . . . I think it will always haunt me. He didn't have to die. If I'd been more cautious, he would have not been in danger. I was responsible for his safety on that journey, and I failed miserably."

He hung his head.

I leaned forward, tipped his chin up, and kissed him lightly. "Some things can never be undone. We can only learn and move forward. And . . . the snake?"

A tear slipped down his face. He bit his lip and hung his head. "You know how my parents don't blame all humans for the slaughter that happened in their families, and how Grandmother Coyote rescued my father and brought him up?"

"Yes. She sent him to live with Kimiko, the nature spirit who rules over the devas and flower faeries, right?"

"Right. Well, we were visiting her when I was in my teens. I loved attending to her shrine, and I loved it when she summoned us to her side. I met a young woman back then— my age. We were both . . . oh . . . teenagers, in our time frame. She was my first." He dipped his head, smiling slyly. "She was brash and independent, and her family tried to rein her in, but it never worked. Anyway, we spent that summer at Kimiko's, and Yoshiko and I fell in love, in that reckless teenage way where every look, every touch means something earth-shaking."

I let out a small laugh. "Like Shamas and I did, before his family separated us."

"Right." Morio frowned. "Let's leave Shamas out of this, okay? I still don't trust that he's not after you."

Rather than argue, I shrugged and bit my tongue.

"Anyway, we were out exploring one day, and we came to a cave. We decided to explore, and when we entered the main chamber, we discovered a nest of magical sea vipers. We were near the cliffs, near the ocean."

I'd never heard of the snakes before. "Were they poisonous?"

"Very." He pressed his lips together for a moment, then let out a long sigh. "Long story short, they separated us. They were quick and large and managed to cut her off from me. I had no choice—if I didn't get out of there, they'd kill me. I had to leave her behind. I can still hear her screams as they swarmed her. I glanced back, but all I could see was a mass of writhing scales and slithering bodies. I ran home to get help. Kimiko herself joined the search party. But we couldn't find Yoshiko. We never even found a trace of her, though we found the nest and destroyed it. I knew she was dead, but the rest of the summer, I went out there every day, looking and hoping that somehow she managed to get away."

"What about her family? How did they take the news?"

He shrugged. "They were pissed that she'd disobeyed them and gone with me. They had forbidden us to be together. They disowned her memory, cut her out of the lineage. They forgot her."

The hairs on my arms stood up. How could parents be so cruel? I still hadn't fully forgiven Father for disowning me, even though he'd been on his best behavior since he came around a few months ago. But it would take a long time to heal the wound he'd left on my heart.

I took Morio's hand, held it tight. "And you've never forgiven yourself. It wasn't your fault. Neither one of you knew that the cave had monsters in it."

"I should have. The area was fraught with danger—Kimiko warned me to be cautious when I first arrived. And if I hadn't encouraged her to sneak out with me, Yoshiko would have still been alive." He paused, then looked up. "Leaving her there, helpless to do anything, I've never forgotten that feeling. And when Hyto captured you—it all came back. I couldn't do anything. I couldn't stop him. We *knew* he was out there, hunting you, and we let you down." He looked up at me, his eyes haunted in a way I'd never seen him look.

And there it was. The crux of his regret. Both of his challenges—the demon and the snake—were all about regret over perceived failures. And he felt he had failed me, too.

"You did not fail me." I took both of his hands, pressed them to my breasts. "My love, listen to me. People die. Monsters are real. As Chase would say, 'Shit happens.' There isn't any way to predict some of the tragedies we'll encounter. You didn't kill the monk—the demon did. You were seduced and deceived. It happens. And you didn't kill

Yoshiko—the snakes did. Both of you were young, in the throes of that youthful passion, and you didn't think—either of you. And that's normal."

He pushed to his feet and held out his hand. "I know that logically. And logically, I know that Hyto would have found a way to get to you, no matter what we did. I know that on an intellectual basis, but emotionally . . ."

I took his hand and let him pull me to my feet. "Emotionally, you feel like you'd be a bad person if you let the guilt go?" It was a suspicion, not a certainty, but I thought I understood what was going on. "You don't have to wear the guilt around like a hair shirt, *especially when it wasn't your fault*. Nobody's going to think less of you if you set it down. Guilt impedes you, makes you weak. Let it go, my love. I don't blame you. Yoshiko and your monk friend? They're long gone, except in your memory."

With a drawn-out sigh, he conceded. "I know you're right."

"Then say it. Tell me that you weren't at fault." Sometimes, saying it out loud made it real.

He straightened his shoulders, standing tall. "This is one of the hardest things I've ever done, you know."

"You are my priest. You need to be as strong as you can— to reclaim the energy and power you gave to those monsters. They hurt you by hurting those you loved."

The Moon Mother filtered down through my body. She was looking through my eyes—I felt like I was standing to one side, listening to her speak, watching her as she watched Morio. "Claim back your power."

Shivering, Morio let out a slow stream of breath and I knew he could see the Moon Mother in the reflection of my eyes.

"Yes, my lady. I . . . I was not responsible for their deaths. I was not responsible for Hyto kidnapping you. There was nothing I could have done to stop any of it from happening. I did the best I could under the circumstances."

As he spoke, a ray of silver light shot down from the

moon, into my body. I raised my hand and pressed it to his forehead. "Be cleansed."

As he shuddered, a black cloud—buzzing like a hundred bees—rose from his body and flew off into the night. Another light, brilliant green and filled with a thick flurry of sparkles—came racing out from the forest. It washed over me, and I raised my other hand and pressed it to his heart.

"Be one with the Lord of the Hunt."

Morio fell to his knees as, from behind a tall cedar, stepped a white stag. His antler tines rose high and dangerous into the air. He was old—so old that moss dripped from the tines, hanging low like it did off the cedars and fir in the forests. His eyes were brilliant red, and he was as tall at his shoulder as I was. He approached Morio and bellowed, nostrils steaming.

A look of wonder filling his expression, Morio reached out and stroked the King Stag as the ancient elk let out a bugling cry. Morio backed up, and I could tell that nothing else existed in this moment. He shifted, turning into his fox form. As the elk bolted away, racing into the wood, Morio followed. I started forward, crying out, worried, but I tripped over a stone and went down hard.

As I sat there nursing my bruised backside, I realized that the ritual was Morio's. I couldn't interfere. It was his to experience, his run to make. Dazed from the evening, I wearily rose and found my ritual garb—somehow it had gotten draped over a nearby bush—and slowly dressed.

The night grew chilly as I waited, and I wondered where Aeval was. Usually she came to get me after ritual. But there was no sign of her now. Nor had Morio returned. Getting a little worried, I began pacing around the perimeter of the glade. Should I wait? Should I go looking for him? Should I go find Aeval?

I had learned to wait for instruction—you couldn't just go your own way when it came to magic, and the training was hard and intense. I'd been subjected to so many all-night rituals and harsh tests over the past few months that I felt steeped in the energy, immersed in it to the point where, on some days, there was little else in my existence.

Derisa, the High Priestess of the Moon Mother back in Otherworld, had told me I was training to become the first High Priestess of the Moon Mother that Earthside had seen in thousands of years. Years of rigorous training loomed in front of me.

But as the night wore on, a chill mist began to rise and the temperature crept lower and lower. The Pacific Northwest was not known for warm springs, and it must have been forty-two and falling by around two in the morning. A glance at the woods where the stag had led Morio showed nothing. And a glance down the trail back to the hot springs and the palace again showed nothing. A stirring here or there told me that I wasn't alone—but when I reached out, all I could sense were the stray animals still prowling the forests.

I looked up at the moon.

"Should I go find Morio?" I asked, quietly, but the Moon Mother wasn't talking to me.

I paced around the perimeter of the glade. Finally, after another interminable time, I couldn't take the waiting. I grabbed my staff and headed into the forest, following the direction in which the stag and Morio had gone.

The passion and drive of the night had fallen off. Now I felt on edge. Warily, I pushed my way through the undergrowth. The foliage was thick, but at this point, I wasn't facing briars and thorn-covered huckleberries. The ferns were huge, and other bushes impeded my progress, but none seemed to be dangerous.

At one point I stumbled, stubbing my toe against a branch hidden by the debris littering the forest floor. It could have been much worse, though, if I hadn't had my staff to lean on when I tripped.

Where had they gone? When I ran with the Hunt, I was gone till morning, unable to tear myself away. But it wasn't a full moon, and the god was wild and unpredictable in ways that the goddess wasn't. She could be merciless, but the god—he was feral and chaotic.

"Morio? Morio!" I called out, at first timid, but then, fear took hold and I shouted his name at the top of my lungs, my voice echoing through the night air, reverberating off trees.

At one point I stepped in something slimy and groaned. It was either a pile of rotting leaves or something that had once been alive. There was nothing else that I could think of. Wiping my foot on a patch of grass nearby, I bent down, trying to see what it was. Oh delightful, a nest of banana slugs.

The Pacific Northwest is famous for its banana slugs— huge creatures that looked like they ought to be in some B-grade science fiction movie, a good four to six inches long and as big around as my thumb. They were colorful, in shades of green and sometimes yellow, and on rare occasion brown, and they were delightful in a slimy, nasty sort of way.

I did my best to wipe off my foot and continued on.

A thousand acres doesn't sound that big, but in the dark, in the wild, it's a huge area. I worked my way farther into the forest, trying to keep myself going in a straight line, but somehow I got turned around a couple of times. After what seemed like another half hour, I knew I was lost. My voice was hoarse—I'd been calling for Morio the entire time, but there was no answer, just scuttling noises from the bushes. Even the devas, the flower spirits and such, seemed to have vanished.

My feet were already sore when my luck ran out and I stepped on a bramble. A large thorn pierced the bottom of my heel. I let out a scream—the pain was shocking, especially when I wasn't prepared for it—and dropped my staff, hopping onto the other foot. Leaning against the nearest tree, I lifted my foot and propped it across my other knee, balancing against the fir as I reached down. In the dark, I gingerly searched for the thorn.

And there it was, sharp and jagged, barbed, firmly implanted in my foot. I tugged on it. Damn it. The barb was just inside the skin. If I pulled it out, I'd rip the bottom of my heel open—or at least a nice little section of it—and bleed like crazy, as well as open myself up to infection. But I couldn't walk on the fucker—it would only drive it farther in.

I sucked in a deep breath, clenched my teeth, took hold of the thorn, and yanked hard. At first it didn't want to give way, but then, with another swift tug, it tore open the skin and came out. I held the thorn up, trying to get a good look at it, but all I could tell was that it was big and sharp, and it had claimed more of my blood than I wanted to give.

My inclination was to toss it, but I was halfway afraid I might step on it again. As I pressed against the tree, my fingers felt a hollow in the trunk—just a little woodpecker's hole—and I dropped the thorn in there. One problem solved. Only a dozen more to figure out.

Next job: figure out which way to go in order to get back to the glade. I tried to gauge the direction by looking at where the moon was now, but the clouds had swept in while I was preoccupied with the thorn, covering the sky, and it was really dark. I could barely see my hand in front of my face.

And I could feel that my foot was still bleeding.

I thought about tearing a strip off my priestess robes to bind up my foot, but that just seemed wrong. I'd worked too hard and too long to get them, and I wasn't about to go ripping them up unless I had a damned good reason. Big honking ax cut or knife wound? Yeah, good reason. Thorn-in-the-foot wound? Not so much.

Grumbling, I balanced with my staff as I felt around the base of the tree, still trying to keep my foot off the ground. I could feel several plants, including vine maple. Vine maple had large leaves—though at this time of the year, they hadn't fully blossomed out, but they were big enough to cover the wound, and I wasn't allergic to them. I picked several in order to provide not only a covering but a cushion for my foot.

Now I needed something to keep the maple leaves plastered to my skin. And then I had an idea. I limped and hopped my way back to the banana slug nest and scooped up some of the disgusting remains.

I wiped the slime around the wound without actually touching it. Banana slugs left a trail of slime behind them that was like rubber glue. This would work perfectly. I managed to smear enough on my foot that when I dropped the slug remains and slapped the largest leaf across my foot, it held, keeping the smaller leaves in place beneath it.

I cautiously tested the makeshift bandage, and it worked. My foot hurt to walk on, so I'd still be limping, but at least now if I set it down flat, nothing would infect the wound. At least for now.

Now, to figure out how the hell to get out of the woods. I was getting tired—oh, so tired—and though I was still worried about Morio, I was also worried about myself. While I doubted there would be anything terribly dangerous in terms of magical beings or traps in these woods, there might be mountain lions or a bear, and they did not enjoy having their space invaded.

Thoroughly exhausted, chilled, and quickly losing patience, I limped around a stand of fir and suddenly found myself on a path.

"Oh thank the gods . . . this has to take me somewhere." Breathing a little easier, I headed in the direction I thought would most likely take me back to the palace and the heart of Talamh Lonrach Oll.

All the while, I kept calling for Morio, but my throat was raw and my words sounded more like a croak. The farther I went down the path, the lighter the sky was getting. Was it almost morning? I was so tired that I couldn't tell how long had passed, but the warm, delicious afterglow from the sex had long faded, and even my thoughts and irritations at Bran had diminished. I just wanted to go home to my own bed and sleep for a dozen hours.

Hobbling unsteadily on my feet, I finally listed to the side one too many times and went crashing down in a pile of ivy. As I sat there, brushing off the pinky-nail-sized jumping spiders that came running out to see who had just destroyed their hiding places, I thought that maybe it wouldn't be so bad just to sit down here, rest for a while. Not in spider-patch central, of course, but up against the nice trunk of a tree or maybe a boulder.

Forcing myself back to my feet, I brushed off the last of the startled arachnids and looked around for a likely bunk buddy. There—up ahead, a flat stone on the side of the road, big enough to sit on. Hell, it was big enough to lie on, if I curled up. That was invitation enough. Morio was a demon—a youkai-kitsune. He could take care of himself. And Aeval, well, if she'd wanted me to wait in the glade, she should have told me.

Exhausted, I hobbled over to the boulder and slipped up on top of it, leaning back with a long sigh. It felt so good to sit down, and not in the middle of a briar patch. I folded my feet in a cross-legged position and lay back, hands under my head, staring at the sky. The stars were still glowing, but the sky was growing lighter, and with a deep breath, I closed my eyes.

I was almost asleep when I noticed a noise. Forcing myself to a sitting position, I yawned and looked around. The woods were just full of visitors tonight, I thought. For, out from behind a giant fir tree, stepped a woman.

Tall and imposing, she had the palest skin, blue-black hair, and the reddest lips I'd ever seen. Her breasts crested abundantly over the top of her corset dress, and she circled me, smiling coyly.

"Well met, again, Camille. I'm sure you've met my son by now?"

At that moment, I realized that I had to have strayed out of Talamh Lonrach Oll, because even though Aeval had invited Bran, I knew she would never invite this woman to touch the soil of the Sovereign Nation.

Cautiously, I eased myself into full sitting position, wondering what the hell was going to happen next. I'd never been alone with her, and I didn't want to. Because, inadvertent ally or not, Raven Mother scared the hell out of me.

Chapter 10

∽⌇∾

Raven Mother stood there, left arm crossed across her chest to hold her right elbow as she cupped her chin. She eyed me, waiting.

Unsure of how to proceed, I slid to the edge of the boulder and hung my feet over. I was too tired for games, but I had to be cautious. Raven Mother was one of the great Tricksters. *And* she was one of the Immortals. She was also the consort of the Black Unicorn, so I had to show her respect, but I also had to make certain I didn't say or do anything that might suggest that she had a hold on me later. Raven Mother had expressed an interest in my coming to live with her in Darkynwyrd and joining her court, and that was the last thing I wanted.

When in doubt, say nothing. I yawned, covering my mouth.

"Tired, are we, young Moon Witch? Tired and weary, perhaps? Oh, pardon me," she added, a feral smile on her lips. "I mean *Priestess* Camille."

I could see Bran in her features—he was his mother's son, all right. A thought ran through my head as I tried to picture just how the Black Unicorn and Raven Mother had managed to reproduce, but some of the possibilities were too scary to consider. Seeing that they were both Immortals, I decided that whatever the truth, I probably didn't want to know.

I nodded. "Yes, I am tired. I am trying to find my way back to the palace." I didn't like admitting I was lost, but it was obvious that I was exhausted, and attempting to lie my way out of why I was sitting here on a big rock, in the middle of the woods, attempting to take a nap, wasn't going to fly.

Raven Mother shifted, and she slipped her hands into hidden pockets on her flowing skirt. She sauntered up to me. I continued to sit on the boulder, too tired to stand and show the proper respect. Usually, I was the first to curtsey or bow or whatever the situation required, but right now? Not so much.

"So, the little priestess lost her way in the woods? A red cloak, yes, you should be wearing. And a red hood, should you not?" And she laughed then, rich and throaty, and I found myself fixating on her gorgeous lips. They were full and pouty, and mesmerizing.

She reached my side and looked down at me—Raven Mother was incredibly tall and bigger than life. She was vivid in an almost unnatural way. As she stared into my face, I forced myself to sit still.

"Oh, my lovely. My lovely Camille, the Moon Mother does choose the most delicious for her Order. You have met my son. My offer still stands. Come away, my lovely, and join me, and my son would be happy to *attend* you. Dragons and foxes are fine, but they are not of our woodland magic. You may bring your Charming one, of course. Svartans thrive in Darkynwyrd."

I sighed. Would she try to woo me away every time we met? And the thought of Bran *attending* me gave me the creeps. But . . . not a good idea to tell her that I found her boy less than appealing. Still, my irritation spilled over.

"You know my pledge is to the Moon Mother. Would you have me break one oath to form a new one? I am no warlock. I am no oath-breaker."

Her eyes narrowed, staring at me with beady focus. Oh fuck. What the hell did I just do? She let out a slow breath, and I smelled worms and soil and early autumn's touch. I blinked, trying to focus on my feet as the morning light began to shimmer brighter. But I couldn't keep my gaze off her face.

"Morning light, it attends us soon," Raven Mother said, her voice shrill and curt.

"Um, yeah. Looks that way." I had no clue what to say, except for the fact that she was right—it was almost morning. Menolly would be going to sleep soon. And if Morio didn't show up soon, I was really going to freak. That was, if Raven Mother decided not to peck out my eyes for my insolence.

But after a moment of staring me down, she looked up at the sky and let out a long laugh. "Oh, my lovely, you are a conundrum. Well, then. Since you still refuse to join me, I suppose I will muffle my disappointment and show you the way back to your precious Aeval. Someday, though, young witch, you will realize your destiny lies with me, and you will come join me in the delights of the dark forest, and dance your nights away under the sparkling stars."

She backed up. "I will lead you. Follow, as the raven flies."

"I'm hurt—I can't walk very fast." Again, not so much wanting to admit my vulnerability, but there wasn't any way around it. She would expect me to accept her offer, and there was really no way I could turn her down. Especially since I was truly lost.

"Hurt, my lovely? What ails the Moon's Daughter?"

"My foot. I sliced up the bottom of the heel on a bramble thorn." I stuck my foot out to show her the slug-slimed leaves affixed to the sole.

Raven Mother stared at my foot, and it was hard to tell whether she was smiling or affronted. After a moment, she sighed. "Very well. Since you are not ready to run with the raven, then the raven shall have to run with you." She stepped forward, prepared to gather me up.

The thought of Raven Mother holding me against her was unnerving, but before she could wrap her arms around me, the ferns to our right parted, and out of the wild wood stepped Morio.

"I will take care of my wife." He was back in his form, scratched and bruised, but looking relatively intact.

Raven Mother let out a low hiss but stepped away from me. "It would seem your demon prince has arrived, to save you from the *big, bad raven.* Ah, kitsune, your fair maiden was in no danger from me, regardless of what her thoughts might be whispering. Run with her; she is tired and sore and with a sadly injured foot."

He quietly stepped between us, and Raven Mother gave him an irritated look. "I warn you, youkai. Do not cross me, nor crowd me. Your lovely was in no danger. If you find yourself running rude, you may find yourself running for your life."

Luckily, Morio kept his mouth shut. I reached out, touching his arm, and he nodded at my unspoken plea to remain silent.

"Bird have your tongue? Perhaps that is best." Raven Mother turned to me then. "My lovely, I will see you again. Give Aeval my salutations, and tell your blessed Moon Mother to guard her daughter well, for there are others who would be only so delighted to play the role of Mother." And with that, a flash of crimson blinded us and when I blinked, a large raven flew to a nearby tree, perched, gave three long cries, and then vanished into the sky, winging away to the east.

"What was she doing here?" Morio asked, turning to me. "I thought she belonged in Otherworld."

"The Elemental Lords and Queens travel where they will. You know that. They cross dimension and plane and portal. But where the fuck were you? I've been looking for you most of the night." I stuck out my foot. "I caught my foot on a thorn, and I can't walk on it until I get some antibiotic or a healing potion or something, and a soft bandage."

He examined the sole of my foot. "My love, I'm sorry, but the Horned One, he ran me through the woodland all night long. I've not had that much fun in a long time, nor reveled in my nature so much."

I frowned. "Where's your familiar? You can't change back without your skull. Where did it go?"

Morio shook his head. "He had to have helped me. My skull is in my bag, back in the cottage near the palace."

That was definitely odd, but then again, he had been running with the Horned One, and so much could happen when dancing with the gods. "Where are we? I got lost when I was looking for you."

"This path? Leads directly out to the front gates. It delineates the eastern boundary of Talamh Lonrach Oll. We're about a quarter mile from the entrance to the Fae Nation." He grinned. "You were almost there." Pausing, he looked at me closely. "Are you okay?"

Tears were close to the surface, and I wasn't even sure why. I ducked my head. "I thought you were hurt. And I'm so tired. I was going to rest when Raven Mother showed up, and she scares me spitless."

Morio murmured softly, then stood back, shifting into his demonic form. "Come, love. No more words, no more tears. Here, let me get you back to Aeval's palace, and then we'll go home."

He lifted me up, and I leaned my head against his shoulder. He carried me as if I were as light as Maggie, and the rocking move of his stride had my eyes closing. Before we neared the gates, I fell asleep, safe in my youkai's arms.

When I opened my eyes the first time, I was dressed in a loose shift and in the car. Morio was driving. He reached over and brushed my hair back from my head. My foot was throbbing, but as I blurrily glanced down, I saw that it was bandaged in a proper fashion now.

"Shush . . . don't even speak. Aeval had her attendant— Tanya? Yes, Tanya. Anyway, Tanya dressed you and the healer attended to your foot. We'll talk more when we get home, but for now, sleep. I'm good to drive."

His voice was already fading out. I glanced out the window at the early sun rising through partial overcast. Streaks of red and orange lit the pale blue aflame, while the cotton candy clouds covered the sky. As I watched, a murmuration of starlings filled the sky, swooping and turning in unison, creating a vision in fluttering wings. Overwhelmed by their beauty and by the night, I closed my eyes again as the swaying of the car lulled me back into a deep slumber.

As we pulled into the driveway, I grumbled and forced myself to open my eyes. "Can't you just leave me here? The seats are comfortable and I can sleep right here." I didn't want to get out of the car and drag myself up the steps to my rooms.

"Come on, Sleeping Beauty. Iris is waiting for us." Morio swung around to my door, opening it.

"What? Why? You called her?" The brisk morning air infiltrated my sinuses, and I groaned as he took my hands and helped pull me to my feet. I stumbled out of the car, blurry-eyed, but at least the half-hour drive had given me a chance to fend off a total meltdown.

"No, she called me. I didn't want to wake you up." He sounded worried now.

Oh fuck. Not another problem. "Don't tell me we have another emergency? I don't think I can handle anything more after last night. My energy is at low ebb." I draped my arm around his shoulder and struggled up the porch stairs. My foot was better but throbbing. However, compared to what it had felt like in the woods, I could tell it was already on the mend. The Triple Threat would, of course, have some of the best healers in the Fae world.

"Yeah, something new has cropped up, but we don't have to address it immediately. You'll have time for a nap. Iris is preparing something to help you sleep deeper, so that you'll recharge faster." He opened the door and we were greeted by chaos, as usual.

I was about to ask what the hell was going on, but before I could open my mouth, Iris was there, pressing a small glass into my hands.

"Drink this. Just do it." She looked harried. So harried that I did as she asked without question. Whatever it was tasted like bitter mud and I grimaced, but before I could ask what it was, or what was wrong, the room began to spin, and the last thing I remember was Iris smiling as I slumped into Morio's arms.

The sunlight was streaming through the window as I woke to sudden consciousness. Blinking, I pushed myself up, trying to figure out where the hell I was. After a moment, it registered that I was in my bed, in a loose nightgown. A glance at the clock told me that it was eleven. I'd been asleep only five hours, but my mind felt remarkably clear. As I slipped out from beneath the comforter, my muscles groaned, but my foot felt a lot better. If it came down to either my muscles being a little stiff or limping because my foot hurt, I'd choose the stiffness.

As I headed for the shower, my stomach lurched. I hurried into the bathroom, reaching it just in time to throw up. Luckily, there wasn't much in my stomach, and as I rinsed out my mouth, I stared into the mirror. My eyes were dilated, and I had a light rash of tiny bumps on the left side of my face. What the fuck? But they didn't itch, so I decided the hell with it and hopped into the shower. The hot water felt good on my back, and ten minutes later, I stepped out, brushed my hair out from the ponytail that had kept it from getting wet, and hurried back to the bedroom.

Someone had set out an outfit for me, and I quickly dressed in a light green gauze skirt and a plum-colored corset top, deftly fastening the hooks and eyes. I looked through my shoes and found a pair of black ankle boots overlaid with silver netting. Their kitten heels weren't my usual height, but they were cute and, more important, they were padded with gel inserts. The boots were the most comfortable pair of shoes I owned. Finally, I put on my makeup and headed downstairs.

As I hustled into the kitchen, Hanna was putting out a platter of sandwiches and a bowl of chips for an early lunch.

She gave me a bright smile. Hanna had blossomed during her time with us, and more and more I caught a glimpse of the woman she had probably been before Hyto got to her. "I heard you stirring. You must be starving."

"Thanks, and now that I think about it, I am." My stomach rumbled, the queasiness replaced by hunger, as I reached for one of the ham and cheddar sandwiches. I slapped it on a plate and added a handful of potato chips, then settled at the table. Hanna glanced at my plate, then quickly poured me a big glass of milk. She also added a fruit salad and bowls to the table and, in a loud voice, headed into the foyer calling out that lunch was ready.

I bit into the sandwich, and it was the most delicious thing I'd ever tasted. Either that, or I was starving. I had already polished off one sandwich by the time Delilah and Shade appeared and was starting on another.

Iris poked her head into the kitchen from the back porch and—on seeing me—slipped through the door and took a seat next to me.

"Are Smoky and Trillian back from Otherworld yet?"

She shook her head. "No, but it's been less than twenty-four hours."

She gave me a sideways glance. "You feeling okay?"

"I threw up when I woke up, but slept like the dead. What the hell did you give me? Whatever it was, it did the trick, but it left me really disconcerted."

Iris nodded. "Yes, that's why I don't usually prepare it. It not only leaves a person disoriented, but can have serious long-term effects on the body, if you take it more than once or twice a year. But given what happened . . . I figured you'd need to be up and strong as soon as you could."

That didn't sound good. In fact, when I looked around at the expressions of the others, I realized that whatever it was, it wasn't good at all.

"So, you all look pretty grim. What's going down? Tell me."

"We have a problem." Rozurial pushed the evening newspaper over to me. I opened it up to find a picture of two zombies splashed across the front, along with a lurid headline: ZOMBIE APOCALYPSE BEGINS?

"Oh, fuck." I took the paper and skimmed the article. It reminded me of a bland version of Andy Gambit's sleaze rag.

"It was bound to happen sometime," Morio said.

"I guess there was no way to keep the existence of zombies and ghouls secret forever. After all, vampires are out of the closet now."

While most of the FBHs knew of the existence of Fae by now, and the vampires had come out of the closet, and Weres were talking about their two-faced nature openly, we'd somehow managed to keep the lid on zombie attacks and other nasty night creatures. Ghost stories had always abounded, but now, with this picture, it looked like the corpse was out of the coffin. Somebody in one of the graveyards had managed to snap the photo early this morning.

"Was another graveyard ransacked?"

"Yeah. Just like the others. And by the way, I took a look out there, at the one that was hit yesterday, and all the spirits are gone." Vanzir shrugged. "Epidemic."

Roz nodded. "Chase is fielding calls right and left. The 911 operators are swamped by people convinced there are zombies lurking outside their doors. And for once, the Fae aren't being blamed."

"No, but the vampires are." Delilah looked grim.

"Vampires? What the hell do they have to do with it?" I frowned. "Vampires don't raise zombies."

"Of course they don't, but since they're undead, like the zombies, once again the Church of the Earthborn Brethren is making waves. They quieted down after the mess with Andy Gambit, but they're back in the news today. They've been picketing outside the Shrouded Grove Suites all morning."

"Not again. That's where Wade lives." The founder of Vampires Anonymous and a former psychologist, Wade Stevens was a vampire dedicated to help new vamps adjust to the "life." Even though VA was now under control of the Seattle Vampire Nexus, run by Roman, Wade had been granted relative autonomy over the group.

"Yeah. Management has been dealing with this sort of crap since day one."

When building started on the protected, vampire-friendly apartments, the picketers had come out of the woodwork. And they'd shown up almost every day since then until Andy

Gambit's death. The resulting scandal over the sleazy yellow-tabloid reporter/rapist had quieted them down for a while.

After the story had broken about what he'd done—a final count of ten confirmed rapes on Fae women, eleven on human women—the hate groups fell silent, not wanting to be associated with the vitriol aimed in his direction.

The resulting glee over his death had left them even more silent. But a few months had passed, and people quickly forgot the flavor of the month, be it bad or good.

"So how do we enact damage control? I'll bet Chase is freaking out right now." Chase's department would be the first to face the fire.

"That's putting it mildly." Delilah rested her elbows on the table and stared at her food. "He asked us to come down to headquarters when you woke up. Menolly doesn't know what's going on—she had to go to bed before this all broke loose, but you can bet, tonight when the vamps wake up, a lot of blood-suckers are going to be mightily pissed at being lumped together with zombies, let alone being accused of causing the problem. Roman's going to have something to say about this, too."

I let out a long sigh. This did not bode well. "Heaven help the reporter who started the rumor. With Roman and Blood Wyne so prominent now, I don't know what the hell they'll do. The Crimson Veil works behind the scenes. The idiot journalist may just end up vanishing off the face of the planet. And no one will ever know what happened."

Roman scared me. He scared Delilah, too—I knew because we'd talked it over out of Menolly's earshot. Granted, she had no choice, and now he was considered her reborn sire, another twist in the whole mess, but that made the son of the Vampire Queen far too close for comfort to our lives.

"We don't have any control over Blood Wyne. And neither does the FH-CSI, regardless of what we'd like to think. If she wanted to, she could reach out and take control of this country. I kind of wish she'd stayed in seclusion." Delilah absently bit into a cookie. "So we head to headquarters in a few minutes?"

"I suppose—" The phone interrupted me. I was sitting

nearest, so I grabbed it. And sure enough, it was Chase on the line.

"Camille? You're awake? Good."

"We're getting ready to come down to headquarters now," I started to say, but he interrupted.

"No. I need you elsewhere. We have an emergency."

The four little words I dreaded hearing but lately heard all too often. Life seemed to be made up of one emergency after another these days.

"What's up?"

"You saw the paper, right?" He sounded harried.

I groaned. "Yeah."

"That's the tip of the iceberg. I need you guys out here, in full fighting armor. You know the house Fritz and Abby had? That burned to the ground?"

The demonic bloody-wall ghost-filled house had been terrifying. We hadn't really won the battle, but at least we'd survived.

"Yeah?" I asked warily.

"There's something on the lot. Something weird that I don't want my men near until we figure out what it is. And it's attracting a horde of zombies. I've got the entire block cordoned off. The few other houses there that are actually inhabited, I've evacuated."

I cleared my throat. "Something weird as in what? A creature? Structure? Portal? Big-ass pony with wings?"

He snorted. "I wish. If I knew what it was, I'd tell you instead of coming out with a vague description. I'd say, 'We have a large wheel of cheese cavorting around town' or 'There's a giant snail on the property squirting everybody with slime.' But I don't have a clue. I think it's organic. In other words: alive. But truthfully? I don't know. And the way I've been losing officers lately, I don't want to take any chances."

I sobered. Chase was right. He'd lost several good cops, and he was feeling the heat from all sides. "Right. We'll be there in fifteen to twenty minutes. Don't let anybody near . . . whatever the thing is. And Chase?"

"Yeah?" He sounded tired.

"We've got your back, dude. Seriously."

"I know, Camille. And for that, I am eternally grateful." As he hung up, I turned to the others.

"Let's roll. Weapons, arms . . . bring it all. We're going in blind." As we hurried to gather everything we could, Iris made up a couple of sacks of sandwiches so we'd have a chance to eat on the run. I told them what Chase had said. Vanzir warned the elfin guards who watched over our property to keep alert, since Trillian and Smoky were still gone. As we headed to the cars, we were all quiet, as a deep sense of apprehension settled in.

We divided up into two vehicles: Morio, Vanzir, and me in my Lexus, and Delilah, Shade, and Roz in her Jeep. The trip didn't take long, even though we hit noon traffic on one of the main streets. I glanced at the clock. We were still ten minutes out and the more time we took, the more danger Chase and his men were in. I finally saw a side street that I knew would lead to a back route.

"Call Delilah and tell her we're going down Bay Street."

Morio punched in her number and, a moment later, I edged over to the right side of the street, nudging in between bumper-to-bumper traffic, with Delilah on my tail. I managed to get into the turn lane right before we hit Bay. A quick, sharp right and we were on our way again.

In another ten minutes, we were on Foster Street, a block and a half out from what had been Fritz and Abby's house, and we were entering the Greenbelt Park District—the most haunted place in Seattle. Now knowing that Gulakah was fueling the fire made it even more nerve-racking.

The cedars and firs overshadowed the streets, and all the houses around here looked weathered and decrepit. As we neared the intersection, we saw prowl cars blocking the way, along with police tape. Chase had cordoned off the area.

I pulled over to the side and we jumped out, looking for Chase. Delilah and her crew were right behind us. After a moment, I caught sight of him—on crutches and looking frustrated. He motioned for us to join him. Next to him stood Yugi, who seldom went out in the field.

"What's going on?" I nodded to Delilah and we joined them. "Yugi, what are you doing here?"

"I was hoping, with his empathetic abilities, that he might be able to get a sense for what this is." Chase sounded tired, and he stifled a yawn.

Yugi shook his head. "All I get is a lot of static—the airwaves are filled with confusion. Either I'm not tuned in enough to hear clearly, or whatever is around here is causing a lot of chaos."

That's the first time we'd seen exactly what Chase used Yugi for, other than his typical duties. We knew he was an empath, but until now, I'd had no clue that the FH-CSI actually made *use* of his abilities.

"Don't sweat it," Shade said. "The energy here is thick enough to cut with a knife, and it's bound to be hard to navigate."

I closed my eyes, trying to tune in myself. "Shade's right. It's like a big hollow brick filled with bees." Try as I might, I couldn't pick up anything other than a loud buzz of static. That didn't mean there weren't any demons around, though.

"I guess we'd better see what it is." Morio glanced at Chase. "You stay here—with that leg, you'd be a sitting duck. In fact, we'll only take one of your men with us, to act as a messenger. I don't want any easy targets."

Yugi started to volunteer, but Chase nixed that idea. "I need you—you're second in command. Keo, please go with them."

Keo stepped forward.

Delilah squinted, then let out a short laugh. "Werewolf?"

He nodded. "Right." And then, with a grin, he added, "Pack mentality makes for good teamwork, you know."

"You've got a point." Delilah glanced at me. "What order?"

"Morio and me first, with Shade and Vanzir right behind us. You, Roz, and Keo take up the rear. Keep an eye out, too. We don't want anybody slipping behind to ambush us." I pulled her to one side. "You keep an eye on Keo. If it looks like he's in danger, get him out."

She nodded.

As we fell into line, I took a moment to gather the Moon Mother's energy. The afternoon was fairly sunny. There was no chance for me to call down the lightning, and so I had to focus her power into an energy blast.

I'd also brought the Black Unicorn horn with me, and it was secreted in a hidden pocket in my skirt. I didn't want to have to use it, if I could avoid doing so. A few good blasts would drain it of energy, although they'd be megacharged blasts. I had to renew it every month under the new moon for it to both retain and recover its power.

Morio was prepping for a spell, too, though I wasn't sure what it was. I glanced back. Shade needed no weapon. He *was* a weapon. Vanzir, too, with his powers recovering in a strange fashion that none of us were sure about at this point, including Vanzir, himself. Delilah had her dagger out, and Roz was fiddling in his duster, probably making sure he had easy access to the multitude of weapons he carried.

"Ready?"

They nodded.

"Then let's go." We ducked under the police tape and jogged down the street. The trees on either side seemed sickly, and as I reached out, a sickly tendril of energy came creeping my way. Snakelike, it was twisted, reminding me of a withered, grasping hand. I yanked my attention away and quickly told the others.

"I think it might be able to latch onto our energy, so please, be cautious. Pay attention to what's going on in your thoughts. We've all been leeched onto at some point, and this is one time we can't afford to go down to some astral freakazoid."

I quickly focused on raising some wards—Morio and I had been practicing our internal shields over the past few months, and I was getting a lot better at them. Protection magic had never been my strong suit, but I worked overtime to learn it now, because our need was so great.

We hit the end of the street and headed through a drive that was bounded on both sides by large iron gates. But the gates had been pulled off their posts and hung loose, a sad statement to what had once been a magnificent mansion.

Across the circular driveway, the rubble remained from Abby and Fritz's house. A demon had been trapped in the house, as well as several nasty ghosts. I nervously glanced from side to side, wondering where the hell spawn had disappeared to. The house had burned to the ground, leaving the cracked foundation and basement open to the elements. The front porch had burned, too, and there was no sign of the vortex that had formed beneath the rotting timbers.

"There it is," Keo said, pointing directly to where the porch and vortex had been.

Chase's *something weird* was a good description, all right. Whatever it was, *weird* definitely fit the description. Standing about ten feet tall, it was a vaguely circular shape—although it wasn't a perfect circle. And it was easy to see why he thought it might be organic—alive.

The thing was a pale gray, almost silver in color. The mass was smooth, almost shiny. But it didn't look extremely hard. Rather, it seemed almost amorphous—smooth, with no protrusions or limbs or anything of that nature. As we stood, staring at it, it *shuddered*, and as we watched, it seemed to grow a few inches.

"The Blob," Delilah whispered.

"You watch too much TV," I answered back, although the same thought had run through my head. But it wasn't like that. It wasn't soft and oozing.

"Fine, but I'm going to call it that, because we don't have a fucking clue what it is, do we?" She took a step into the driveway and the blob—for lack of a better term—shuddered again, and again, grew.

"Okay, this thing is getting bigger as we watch. And I'm not sure that's a good idea. Whatever it is, it can't be good—oh fuck, look." Morio pointed across the lot. I shaded my eyes and followed his direction.

There, shuffling across the grass from the back of the lot,

were a host of zombies. But they didn't seem focused on us. Instead, they were headed directly for the gray .. thing.

Shade jolted forward. "I have a hunch that it would be a very bad thing to let the walking dead touch whatever that is. Keo, stay here." He headed across the drive. The rest of us, except for the werewolf, followed. We'd gotten no more than four feet when a group of people emerged from behind a group of large rhododendron bushes to the left.

I stopped. "Who the fuck are *they*?"

"I don't know, but looks like a mix of humans and Fae and maybe a couple of others in there that I can't identify." Delilah stopped beside me as they formed a living shield in front of the creature and the zombies.

"Are you crazy?" I yelled at them. "Zombies—those are zombies and they will *kill* you!"

But the line of about twenty people—give or take a few—joined hands and stretched out, forming a half circle around the thing. Mostly women, they said nothing, just smiled with vacant gazes, and held tight. A hum began to rise from the group, and at first I thought they were embarking on some bizarre form of sing-along, but then I realized they were raising energy, and they were directing it at us.

"Fuck, they're casting a group spell. Hit the dirt!" I dropped, not able to see who else made it to the ground. Seconds later, a wave of energy came racing our way, crackling with static. I heard a scream—it sounded like Delilah, and then the air exploded into flames, which burst brightly over my head, then faded into vapor.

Stunned by both the sound and the force of the magic, I pushed myself up. A glance told me Delilah had gotten caught—she looked singed and burned along one shoulder and her right cheek. But she was up and moving.

Within seconds, we were all on our feet and facing our opponents, and I suddenly knew just who the hell they were, and why we couldn't fight them.

Chapter 11

~~~

"Don't attack!" I frantically waved the others back. "Retreat. Get out of their line of fire." I raced behind the nearest cedar, hoping to hell everybody was behind me. I leaned against the tree, shaking. The others were right on my heels. As soon as I was sure they were out of danger, too, I motioned for Shade to watch our backs.

"Are you hurt?" I asked Delilah as Keo took a look at her burns.

"Yeah, they sting, but the burns are superficial. What's going on? Why did you tell us to get out of there?" Delilah was digging her blade into the tree.

"Because those people are some of the witches from the Aleksais Psychic Network. I recognize a few from seeing them in Mystic Charms. We *can't* attack them—they're under a spell, or brainwashed, or something like that."

A thought occurred to me, and I darted a quick look back around the tree trunk, hoping to see Faerman's wife, but she was nowhere among the group as far I could see. Couldn't have it easy for once, could we?

I leaned against the tree. "So what do we do? We can't attack them, even if they attack us."

"I agree." Delilah frowned. "Is there a way to break whatever spell they're under? To free them from whatever is controlling them?"

"No, because we have no clue of how they're being influenced. It might be a spell, but it also might be simple brainwashing techniques. Or maybe . . . some sort of psychic leech connected to them? We really have no way of knowing without capturing one of them to find out. And considering they seem to be wielding magic beyond what most FBH pagans and witches can work, we'd be in danger if we tried." I bit my lip.

Morio crossed his arms. "Well, we can't just stay here the rest of the day. What about that gray orb? Any clue as to what it is?"

Shade stepped to the side. "I'll see what I can find out." But after a moment, he let out an exasperated noise. "Not enough shadow for me to work in, damn it. I was going to shadow-walk over there, but for once the sun is out and there aren't enough areas in the shade for me to manage it."

"Let me take a look on the astral." Vanzir vanished before we could say anything. I hoped to hell he could find something. It sucked to be stumped like this. If we could just take the witches down, we'd have no problem, but we were the good guys. And good guys didn't take out innocent pawns.

A moment later, Vanzir reappeared. He looked shaken. "Okay, so look over there and tell me what you see now."

I glanced back around the tree trunk. The zombies had reached the line of witches but instead of attacking them, they were walking toward the gray mass and . . . and what the hell? They were disappearing into it. As each zombie walked into the blob, there was a spark of light and it vanished. The human shield was standing there, staring across the drive, waiting for us to return.

More confused than ever, I stepped back. "Um . . . guys, take a look. I have no clue as to what's going on. Is the thing an illusion?"

Vanzir shook his head. "That orb is no illusion. And on the astral plane? It's very much alive and growing. Be right back." Once again, he vanished. We waited until he reappeared. There was nothing else we could do.

"Okay, here's the thing. Every time a zombie walks into that creature? It eats it and absorbs the energy. My guess is that—whatever that thing is—it's eating dinner. I just hope whoever's holding its leash isn't going to drop those witches into the mix." Vanzir looked a little queasy.

"Can you get to it from the astral?" I looked at him. I knew that Vanzir's powers had returned, albeit somewhat twisted. And the Triple Threat had something to do with it.

He gave me a long look. With his Jareth-via-David-Bowie's spiky haircut and gaunt face, and the kaleidoscope of colors that whirled in his eyes, Vanzir gave off a haunting, edgy presence. The dream-chaser demon and I had a convoluted history and an odd bond that neither of us had asked for.

"I might be able to. In fact, we all might want to approach it from the astral, considering that we don't have many other options." He glanced around. "Roz can take you over to the astral but only one at a time. I can hop over there but can't take anybody. Shade?"

Shade let out a sigh. "It's better if I don't carry living beings with me, unless they are connected to the Netherworld in a strong way, but . . . we can give it a go. I warn you, though, it will have an effect on whoever I take with me."

Morio shrugged. "I'm youkai . . . I doubt it will bother me too much. Take me, while Roz takes Camille and then Delilah. Vanzir, you wait here with Delilah till Rozurial comes back for Delilah. With Camille and me over there, at least we can work our magic together if need be."

With a shrug, Shade agreed. "If you're willing to chance it, I'll take you."

"Whatever we're going to do, let's get moving. We can't wait around here much longer. Keo, go back to Chase—tell him to keep his men back. Tell him what we're doing and that we'll return as soon as we can. If he doesn't hear from us in an hour, let Smoky know what's going on."

The werewolf nodded and took off, running back down the street. Once he looked to be safely away, I moved over to Roz, who arched his eyebrows in a joking leer. I grinned back at him, then leaned in. He opened his arms and I pressed against his chest, which was extremely lumpy thanks to the multitude of weapons he had hidden under there.

"Dude, you are the most uncomfortable hug I've had in ages." I wrapped my arms around him, and he enfolded me in his embrace.

"Try it when I'm naked," he whispered, but before I could smack him, we shifted into the Ionyc Seas, and the familiar sleepiness began to claim me. I closed my eyes, secure in Rozurial's arms, as the heavy drag of interdimensional traveling began to wear on me.

A moment—or a lifetime—later, we set down and I opened my eyes. A misty plain spread out before us, where I could see vague shapes representing the physical bodies of the trees and structures and people back on the physical. The tree behind which we were hiding was glowing wildly—its spirit was vibrant and tuned into magic.

I stepped to the side and peered around the "trunk" to see what Vanzir had been talking about. Sure enough, behind the astral bodies of the people forming the human shield, I saw a brilliant, shimmering circular being—only the colors were chaotic and wild, and it felt bloated and squishy from here. Dark forms—glowing so faintly that I knew they had to be the zombies—were making their way to the thing, and every time one of them stepped into the creature, a spark flared and the blob grew stronger.

"Fuck. What the hell is that? It's brighter than a hooker in sequins." I cocked my head. There was something . . . something that was on the outskirts of my thoughts, but I couldn't pull it into focus yet. "It reminds me of something."

Just then, Shade appeared with Morio, and Roz vanished to get Delilah.

Morio looked vaguely queasy, and as Shade let him go, he turned to the side and vomited. Shade produced a bottle of water from the inner pocket of his calf-length duster and handed it to him.

"I thought that was going to hit you. Drink. It will help."

Morio wiped his lips on his sleeve, then poured a shot of water into his mouth, rinsing and spitting before taking another drink to settle his stomach.

"Fucking A . . . you really travel in some squirrely places, dude." Morio shook his head. "Let me clear my thoughts."

"I warned you. Even though you work with death magic, the ebb and flow of the Netherworld forces are harsh on those who don't spring from its energy. I'm pretty sure Camille found that out when she was in Gulakah's mind." Shade glanced over at me, a faint look of pity washing across his face.

I gave him a little shrug. "It was bad, that's for sure. But I've been through worse."

"That you have, Mistress Camille. That you have." Shade inclined his head, giving me a small salute.

Just then, Roz returned with Delilah, and Vanzir followed. We got our bearings and began to make plans.

"Here's the thing: Most of the human shield won't be able to fight us here. I know they have stronger powers than most FBH pagans, and there are some Fae with them; however, they don't appear to have an awareness that we're here. And even if they knew, I don't think there's much they could do about it."

Vanzir shrugged. "So, we can skirt around them and attack the creature from the back. The zombies won't be able to affect us, either, so we just might manage to trace the energy signature of whoever raised them, while we're at it."

I whirled around. "Do you think we could trace the signature from here?"

He pursed his lips, considering. "Maybe. Depends on who cast the spell and how adept they are at hiding their whereabouts."

Delilah peeked around the trunk, then darted back. "Do we have *any clue* what the hell that thing is?"

"I recognize something about it, but for the life of me I can't quite bring it to mind." I strained to find the words for what it resembled.

"Looks like a silver squishy orange," Delilah said, grimacing.

And then, it hit me. "Not an orange! An *egg*. Reminds me of a giant fish egg or something like that. You don't think . . . that couldn't be . . ." A sudden rush of fear hit me. If that thing was actually the egg of some creature and it was sucking up zombies right and left, what the fuck could it be? "Shade, that's not a dragon egg, is it?"

Shade let out a strangled "Ugh" and gave me a look that said he thought I was crazy. "*Dragon egg? No*, not dragon. However . . . you may have a point. That might just be an egg. The questions are: What's inside, and when is it going to hatch?"

As the last of the zombies disappeared, the witches turned and began walking toward it.

"Fuck! We have to do something now, or it's going to destroy them, too!" I raced forward. "We can't let it absorb all those people."

And then a cold thought struck me. What if Gulakah was intending to use the entire magical community as food for this thing? And what if there were more of them?

All these thoughts ran though my mind as I raced through the mist. On the astral, I could run faster than just about anybody in our group except for Roz. Smoky, in dragon form, could barely keep up with me. So I was through the mist and at the side of the egg—if that was what it was—before anybody could react.

I stared up at it as the ghostly auras of the witches moved toward it. I had to do something, break the spell somehow. And then I knew. I pulled out the Black Unicorn horn.

Crystal, with threads of gold and silver running through it, the spiraled horn was a powerhouse. It contained Eriskel, a jindasel, both an avatar of the Black Unicorn and yet a being in his own right. Not a djinn but similar in nature, the jindasels were a mysterious symbiosis.

I didn't have time to stand on formality, nor did I know

just how the horn would work over here on the astral. I held it up and called on the four Elementals who also were locked within the horn.

"I don't know how to fight this—I don't even know what it is, but help me." As I focused the energy, a dazzling blast shot out, and the next thing I knew, I was standing inside the horn, with Eriskel by my side, looking horrified.

"I don't have time to talk—we're fighting . . . something. It's going to kill a lot of innocent people unless you let me get out of here." I stared at the jindasel, both pissed and frightened.

Today, he was standing a good seven feet tall, though that was relative considering we were in yet another interdimensional space that existed only within the Black Unicorn horn. His dark hair was tucked back in a neat ponytail, and golden rings hung from his ears. He was wearing green—a brilliant, almost blinding green.

He waved away my concerns. "Time has no meaning here. You know that."

"I also know that I've lost plenty of time before on the outside, when I've been talking to you." I didn't have the energy to argue. All I could think about was getting out there and destroying whatever the creature was.

"I promise you, that won't happen. Just calm yourself, Mistress Camille, and tell me what you're doing." He didn't look happy. In fact, if I had to pin an emotion on him, he looked perturbed.

I sighed. It did no good to argue with creatures like Eriskel—they did as they pleased. A glance around told me that all four of the Elementals were watching. Huge screens splashed across each wall of the chamber, and from one, the Lady of the Land watched from a verdant forest. From the second, the Master of Winds stood beside a giant eagle, gazing down from a mountaintop. The third was occupied by the Mistress of Flames, who was sitting on a chunk of glowing lava. And the fourth contained an ocean and, with his shoulders rising above the surface, the Lord of the Depths. They all waved at me.

A table and two chairs were in the center of the chamber, as usual, and with a huff, I sat down. "Seriously, Eriskel, if you make me too late to help those people out there, so help me, I'll make you so miserable you'll wish you'd never met me."

I was dead serious. We'd had enough collateral damage, and even though I didn't know most of the witches in danger, I wasn't about to let them become lunch for some bloated embryo of unknown origin.

Eriskel took the other chair. He straddled it, resting his arms on the back. "Do not fret, Mistress Camille. I promise you, no time will pass. I can slow it down when I wish, within this chamber."

"I just need your help in destroying that . . . that . . . thing. I don't even know what it is, but it's about to hurt a lot of innocent people who are either under a spell or brainwashed. It just ate—absorbed? Whatever it's doing, it devoured a bunch of zombies, and now it's luring in the people who were sent to protect it."

Eriskel cocked his head. "You don't know what this creature is?"

"No. We haven't been able to figure it out yet. We think it's an egg, and we're pretty sure that it's connected to Gulakah, the Lord of Ghosts. He was a god in the Nether-worlds until—"

He held up one hand. "I know who Gulakah is. The Black Unicorn knows all about the god."

"Well, he was demoted and sent to the Sub-Realms. Now Shadow Wing's using him. Did you know that, too?" I was antsy. All this talk was getting me nowhere. I wanted to get back out there and fight. But the jindasel stopped me cold with his next words.

"I did know that," Eriskel said softly. "And I know what's in that incubator you're fighting."

"Seriously?" I stared at him.

He nodded. "Yes, which is why I pulled you in here once I realized what you were attacking. Camille, it isn't just one creature. It's housing a nest of demons—but they aren't from the Sub-Realms. Gulakah would have a hard time gating them over if they were, and he'd also have a hard time controlling them. No, these spawn from the Netherworld."

I paled. Gulakah specialized in a certain type of demon, all right. "Bhouts? Is this how bhouts reproduce?"

"No, not bhouts. Those *must* come through a Demon Gate. No, these are worse. Spirit demons. A whole nest of them."

Spirit demons. I shuddered.

Vanzir had described them some time back when we thought we were up against one, although it had turned out to be a false alarm. That was when I'd gotten my scar from hellhound blood. But the hellhound had been child's play compared to the spirit demon Vanzir thought it was.

"Do you know what a spirit demon is?" Eriskel gazed at me, then softly said, "I think you do."

I nodded, my mood plummeting. "Magic won't do anything but feed them. That's why you stopped me."

"That's why I stopped you."

"Can we attack them on the astral, though?"

"No, you're going to have to get back over to the other side. The egg is about to hatch. This is the way they're fed until they break open the shell. Then the demons run rampant, feeding like ravenous dogs. Go now, tell your friends, and do what you can."

The next thing I knew, I was standing beside the egg again, the horn in my hand. Disoriented, I shook my head to clear my thoughts as I slid the horn into my skirt's hidden pocket and firmly zipped it up. The weapon would be of no use to us, nor would my magic. No, we needed silver to fight these creatures.

As the others caught up to me, I motioned frantically. "We need to get back over to the physical. This fucking egg is housing a nest of spirit demons."

"Crap." Vanzir paled. "We can't fight them on the astral. "Meet you on the other side." He immediately disappeared.

Roz said nothing, grabbing me around the waist. "Shade, you wait till I return for Delilah." And—with a lurch and me clutching at his duster—we launched back into the Ionyc Seas.

The shift was even more disconcerting because of my panic over the spirit demons, but at least the fear and worry kept me from drifting. The moment we set down, Roz let me go next to Vanzir and then disappeared again.

I turned around, waiting for the blasts of magic from the line of witches, but they were processing toward the egg, now oblivious to Vanzir's and my presences. I just hoped that would last.

Vanzir pulled out a blade, but it wasn't silver and he grumbled and shoved it back into the sheath. "I need a silver blade."

Spirit demons fed on magical and psychic energy, much like bhouts, but they were far more dangerous and far harder to disrupt. Magic wouldn't work on them unless you knew a snare spell—and that would only entrap them. Neither Morio nor I was powerful enough to create one. No, we needed silver weapons.

"Wait for a moment. Roz may have more. Damn—they're getting close!" I shouted at the line of FBH pagans and Fae, but they ignored me. "We have to stop them!"

Vanzir pursed his lips, then shoved me back a few steps. "You wait here." He raced across the lawn, intercepting the one closest to the egg, tackling her and knocking her to the ground. I cringed, waiting for her to return fire, but she merely stood up again and began marching toward the egg again as Vanzir went on to the next.

Realizing they were fully enrapt in their purpose, I joined him, darting across the lawn to bowl over the nearest person, who happened to be an older lady. I cringed as we went rolling to the ground, hoping to hell that I hadn't broken anything. But she didn't look hurt, and she was struggling to get up, so I jumped up, going on to the next.

About that point, we heard shouts and turned. Morio, Delilah, Shade, and Rozurial stood there. Vanzir and I hurried back to their sides.

"They're in a trance so deep I doubt if they realize we're here. They seem to be totally focused, so we have to make quick work of it. The minute they touch that egg sac, it will suck them in and drain them dead." I pulled out my dagger, which was silver if not the most lethal-looking blade. "We have to have silver to hurt them, and magic will only make them stronger."

Delilah held up Lysanthra, her dagger. "I'm armed."

Roz opened his duster and quickly sorted through the pile of weapons. "I have two silver blades and—oh, I have a silver spike, too. It ought to be good for something. Who all needs one?"

Morio shook his head, dropping his pack. He stood up, shurikens in hand. "These are silver. I also have a silver blade."

But Shade and Vanzir raised their hands. Roz tossed Shade the spike, and Vanzir one of the daggers, arming himself with the other. "I guess this is as good as we get."

As we turned to the egg, Delilah shivered. "Remind me again what these things can do. I remember their name but not so much about them. There are so many kinds of demons."

Vanzir's voice was raw. He actually looked scared. "Spirit demons are one of the worst. They're from the Netherworld, because they are more of a spirit than just a corporeal demon. They have a hole where their heart was, with a vortex in it. Their tendrils emerge from there, and they feed on any magical or psychic energy around. They'll kill you if they drain you."

"Magic doesn't work on them," I added. "It's like throwing gasoline on fire. We can only attack them on a physical level using silver. Whatever you do, don't let them attach to you."

As I spoke, one of the witches managed to get past us and reached the egg. I lunged forward, but Shade streaked past me. He leaped for her, catching her by the knees. She tripped and sprawled against the egg, her torso vanishing through it. Shade hollered as he tried to pull her back. Yanking, he tumbled back, and she came with him, but the moment we saw what had happened to her, I wished he'd let her go. I stared at her in horror.

She was lying there, her torso, head, and arms looking

rubbery—almost like she'd been melted. But she was still alive. Holes riddled her body, as if she'd been pumped full of huge bullets, but no blood flowed, and no body fluids. Only a pale current of energy. My stomach knotted as she writhed on the ground, mouthing screams that would never be heard.

"She's bleeding out on a psychic level." I raised my dagger, unsure. There was no way to save her. No way to fix her.

"Do something!" Delilah screamed.

Shade started to move, but I was quicker. Wincing, an ache threatening to swallow my heart, I plunged the dagger into her chest, driving it swiftly and cleanly through her heart. She convulsed once . . . twice . . . and then was still. I looked up at the others, horrified.

"Destroy that motherfucker. And somebody—I don't care who it is—keep the rest of these people from getting near it." I growled at the egg. "I'm calling in reinforcements."

I pulled out my cell phone and speed-dialed Smoky, hoping to hell he and Trillian were home from Otherworld already. While I was anxiously waiting, Roz moved to intercept the next witch. She—like the others—seemed totally oblivious to what had just gone on. It was as if they didn't even register what was happening.

This couldn't be brainwashing, not if they were totally ignoring their self-preservation instincts. And if they were exhibiting hive mentality, they would have swarmed to protect the egg once they noticed we'd returned. No, my guess was that they had been magically programmed, like living zombies. When we'd vanished the first time onto the astral, our threat had vanished and they could feed the spirit demons.

To my relief, Smoky answered the phone. "What's happening? We just got back."

"I'm so damned glad to hear your voice. We need all hands on deck. Do not bring Iris. Tell her to take Maggie and Hanna and lock themselves in Menolly's lair—they'll be safe there. We're facing an egg full of spirit demons that's about to hatch, and we've got a bunch of magically brainwashed FBH pagans and magical Fae throwing themselves at it like cattle feed."

Smoky let out a slow whistle. "Trillian and I will be there in a few moments. Shamas is out in the yard. He'll come, too. Where are you?"

I gave him the address. "Can you come through the Ionyc Seas? We need you here fast."

"I've never been there, but I know a park nearby. I can carry both Shamas and Trillian. Five minutes . . . ten at the most."

"Make it five. And bring silver weapons. That's the only thing that will touch these creatures." I hung up and turned back to the egg.

As Roz did his best to fend off the would-be sacrificial offerings, a vibrating hum began to fill the air. The noise started like a faint ringing in my ears, quickly increasing in volume as the egg began to rock. I dropped to my knees, holding my hands over my ears. Delilah was doing the same. The piercing wail was unrelenting, but still the supplicants attempted to get to the egg. Roz was doing his best to stop them, ignoring the sirenlike shriek.

Morio yelled something at me, but I couldn't hear him between covering my ears and the wail of the egg. He pointed to a spot high on the silver orb, and I squinted; the pale sun was glaring in my eyes. But then, as a cloud passed between the light and us, what he was looking at became clear.

Fuck. Narrow veins began to appear, the cracks slowly rippling across the egg, like a spiderweb or an intricate mosaic. A glowing violet light began to shimmer from the hair-width fractures, and in my gut, I knew it was the energy of the Netherworld peering out. The energy of the spirit demons.

My stomach knotted. The thing was about to hatch. I tried to stand, but the noise drove me down again. Roz, Morio, Shade, and Vanzir were all on their feet—it must have been just Delilah and I who were affected.

"Please, Moon Mother, let it hold off until the others get here. We need all the help we can get," I whispered, unable to hear myself but praying still the same. I couldn't use her magic in this battle, but maybe—just maybe—she'd send us a little luck, a little boost.

And then the sirens fell silent, and—disconcerted—I pushed to my feet, Delilah doing the same. We gathered up our blades and turned to face the egg. The cracks had nearly covered the surface now, and the violet veins of light were shining through them, but so far, they hadn't gotten any wider. I had no idea whether it was like a chicken's egg—were the spirit demons pushing against the inner walls of the shell? Would they emerge one by one, or in a huge, writhing mass? And how many were in a nest, anyway?

So many questions, and unfortunately, we were poised to find out the answers. *The hard way.* I glanced at the others, uncertain.

"Should we rush it now, while they're still inside? Smoky, Trillian, and Shamas are on their way. Should we wait for them? I don't know what to do!" Frantic, I turned to Vanzir. "You know the most about them—what do we do?"

He looked just as terrified as I felt. "They'll go for the magic users first. I'd say for you and Morio to get the hell out of here, but you wouldn't be able to run fast enough. A nest contains dozens of the demons—but they won't be at full strength yet. They'll be fast and they'll be ravenous, even though Gulakah has been sending them food."

"When should we attack?"

Shade interrupted. "Not till they come out. If we break the shell now, they'll all pour out at once. If we're lucky, then they'll only be able to come out a few at a time. I don't know for sure, but I say we don't give them any help." He gazed up at the sky. "Pray for more clouds—there are a few but not enough for me to slip into shadow. I may not be able to attack them with my magic, but I could use it to navigate."

Finally! Something I could manage!

"Hold on." I sheathed my dagger and raised my arms to the sky. I couldn't call the lightning to fight, but I could gather the clouds. The sky was overcast enough now for me to summon them.

I inhaled deeply, pulling in the scent of rain on the horizon. A storm was on the way, and I could bring it faster. Not strong enough to give us a deluge, but a bank of nimbostratus clouds was near enough to summon. They were low-level and dark and filled with enough precipitation to spur on moderate showers. I quickly unzipped the pocket and pulled the horn back out, thrusting it into the air.

"Master of Winds, Lord of the Depths, hear me. Bring the storm, bring the rain, bring the cloud cover, not to attack but to help camouflage and protect!"

As I spoke, a loud crack of thunder rumbled in on the currents as the clouds began to move, shifting rapidly, piling up as if we were watching a time-elapsed film. The wind picked up, whipping my hair, the faint taste of rain caught in the gusts. I laughed—the sheer joy of the elements washing through me, cleansing my fear.

Replacing the horn in my pocket, I zipped it up and turned to Shade. "Will that be enough?"

He gave me a sultry smile. "You're the best," he said, and vanished into the sudden glut of shadows that spread across the lawn.

As the clouds continued to build, I realized that I'd called more than a simple storm. Something big was going on up there. But there was no time to worry about it now—because as Smoky, Trillian, and Shamas came racing up the street, the egg began to shatter—shards of pale gray shell falling every which way. A host of shadowy creatures began to rush out, nebulous but visible, and they descended on us with a fury. I raised my silver blade. The fight had come to us, and we were sorely outnumbered.

Chapter 12

The rush of spirit demons was an eerie sight against the backdrop of darkening sky. We watched as a fountain of light shot up, sparking with the violet flames of the Netherworld and, flying out of that fountain, the nebulous forms of the spirit demons.

We'd never actually fought any of the creatures, though I wondered how much worse than the bhouts could they be, but that question was answered all too quickly as one landed in front of me.

While it was ethereal, I could see its face and body, and the hollow sockets were filled with glowing fire—burning brilliant orange. The body itself was vaguely bipedal, resembling a human though not of human descent. But where the heart would have been was a hole of swirling mist, and out of that hole, feelers emerged—thin tentacles that reminded me of Vanzir's neon feeding tubes. They were silent as they writhed toward me, and I dodged as one of them swiped toward my head. It missed me by inches.

Holy hell! The things were fast, and there were so many

of them it was hard to estimate the horde we were fighting. I slashed at the one in front of me. It was close enough to touch, and I managed to score a direct hit. It screamed as the silver bit into its side and launched itself at me again. Again I ducked and countered, and again, I managed to hit. The second time, the spirit demon vanished in a whiff of flame.

I killed it? That had to be a joke! But then I realized that we were dealing with newly hatched creatures and, demon or not, they were still vulnerable. Once they began to feed now that they were outside, they'd become much more dangerous.

Roz's voice echoed over the fray. "No! Damn it to fucking hell!"

I darted his way—I'd been close to him anyway. The path cleared just long enough for me to see a group of the spirit demons diving for the FBH witches and the Fae. They were doing nothing to protect themselves—lambs to the slaughter in their magical possession. Roz was butchering the demons right and left, but still they came.

Several of the women were dead—rather than vanishing, as they had into the egg, they looked like they were riddled with bullet holes. The carnage spread out across the lot. I rushed in to help him try to protect the rest, but a glance at the egg told me we were fighting the clock.

Spirit demons were still pouring out. There was no way we could kill them all before they feasted. And the demons who were draining the magic and life force from the witches were stronger. Their bodies became more solid; they looked bigger and tougher.

What the hell were we going to do?

But there wasn't time to dwell on questions. Another spirit demon—still searching for food—came at me, and one of its feelers hit my arm. An electric shock raced through me as the thing sought to latch hold. It was then that I saw a round row of needle-sharp teeth in the end of the tube—a lot like a lamprey's mouth.

"Oh hell no you don't!" I pulled away before it could sink its teeth into me and whirled around, slicing through the feeler with my dagger. It did not flinch, did not scream, merely came at me again. The silence and grace of its movement was almost more frightening than the creature itself—everything was done in a hush, the movements barely perceptible except to the eye.

I tried to anticipate the spirit demon's action, whirling to match its advance. The first time, I lucked out and managed to slice through another feeler. The second time, I miscalculated and it slammed two of its tentacles against me and one managed to grab hold. The teeth dug in and I screamed, trying to shake it off. Maneuvering a blade so close to my skin was difficult, but I had to get the thing off me, and everybody else was caught up in their own battles.

Using the dagger, I began prying at it, digging into my arm with the tip, trying to break the suction of the spirit demon. It was holding fast, so I gritted my teeth and slid the blade into my skin, just under the top layer—I kept the dagger extremely sharp—and then shoved it beneath where the feeler had hold. With a sharp jab, I turned it upward and shoved, ripping through my flesh, but managed to aim right into the mouth.

The spirit demon jerked the tentacle away, again in silence, and as I yanked my dagger away and aimed for the other feeler, it pulled off me. I was bleeding and it hurt, but I'd hurt a lot worse before. Angry, more than anything, I slashed at the demon and my dagger met its mark, plunging directly into the creature's core where the heart should have been—into the swirling vortex from where its tendrils emerged.

I didn't let up, driving the blade farther into its core. It struggled, but I threw my weight against it, and with a slow ripple the spirit demon collapsed and vanished.

As soon as it was down, I turned back to the carnage going on with the spellbound members of the Aleksais Psychic Network. Most of them were dead, and we were fighting a bloody and failing battle, just trying to keep the collateral damage as low as we could.

The spirit demons had filled the area, their shadowy

figures haunting the lot. I glanced around, panicked. We were too few, and though the others were doing their best, because it took silver weapons to harm them, we couldn't fight at our best advantage.

But there wasn't time to focus on the big picture. Another pair of demons came my way. Luckily they were fresh and young. As I backed up, trying to gauge the best way to keep one at bay while I fought the other, the roiling clouds shuddered as a wave of thunder rolled through, rattling the ground. Lightning followed, a fraction of a second afterward—it was right above us, the storm; I'd called it in, perhaps a little too well.

As the afternoon sky shifted, thanks to the rising power of the storm, a jagged shard of lighting crashed to the ground and hit the egg dead-on. Since the lightning itself wasn't magical, it appeared to do damage rather than help the demons. The remaining shell shattered, sending debris every which way. I was out of reach, but Delilah yelled, and I saw that she had several shards of the orb stuck in her arms. But she yanked them out, tossing them on the ground, and went back to fighting one of the spirit demons.

The smell of ozone trickled through the air, scorching my nose.

I turned back to my own opponents. They were bearing down on me, and I wasn't sure just how I was going to manage keeping them away.

And then there was a howl from down the street, and the sound of running feet, and before I could react, a group of about twenty-five members of the Supe Community Council came charging in—all big, burly men with silver swords. Bear shifters and werepumas mostly, though I recognized a member of Marion's coyote shifter clan. They rushed in, sweeping through to help us.

I found myself beside Jonas—a burly hulk of a man— well, werebear—with curly black hair, and a trim, neat goatee. He was an ex–football player, and he looked it. But he was also an ex-Marine, and he fought like it. I had no idea how he'd managed to hide his heritage in the service when the moon went full, but the question vanished as one of the spirit demons launched another attack at me. Jonas shoved me out of the way and lopped the spirit demon in half—right down the center—with a badass silver sword.

It occurred to me that there wouldn't be any werewolves around—they had a problem with silver just like vampires, but none of the other Weres were allergic to it.

As Jonas finished off my second opponent, I stumbled back, tired from the constant fighting. I was used to battle, but using magic was different from fighting it out hand-to-hand. I was trying to clear my head when Smoky suddenly came rushing past, sweeping me up under one arm. I barely had time to let out a "Huh?" when two more spirit demons descended on the spot where I'd been standing. I hadn't even noticed them coming.

He pulled me out of the fray, running me across the street. I groaned as he set me down next to another group of perhaps ten Weres. "Watch her. Don't let her get hurt." And then he was off.

I turned to find myself staring at Frank Willows, a were-wolf who had recently taken on a bigger role in the Supe Community Council. He gave me a slow nod. Frank was an urban farmer and one of the good guys. We bought our pork from him and also some of the blood that Menolly kept around for reserves. Most werewolves didn't like magic or vampires, and Frank was no exception, but he'd never been anything but polite to Menolly and me, unlike some of the lycanthropes we'd met. We were on friendly terms.

"Frank, what are you doing here? *You* can't use silver." I fretted. He, as well as any other werewolves, wouldn't be able to defend themselves if the spirit demons crossed the street.

"Plenty of Weres here who can, though. Since Johnson called us up for active duty, and since I'm the leader of the Supe Militia, I felt it was my duty to come. Camille, you need to distance yourself from the battle. It's not safe for you. Chase said those things eat magic, and you're . . . filled with it."

He was soft-spoken, even though his voice was a little gruff, and his apprehension made me smile. I'd faced, and defeated, worse threats than Frank could imagine. But I didn't want to bruise his ego, or make him think I wasn't grateful for his concern.

"I think we'll be okay here. They seem to be making inroads now that we have your men helping us." And it was true—the swarm of spirit demons was thinning out. In fact, I was able to count the number left from here, and it looked like only twelve remained. I had no clue how many we'd killed, but it had to be nearly seventy-five, if not more.

After a moment, I cocked my head and glanced back at Frank. "Dude, you said Chase called you?"

"Right. Johnson told me that Smoky said you guys needed fighters who didn't use magic and who could land a good punch with silver blades. That's all he knew. So I set the phone tree in motion and we called in all available men who could get here on the fly." Frank let out a slow breath. "That dragon husband of yours knows how to wield a sword, that's for sure." He was staring at Smoky, who—for the first time, I noticed—was carrying a long silver sword. A wickedly nasty long silver sword with one serrated edge and one flat.

"Cripes, I had no idea he owned that." I blinked. "I wonder if it was his grandfather's?" Smoky's grandfather had bequeathed him a great many treasures, and I wondered what else might be hiding, tucked away in Smoky's treasure trove. But the sword was magnificent. It gleamed, even in the dim light of the storm clouds, and every time it hit against one of the demons, a pale blue glow would flash.

As the men continued mopping up the last of the demons, Delilah came trudging over, looking weary and covered with mud and welts.

"What happened to you?"

"The spirit demons tried to latch onto me, but I guess this is what happens when you don't have much innate magical power. They left rows of bite marks because they couldn't damage me on a psychic level. I guess the powers of a Death Maiden aren't tasty enough for them."

"Yeah, either that or . . . perhaps they can't handle your energy because it's connected to the Autumn Lord? Maybe that's an avenue we should explore."

"You might be right." She nodded at Frank, an easy shake of the head, and dropped to the grass while we waited. I joined her, resting my head on her shoulder. "You okay?"

"I think so. I got hit a couple of times, and believe me— it's jarring to have those things trying to suck out my energy."

"Was it like when Vanzir . . ." Her voice trailed off and she arched her eyebrows.

I shrugged. Vanzir had tried to feed on me once, though to be fair, it wasn't really his fault. We'd been under pressure, he'd been using his powers, and I was radiating so much magic that he'd been unable to control himself. I'd ended up fucking him to stop him from invading my mind, and that had led to another can of worms.

"A little . . . only with Vanzir, I knew he wasn't doing it deliberately. These things are out to hurt—they're out to destroy. And though the end result is the same, there's definitely a different feel to it. I'd never liken Vanzir to the spirit demons." I plucked a blade of grass and chewed on it.

"You might not want to admit it, but I guarantee you, any other dream-chaser demon wouldn't show the restraint he does, and I have no doubt that they would be out to feed on you. Deliberately." She shaded her eyes, trying to see what was going on. "Almost done, it looks like."

"Maybe so, but Vanzir's not just any other demon. He's been a huge help to us, and he didn't have to stick around once the soul binder vanished."

She sighed, pushing herself to her feet and dusting the back of her jeans. "Listen, I know Vanzir's not like the rest of his kind, but you can't deny he's dangerous. Never, ever forget that." She reached down, offering me a hand, and pulled me to my feet.

"I know that. I never forget the strengths of my enemies. Or my friends." Vaguely annoyed, but too tired to do anything about it, I jumped as another crash of thunder echoed through the area and the clouds opened. A sheet of rain so thick you could barely see between the droplets came gushing down, a real deluge.

After a moment, another crack of lightning split the sky, and thunder rumbled through just behind it. The rain turned to hail and we were inundated with pea-sized ice pellets. I yelled as they sliced against my skin, the sting bad enough to make me wince. Frank glanced around, then grabbed my hand and pulled me beneath a nearby cedar. He motioned for me to crouch beneath the lower branches. Delilah followed, and we covered our heads with our hands as the hail went on and on.

Frank stood straight, face front into the hail, guarding me. I wanted to tug on his jeans, make him hide under the boughs with us, but I knew he wouldn't budge. It was a matter of pride for him. Smoky had entrusted him with my care, and even though Delilah was here now, he felt like he had to honor that promise. If I tried to persuade him to protect himself from the weather, he'd take it as a personal insult.

Unable to see what was going on across the street from here, we knelt beneath the cedar, breathing the fresh, crisp scent, as I sent up a whispered prayer to the Moon Mother. *Please, let them find all of the spirit demons. Please don't let any of them escape. Please, let our friends be okay.*

Another minute or two and the hail let up, fat raindrops replacing the shower of ice. Delilah crawled out from beneath the tree, and then I stumbled out. Frank helped me up. As we stood there, the others made their way back across the street. Rozurial looked exhausted. Vanzir had fallen in the mud several times. Shade and Morio looked tired but no worse for wear. And Smoky, of course, was pristine and clean, as always. But none of them were smiling.

Behind them, the Weres followed, some limping or leaning on their buddies, but most looked okay. I anxiously waited as Smoky walked up to us, Jonas by his side.

"How did we fare?" I almost didn't want to know—if we'd lost any of our Supe Community friends, it would be too much. We'd already lost all of the witches who had formed the human shield against us.

"Several men down, but alive. Chase is sending help. The spirit demons are all gone. And the witches . . ." Smoky stopped. He let out a long sigh, then lifted my chin, his fingers gentle on my skin. He gazed down at me, his frosty eyes a swirl of snow and mist. "They're all dead. But you knew that, my love."

"Yes, I knew that." I leaned against him, resting my head on his chest as I slipped my arms around him. He smelled musky, and yet fresh, like newly fallen snow. I knew that scent—I knew it so well, I dreamed of it. Each of my men, I loved in a different way, but none of them any less than the others.

"I'm sorry," he whispered, rocking me gently back and forth. "I know it hurts you to lose people who aren't directly involved in the battle. I do understand, even though I'm a dragon. War is a horrible thing, and good people die, and children, too. It is the way of the world. If war were simple, we'd never strive for peace."

"We don't seem to be doing a very good job in finding peace." I wanted to cry. How were we going to tell Lindsey that a group of her friends were dead, their life energy fed to a horde of ravenous spirit demons?

"All we can do is our best." Smoky found my lips, his tongue slipping deep into my mouth, probing gently as he kissed me. Long strands of his hair reached up to caress my shoulders and curl around my back, pulling me even closer to him. As the kiss went on, I melted into his arms, wanting him, needing him. Sex was one of my greatest stress relievers, and right now, I was stressed to the max. I moaned gently as he cupped my butt with one hand and lifted me up to meet his height.

"I need you, my wife. Morio and Trillian and I will take you away from this carnage, if only for a while."

I held tight to him, breathless, wanting the moment to never end.

Smoky whispered in my ear. "I *could* take you away now—you and your family. All of us. I could fly us to the Dragon Reaches. You would be safe there—and your sisters, and Maggie. Iris, Bruce . . . everyone. Mother would welcome you. She has developed quite the fondness for you."

It was so tempting. Leave this war, run off and live life at the top of the world. But there was no way my conscience would allow for that, and I knew that Delilah and Menolly felt the same way. We were stuck in the trenches, for good or evil. This was where we belonged right now. So many people depended on us, and we would not shirk our duties.

"I truly am fond of your mother, too, but no. We can't do that and you know it." I kissed his forehead and placed my hand against his chest. "In your heart, you know it. Even though you are a dragon, you care about these people."

I seldom broached that subject. Smoky, like all dragons, was touchy about his emotions. He didn't like my pointing out that he actually gave a damn about the humans, or about Earthside. Whether it was from not wanting to appear vulnerable, or whether he just didn't like to talk about his feelings, I didn't know. But regardless of his protests, I knew I was right. He wouldn't take care of my family and friends the way he did if he hated humans or the Fae.

He wouldn't stay with us, put up with all the ribbing and the joking and the tight quarters of our house. He wouldn't be here, fighting to help us against the demons, if he didn't care. And right now, I needed to hear him say it. Needed to hear him validate my choice.

He looked long into my eyes, the smile gone from his face. "My love . . . yes, *we* need to stay here." And then he set me down. "Come, we have work to do. Let's go talk to Chase. It's easier for us to go to him, while he's on crutches."

Without another word, he turned and motioned to Delilah and the others. We started down the street, leaving Keo and Yugi to cope with the cleanup. They were directing the Supe Militia in sorting out the aftermath and preparing the dead bodies to be transported to the FH-CSI morgue. Fourteen FBH witches and four Fae had died, thanks to the Aleksais Psychic Network. And we had to figure out what to tell eighteen families about their loved ones.

* * *

By the time we reached home and had all washed up, it was nearing four P.M. Chase had decided against contacting any family members for a little while. They weren't expecting their loved ones to come home immediately, so we had a little while in which to figure out what to tell them. I knew it ran against his grain to keep information like this under wraps, but we had to sort out what had happened and make sure it didn't happen again.

As we slumped at the kitchen table, Iris and Hanna silently brought over a late lunch or early dinner. They quietly set a bowl of salad, a big basket of sliced French bread toasted with Parmesan, a meat platter, and a tray of cookies down for us. Hanna brought over a pitcher filled with iced raspberry tea.

Everyone seemed spent. Delilah was staring at the table, Shade's arm draped around her shoulders. Rozurial and Vanzir were unaccustomedly silent. Morio and Trillian slumped in chairs next to Smoky and me. Even Shamas was quiet as he took a chair across the table from me.

Iris waited for a moment, then, hands on her hips, said, "Eat." As we slowly reached for the food, she added, "Tell us what happened. It can't be good, not with as quiet as you all are."

I caught her gaze. "It isn't. We lost eighteen people today—four Fae and fourteen FBH pagans who had been sucked in by the Aleksais Psychic Network. They, along with a host of zombies, were used to feed a hatchling nest of spirit demons."

"Not good." Iris frowned. "Do you think that's the only egg around?"

I hadn't even thought of that possibility, but it wouldn't have been long before the question came up. My head began to pound and I rubbed the back of my neck, trying to work out the knots.

"I doubt it. And if it *wasn't* the only one, and Gulakah has more of those stashed away, when they hatch, the spirit demons will go through anyone and everyone who even has a *limited* psychic or magical ability. They could devastate the world if enough of them got loose."

"How did you stop them?" Iris lowered herself into the rocking chair as Hanna brought out Maggie and handed her to me.

I took the little gargoyle in my arms, burying my face in her fur. Maggie was solace for us on days when everything seemed to overwhelm, but she couldn't solve our problems. I kissed her softly on the head.

"If it weren't for the Supe Community Militia, we wouldn't have been able to contain them. But I hate to have to call them out—Weres are strong, but the spirit demons are stronger, at least once they've had a chance to feed. They're only affected by silver weapons, so we had to go in hand-to-hand." I tickled Maggie under the chin and she giggled, grabbing my finger and licking it.

Shamas leaned forward, resting his elbows on the table. "There might be other ways to deal with them, but if there are, it would take a demon far more powerful. Or . . . well . . . someone like Gulakah."

Delilah snorted. "Gulakah? Yeah, he's likely to help. We have to find a way to get to him."

I handed Maggie back to Hanna. "There's no other way. I'm going to infiltrate the Aleksais Psychic Network tomorrow night. I'll find a way to get to Gulakah." I turned to Trillian. "I didn't have a chance to ask, were you able to get hold of one of the talismans of disguise?" *Please, please, say yes.* I couldn't take one more piece of bad news.

Trillian gave me a tired smile. "I managed to hook up with one of my old buddies who has deep connections with the Svartalfheim sorcerers' guilds. Yes, we have a talisman. And it will work until you break the spell or until you're attacked. Which better not happen or I'm coming in there and ripping the heads off every person in sight."

"And I'll be there to help." Smoky shook his head. "I still don't understand why you didn't bargain with the shyster."

Trillian snorted. "That shyster could have burned me to a crisp with one word. He would have put *you* to the test, that's for sure. Don't underestimate him because he's Svartan. Some of *my* people could take on *your* people and actually win." His eyes flashed, and I knew he was dangling bait.

And, of course, Smoky took it. "I never underestimate anyone—"

Trillian let out a snort. "Right. You underestimate *every-one*. You're the *big bad Dragon-Dude* so nobody can touch you, nobody can—"

Smoky laughed, but it wasn't an altogether friendly laugh. "And how many really can? Well, demons, yes, but humans? Most of the Fae? Even you have to admit that very few people can harm me, while *you*, on the other hand—"

"Right, I *can* be hurt and I *know* it. But you won't even admit the possibility, you big lizard—"

I jumped up. "Enough, you baboons! Seriously. *Enough.* You managed to make it all the way to Otherworld and back without killing each other. *Now* you go at it? *Really?* You think I want to hear this? Trillian, stop baiting Smoky. And Smoky, do you always have to fall for his games?"

And then Morio had to get into it. He coughed. "What I want to know is how did the two of you actually manage the trip without Camille along to keep the peace?"

Smoky let out a *hrmph*. "I'll have you know . . ." He stopped, and a smile cracked his face. "We made a pact before we left. We agreed on a truce."

I stared at the two of them. "You actually had to form a truce in order to coexist for a twenty-four-hour trip?" With the stress of the day wearing on me, the ridiculousness of the situation was too much. I dropped back in my chair, laughing so hard I started to cry. "Sometimes, I feel like I'm married to a couple of teenagers."

"Teenagers, you say?" Trillian gave Smoky a long look, who nodded.

A tendril of his hair rose up and crept across the back of my shoulders. I jumped, but the soft creep of the strands played across my skin, tickling me, stroking so gently that it sent shivers down my spine. I tried to shrug it off, but Smoky kept on, grinning the entire time.

"Okay, you stop it right now!" Though I wasn't entirely sure I wanted him to stop. There was something sensuous about the feeling, and I was tired and the stroking felt good, in an annoying way.

Smoky reached over and gently took hold of one of my wrists as Trillian held the other. Another strand of Smoky's hair slipped under my skirts to coil around my thighs.

I shrieked. "Okay, okay! I give up."

"Do you really want me to stop, Camille?" The huskiness in his voice as it lingered over my name made me catch my breath. His hair slowed its caress, the tendrils trailing along my inner thighs. "All you have to do is say the word."

I blushed as Delilah started to laugh. She leaned her head against Shade's shoulder; he was trying to keep a straight face but failing miserably. Vanzir and Roz were eating with snarky grins on their faces. But Shamas was scowling, intent on his food.

"*Do you?* Want me to stop?" Again, the steady tap, tap, tap, of Smoky's hair on my thigh, like fingers gently rapping on a table.

I was tired, and my bruises had bruises. I glanced at all three of my men. They waited, expectantly, and I could feel their anticipation. A wave of heat made its way up my body, emanating from the point where Smoky's hair was stroking me, and I realized I was wet and hungry for them. It was all I could do to not squirm in my seat. I sucked in a deep breath. Their desire had transferred to me, and now all I wanted to do was race upstairs and fuck their brains out. *Thank you, Soul Symbiont ritual.*

I glanced sideways at Morio and Trillian. Morio slowly, deliberately mouthed, *Bed. Now.*

"What the hell. We need a nap. If Chase calls, tell him we need an hour or two to regroup. Nothing else better happen, because for the next twelve hours, I can't take another emergency situation." I slowly rose. "We'll be in our rooms resting—"

Shade let out a burst of laughter. "Oh, we *know* what you'll be doing." But he winked again and went back to his meal. "Meanwhile, we'll clean up, and get some rest ourselves. Won't we, Pussy-Cat?" He purred at Delilah, who blushed but grinned back at him.

"Just as long as *clean up* means a shower and *not* a bath. You know I hate baths."

And with that, Smoky let out a throaty laugh and swept me up into his arms. "Come on, wife. Your men have needs. And so do you."

Trillian and Morio pushed back their chairs, and amid a roomful of laughter, we headed up the stairs. All the way, the only thing I could think about were my men, their hands, and our bed.

Chapter 13
〜✦〜

The bedroom was warm, so Trillian opened the window. Smoky set me down and turned me around, resting his hands on my waist. Trillian stepped in front of me. Slowly, with a firm hand and a faint smile playing across his face, he unhooked the metal busks of my corset.

The energy in the room was thick and heavy, like right before a thunderstorm, and I quivered under his touch. Smoky caught hold of my corset when it fell open and set it aside.

I stood there, breasts heavy and waiting, nipples rising as Trillian thumbed one, squeezing it just hard enough to make my stomach lurch. He turned me a quarter turn, and Smoky took hold of my skirt's waistband, unzipping it, easing it down to the ground. Holding Trillian's hands for balance, I stepped out of the garment.

He kept my hands in his, his gaze locked on my face, his lips curved up at the very edges. As I stared at him, the images of the dead witches and Fae sprawled through my thoughts. I couldn't shake them out, couldn't shake them loose. It was too reminiscent of Henry Jeffries's death. He'd been a friend, he'd worked for me in the Indigo Crescent bookstore, and his love of my store had gotten him killed. Aching with the weariness only a long, protracted battle can bring, I let out a little cry as the stress and strain of the day welled up.

"I need to stop thinking. I need to get out of my head." My words were more a plea than anything.

"You need us to take over?" Trillian asked, still holding my gaze.

I nodded. "Please . . . please . . ."

He gave Smoky, who was still standing behind me, a particular look that I'd seen only a few times. As I stood there, wanting to cry because I was so tired of the whole fucking war, Smoky wrapped his hair around my waist and lifted me up. I gasped as he sat down in a chair, still fully dressed, and gently laid me face down across his knees.

Morio knelt by my head, and before I realized what he was doing, he slid a blindfold over my eyes. The blessed darkness calmed me, removing distractions. The velvet pads were soft against my skin, and I inhaled deeply, letting out a stream of worry. As I lay against Smoky's lap, I could feel his erection beneath his tight white jeans, and it gave me a little thrill. I squirmed a little, and a rope-thick section of his hair caught my arms in back of me, gently wrapping around my wrists to keep them together. Again, a jolt of desire ran through me as he shifted me into a slightly different position.

Someone's finger—Morio's, by the smell of him—traced a line around my lips. I reached out the tip of my tongue, darting a taste. He slid his finger into my mouth and I began to suck.

"Give her what she wants," Smoky commanded.

The next thing I knew, I felt the tip of a cock pressing at my lips. Eager now, I opened just enough as Morio slid into my mouth. Tightening my suction around him, I ran my tongue over the rigid skin, the musk of his scent filling my mouth. As he began to gently thrust, I sucked harder.

"I love watching you give him head," Trillian's voice whispered in my ear. "I love watching you fuck, baby. I like watching you fuck other guys—as long as you remember that I'm your alpha." He pressed his lips to my neck, then

softly trailed them down my back, and over my ass, lingering to give me a gentle nip on the right cheek.

My pussy was so wet that I wanted to scream, but with
Morio in my mouth, all I could do was moan lightly around
the shaft of his cock. I squirmed ever so slightly.

"Hold still." Smoky's command was firm but hard to obey.
Trillian was working his way down the back of my leg now,
licking, tickling, kissing. As he reached my calves, I suddenly
felt his hands grip my ankles, spreading my legs. The next
moment, ropes—Smoky's hair, no doubt—wrapped around
each ankle, keeping my legs wide. A rush of cool air washed
past my cunt and, without thinking, I squirmed again.

"You disobeyed, my love." Smoky's voice was soft, but
firm. The next thing I knew, I felt a resounding smack on my
butt.

Morio kept up his gentle thrusting, and I couldn't cry out.
The second blow fell, radiating a heat through my body, and
all I could think about was wanting someone inside me,
someone to fuck me—to calm the rising flames.

"I have to punish you for disobeying, you know that, don't
you?"

I nodded. Usually I played along because Smoky enjoyed
spanking me, and I found it somewhat titillating, but today, I
needed it—seriously needed the sting of my flesh to jog my
feelings out of me, to get the images out of my head.

And then, because he always offered me an out, he added,
"You know the word. All you have to do is say it."

I nodded again. One word from me, and they would stop.
But I didn't want that—I didn't want anything except pure,
sensual feeling. I wanted to be swept under, dragged down
into the depths of my sorrow and freed from the weight that
anchored me there.

After a moment, I once again felt a blow to my ass, and I
closed my eyes, focusing only on the taste of Morio in my
mouth, the feel of Smoky's hand on my ass as he spanked me
a third time, a fourth, a fifth. I quit counting and fell into the
rhythm of the blows, but they weren't so hard that I couldn't
take them.

And then, Smoky paused. A moment later, I gasped as Trillian thrust himself inside me from behind, into my pussy, as the hair ropes held my legs apart. He was thick, and hard, and he drove his cock deep inside me, grunting as he did so. Slowly, a lubed finger worked its way into my ass. I squirmed again, moaning around Morio, who was picking up the pace.

Another hand found my clit, and began fingering me, stroking first slowly, swirling around in circles, then picking up the pace until I couldn't think of anything except my growing need. Unable to move, unable to do anything except let these men tend to me, as the last lingering strain from the day welled up, tears rose, a gathering storm of sadness and fear and anger.

Morio let out a loud groan, filling my mouth with his cum. Salty on my tongue, it was thick and musky, but not unpleasant. I swallowed, taking every drop inside me, licking his penis clean. The next moment, he pulled out and then he was kissing me, his tongue playing over mine, his hands holding the sides of my head. I couldn't see him, but I knew it was my youkai, my fox, my love.

"Camille, oh my Camille . . . my priestess . . ." He kissed me deep and dark, and I began to fall into the well of emotion that had bottlenecked in my throat. As Trillian continued to drive himself inside me, Smoky's fingers deftly played me higher and higher, as I rose on wings, flying high to the ceiling,

I spiraled, dizzy, as heavy sobs worked their way to the surface. Toppling over the precipice as the dam burst, tears streaked down my face from behind the blindfold. Weeping, I came, the sharp jolts of orgasm painful in their strength. Trillian drove harder, faster, then stiffened as he joined me, creaming my pussy, clutching my waist to keep himself steady. Again, another jolt, and this time, I came again, hard and fast. Panting, he slowly pulled out.

I moaned gently as Morio slid the blindfold off, and Smoky's hair unwound from around my wrists and ankles. He caught me up and carried me to the bed, laying me gently on my back. As he stripped, a delighted look on his face, Morio and Trillian joined us.

"Open to me, you wanton wench. You beautiful wife of mine." Smoky loomed over me, and as I slid up on the pillows and spread my legs, my knees bent, he dove for me, sliding neatly into my pussy. I moaned, squirming happily. Now that the tension had been released, I was ready to play. I let out a purr, content and able to focus on the four of us without the fear and worry interfering.

Morio laughed. "Got room for me, babe?"

"Always." I glanced up at Smoky. "Lift me up?" And he did. Still inside me, he lifted me up, so Morio could slide beneath me. Trillian tossed him the lube and I heard him lubing up, then Smoky cautiously lowered me, still holding me as Morio's fingers widened my cunt and, very slowly, slid his cock into me, next to Smoky's. It was a tight fit, but they were both inside, filling me so full it almost hurt. *Almost* . . . but not quite.

A delicious sense of being absolutely possessed, of totally belonging to all three of them swept over me, and I reached out to touch Trillian, who was curled next to us. He kissed my fingers, and I took him in hand, stroked him long and hard again, squeezed, delighting in the feel of his cock thick and warm and alive in my hand.

Smoky began gently thrusting, cautious and careful, and Morio responded from beneath me. Together, they set up a rhythm, one gliding in with long, slow strokes as the other glided out. It was delicious and decadent and my pussy was so wet that the lube only made it that much easier. We didn't do this often, but once in a while, it was exactly what I needed.

The feel of Morio's chest against my back, of his arms wrapped around my waist as he drove himself into me time and again; the sight of Smoky bearing down on me, his hair stroking my body as he stroked my pussy with his cock; the rigid tumescence of Trillian's shaft as it pulsed in my fist, all entwined to drive all thought and reason out of my head, and I finally, fully let go, soaring, as a series of little screams

came echoing into the room, and I realized it was me—
laughing and shrieking as I came, and came again.

Blinking, I opened my eyes, forcing myself to a sitting position. The light filtering in through the room showed the pale
glow of the approaching sunset. Apparently my storm had
worked its way through and out. The window was cracked
open and a gust of fresh air rushed through, invigorating my
mind. I stretched and yawned, shaking the cobwebs from my
brain.

Morio was sitting on the bed next to me, legs crossed,
meditating. Smoky and Trillian were nowhere to be seen.
Without opening his eyes, he whispered, "Good evening,
sleepyhead."

"How long was I sleeping? I had no idea I was that tired."
I looked for the clock. Seven thirty. Forty-five minutes till
sunset.

"You slept like the dead." Morio opened his eyes as he
reached for me. I crawled across the bed, through the blankets, and he pulled me into his arms.

"I'm a little sore," I whispered. "But I loved this afternoon. Thank you."

"We should be thanking you." His lips were soft on mine
as he gave me a long, lingering kiss, and his hair tickled my
breasts. His scent was musky, but he'd taken a shower after
sex, that much I could tell, and I wanted to just slip into his
arms and curl up and snuggle. "I love you, Camille. And so
do Trillian and Smoky. We all love you."

I knew they loved me, they knew I loved them, but we
didn't always talk about it. Worried a little, I bopped his nose.
"Of course you do. And I love you. But . . . is anything wrong?
Has something new and extraordinarily bad happened?"

"No, nothing," he murmured. "We're just lucky to have
you. *I'm* lucky. Sometimes I don't think we say it enough.
You are an incredibly difficult woman, you know. You're
stubborn, you're bossy, and you've invested a fortune in corsets and makeup." He grinned.

"And this is supposed to win me over *how*?" I cocked my head at him, waiting. I couldn't deny any of it, everything he said was true, but there better be a *but* coming up soon.

He didn't disappoint me. "*But* . . . you're also an incredibly strong woman. You're loving, sexy, and you never, ever quit. And all of those qualities—*all* of them, including the bossiness, they make you who you are. The only woman I know that I'd ever want to marry." And once again, he kissed me, his hand running up and down my back.

"*I'm* the lucky one," I murmured, meaning every word. I was a lucky, lucky woman. Three times over.

Morio reached up and caressed my face, staring into my eyes, his own flashing dark, with flecks of topaz. The curve of his eyelids, the long silky black hair, the slight upturn of his lips—he was a gorgeous man.

I traced my finger over his lips. "What did Aeval say to you? When they brought you out to Talamh Lonrach Oll?" I wanted to know. Wanted to understand what they had in store for us, and Aeval sure as hell wasn't telling me.

He lightly bit the end of my finger, nipping it gently, then kissed it. "There are things I can tell you, and others I can't. I promised Aeval that—as long as it wouldn't hurt you—I would keep her secrets."

"I'm not sure I like you having secrets with the Queen of Darkness." I sat back against the head of the bed and pursed my lips as I drew my knees up to my chest and wrapped my arms around them.

"Can't be helped, babe. Deal with it." He winked at me. "You know no one can replace you in my heart."

"My sister almost did." The words slipped out before I could stop them, but I realized how unfair they were even as I said them. "I'm sorry. That was uncalled for. It wasn't your fault, or hers, what happened. And it's resolved now. I promise not to mention it again."

Morio rolled his eyes. "If it's all the same to you, I'd rather forget all about that. I like Menolly, but you're right— it wasn't my fault, or hers. And she took care of the issue before anything happened."

"Right," I said, frowning. I didn't like jealousy in myself. It wasn't becoming, and it didn't feel right. Mostly, it was Mother's blood that brought it out in me, but I preferred to mute it when I could. Jealousy had caused too many heartaches over the years, and I knew Morio loved me.

After a moment, I gave him a please-forgive-me smile. "Back to what we were talking about . . . so, before I take a shower, dish, babe. And don't leave out any details you're allowed to tell me."

Morio let out a long breath and then leaned back, resting on his elbows. "Okay. Here goes." He leaned his head back and stared at the ceiling. "There is a reason you have to be paired with a priest—and no, they didn't tell me why, so don't ask. But whatever the case, you need to be paired up. And since you are already married, to three men, and one of them—namely me—happens to work death magic with you, it would be an . . . inconvenience . . . to match you with another man." He looked up, and I could see the dark shine to his eyes. His demonic form was close to the surface and I could practically smell the jealousy.

And then I knew. "*You* went to *them*. They didn't call you."

He considered the question, still gazing into my eyes. When I'd first met him, I'd thought Morio wasn't the jealous type, and to some extent I was right. As long as I was happy, he stood back and let me have my way. But he wasn't a pushover. He wasn't afraid of me, either.

Once we had gotten married, he'd changed. It was like he'd staked his claim, and during the Soul Symbiont ritual he had also bonded with Smoky, and then with Trillian. The three of them formed a protective triangle around me, in silent agreement—or maybe they'd actually talked it out—to keep me as safe as they could, given the circumstances. I was their wife, and they were my protectors and consorts.

"They did call me. But it was to ask my opinion on the subject. I told them that while we support you entirely, I also understand how deep magic can create a bond between a man and a woman. And that while I might understand, I wouldn't be happy about it. And Smoky? He would never accept the possibility that you might have to be intimate with another man in the name of the gods."

Morio cleared his throat as a slow smile washed across my face. I rested my chin on my knees. "So you volunteered." But I didn't need an answer. His expression said it all. "You did, didn't you?"

After a moment, he gave me a slight nod. "Yes, I did. Because babe, I'm going to tell you something and I want you to listen. You are a priestess of the Moon Mother. You have certain obligations to fulfill. But you and I—our magical connection goes soul deep and we have a bond that I won't allow any other man to interfere with. This is our special place. You can't give up being who you are. I would never expect that. But I won't allow another man to interfere with our magic."

I wanted to smile. Now, I understood. He would share my body with Smoky and Trillian, but my magical side—it was his. Just like Trillian would share me, but I always acknowledged he was my alpha. And Smoky shared me as long as nobody else was brought into the mix.

A thought popped into my head, and I grimaced. "Not Bran. They weren't thinking of . . ."

Morio shook his head, grinning, and jumped off the bed. "Don't even go there, because it's not going to happen. All I can tell you is that I agreed to undergo initiation. While I'm not a priest of the Moon Mother, I am now a priest in Aeval's Court, and therefore able to officially stand as your consort in magic for the Triple Threat."

And that was that. If he said he couldn't tell me more, then he couldn't tell me more. I slid from beneath the covers, padding across the floor toward the bathroom door. Pausing, I glanced back.

"Thank you."

"For what, babe?" Morio was making the bed.

"For . . . being you. For caring. For sharing a part of me that no one else has ever shared. I'm going to go take a shower. I'll meet you downstairs." As I left the room, he was standing there, watching me, eyes glittering.

* * *

Once I was clean and dressed, I headed down the stairs. Menolly would be up soon, and I wanted to find out if Chase had discovered anything new. I also wanted to examine the talisman that Trillian and Smoky had brought back with them, because in twenty-four hours, give or take an hour, I'd be ferreting an undercover path into the Aleksais Psychic Network and I'd damned well better be able to bluff my way through. Plus, we still had to attend to the zombie panic that was spreading through the city.

I found everybody gathered in the living room. Another fifteen minutes until sunset, and Menolly would be up then. It seemed easiest to wait till she was awake to discuss what we were going to do.

Trillian, Smoky, and Bruce were examining the blueprints to Iris and Bruce's house, going over their plans for the next day. Nerissa and Rozurial were folding laundry with Hanna, and Vanzir was looking up something on the computer. Shamas was apparently still at work. Delilah played with Maggie, and Iris was in the kitchen.

Smelling cookies in the air, I wandered in to give her a hand. "Hey, Little Mama. How are you doing?"

Iris was about to take two pans of cookies out of the oven, and I took the oven mitt from her and shooed her away from the stove. She was almost four months pregnant by now. As she backed away, I did a double take. Her boobs were definitely starting to grow.

She noticed my look and grinned. "Yes, Bruce is a very happy leprechaun. But I'm going to need new bras very soon. Twins seem to speed up the . . . enhancement." As she dropped into the rocking chair with a grateful sigh and put her feet up, I also noticed the dark circles under her eyes.

I took the cookies out of the oven and set them on the hot pads, then used the spatula to loosen them and place them on the racks. Peanut butter chocolate chip. Delilah was going to be overjoyed.

"You aren't sleeping, are you? How's the morning sickness?"

"The morning sickness has died down a little, but I get tired a lot easier now. I take more naps. And no, I'm not sleeping all that great." She stared at her hands. "I can't seem to sleep deep, or stay asleep."

"What seems to be the problem? Does Bruce snore?"

"No, he doesn't snore." She paused, then laughed. "At least, not much. No, I think . . ."

"What is it?" I could tell she didn't want to talk about it, but I had the feeling that it was important. "Tell me, or I'll tell Menolly you're hiding something." I didn't like using blackmail, but I sure as hell wasn't above it when necessary.

Iris sat forward and stopped rocking. "You wouldn't dare."

I leaned down and planted a kiss on her cheek. "Try me."

She grumbled, and then with an irritated shrug she leaned back again. "Okay, but don't you make a big deal about this."

"Just tell me what's going on. The more you dance around this, the more I'm going to worry. And I do *not* need to worry any more than I already do." I knelt by her side. "Tell me."

"If I do, you have to promise me—"

"No promises. *Tell me*."

"Oh, all right. I can't sleep because of the damned trailer. It's the most uncomfortable piece of crap I've ever lived in. It reminds me of a big tin can." To my horror, she burst into tears, and I recognized them as hormone-enhanced.

"I hate it—I hear every noise at night and it keeps me awake. Now that I'm pregnant, it seems like I can't control anything happening to my body. I can't wait till my house is built, but to be honest, I miss living with the rest of you! I feel like I've been exiled, and I know I did it to myself."

As her expression crumbled, I gathered her in my arms and let her cry against my shoulder. "Oh honey, oh, Iris. I'm so sorry. If you want, we can make up the parlor for you now that Douglas and Marion moved out."

Iris sniffed, then sat back, a sad smile on her face. "You are so sweet, but no. We've got a perfectly usable trailer and we've paid for the rental already."

I shook my head. "The month is almost over. Move back in here. It will only be another month until the house is ready. Sure, we're crowded, but aren't we always? No problem with that! Bruce is rich, he's not going to care about one month's trailer rental—"

The kitchen bookshelf opened, along with the steel door behind it as Menolly appeared. She grinned. "Before you even try to cover your tracks, Iris, I overheard what you two were talking about. Camille is right. You and Bruce will sleep in the parlor until your house is done. The trailer can go back tomorrow. No arguments or I'll get pissed and you really don't want me pissed at you."

Iris blushed, then ducked her head. "If you're sure it won't be too much trouble . . ."

"Go tell Bruce right now, so the guys can bring in some of your clothes for the night." Menolly waved her off and, smiling, our house sprite took off for the living room. After Iris was gone, she laughed. "Hormones. Gotta love them. That's one thing I'll never have to worry about." But her voice was wistful.

I stared at her. "You want children?" My biological clock had never gone off, though I'd half-promised to think about kids with the guys, if Smoky could find a way around the fact that we were from different species. But if I had a child with him, I'd have to have one with Trillian first, because he was my alpha. If we ever did end up parents, I had the sinking feeling I'd be the mother of three. And I really wasn't keen on the idea. At least not right now. But we had a long, long time to decide, and I wasn't about to let anybody rush me into it.

Menolly shrugged. "I don't know. I guess . . . I wish I had the chance to make a choice. But Dredge killed any options I might have."

"Nerissa can have a baby. You guys could still parent." I began putting fresh dough on the cookie sheets and slid them into the oven. Menolly picked up the tray of warm cookies and followed me out of the kitchen.

"Well, that's an idea. Maybe . . ." she said, dropping the subject as we reached the living room.

Hanna was following Iris and Bruce toward the kitchen. "I will help them bring in their clothes and make up the sofa

bed." She smiled knowingly at me, and I realized she'd suspected Iris's unhappiness. "Maggie will need her cream
drink in twenty minutes."

"We'll take care of it." I glanced over at the corner of the
living room, where Maggie was playing with Misty. Both of
them missed Snickers—Marion's cat—and I had a feeling
Delilah did, too. Maggie trailed a string around, and Misty
was chasing it, both of them in heaven.

We settled in, me in the rocking chair, curled up on
Smoky's lap, and Menolly in her usual place, hovering near
the ceiling. Nerissa was carrying the baskets of laundry off
to each room.

"Okay, I guess it's general meeting time. We have several
things to go over—infiltrating the Aleksais Psychic Network,
trying to figure out how to find out whether Gulakah sneaked
in any more spirit demon eggs, dealing with the zombie scare
that is gripping Seattle. Oh, Menolly—you haven't heard yet.
You may have to calm Roman and Blood Wyne."

At her look, I launched into a quick recap of what had
happened, while Roz handed her the paper. She glanced at
the story and rolled her eyes.

"So now, the vampires are responsible for zombie upris-
ings? How stupid can these people be?" She let go of the
paper and it came fluttering down to the floor, where Maggie, distracted from Misty, grabbed for it.

Roz managed to snag it out of her reach, and she started
to cry. Delilah picked her up and walked her back and forth,
soothing the bereft baby.

"They aren't stupid. In fact, Earthborn Brethren are smart.
Pin the blame on the vampires and they've got a new little
hate war going—one that's easier to fan the flames on, when
people start dying. Most of the citizens of Seattle had no clue
zombies actually existed. Now they know, but they have no
idea of how they're made or born or whatever—for all they
know, some demented stork might have dug them out of the
grave."

Morio snorted. "Zombie stork."

"Right . . . I wouldn't put it past them to come up with that one. Anyway, the story that vampires raise them? It's as plausible as any, given the general level of knowledge about how magic works, at least among the basic populace."

I took a deep breath. "We can't blame them for being afraid. It's like . . . well . . . George A. Romero's worlds come to life. *Night of the Living Dead* is imprinted on people's memories. And the *Walking Dead*. And . . . hell, even *Zombie Strippers*."

Menolly lowered herself to the floor. "Yeah, yeah, I know all that shit, but fuck, it just infuriates me that the freakshow minority has to stir things up every chance they get. They'll use anything—including the lives of the innocent who are killed—to prove their point. Or at least, to try to prove it."

"Remember, they think of *us* as the freakshow minority. But they have no compassion." I sighed, leaning forward to rest my chin on my hands. "We need to put a stop to them before they gain a foothold in society."

"So what do we do?" Trillian looked over at me.

I didn't want to go out again. I just wanted an evening at home, doing nothing but eating cookies and playing a game or watching a movie. However, movies didn't solve the problem; they just offered a temporary escape.

"I want to discuss how to use that talisman, but first, we should head over to the Shrouded Grove Suites. The protesters are currently there." I pushed myself to my feet. "We don't all have to go. I will. Who else is up for some picketline busting?"

Menolly raised her hand. "Count me in."

Trillian shook his head. "I'll come along. I usually stay home, but tonight, I feel like getting out. Even if it is to bash some sense into a few people's heads." He headed to the hall closet and pulled out his long leather duster.

Smoky nodded. "I will come, too. Shade, you stay home for a change."

We ended up leaving Shade, Vanzir, and Delilah home to watch over the house, while Morio, Trillian, Smoky, Menolly, Rozurial, and I headed for the cars. We had no clue what we'd be facing, so it seemed better to bring a larger group than just a couple of us.

Menolly climbed into her Jag, and Roz rode with her, while my men rode with me. As we pulled out of the driveway, the sky was overcast and it started to pour rain. Once again, we headed out into the night.

Morio put in a call to Chase when we were on the way, to let him know of our plans. When he hung up, I could see in the rearview mirror that his expression was strained.

"Chase said things are getting worse. They've found another egg, though not nearly as big as the one this morning, so we have a little time before it hatches. There are more zombies incoming . . . feeding it like they did the one this morning. I guess we should swing by there after we disrupt the protesters."

Glad I'd had a couple of naps during the day, all I could do was nod. The last thing I wanted to do was encounter another batch of spirit demons. Even though I didn't want to involve them, I glanced at Morio through the mirror again.

"Call Delilah. Have her get in touch with Frank Willows and tell him to start up the phone trees, but also make sure they know *not* to arrive until we get there and scope out the situation. She'd better come, too, given we'll be dealing with the Supe Community werewolves again. I guess . . . call Menolly and tell her to double back and pick her up? We're not that far out from the house yet."

As Morio set to calling, I steeled myself for another rough battle, keeping my eyes on the road as we sped through the rain-soaked night.

Chapter 14

Built by investors who'd seen the profit margin above the fear, the Shrouded Grove Suites apartment tower was in a posh part of the city. With landlords who were Fae taking the day shift, and vampires for the night shift, the building was vampire-specific. The development had been a stroke of genius, and both towers were filled to capacity, with a long waiting list. We had heard there were more in process.

Each apartment offered at least two windowless rooms, and throughout the rest of the apartment, shuttered windows kept out both UV rays and the sunlight in general. The rooms were tiled, for easy cleanup, and had security locks on the bedroom doors.

Wade Stevens lived here, and so did a number of prominent vampires who didn't want to go to the trouble of keeping guards posted. Vamps who weren't publicly known could afford to go without guards, but there were too many hate groups to trust to fate if a vampire had any sort of notoriety.

We pulled into the parking lot, somewhere near the

middle. I wanted to get a scope on things before we went marching up there. We could see the picket line from here. It was long, too long for comfort.

A few minutes later, Menolly pulled up alongside my Lexus, with Rozurial and Delilah in the Jag with her.

Grimacing at the steady rain, I shrugged into a light jacket. It was chilly, and I didn't want my bustier getting ruined. It was jacquard and I'd have changed if I'd thought we were going to be doing more than talking to these bozos, but once we were on the road and had talked to Chase about the second egg, I really didn't want to take the time to go back to the house to change clothes. I needed to start keeping a set of fighting clothes in the car. The very thought of that depressed me.

"What's the game plan?" Menolly shaded her eyes to stare at the crowd. "They don't look so tough from here."

"They may not be tough, but we can't just go in and rough them up, either. I don't think that would play too well with the crowd. Besides, given the headlines, I have the sick feeling that the *Seattle Tattler* may start up again under new management. Don't ask me why, I just do."

"That would figure." Trillian sighed. "What say we mosey on up, tell them they need to dial it back, and if they protest, we threaten them with a lawsuit for harassment? Isn't that a hate crime, if it's directed toward a specific minority?"

"Yeah, but free speech isn't a crime. Let's see what we're dealing with before we do anything." As usual, I had the feeling we were probably walking into more trouble than we actually were prepared for, but then—why spoil our batting record?

Menolly snorted. "Free speech isn't a crime, but what they're inciting is. Look at those fucking signs." By then we were close enough to see them under the streetlights along the condo tower.

While not located in the best part of the city, the Shrouded Grove Suites tower was well placed and had been constructed to keep out an army. In addition to the internal amenities, reinforced steel surrounded most of the apartments, hidden beneath the concrete and drywall, and although not visible to the public, steel gates were prepared to slam down if anybody tried to storm the front door.

The building was fireproofed, with all outside vents and exits guarded by security monitors. All workers who came in or out of the building had to be vetted with background checks, and most were Supes of one kind or another. Anybody with even remote affiliations to the anti-Supe hate groups was automatically weeded out. Silver and garlic were forbidden.

Each twenty stories tall, the twin apartment buildings were aesthetically soothing to the eye, dark and mysterious, but they lent an upscale air to the surrounding neighborhood, and since they'd opened up, real estate prices in the surrounding blocks had skyrocketed. People loved vampires as much as they feared them. Only now—if the Earthborn Brethren had their way—that would rapidly change. It occurred to me that the Seattle chamber of commerce, as well as all the local real estate agents, had a vested interest in keeping the peace.

Menolly and I took the lead, with Delilah and Roz behind us, and Smoky, Trillian, and Morio brought up the rear. As we headed through the parking lot, the protesters saw us coming. Immediately, they closed ranks and formed a line. What was this? Human-shield day?

I decided to take the lead, since Menolly would just antagonize them. As I glanced over the group, I realized I didn't recognize anybody. By now, we knew some of the locals who were big in the wacko groups, but nobody here looked familiar. Maybe we had a new crew to deal with, or maybe those who'd been Andy Gambit's supporters didn't want to hurt the "cause" by appearing up front.

Although that thought might be giving them too much credit. They weren't the brightest bulbs in the sockets.

As we approached them, one of the bigger lugs pushed his way through to the front. He looked like a quarterback with a buzz cut, and he was wearing jeans and a suit jacket over a button-down shirt. The sign in his meaty hands read, "Stake the Bloodsuckers!" He looked us over, stopping when he came to Menolly.

"Your kind aren't welcome here." His voice was raspy, and he smelled like stale cigarette butts.

Uh-oh, this wasn't going to be pretty.

Menolly's eyes narrowed. "I think you're mistaken. My *kind* are welcome here—these towers are built for vampires. You're the intruders."

"You're unclean. You're an agent for the devil—"

Menolly snarled and her fangs came down. "I advise you people to back off. *Now.* Or you're going to *wish* I were an agent for the devil."

I pushed in front of her and stared up at him. He towered over both of us. "Dude, you need to move on." I glanced at the signs. They were vicious, inciting violence. Some claimed the vamps had reanimated the zombies. "I could so easily call the cops and say you're instigating hate crimes."

"I'd be back on the street in an hour." He sneered at me. "You're not a vamp, but you aren't one of the earthborn."

"Big fucking deal. Apparently, being one of the earthborn doesn't guarantee intelligence, if we use you as an example." Apparently, my diplomatic skills weren't as up to par as I thought they were. I held my breath, then slowly let it out, trying to calm down.

Buzzcut, though, wasn't having as much luck with self-control as I was. "Listen, bitch . . . we have a right to voice our opinion."

"Your opinion is bullshit. It's . . ." And then I stopped. Maybe Trillian was right. "Menolly, call Roman and ask him to get his lawyer down here. These signs are libeling the Vampire Nation by claiming you're responsible for the zombie uprising. We know this isn't the truth, we know it's not even *possible*. Therefore, I suggest we slap a multimillion-dollar lawsuit for libel on the Fellowship of the Earthborn Brethren right now and ask for a restraining order to prevent them from picketing here. We could probably bankrupt them."

At this point, Buzzcut was starting to look a little nervous. Menolly snapped out her cell phone and punched a speed-dial number. "Roman? I need you and your lawyer down here at the Shrouded Grove Suites immediately."

My hearing was keen enough to hear the recorded message playing on the other end, but no FBH would be able to pick it up.

"Wait—wait!" Buzzcut glanced at his fellow picketers nervously. "Can't we deal with this peacefully?"

I stifled a snort. "Yes, we can. By you and your happy little troublemakers removing yourself from the premises and by the cessation of any libel or slander against the vampires. Do your research next time before you go targeting a target to hate. Better yet, get a life of your own and quit trying to ruin others' lives."

He glowered at me. After a moment, he motioned for the others to put down their signs. "Come on. We'll figure something else out." As they headed away from the building, I watched them.

I couldn't resist one last parting shot. "Oh, and by the way, if any hate crimes happen against any of the vampires or their allies, we know where to look. So you'd better be on good behavior!"

He shot me the finger, but I ignored it. We'd made our point, and they were walking away, deflated. We'd won the battle, albeit a small one, but hell, in this war, every victory counted.

As they headed off in their vans and trucks, I turned to the others. "What now? Do we go in, talk to Wade? Does Roman know about what happened?"

Menolly shrugged. "If he doesn't, then I'm sure he will soon enough. Roman has an intricate networking system set up throughout the entire region. Anything to do with vampires—in the news or in the gossip mill—he's going to know about. But he hasn't said anything to me yet."

I looked around. The security guards inside the building waved to us. We could either go up and see Wade or we could book and go check out the second egg. Wade was nice, but right now I had the feeling he wouldn't have anything to add to our investigation. And the sooner we dealt with egg number two, the better.

Making up my mind, I turned back to the cars. "We've

done what we set out to do. I doubt it will keep them away for too long, but it cleared them out for tonight. Let's go. Chase is waiting on us, and I'm pretty sure he's had a long, hard day. I don't want to keep him waiting longer than necessary."

"Okay, but I have a feeling this mess with the Earthborn Brethren isn't over with yet." Morio shook his head. "It feels unfinished."

"That's because hate is seldom ever conquered. It just goes underground. Or changes form." With a sigh, I turned back to the car, and the others followed.

As Delilah, Menolly, and I entered Chase's office, he was waiting for us, looking exhausted. His leg was propped up and he appeared uncomfortable.

He waved tiredly as we crowded into his office. "Hey, glad you made it. I'm just about stick-a-fork-in-me done. What news do you have for me, and it better not be bad? I'm not going to have to lock you three up, am I?"

"We sent the Earthborn Brethren packing away from the Shrouded Grove Suites via threat of a lawsuit for libel. But I doubt if it will be long before they're up to some new trouble." Menolly hopped up on a side table, her legs dangling over the edge.

Chase gave her a nervous look. "You didn't put the fang on them, did you?"

"Bite me." She stuck out her tongue at him. "No, I didn't even rough any of the suckers up, though I wanted to. Camille was nastier than I was."

"I couldn't help it," I said. "I'm blunt."

"Yeah, we know. We know. Well, good." Chase glanced around. "Where are the others?"

"Waiting for us out in the cars. They can come in if you need them, too, but it's late and we figured we'd just get the info on where the other egg is and go check it out." Delilah stopped. "You look exhausted."

"I am." He paused, toying with a pen on his desk. Finally, he met Delilah's eyes. "I've asked Sharah to move in with me and . . . she accepted." A smile broke through his weariness, and he practically beamed his joy.

I caught my breath, waiting. I knew that my sister was in love with Shade, and they were engaged. But she and Chase did have a history, and this was a big step for him.

Delilah paused, and an indecipherable look crossed her face. Then, she broke out in a big smile and clapped her hands. "That's wonderful! Congratulations. It will be easier that way when the baby comes."

Chase nodded, looking pleased. He was blushing, but his happiness was palpable. "Yes, it will. Sharah and I had a long talk over lunch. I told her . . . I finally got it through her head that I want to be there for her. For the baby. That it's the most important thing in the world to me to be a good father. And a good match for her. We're finding a new apartment together. Or maybe a house with a yard, so the baby can have a place to play."

His voice was soft as he picked up a framed photo on his desk. He turned it around to show me. It was of Chase and Sharah, his arms wrapped around her, and they were both smiling. Her pale blond hair was blowing in the wind and she had a free, easy look on her face that I'd never seen before. Chase was relaxed, leaning into her, and there was something comfortable about their stance. They fit together.

I took the photo, holding it for a moment. Suddenly, I wanted very much for them to be happy, to have their baby and a whole houseful of other kids, and bring them up in a peaceful world where the demons were a distant memory.

As I handed it back to him, I touched his fingers, hoping to convey something of my feelings. He glanced up at me, then ducked his head, a shy smile creeping over his face. Delilah peeked over his shoulder at it, then gave him a hug.

"You and Sharah should come out to dinner with Shade and me. I think . . . I think it would be a good thing for all four of us. Maybe when this ghost crap has calmed down again?"

He snickered. "How about when I'm in a walking cast

and not so dependent on these damned crutches? And, Delilah? I'd like that."

I yawned. "Okay, let's get on with it, as nice as it is to talk about something other than death, demons, or dismemberment. So, we have another egg to deal with?"

Back to business, he leaned his elbows on his desk and nodded. "Unfortunately so. And who knows how many others might be out there? This one, Shamas and another officer found this afternoon. Not as big, doesn't look ready to hatch, Shamas said. But eventually, you know it's going to. And then we'll have another round of spirit demons on hand."

"Not if we can destroy it first."

"What happens if we crack it open before it's ready?" Delilah picked up an apple off the bowl of fruit sitting on Chase's desk. She stared at it a moment, then put it down. "Cookies?"

Chase snorted. "No cookies. Eat the apple. Sharah's taken me off most sugar. And she's made me cut out almost all junk food except for my tacos—which I might add, she can't stand. But she gives in on those, and I give in on the rest. I've lost a few pounds and I actually feel better." He pointed to his foot. "Except for that."

Menolly frowned. "I want to go check this thing out. I missed all the action today and I should know what they look like, if nothing else."

"*You* can't even attack the spirit demons. It takes silver to hurt them and you can't even touch silver." Delilah tossed the apple into the air, caught it, and then polished it on her shirt before biting into it.

I thought over her question. What would happen if we cracked it open before it was ready to hatch? Would a bunch of immature spirit demons come pouring out? Apparently, they needed to be fed before they grew enough to break out of the shell.

"You said there are zombies there already?"

He nodded. "Well, skeletons, actually."

"They'll probably do just as well as zombies because

they're animated and contain magic. Which means some-body's feeding it. We better get over there. Menolly, you can attack the bone-walkers and keep them from feeding it while we go after the egg. If they have a human shield there again, we have to keep any more of the Aleksais Psychic Network members from becoming demon chow."

I pushed to my feet, not really wanting to head back out into the blustery night. But there was an egg out there, and we had to take it apart. "Give us the address. Then you go home and rest. We may need you later."

Chase handed me a piece of paper. "You might want to call in the Supe Community Militia again."

"We've got them on standby. One phone call and they head out to meet us." Delilah headed to the door, with Menolly following.

I lingered behind for a moment, waiting till they were out on the main floor. "Chase . . ." I wasn't sure what I wanted to say, but I knew I had to say something. So much had hap-pened since we'd first met.

"Yeah?" He wearily moved his foot onto the floor, hold-ing his leg by the knee so the splint didn't come down too hard.

I stopped by the side of his desk, leaning on the edge. "A lot's happened since you brought me that rope that Bad Ass Luke used to garrote Jocko. I remember that day, you were trying to look up my dress."

He snorted. "Yeah, I was. I admit it." He held on to his crutches, staring at them. "I remember the first day I met the three of you. I couldn't believe how full of life you were. Delilah made me nervous, and Menolly scared the crap out of me. But . . . I couldn't take my eyes off you. I was totally caught up in fantasies of how I would seduce you and then . . . and then . . . well, back then, I didn't have an 'after the act' in mind."

Laughing, I shrugged. "I've been there. Hell, I didn't expect to end up married."

"To three men, no less?" He winked at me.

"Oh, I could see myself with three men. But *married*?

That was something I didn't plan on." I paused, trying to find the words for what I wanted to say. "Chase . . . you've grown. So much has happened to you—to all of us. I just want you to know that whatever happens . . . with the demons, with anything . . . we're here for you. Sharah, too. We've got your back. Whatever you need, you're part of our family, and so is *your* family. Because, unexpected or not, with a baby on the way and Sharah moving in, that's what you have now."

He caught my hand as I stood. "Thanks, Camille. We've been through hell and I have a feeling it's only going to continue. I have no clue what the future holds, except that— barring a deadly accident—it holds a lot of long years for me. But I know that *right now*, in the present, I'm damned glad we're all in this together."

"Just think. You're going to be a *father*, Chase." I smiled at him.

"Wow. Yeah," he said, a look of wonder on his face. And with that, he let go of my fingers, and I patted his cheek and followed my sisters out the door.

The rain hadn't let up. In fact, it was worse. The night was relatively warm, though, and at least we weren't going to be fighting in the freezing cold. We'd long ago resigned ourselves to getting soaked while working, and now I made sure everything I bought—bustiers to skirts to boots—could take a little rain, if not a deluge.

"So, the egg's in another cemetery?" Smoky asked.

I nodded, my eyes firmly on the road. "Yeah, but it's an old one; there hasn't been anybody planted there for years. It's tucked back behind an abandoned church. And guess where it's located?"

Morio groaned. "The Greenbelt Park District?"

"Bingo. That place has a lot of cemeteries, which is creepy. Although technically, most of them are on the outskirts. This one? Smack in the center." I zigzagged through the streets, skirting the cars parked along the narrow street.

Abby and Fritz's house had been on a relatively spacious

street, but we were now in the older part of the district. Here, the houses were falling apart, with few of them occupied. The yards and trees were so overgrown that it was difficult to make out the paths leading to the doors. Few lights shined through the night, and what few did were shrouded behind blinds and ratty-looking curtains.

We silently glided through the maze of streets until we came to a turnoff onto a side street filled with potholes. It was barely wide enough for one car at a time. We bumped along, with me struggling to see the road in the rain, under the streetlights that were spaced few and far between.

Eventually, to the left, I saw the broken gates to an overgrown cemetery. The sign had long ago disappeared, but I knew it was the right one—it was exactly where Chase had told us it would be.

I pulled through the arches, cautiously entering the parking circle. As I slowed, then turned off the engine, Menolly's Jag pulled in behind me. I glanced at the guys.

"Time to get this show moving." With a sigh, I opened my door. Morio grabbed the bag of gear from the backseat and we all climbed out.

Menolly and Delilah wandered over to me, as we squinted, trying to figure out where we were. Chase had told us that the egg could be found about a block down the main path, but which was the main one? There were paths going in five different directions.

Menolly stood back. "Hold on." She closed her eyes, slightly unsteady on her feet, and the next thing we knew, she'd turned into a bat.

I blinked. Ever since Roman had re-sired her, she'd made remarkable leaps in some of the old-school vamp stuff that seemed to be the domain of mostly the elder vampires. Of course, with Roman's blood in her now, along with Dredge's, Menolly was turning into one scary-assed dead girl.

She swooped off into the night and we waited, sorting out our weapons. We'd brought enough silver to arm a small militia, just in case we had to call in the Supes again, although most of them would have their own gear.

After a few minutes, Menolly came sweeping back, landing gracefully to transform back into her natural form. She reached out, steadying herself on Roz's arm, then cleared her throat.

"It's getting easier, but damn, the landings still get me." With a toothy grin, she shrugged. "I'll master it in time. Meanwhile, the egg is down the middle path. From up above, even in the dark, it shows as being wider than the rest. It's hard to tell down here on the ground, though, especially since *all* the paths are overgrown."

"Then I guess we head in. Delilah, you have Frank on speed dial?"

She nodded. "All I need is five seconds. The minute he gets my text with the address, he'll start the phone tree—and everybody on the other end is waiting for the call."

There was no more procrastinating. "Let's get a move on, then." And with that, I took the lead and, with Smoky by my side, headed down the middle sidewalk, hoping like hell this was going to be easier than this morning.

The egg was no more than five minutes' walk away, around a curve in the sidewalk behind a clump of overgrown rowan trees—also known as mountain ash in the area. The branches were covered with ghostly white berries that would turn red in a few months, and bright orange by late summer. For now, though, they were just ghosts of color against the rain-soaked sky.

Tombstones littered the field, and I do mean littered. They were scattered haphazardly, as if they'd been tumbled every which way. Some were rubble, long ago fallen into heaps of broken rock; others looked weatherworn and were covered with moss.

Mounds of earth showed that the inhabitants of the graves had dug their way up, through rotting caskets and dirt, to the surface. The grass was knee high, making it difficult to see if there were any twigs or rocks in our way.

The egg stood in the center of the boneyard, looking very

much the same as the one this morning, though a lot smaller, with a group of bone-walkers clustered around it. That alone told me the age of the graveyard—the flesh had long ago rotted away, leaving only the skeletons of whoever had been buried here.

One at a time, they walked forward, vanishing into the egg, sucked in and sucked dry. A sickening thud hit my stomach.

"We have no way of knowing what's going to happen when we crack open that egg." I stared at it, almost afraid to try. But if we didn't stop it now, the carnage would be worse later. At least I didn't see any of the Fae or FBH witches hanging around. Maybe Gulakah didn't realize we'd found this one, or maybe their energy wasn't useful until the egg was almost ready to hatch. Whatever the case, the fact that they weren't around meant one less worry for us.

"We need to stop the bone-walkers. Menolly, can you and Roz and Delilah go after them? Smoky, Morio, Trillian, and I will take on the egg." I wasn't sure just exactly how we were going to do that, but lack of a plan had never stopped us before.

Menolly nodded, and the three of them moved toward the bone-walkers. As we watched, they began trying to herd the shuffling creatures away from the egg. The skeletons, which had paid no attention to our presence before then, suddenly seemed to notice that yes, there were obstacles in their path. Rather than fight back to harm, they fought to get past my sisters and Roz. Which meant they were just as dangerous as any unbewitched bone-walker.

Meanwhile, my men and I headed over to the egg. We walked around it, staring at it. Smoky reached out to touch it, but I yelled at him, startling him enough for him to step away.

"Don't touch the shell—that's how it sucks you in, and I don't know if a dragon can resist the pull." I was pretty sure that Smoky would be okay but didn't want to find out. After all, we *were* dealing with demons.

"Well, there's no other way to do this." Smoky pulled out his silver sword.

"Was that your grandfather's?" I asked, as we waded into the fray.

He smiled. "You presume correctly, my love. This belonged to my mother's father. Remind me when we have more time and I'll tell you the story of how I came to possess this, and what my grandfather used it for."

And with that, he swung it against the egg. The silver of the blade contacted the egg, and a shrill reverberation echoed through the rain. I winced, wanting to cover my ears, but it was too dangerous to set down my blade to do so. I sucked in a deep breath and waited for any sign that the spirit demons were going to come racing out of the shell.

The egg pulsated—that's the only way to describe it—and then shuddered. The shell shifted, reminding me of a pregnant woman's belly when her baby was pressing against it. Or rather, more like Kane's chest in *Alien*, when the alien was writhing beneath the skin, ready to burst out into the room. Only with the egg, there were dozens of baby aliens beneath the shell, moving and twisting against the outer membrane.

My stomach lurched. Watching the movement and shifting shadows against the silvery surface of the orb made me queasy.

Smoky took another whack at the egg, and Morio and Trillian joined in. Again, the violent movement, and again the high-pitched shriek. I started to back away, a sick feeling rushing over me.

Meanwhile, Delilah, Menolly, and Rozurial were engaging the skeletons in an easier-than-usual battle, since their main goal was to get to the egg and feed it. In fact, the two shrieks seemed to have spurred the bone-walkers on, and they were frantically trying to fight their way past.

It was making for easy pickings. Menolly swung in from behind, and as long as she was carving them up as they ambled forward, and didn't try to stop them from moving, the bone-walkers ignored her. Delilah and Roz saw what she was doing and adopted the same strategy.

I turned back to the egg. Fractures were beginning to show in the skin. Raising my dagger, I waited. Smoky landed a tremendous blow to the top of the orb—this one was only about six feet compared to the ten-foot diameter of the one we'd fought earlier—and one last shriek rang through the air as the egg shattered. Shifting shadows began rushing out, but they were malformed—looking like blobs compared to their fully gestated brethren we'd already killed.

The spirit demons swarmed over us, feelers wriggling out of the holes where their hearts should have been, but this time, the teeth weren't fully formed. One managed to land a hit on me, but instead of latching on, it scraped against my skin. A jolt startled me, but the demon couldn't gain full purchase and I managed to skewer it with my blade before it could try again.

We fought. There were probably about thirty in this egg, and this time we managed to wade our way through without calling for outside help. After a few minutes, Roz and Delilah joined us, leaving the rest of the skeletons to Menolly. Now, with the egg broken open, they were attempting to get to the demons themselves.

One of the spirit demons managed to land on one of the bone-walkers, and it struggled, finally making contact. The bones began to crumble as the demon drained the magical energy from it, and then the shattered remains fell to the ground, once again a mere framework of what had once been a living person. The demon looked stronger, but it still looked malformed.

As it came toward me, Roz swung in from behind and landed a firm blow to it with a long silver spike. The spirit demon turned on him. I raced forward and plunged my dagger into its back, and this time it vanished with a silent hiss.

The stillness of the creatures still bothered me. Other than their egg shrieking, they made no noise, fighting in an eerie silence, never screaming when hit, making absolutely no noise.

I ducked another attack, wading through a snarl of weeds in order to parry again. Once more, I brought down one of the shadows. I was getting pretty damned good with the dagger. As yet another spirit demon moved in, I moved to attack, but the toe of my boot caught on a rock that was hidden by the patch of dandelions and tall field grass and whatever else was tangled in the mire of undergrowth.

Losing my balance, I fell forward, landing hard on my knee. With a groan, I rolled over onto my back, just in time to see the shadow of the spirit demon come barreling for me. I dodged to the side, rolling to the right, quickly enough to avoid the feelers seeking to latch hold of me. As it came in again, I turned to the left and this time it managed to clip my arm, but again, it was too immature to do anything but graze my skin.

And then Smoky was standing there, his sword thrusting through the demon, and it vanished in the night. He leaned down and took my hand, lifting me to my feet.

I looked around. Nothing in sight. No bone-walkers, no spirit demons.

"You're kidding. Did we get them all?"

"I believe so," Smoky said. He draped his arm around my shoulders. "Come on, sweetheart. Let's go home."

As Delilah called Yugi to ask him to send out a team in order to clean up the remains of the egg and the scattered bones, we set off for the car. I was tired, and irritated. Enough was enough.

Tomorrow night, I was headed into the Aleksais Psychic Network, and I wasn't coming out until I had Gulakah's head on a stick.

Chapter 15

On the way home, we stopped to pick up some chicken. All I could think about was grabbing a bucket of KFC and diving into it as soon as we got home. It was late, but there was still one open near the Belles-Faire district.

I leaned out the window and shouted into the intercom. "We want four twelve-piece meals."

A silence, then, "Did you say *four* twelve-piece meals?"

"Yes, extra crispy, with mashed potatoes and coleslaw for sides on all of them."

Another pause, and then he gave me my total and I pulled up to the window, handed him two fifties that Smoky handed me, and passed the chicken into the backseat with Morio.

By the time we got home, I'd managed to shake off the lingering creeps that the bone-walkers and the spirit demons gave me. We hauled our treasure trove of chicken into the house. The kitchen smelled like lemon, and Iris and Bruce were busy putting the finishing touches on the swoops of meringue covering several lemon pies.

The guys set the chicken buckets and sides on the table as I peeked into the parlor. Nerissa was there, helping Hanna as they finished making the bed for Iris and Bruce. Everything looked cozy.

"You're home safe!" Nerissa asked. "Is Menolly with you, or did my wife head down to the bar?" The blond bombshell who had married my sister was the most annoyingly happy newlywed I'd ever seen. And Menolly had become more cheerful than I ever expected her to be.

Menolly squeezed past me and threw herself into Nerissa's arms, planting a huge kiss on her. Nerissa breathed in a contented sigh, and when she looked over at me, the glow in her eyes was almost blinding.

"Come on, dinner's on the table and we need to talk over plans." I motioned for them to follow me back into the kitchen.

As we entered the kitchen, I saw that everything had been laid out, along with plates and forks and knives.

Nerissa leaned over to sniff one of the buckets of chicken. She clapped her hands and licked her lips. "Chicken! So," she added, looking up at me, "was it rough out there tonight?"

"Well, it wasn't a picnic. It was easier than this morning, but it was still a mess. Bone-walkers everywhere, yanked out of their graves. My only hope is that the cemetery was so old that whatever raised them wasn't able to find any spirits around the graveyard to suck up through their astral straw. And now, I'm wondering if the ghosts who were . . . well . . . ghostnapped . . . weren't used in the ritual to gate the eggs over here."

Shade returned from the bathroom off the utility room. He sat at the table and motioned for Delilah to sit next to him. "It is possible—the amount of psychic energy it took to bring those eggs over here had to be tremendous. While Gulakah's perfectly capable of gating them over from the Netherworld, it might make it easier on him if he uses the extra energy from harvesting ghosts."

Trillian was standing at the counter, filling a pitcher with lemonade. He motioned for me to join him, and when I did, he handed me a small pouch. I opened it and a silver medallion fell into my hand.

A round coin, the size of a quarter with a hole in it for feeding a cord through, it looked similar to the one I'd worn so many years back, but there were subtle differences. It was heavier, and stronger. I held it in one palm and closed my other hand over it, trying to read the energy signature, but—even though I was a seasoned witch—it was hard for me to detect the magic within the charm. And that was a very good thing. It meant it would be harder for others to sense that it was magical as well.

I held it up to the light. "You say this will last until I'm attacked?"

"Yes, it's stronger than the ones we had back when we were chasing Roche. This will last longer."

Menolly swiveled around from where she was carrying the pies over to the table. "*You* were chasing Roche? Are you saying you belonged to the OIA?"

Trillian stared at her for a moment, and then he looked at me. "Ask your sister."

"I guess the time's come to tell them," I said.

"Tell us what?" Menolly looked confused.

At first, we'd kept it quiet that Trillian had saved my ass. Lathe, my boss, was looking for any reason to get rid of me because I refused to give him a blowjob or sleep with him. He'd done everything he could to make my life miserable. I'd met Trillian, fallen hard for him, and he'd joined forces with me to bring in Roche, a serial killer I was hunting.

I'd wanted to tell my sisters, but Trillian told me to keep it a secret. He wanted them to like him for who he was, not because he'd helped save my career. I'd felt odd about it, but agreed, and shortly after, with Menolly getting turned into a vampire, the issue faded into the background and we never had gotten around to telling them what really happened.

I turned around. "Okay, you remember the case I was on? The one that scared the fuck out of me because Roche was a demented serial killer and Lathe wouldn't assign anybody to help me?"

They nodded. Smoky and Morio were staring at me now, too.

"That's when I met Trillian. And he . . . the truth is that without Trillian, Roche would have killed me—that is, if I could have tracked him down in the first place. Trillian not only helped me catch him, but he saved my life doing so. And then, he refused to let me tell anybody because he didn't want Lathe to use it against me."

Delilah and Menolly glanced at each other. Delilah started to blush. They'd treated Trillian like dirt when we were first together, and it had driven a wedge between the three of us for a while.

"Well, now I feel like a crap bucket," Menolly said. She set down the pies and walked over to Trillian, where she gave his ponytail a gentle yank. "We gave you a lot of shit and we're sorry. But you have to admit, you can be an asshole sometimes."

Trillian leaned back and folded his arms as he leaned back against the counter. "You and Delilah *did* give me a lot of shit. And of course I'm an arrogant ass, but *you* have to admit, I have the goods to back it up." He smiled, and then Menolly smiled, and everybody took a deep breath and started moving again.

Menolly flicked his nose. "Sit down, eat."

"We were pretty bad." Delilah started filling her plate. "But you know what? Water under the bridge. We're all one big happy family now."

"One big happy family?" I glanced around the room. Everybody was busy, the food was being passed around, Trillian went back to handing pitchers of lemonade over to the table, and even though the demons were outside the gate, I realized that Delilah was right. We were one big happy family.

I slid the talisman back into the pouch. "I'll put this on tomorrow afternoon to give myself a couple of hours to settle into my new looks. What are the specs on it? No dwarves this time, I hope."

Trillian snorted and took a chair beside me. Smoky was on the other side. "No dwarves. I promise. You'll look mostly human, though gorgeous as always. But you won't look like you."

Wondering what the charm would do, I reached for a chicken thigh and then piled mashed potatoes and gravy on my plate. Besides the coleslaw and biscuits, Iris had added a platter of carrot sticks, cucumber slices, and cherry tomatoes to the table, and soon we were all busy eating, telling them about our day. And for once, the rest of the evening proved to be just as calm, and we took full advantage of the downtime.

Shortly before bed, I closed myself into my study, where the Whispering Mirror was. It had been a long time since I'd had any time to myself and, with the upcoming foray into the Aleksais Psychic Network, I wanted to meditate.

My study had evolved over the past couple of years. When we first moved here, I'd furnished it with a desk, the table that held the Whispering Mirror, a couple of chairs, and a bunch of shelves and drawers to hold spell components. I also had a small table where I could blend oils or brew potions.

Now the desk had been replaced with a huge wonder in solid oak, thanks to Smoky, who had decided the room needed an overhaul. He'd also come up with matching bookshelves; a credenza in place of the particleboard dressers; an apothecary case with a hundred little drawers, perfect for holding bits of herbs and bones; and a matching table to replace the cheap one originally holding the Whispering Mirror. A polished wooden rocking chair, a burgundy velvet love seat, and a Tiffany-style lamp in either corner completed the look, and now my study truly looked like a study.

I ran my hands along the spines of the books on the shelf. Some were in English—Earthside books. Alongside them were a few from Otherworld, hand-bound volumes I'd studied from over the years when I was first accepted into the Coterie of the Moon Mother. The books had been so big I could barely carry them when I was little. I'd finally resorted to using the toy wagon my father had given me to drag them around.

I pulled one off the shelf and settled into the rocking chair. As I flipped through the pages, I came to one in particular that made me stop. There was a pressed rose between the pages—paper-thin now. It had been forty ES years since I'd held the flower to my nose and breathed in the scent. It had been back when I was just into womanhood—still the equivalent to a young teenager, if I'd been full-blooded human. I'd fallen in love for the first time. Only it hadn't been with a boy . . . no, it had been with the Moon Mother herself.

Leaning my head back against the slats of the rocker, I gently lifted the rose out of the book, then closed my eyes, remembering the night when I knew—absolutely knew—that I was in love with a goddess.

The night was warm, and I was sitting outside. I'd climbed up a ladder to the roof, where I could see the sky and the stars. Menolly and Delilah never understood the draw, and I was just as happy they decided to stay inside. Between taking care of the house, studying with the Coterie of the Moon Mother, and my studies to eventually enter the Y'Elestrial Intelligence Agency, I never had any time to myself. I leaned back on my elbows and stared up at the sky.

The moon was full tonight, and Menolly had promised to watch over Delilah, who had already turned into Tabby for the night. A light breeze wafted by, playing with my hair, and I inhaled deeply, lingering over the scents riding the wind.

The moon was full and shining, a silver orb hanging in the sky. As I watched her, silent and in awe, a rush of love welled up in my heart. I'd always envied Derisa, the High Priestess, as she led the weekly rites, but tonight . . . tonight I knew she would be running with the Moon Mother as the

Hunt raced through the sky. And I wanted to be there, wanted to taste that freedom.

I was due, in a couple of years, to face the test, to be either given full entrance into the Order or turned away forever. I'd trained for so long, tried so hard, but the fear that I might not be good enough raged through my heart. I'd tried to talk to Shamas about it as we walked through the fields, but he never wanted to hear about my studies with the Coterie. I cared about him, even suspected I was beginning to have feelings for my cousin and that they were reciprocated, so I let the discussion drop, since it so clearly made him uncomfortable.

And I'd locked away the fear, deep inside. But tonight, it rose thick in my throat, choking out my joy. As I watched the Moon Mother's glowing gem rise into the sky, I started to cry.

"What are you afraid of?"

The woman's voice startled me and I sat up, looking around, but no one was there. Not sure whether I'd imagined it, I tried to relax again, to take my thoughts off the fear.

"I repeat: What are you afraid of? What do you fear?"

Not sure where the voice was coming from but feeling compelled to answer, I wrapped my arms around my knees and stared up at the moon.

"I'm afraid . . . of not being good enough."

"Is that all you fear?"

Biting my lower lip, I struggled with the question. Was it all I feared? And wasn't it enough? But then I let out a long breath and lowered my gaze, staring at the roof. "No, it's not. I'm afraid . . . of losing the chance to walk under the Moon Mother's light."

"You can always walk under the moon."

"No—it's not that. I'm afraid . . ." I wasn't sure how to phrase it, especially since I had no clue to whom I was talking, but I had to answer. That much I knew.

"What do you fear, Camille?"

The voice was ancient, echoing through the night. I picked up a pebble and chucked it off the roof. Finally I said, "I'm afraid . . . that she won't want me. And I couldn't bear that."

"Why? What is so special about being part of the Coterie

of the Moon Mother?" There was no judgment, almost no emotion behind the words. The questions were just that— questions—but they were skidding through my mind like a runaway cart.

"Being chosen by the Moon Mother . . . it means *everything.* I've never wanted anything else. I never expect to be a priestess—I know my heritage keeps me from being strong enough for that, but to be one of the Moon Mother's witches? That would mean more than I can ever express."

"Why?"

"To have her love . . . to be able to give her mine." And then I knew. "I love her—unreasonably, without logic, without hesitation. It doesn't matter why. The fact is, I love the Moon Mother and she is my everything, my all. I want to be part of her world, to dance under her glowing radiance, to revere her, to worship her, to make her magic."

"You can do all of those things without belonging to her order."

"Yes, but I want her to love me." I began to cry. "I want her to smile down on me, and say, 'You're mine. You're my daughter. Stay with me always.'"

"You love her."

"I love her. I would give my life for her if necessary."

I looked down to find a rose there. A beautiful deep red rose. I picked it up and smelled it, holding it to my nose. I'd never smelled anything so incredibly intoxicating.

"It will be a long journey, and you may regret it . . ."

Lying back, I stared up at the sky as I laid the rose between my breasts.

"No," I whispered. "I never, ever will regret it." And the voice vanished, and I realized that I'd just promised my life in an unofficial compact to the Moon Mother. And she'd answered.

I opened my eyes, staring at the rose. It had been a long journey, yes, and dangerous, but I had been truthful. I had never regretted it. Not once. As I gently replaced the rose into the book and placed it back on the shelf, a chime rang, alerting me that the Whispering Mirror had activated.

Sliding onto the chair in front of the table, I whispered the password that opened up the mirror and waited. A moment later, the mirror swirled with mist and then cleared, and I could see my father, staring out of the mirror at me. Behind him, stood Trenyth, looking through a sheaf of papers.

I caught my breath. I hadn't actually spoken to my father since we'd been in Otherworld for Menolly's wedding. At least we were on speaking terms again, and so far he'd shown nothing but remorse for treating me like dirt. I wasn't holding my breath—Sephreh could change his mind at any time—but I was giving him a second chance.

"Camille, good evening." He was always formal, always the soldier, even though I knew he cared. But sometimes his training as a guardsman overshadowed his role as our father.

"Father. Is anything wrong?" Yeah, I'd inherited his bluntness.

He leaned forward. "We have news on several fronts. I'll let Trenyth speak to you first—his news is the most urgent." Without another word, he slid out of his chair and Trenyth, nodding to him, sat down.

"Trenyth, what's going on?" I didn't like the look on the advisor's face. Trenyth was the advisor to Queen Asteria, and he probably knew more about what was going on with the demonic war than anybody. "Should I get the others?"

"Just take good notes. We don't have a lot of time, and I'd rather not waste it by waiting for them to join you."

I grabbed the voice recorder I kept in a docking bay near the mirror. At first we'd jotted down notes when talking, but this preserved more of the information, and Delilah transcribed them onto her computer. I tested it, then turned it on and set it near the mirror.

"Speak up, if you would. Go ahead. I'm ready."

Trenyth gave me a bare nod. "Good. Darynal's group has managed to infiltrate Rhellah. Quall hasn't approached his father yet, because we're unsure how that might go, but Taath has joined up with a new guild down there."

"Do I even want to know what the guild is?"

"Probably not, but you have to. It's a guild that Telazhar has started—the Guild of the Flame Serpents. It's a sorcerer's guild, and it's aligned with the temple of Chimaras. And from what Taath has seen so far, they are planning an assault on Ceredream. They're planning to march through the Southern Wastes, gathering up as much of the rogue magic as they can, and first take Ceredream, then move north and northeast."

"The Moon Mother's Grove."

"We don't know that for sure—I believe they are far more focused on Elqaneve because of the spirit seals. Telazhar seems to know they're here, in Otherworld, and he seems to have an idea of where they're being hidden."

Trenyth's face looked so despondent that I wanted to reach through the mirror and give him a long hug, but even if I could, it wouldn't do any good. Hugs were Band-Aids at this point.

"Okay, then. What's Darynal's group doing about it?"

Trenyth stared at me, then shook his head. "Doing about it? There's nothing they *can* do about it. Taath has caught sight of Telazhar, but he can't get near enough to dare staging an assassination. What they *are* doing is feeding us information. We are debating on how to approach the leaders of Ceredream to discuss this—the city has no real love for the elves and is home to a lot of rogues and sorcerers who might have found their way into the court. We are, however, now aligned with King Vodox of Svartalfheim, and the dwarves have come around. The kingdom of Nebelvuouri is our ally."

"Well, that's something, at least. And we have Y'Elestrial on our side."

Another pause, and then Trenyth held up a piece of paper on which I could see some faintly written decree. I couldn't read it, but I could make out the official seal of Y'Elestrial.

"One more thing. Queen Asteria and Queen Tanaquar have agreed to send your father to Aladril, to speak to the seers and see if they can help. He leaves in the morning."

That was a surprise. Dropping in on Aladril was no small feat, and to dare ask them for help meant that both queens felt the impending war might not go their way. I shot a glance at my father, who was standing, arms behind his back, in typical guardsman stance.

"So, that is our news. Taath says the sorcerers are creating magical weapons—spells, charms of all sorts, anything they can to do as much damage as possible. And they are attempting to harness the magic of the sands—dangerous, unpredictable . . ."

"The magic left over from the Scorching Wars." I softly let out my breath. The rogue magic of the sands was inherent in the lands down there, long ago imprinted during the Scorching Wars when the sorcerers laid waste to vast swaths of forest and grassland, leaving only charred, burned desert in their wake. The magical residue of battle had sunk into the land, turning it into a wild, dangerous place.

"Yes, and it's not hard for them to harvest. Especially with someone like Telazhar. And especially since he does, indeed, possess one of the spirit seals." Telazhar put down the papers and sat back. "Okay, so that's where we're at."

I smiled softly. Since being around us, Trenyth had picked up some ES slang, but if I pointed it out, he'd find a way to deny it. So, instead, I just leaned forward and turned off the voice recorder.

"Got it. Thanks, Trenyth. And I suppose . . . well, I'll fill in the Triple Threat on what's going on. We're all in this together, especially since Gulakah is putting the pressure on over here."

I told him what was happening with the eggs and ghost harvests. "I'm going in tomorrow night to infiltrate. I'll let you know what I find out."

"Be careful, Camille. Gulakah is smart. You can't trust anyone at his network. They're all in his pocket, one way or another." Trenyth stood up, letting my father take the chair again.

Sephreh just sat there, staring at me, a solemn look on his face.

"What?"

"Leethe is dead." He lowered his gaze. It was the first time I'd heard his voice crack in a long, long time.

I stuttered, unable to speak. Leethe, our housekeeper and cook. She'd taught me how to manage the house after our mother died. She'd done her best to comfort me when he yelled at me for not keeping things just the way Mother did, and she'd covered for me when I came in late from partying. Leethe had been old when Father brought Mother back to Otherworld. But she hadn't been old enough to die.

"What happened?" I didn't want to hear—didn't want to hear of a horrible death. Didn't want to hear that she'd suffered.

Father let out a slow breath. "She was hanging out the washing. Apparently, when the new girl—she hired a young girl to help her lift the water and carry things—dumped the washing water, she spilled some on the flagstones in back of the house. On her way back inside, Leethe was carrying the clothes basket, and she didn't see that the stones were slippery. She stepped on a slick spot and fell. She . . . hit her head on a sharp stone. It killed her instantly."

I sat very still, searching for something to say. I was so used to deaths from battle and collateral damage. I'd seen eighteen people mowed down by the spirit demons earlier today, and while it wrenched me, it didn't hit me like this news. Leethe had been comfort and home, and her arms had been big enough to embrace all three of us girls when we returned from Mother's death ceremony. Leethe had been *foundation*.

Father cleared his throat. "Camille? Did you want to say anything to her family? They're coming to pick up her body tomorrow."

Of course they were. They'd seen the shattered soul statue and knew she was gone, just like I'd seen Mother's and knew she had died. I wondered who had found it. Maybe her sister, or her niece? Leethe had been unmarried, and while she'd had numerous lovers, she'd never borne a child.

"Camille . . . Camille?" Sephreh's voice cut through my thoughts.

Shaking my head, I tried to snap myself out of the fog. "Um . . . please, tell them . . . I don't know what to say. There's so much . . . she was such a part of our lives. I wish we could make it home for the funeral, but I don't think we can." I paused, and then, pressing my hand against the glass, I said, "Please tell them we loved her. She was family."

Sephreh reached out then and pressed his fingers against the glass to meet mine. "I will, daughter. I'd better go now. But . . ."

"Yes?" My hand was still pressed against the reflection of his.

"When the civil war was going on, I kept thinking, if we win this, then I'll bring my daughters home. And we won, but then Shadow Wing loomed larger and you couldn't even think of coming back. I understood. But every day now, I think about you and your sisters and the dangers you face, and I worry."

He leaned forward. "Camille, I want you to promise me, stay as safe as you can. Lean on your husbands when you need to. Tell your sister Delilah . . . she needs to let Shade help her. And Menolly . . . well, she needs to protect her wife." Pausing, he waited for me to say something, anything.

After a moment, I said the words I'd been longing to say for months but had shelved on ice, believing I might never say them again. "I love you, Father."

He leaned back, straightening his shoulders, and slowly withdrew his hand from the Whispering Mirror. "I love you, and your sisters. More than you will ever probably know. And now, good night."

"Good night. Sleep well."

The light in the mirror faded back into a milky swirl of fog, and I covered it with the black velvet cloth. I picked up the voice recorder and, carrying it with me, opened the doors leading out on the balcony. My floor was the only one that had a balcony, and we often gathered here when the weather was good, to watch the stars and talk.

But tonight the rain was coming down in torrential sheets, and I stayed out for only a moment before darting back inside and locking the doors. I quietly exited the study and, hearing Delilah and Shade on the steps, hurried to the landing to stop them before they rounded the curve leading up to the third floor.

"Father called. Trenyth was there. We have news of the war." I paused, then went on. "And Leethe, she had an accident. She died."

Delilah uttered a little "Oh," but I knew that Leethe's death would hit me the hardest. I'd been the one to turn to her time and again, just as my sisters had turned to me.

"I'll take this and transcribe it before bed." Delilah took the voice recorder from me. "You go rest. I know . . . you go rest." She leaned down and kissed my forehead, then motioned for Shade to follow her up. I heard her explaining to him who Leethe had been as they vanished around the corner.

Turning back to my rooms, I opened the bedroom door. Smoky was reading—some suspense thriller by J. A. Jance. Trillian was doing sit-ups on the floor, and Morio was sprawled across the bed, one arm over his face.

Grateful for their presence, grateful they were in my life and that I didn't have to face the night alone, I shut the door behind me and shut out the world.

Chapter 16

The winds were playing around me, and I opened my eyes. The ocean next to me sloshed against the beach, the gray sheen meeting the silver of the skies, to blend into one long, merged watercolor landscape.

Fuck. Not again. The Ocean of Anger...

I was barefoot, struggling through the sand that shifted with every step. There was something I needed to know. I also realized that I wasn't inside Gulakah's mind, because the overwhelming fear wasn't present.

Stopping, I turned to the choppy water, shading my eyes as I gazed over it. There were waves, cresting against the shore—breakers coming in.

I loved the water, loved the restless energy of the ocean and the depths of emotion buried beneath it. But the ocean was as joyous as she was volatile, as generous as she was demanding.

Here, this particular ocean was filled only with anger. There was no joy, no frolicking dream—only a brooding nightmare. Here, spirits didn't haunt the waves on ghost ships—they *were* the waves.

And then I saw it—saw something I recognized. Gulakah, rising from the depths. As I watched, he began spitting something into the sea, spraying it like a battery of bullets. Orbs . . . silvery orbs. Silver orbs—oh hell, *this* was where the spirit demons came from.

Created from the very depths of the primal pool, the eggs—and the spirit demons—must be a manifestation of all the resentful ghosts and spirits that inhabited the realm. Somehow, the imbalance must have given them the power to manifest. And Gulakah was able to use that power, drawing on the vast sea of fury and wrath to which he was tied.

I squatted down, watching. No wonder the spirit demons and bhouts fed on magic—they thrived on it here.

Here, it was easy to see he was a god. He was huge—towering over the landscape, with his olive green reptilian scales and serpent-infested hair. His roving eyeballs, now fully in their sockets, were a dull black, and his face, a snout, much like that of an alligator's. Jagged, razor-sharp teeth filled his mouth as he opened it and let out a long shout that reverberated through water and shore.

Petrified, but reminding myself that I was *not actually in his mind*, I watched, looking for some clue that might help us. And then I saw it. A thick, pulsating, silver cord ran from the back of his tailbone directly into the ocean—and I knew that was how he was getting his power. And if we could disconnect that cord . . .

"You understand now." Pentangle stood beside me. She crossed her arms over her chest and stared at the Lord of Ghosts.

"We have to cut the cord that binds him here. But will that help us destroy him?" I rose to my feet, standing beside her, basking in the crackling energy that flowed off her.

She nodded, her headdress perfectly aligned, though it looked far too heavy to wear comfortably. "A god without his energy source is a wounded god. Remember, his power does not come from the Subterranean Realms. And even the gods can die. But you must attack him from his own realm. The realm of the dead."

"And how do we do that? Even if we can find him, how do we get him over to the Netherworld? We aren't strong enough."

"The balance must be restored." She handed me a small silver orb. "This . . . will help you when the time comes. You cannot use it except for the task I appoint to you. This will gate you and Gulakah into the Netherworld. But you must touch him."

Before I could say another word, she vanished, and I looked back at the orb in my hand. It began to melt and then absorb into my palm, and I felt a rush of energy as the charm became part of me.

A loud roar caught my attention, and I looked back out over the ocean. Gulakah was wading into the ocean. He dipped his snout in the water and caught up a spirit orb, tilting his head back. And even though I knew I wasn't really in his mind, I shivered as he began to crack open the egg and devour the demons inside, and grow stronger.

I struggled to wake, blurry from the dream. Quickly, I sat up and looked at my hand. Sure enough, a shimmer of silver flickered from a strange rune imprinted on my palm. It had been real. Pentangle had given me a gate spell.

A glance at the clock told me that I'd slept in. When I came downstairs, it was almost noon. Tomorrow was Beltane. Tomorrow night, Morio and I were due out at Talamh Lonrach Oll for the full moon.

I hurried through the kitchen and out back. The rain had departed and the day was actually rather warm—the temperature was nearly sixty. I wandered over beyond the trailer, stopped short by the sight of Morio, Smoky, Rozurial, and Trillian as they worked on the house, with shirtless, glistening backs as they hammered and nailed and built a home for our Iris.

They looked up, and all of them waved. I stood there, smiling, leaning against the side of the trailer—which was going back to the rental agency today—and soaked up the sight of my men. Even Roz—though he was just a friend— all of them were family.

Waving for them to come in, I turned and headed back to the kitchen. I wanted to tell them my news, but it would be easier when everybody was gathered inside. And it wasn't like I could run out in the next five minutes, find Gulakah, and gate him over to the Netherworld where we could . . . garrote him or whatever it was going to take to kill him. I forced myself to sit at the table while Hanna set a plate of waffles and bacon in front of me.

As I started to eat, caught up in my thoughts, I realized that Delilah, Iris, and Vanzir were all being oversolicitous. After about the third "How are you feeling?" I pushed back my plate and set down my fork.

"I'm not eating another bite until you tell me why you're all being so nice. I'm not sick, so what gives? It's not like I don't appreciate your concern—because I do—but I'd like to know what the hell is going on."

Iris and Hanna glanced at each other, then at Delilah, who blushed.

"I thought, with Leethe's death, you might be . . ."

"Yeah, right. *That*." I slowly went back to my waffle. "Leethe's death hit me hard. But there's nothing I can do about it. It was an accident. I've got to be focused for tonight, so I need to not dwell on it. I asked Father to send her family our condolences. By the way, Father . . . he said that he loves us and misses us. All of us."

Delilah gave me a sharp look. "He said that?"

"Yeah, he did."

"He never says—"

"Well, last night he *did*. Seriously, he was one second shy of crying. I think Leethe's accident affected him a lot more than it did even me. She's been looking after him since he first took Mother home to Otherworld. He said he thinks about us every day."

Before she could make a big deal about it, and more for my sake than anybody else's, I said, "Iris, can you gather everyone in here? I need to tell you something that relates to tonight."

Iris gave me an odd look. "I'll fetch them."

"Good." I attacked my waffle.

"I still don't like it," Delilah said. "You're going in there *alone*, Camille. What if something happens? It won't be like we'll be right there to help you out. We're going to keep close, of course. And I know you talked to the guys about it and somehow, you got them to agree. But close isn't the same thing as *there*."

Vanzir came wandering into the kitchen, where he straddled the chair next to me. "She's right, babe. It's a dangerous game you're playing. With dangerous playmates. As we saw with the eggs, Gulakah's followers are bewitched, ready to give up their lives at his command. They'll do anything he asks, and that includes killing. Are you sure you want to take the chance?"

"There really isn't a choice, is there?" I caught his gaze and held it.

Vanzir tilted his head to the side, a knowing look on his face. He reached out and, with his finger lightly tipping up my chin, nodded. "There's always a choice. It just depends on what you choose to do."

"True," I said slowly. "But I'm not willing to take the safe route when I have such a good chance to find out some much-needed information." And with that, I finished my breakfast as the others drifted in.

"What gives, wife?" Morio asked.

I pushed back my plate, really wanting another waffle. "Hanna, can you bring me another?" To the others, I said, "Okay, here's the thing."

As I finished telling them about my vision and the gate spell, the phone rang, and Shade went to answer it. "So, Pentangle told me we can kill Gulakah, but we need to do it in the land of the dead. The Netherworld."

"Even the gods can die," Smoky murmured. "She seems

intent that we have to kill Gulakah and not just dispatch
him."

"Yes, she does. I don't like it, but the more I think about
it, the more I think she's right. If we just send him packing,
he'll be back. We can't banish him—we don't have the power
for that. Nor can we trap his soul."

Delilah didn't look too happy about the news. "Why does
Pentangle think we can kill him easier in the Netherworld?"

"Because of the silver cord. Because without severing
that cord, Gulakah still has access to all of his power. And
we can only sever it in the Netherworld. No, the question
isn't why, but *how* we do it."

"I can help with that." Shade looked troubled, coming into
the room. "I just got off the phone with Carter." Before we
could ask, he said, "Carter did some research for us. Here's a
little more information. Any attacks on Gulakah here are
useless. They may disempower him briefly, but he can't be
harmed on this plane. So Pentangle is right—we have to do it
in the Netherworld."

Delilah frowned. "So we have to find out where he's hiding, and then Camille slaps her hand on him and gates him to
the Netherworld with her? And after that, we just mosey up
and kill him? How the hell are we going to do that?"

Shade cleared his throat. "Carter says he's pretty sure that
a spell will work on him—a spell that you, Morio, might be
able to cast, with Camille's help."

Morio paled. "I know what you're talking about, and I've
never tried to cast it, though I know the procedure. It's
dangerous."

"What spell?" I turned to them. "Tell me."

"The Greater Asa Mordente spell. The *final death*."

The Greater Asa Mordente spell was insanely powerful,
but highly dangerous, and it involved summoning, among
other things, the phoenix—not exactly child's play, and so
many things could go wrong. But it was the only hope we had.

"That means you have to be in the Netherworld with me."
I held up my hand as Smoky and Delilah started to protest.
"We have no choice. We have to make this work. Morio, you

spend the afternoon preparing for the spell. Have everything ready. I'll spend some time reading up on it again after I check out the talisman."

Smoky stared at me, his lips pressed together, but he said nothing. Delilah looked stricken, but I gave her a shake of the head.

Vanzir shrugged. "It's the best plan we have."

After a moment, Morio leaned forward, resting his elbows on the table. "We can do this, my love. We've progressed far enough with the death magic to do so. Aeval . . ." He stopped.

I stood, irritated. "Aeval what?"

"Nothing. Never mind."

"No, there will be no 'never mind.' Aeval *what*? No secrets. Tell me, now. Especially if it will help."

He hung his head for a moment, then apparently decided I wasn't going to give up on this. "Very well. Remember when you found out that the order of the Moon Mother trains their own sorceresses—and that they use dark Moon magic and death magic?"

I slowly nodded, Queen Asteria's words lingering in my ears. I hadn't wanted to think about them but now, they were coming home to roost.

"Perhaps now is the time to tell you. Your beloved Moon Mother trains her own sorcerers, although she will not call them that. They wield dark Moon magic . . . death magic. Why do you think Morio's magic comes so easily to you?"

"I remember . . ."

"Just what do you think you are becoming? Her priestesses are divided, Bright Moon and Dark Moon. Derisa is High Priestess of the Bright Moon Mother. When you take the role of the first Earthside high priestess, you will be taking the role of the Dark Moon High Priestess . . . and you will evolve from being a witch into being one of the Moon Mother's sorceresses. Your powers are already greatly increasing . . . more than you realize."

I stared at him, unable to speak. I hated sorcerers— I'd been brought up to hate them. And now I was to become one?

"It's just a word," Morio whispered. "Just a word, sweet-heart."

Breathing deeply, I pushed aside my fear and distaste. We didn't have the luxury for me to angst over something that I had no control over. I'd deal with the ramifications of it later, once we'd killed Gulakah. And apparently I was more capable of doing the latter than I'd believed. For my beloved Moon Mother, I would do anything.

"Fine. So, Morio and I can handle being in the Netherworld easier than anybody here, except for Shade. I still don't like those odds. Who else can go?"

"I can," Vanzir said. "But it's harder for anybody else here to manage. Smoky might be able to . . . and Roz."

Smoky grimaced. "Yes, and I will. But I can't stay for long. I am of the white and silver line of dragons. The Netherworlds is the domain of the shadow dragons, and we do not mix well with the energy there."

"What about vampires?" I asked Shade.

He shook his head. "Weird crossover problem. Menolly can't go physically into the realm of the dead, since she's undead. Neither can she go in spirit, since she's a vampire and trapped in her body. And she can't go on the Dream-Time because the Dream-Time is not the same realm."

"Then once we find him, it's Shade, Roz, Vanzir, Morio, and me. And Smoky for as long as he can hang out. We try to kill him with the Greater Asa Mordente spell."

When nobody said anything, I shrugged, and, over Delilah and Iris's protests, I pushed the discussion on to our plans for the night, which mostly consisted of where people were going to be. I picked up the talisman.

"I guess it's time to try this out. Here goes nothing," I said. "Just nobody hit me or anything, even playfully." Before I draped it over my head, I kissed Smoky, Trillian, and then Morio.

As the medallion settled down around my neck, a surge of energy raced through me. It was disconcerting, like going through a portal, and as I watched the others, their reactions almost made me laugh. Delilah began to cough as Iris and

Hanna clapped their hands to their mouths. Nerissa—who had the day off—let out a low whistle. Smoky was scowling, Morio had a curious grin on his face, and Trillian just stood, leaning against the kitchen counter, nodding. Shade, Vanzir, and Rozurial all just stared.

"What? What? Tell me I'm not covered in warts. Please." I did have my vanity, even when under a spell.

"Um, no. No warts. Definitely not," Roz croaked out.

I couldn't stand it anymore and headed to the mirror in the hall bathroom. There, staring back, was a complete stranger. I was still a little busty but appeared to have lost about thirty pounds and was more athletic. I was shorter, about five feet, two inches, and though my hair was still long, it was a pale wheat color—almost tawny, like Nerissa's—and was sporting a Farrah Fawcett look. My eyes were no longer violet but a rich, vibrant green. My ears still had the faintest of points to them. I didn't look human, but then again, Gulakah was also recruiting Fae.

Almost more shocked than when the talisman had turned me into a dwarf, I cocked my head to the side. It wasn't bad, but it sure as hell wasn't me.

"What am I going to wear?" I returned to the kitchen, trying to keep my clothes on. "My clothes won't fit me now, and Menolly's are still too petite, and Delilah's are far too tall. Same with you, Nerissa." And it was true, my corset was sliding down my torso, and my skirt almost grazed the floor. "Cripes, I'll be glad when this is done."

"Me, too," Smoky said. "I love you no matter what, but . . ."

Trillian shrugged. "It's a change . . . I guess change can be a good thing."

Turning to Morio, I said, "And you? Do you have something to add?"

He pursed his lips, trying not to laugh. "You definitely don't have the personality for a blonde. Just saying . . ."

"Oh hush, the lot of you." I snorted. "Well, don't just everybody stand there. Somebody, find me something to wear."

Nerissa jumped up. "One of my dresses might actually fit you—if I get a minidress, it would come down to your knees. I'll find one that's really tight and doesn't have built-in bra support. It might be a little loose on you, but it should work. One of my sweater dresses."

The woman wore dresses as short as my bustiers were tight. I nodded. "Whatever you think. And what should I do with my hair? It's so . . . so . . ."

"So retro," Nerissa said, laughing as she darted into the kitchen. I heard the bookcase sliding and leaned back, studying myself.

Vanzir stood up. "Yeah, nobody would ever know it was you by looking—but you're going to have to watch your mannerisms. Some of those people know you as Camille. They may sense a familiarity. What are you going to call yourself? Better get used to it now."

"That's a good point." I sat down. "It needs to be simple, and easy to remember. Since I don't fully look human, better if it's not a recognizable human name." I paused, thinking. "What about my middle name? I don't think I've ever really told anybody outside the family what it is. Sepharial."

Delilah let out a little laugh. "You do realize, that's a combination of Father's name and Arial's name? Though you were born before she was."

Delilah's twin, who had died at birth and now lived at Haseofon, the home of the Death Maidens, was named Arial. We hadn't known about her until the past year or so. Now, when Delilah trained, she was able to meet her and talk to her. Any time Arial left the temple, she had to leave in her Were form—as a spirit leopard. Menolly and I had seen glimpses of her in that form, but we'd never been able to meet her otherwise.

"I wonder . . . did Mother and Father just like the name Arial? And was it deliberate, naming me after Father?" Distracted, I looked up as Nerissa returned.

She thrust three outfits into my arms. "These might work. Try them."

I held up the first. A sweater dress, all right, in a brown-

and-white tweedlike pattern, with a low-cut neck and long sleeves. I motioned for the others to stand back and tried it on. The sleeves were too long, but I could roll them up. The dress fit loosely, but a belt would cinch it in. The hem landed about an inch above my knees. I'd seen how short it was on Nerissa, so that didn't surprise me.

"Um . . . it's okay. Try the others." She seemed to be having fun playing dress-the-witch as she thrust another outfit my way.

I stared at it. At least this one was green, but it reminded me of an outfit off some anime schoolgirl. The top was a knit V-neck tank top, and the skirt flirty, with panels of green and pink. I grimaced at the color combo but stripped off the sweater dress and pulled on the top, then the skirt. It zipped up with no problem, and though it was a little loose, it actually fit better than the first. The skirt came down to two inches above my knees. Again, it barely grazed Nerissa's panties when she wore it.

"Not bad, not bad," she said, circling around me. "But try the third."

Holding up the bubblegum pink dress, I shook my head. "I don't do pink."

"Try it. It will look good with your hair."

Groaning, I once again stripped. Roz was staring at me, grinning, but saying nothing. Smoky was glowering at him, and I rubbed my forehead. All we needed was another fight.

The pink dress was sleeveless—a simple tank dress, in a light knit. I slid it over my head and was surprised to find out how well it fit me. Nerissa handed me a white patent leather belt, which I buckled around my waist. The dress actually fit and came down to a little above my knees.

"That's cute." She stood back, nodding her approval.

Delilah cleared her throat. "I hate to say it, but she's right. The dress looks good on you." Her eyes were laughing, but I could tell she was telling the truth. Delilah couldn't lie very well. She'd never been good at it.

I glanced down at the outfit. It was something I'd never

wear, but for tonight, apparently, this was it. "Okay, then. I'm wearing pink."

Trillian crossed his arms across his chest. "I've been thinking about your idea of using your middle name. Not a wise move. Suppose Gulakah has had his spies do research—it wouldn't be hard to learn what your full names were. I'd pick something else. You look like Earthside Fae. I'd name yourself after a tree or something like that."

When it came to subterfuge and manipulation, Trillian was a master. I trusted his instincts. "All right. I'll be . . . Morning Glory. Do ES Fae have last names?"

"Not so much if they're from the woodlands. Morning Glory it is."

After that, things went quickly. We figured out that my feet were now the same size as Nerissa's, too, so she brought me a pair of white canvas flats. I stared at them, then slid them on. I could run, at least, if I needed to.

For the next hour, I had them practice calling me Morning Glory until I got used to answering to the name. We went over and over the schematics—Delilah had managed to scrounge up the plans to the building that the meeting was being held in.

The Greenbelt Community Center was still used, on occasion, though mostly for church bake sales, an occasional community theater production, and—apparently—the Aleksais Psychic Network meetings. Delilah had asked Tim Winthrop—a good friend and the computer guru for the Supe Community Council—to hack into the records. Apparently, though the center was not the official headquarters for the group, they rented it out fairly cheap for both psychic fairs and general meetings.

"Here—memorize the exits. Double doors in the front, two side doors, and one fire exit that's kept shut but can be opened." Delilah pushed the floor plan over to me. "There's the main chamber, and the men and women's bathrooms on either side of the event floor. In back, on the other side of the hall, are three smaller event rooms, three offices, and a supply closet that houses the heating unit, janitor's supplies, stuff like that. The main office is open to the public; that's where people go to rent out the space. The smaller offices are for the managers."

I studied the plans. "Parking in the front and the back. Sidewalks leading on both sides to both parking lots. Alley in the back, main street in the front. Basement? Attic?"

"No. The heating and cooling unit is in the supply room. There aren't any hidden tunnels, or anything as far as we can tell, but that's just what we know from the official plans. Who's to say if they haven't created their own network."

"I doubt it," Morio said. "Their headquarters are elsewhere. They don't own the building, so it would be hard for them to alter it. I'm going to say it's a fair guess that what we see here is what you'll find. And since they advertised the meeting, I'm also guessing that it's a net—they're trying to find more victims. Once they do . . ."

"They'll persuade them to go back to headquarters. I have to be so appealing they'll do anything to get me back there, and soon. Which means I have to appear vulnerable and let my magic shine through."

I frowned. "Most of the ES Fae aren't particularly prone to brainwashing or enchantment, so what the hell are they using to rope them in? There has to be something that they've got . . . they were using the bhouts, but the well for those has dried up. And the spirit demons are a whole different type of creature. They aren't used for control, so much as destruction . . . and to feed Gulakah."

Iris slid in beside me. The chair was too low for her to effectively see the charts, but she got up on her knees on the seat, leaning on the table. "I know something that they might be using."

"What? Any idea would help, so I know what to look out for."

"There's a tincture that I know about . . . my mother used to warn me when I was little never to accept a drink from a human until we'd formed a contract. Once agreed on, the contract is binding and then we—at least those of us who are sprites—can't be charmed. But if you drink the tincture before you've agreed on service details, then you can be bound. Sort of like a djinn in a magic bottle."

"But does that only work for sprites? Does it work on other Fae?" I'd never heard of the drug.

"I don't know, but they might be able to adapt it. The potion is difficult to make and uses some obscure herbs found in very remote areas. But someone like Telazhar would have the knowledge of how to make that potion. He could have made it before he headed to Otherworld." Iris motioned to Delilah, who pushed the laptop over to her. "Do you have a list of witches who've aligned themselves with the Aleksais Psychic Network? How do you work this thing?"

"Wait!" An idea occurred to me. "Halcon Davis. He was with Jake Evans in the cemetery. And he's one of the organizers of the Aleksais Psychic Network. Maybe he's more powerful. Maybe he has some sort of magic that can charm the Fae. Did we ever find out anything on him? Do we know if he was the guy whom Nerissa encountered at the conference?"

"Crap. I knew there was something I was overlooking." Delilah pulled the laptop back from Iris and started tapping the keys. "Not much online . . . however . . . here we go. Halcon Davis was born in . . . no, that's not possible." She looked up, shaking her head. "This has to be somebody else."

"Why?"

"Because it says here that Halcon Davis was born in 1825. He lived in the Seattle area, and he went missing in 1857. No one ever saw him again. There's a picture here—actually, it's a daguerreotype. I wonder if this is the same man Lindsey saw at the fair. But it couldn't be."

The image showed a rather nondescript man, wearing glasses, with short hair parted in the middle. Nerissa leaned over Delilah's shoulder.

"That's the man at the conference! There are some differences, but that's the man who bumped into me, who was watching all day. I'm sure of it." She shook her head. "He's . . . almost one hundred ninety years old? How is that possible? Could it be a family member?"

Delilah shrugged. "Maybe, but . . . it says here Halcon

was researching into Faerie lore—well, it says the "little people," but they weren't talking about dwarfism." She let out a little gasp. "What if he . . . what if he somehow ended up getting hold of the Nectar of Life?"

"I wonder if Titania met him—she's been living in this area for a long, long time. She was drunk off her ass for a lot of that time, and look . . . she had Tam Lin with her. Maybe she tried to turn another human. She never mentioned it to us, but there's one hell of a lot they've never told us." I was wondering just how I might broach the subject with the Fae Queen when Delilah tapped me on the arm.

"Can we send Lindsey a copy of this photograph? I just downloaded it."

I pulled out my cell and gave Lindsey a call. She answered on the first ring. "Lindsey, we don't have a lot of time, but are you near a computer, or can you get e-mail on your phone?"

She laughed. "I'm playing Plants vs. Zombies right now, so yes, I have my e-mail at hand. What's cooking?"

"Take a look at the e-mail that—" I glanced over at Delilah, who punched the Enter key and then nodded to me. "Delilah just sent you an e-mail. Do you recognize the man in the picture?"

A pause, and I could hear her tapping on the keyboard. Then, a gasp.

"That's the man at the psychic fair! Halcon Davis."

Now we were getting somewhere. "You're *sure* it's him?"

"I'm positive. That's him." Lindsey hesitated, then asked, "What's going on, Camille? Something's going on. I can feel it. And what about the zombies? I know that the magical community around here—the FBH pagan community—is nervous. We're worried about backlash on us, to be honest."

I sorted through my thoughts, trying to figure out just what I could tell her. "Lindsey, there's a lot of freak show things going down right now. I want you and your coven to lay low. Do protection magic for the city right now. Don't go to—or hold any—public events right now. Tell your friends in other Circles to do the same. We've been dealing with creatures worse than the bhouts. We destroyed two nests of them, but we aren't sure if there are others. And Halcon Davis and the Aleksais Psychic Network are right in the thick of things."

I wanted to tell her that I was going in undercover, but it was just safer to keep that information under wraps. As I said good-bye, she sounded concerned. I hated worrying her, but the truth was she *should* be worried. And the more protection magic aimed around the city, the better off we'd be.

"So Halcon Davis was doing research on the Fae. Want to bet he managed to find out about the potion you were talking about, Iris? And maybe found a way to alter it. And somehow, his own life has been extended. We need to ask Titania if she remembers him. I wish they carried cell phones out there, but I don't think the Triple Threat has any intention of being on the end of anyone's speed dial."

"We can find out, but not right now. I don't want anybody wandering off on their own until tonight's over and done with." Trillian spoke up, and the tone in his voice told me he wasn't about to be argued with.

"Fine. We'll ask tomorrow." I turned back to the plans. "So, I'm going to figure on Halcon being there tonight. They just wasted a sizable number of their members in feeding the spirit demons, so they're going to need more recruits. Chances are I can wrangle my way into the inner circle, because I can guarantee you, I'll have more magical energy for him than anybody there."

"If he did take the Nectar of Life, then he's going to be unpredictable, because I doubt if he'll have been guided or counseled in how to use it. But . . . are there any other possibilities for his age? Halcon was human, as far as we can tell. There's no way he could be this old without some sort of magical intervention." Delilah kicked the table leg, frowning. "I wish we knew more about what you're getting into before you go there."

"As usual, we have more questions than we have answers, but I think that's just the way the cookie crumbles. As far as Halcon . . . I don't know. Shade, Smoky? Morio? Do you guys know of any way he could be this age and still be human?"

"There's one thing you haven't considered," Nerissa said. "He might be Were. Weres are good at passing, and we live to quite a long age."

That was a possibility, but something didn't ring right to me. "If he were Were, wouldn't you have sensed it at the conference?"

She shook her head. "There were so many people there, and I only saw him here and there. I was focused on work, and I doubt that I would have noticed if he was wearing a clown suit."

The clock chimed and I glanced up. Six P.M. Half an hour and I needed to head out in order to be there by seven. I didn't want to arrive early because the less time people had to meet me before the meeting, the less chance there would be that I'd be discovered.

Nervous, I locked myself in the bathroom. Logically, I knew it was me, but standing there, gazing at the face in the mirror, there was a part of me that felt like I'd lost myself. I didn't connect with the person in my reflection. I stuck my tongue out at myself, then winked, then shook my head. Feeling uncomfortable and out of sorts, I returned to the kitchen after washing my hands and holding a cool wash-cloth to my neck.

The clock seemed to drag—the second hand slowly ticking around. I wanted to go, to be off, but it would be a mistake to go early and I knew it. Pacing, I went over everything again.

"So I get there. I find whoever's in charge—hopefully it will be Halcon Davis. I gain his trust. I express an interest in becoming part of the network. And . . . then we see what happens." I looked up. "I guess that's about the extent of things."

"We'll be outside, waiting. If there are enough people there, we'll hide in the parking lot. If not, we'll park on the street, a few car lengths away. We won't be able to contact you without giving you away, so you need to be able to get through to us."

Shade cleared his throat. "I think you all are forgetting something. It's dark. I can walk in the shadows and get a lot closer than the rest of you."

I groaned. "And why didn't you remind me of this beforehand?"

"You didn't ask." He grinned, then shrugged. "I thought it was a given that I'd be up there, keeping guard, so I didn't think to say anything."

I stared at him. "*Seriously?* You give us more credit than you should. But I feel a whole lot better knowing you'll be that much closer. If there's enough shadow inside, feel free to come in—"

"Not a good idea." Shade shook his head. "If Davis is as strong a sorcerer—or whatever he is—as we think, then he might be able to sense me. But I'll be right outside, listening in, and I'll be able to get inside within seconds if I hear you scream."

Smoky let out a long sigh. "I should be there. I'm your husband."

We'd already gone over this several times in the past couple of days. Smoky didn't want me in danger—as usual. And I understood. But I also knew that this was our best way to get inside the Aleksais Psychic Network. If they so much as smelled us, they'd back off and tell Gulakah we were getting close.

"You know why I'm doing this. Just stay close enough that you can come in on the run." I leaned up to kiss him, stopping at the strange look on his face as he pulled away before my lips could meet his. "What's wrong?"

"I . . . I . . . you aren't . . . you are, but . . ." He stuttered, looking totally confused. "I'm sorry—I didn't mean to pull back."

I cocked my head. "You're blushing." I'd never seen Smoky blush before, and I rather liked it. Then it hit me. "You feel uncomfortable kissing me because I don't look like myself!"

He glowered. "No—I just . . ."

"Dude, she's totally right." Vanzir snickered, quickly sobering as Smoky whirled on him.

"You have something to say, demon?" Smoky might think he hadn't fully forgiven Vanzir, but the truth was, after Hyto had stolen me away, Smoky had never fully forgiven *himself*, even though we all told him it wasn't his fault. He blamed his temper for leading to the disaster that had followed.

Vanzir shook his head and held up his hands. "Peace, dude. I'm not saying a word. Nothing."

"Enough. It's time to book." I picked up my purse—another loaner from Nerissa—and headed toward the door.

Smoky stopped me. He pulled me into his arms and leaned down, brushing my lips with his own. "Whatever you look like, wherever you are, you're my love. That's all that matters."

And with that, we were off.

Chapter 17

～✺～

The Greenbelt Park District Community Center was as ratty as I'd been warned. I stood outside the double doors, steeling my courage. I was Morning Glory ... Morning Glory ... and I was alone, and worried, and lonely. Sucking in a deep breath, I pushed open the door and walked in.

The room was large, the walls a pale brick. I scoped out the exits—right where they showed on the map. And the men's and women's bathrooms, too. Two sets of double doors against the back wall should lead to a hallway running parallel with the event hall, as well as the other event rooms and offices, and two more exits.

The room wasn't full, exactly, but there were at least fifteen people milling around, and I could tell they weren't already members of the Aleksais Psychic Network because they all looked rather confused and unsure, just like I was supposed to feel.

A table to one side held snacks—chips, cookies, several pitchers of neon pink juice. Staring at it, I remembered Iris's warning and decided to leave the food and drink alone.

A group of chairs were set up in a semicircle, with a table and a chair in front. Three high stools sat behind the table. And a banner hung over one set of the double doors leading to the hallways that read: WELCOME TO THE ALEKSAIS PSY-CHIC NETWORK. JOIN US!

As I made my way over to the chairs, a figure came through the other set of double doors, and I stopped cold. Halcon Davis, and he had three people with him who weren't people at all, but Tregarts. I could smell a Tregart demon a mile away. But rather than looking like bikers, they looked like hunky Fabio types. And that was when it dawned on me that every one of the people who had shown up were women. I didn't see a single man around, except for Halcon and his glam-groupies.

That made sense. Among the FBH population, more women were likely to seek out others when they had questions about their psychic abilities, and men still weren't encouraged to explore that side of themselves. There had been very few men during the assault on the spirit demon egg yesterday, and they'd died just as quickly as the women. But overall, the group of victims had been mostly female.

I made my way over to them, smiling hesitantly. I couldn't appear too confident. I needed to convince Halcon that I was searching for something to give my life meaning. I needed to become a victim, and that wasn't an easy act for me. Even with Hyto, I had kept hold of my dignity. I hadn't let him beat down my soul, even though he'd beaten my body. Now I had to mute myself, muffle my natural inclinations.

I stood on the edge of the group, checking out their energy. Some were bored, looking for something to do. A few seemed to have some sort of power, and a couple of them were just difficult to read. I edged back, trying to look interested, but standing apart so Halcon would notice me. I turned on my glamour but was cautious about how much I unmasked, because if they sensed I was using it, they'd suspect something. The Fae who had come here had probably not bothered to cloak up, but they'd been genuinely interested.

I summoned energy from the Moon Mother. After a moment, when I felt the power build, I glanced over at

Halcon. He was staring in my direction. Forcing a wide-eyed, slightly confused look onto my face, I flashed him a tentative smile. And that was when I saw it. Hanging around his neck was a smoky quartz pendant, and it radiated an energy that made me want to run up to him, to be his friend at all costs.

The eighth spirit seal. Motherfucking son of a bitch. *Halcon was wearing the eighth spirit seal.* And the damned thing was emanating some sort of charm energy that worked on Fae as well as mortals. Holy crap, so that was how he persuaded people to leave their families and to give him all their money. And that was how he had lived so long.

He conferred with his bodyguard groupies and then headed in the group's direction, but I knew he was focused on me. Nervous now, not wanting to get caught in the trap of his bewitchment, I stepped forward, just a half step, but enough for my body language to say hello.

Halcon looked so much like his picture that it was hard to believe he was almost two hundred years old.

"Welcome, ladies. Welcome to the Aleksais Psychic Network. This is a recruitment meeting, so we'll be joined by some of our regular members in a bit. Meanwhile, would you like some refreshments before we get started? That will give me a chance to say hello to each of you and get an idea why you're here. "

This wasn't the way he usually ran things. I could tell by the startled looks on the Tregarts' faces. They were eyeing each other, as if trying to figure out what to do.

As we allowed him to herd us to the buffet of chips and desserts, I left just enough room beside me. Halcon took advantage. He slipped in between me and the nearest guest.

"Hello, I'm Halcon Davis. And you are . . .?" He held out his hand.

Grateful the rune was implanted in my left hand, I offered him my right, making sure my grip wasn't too firm. A wave of revulsion ran over me and I shivered, wanting to back away. Even the spirit seal couldn't mask the slimy, grasping energy of his aura. It made my skin crawl.

"My name is Morning Glory." I gave him a gracious

smile. "I'm so excited to be here. I've been . . ." I let my voice drift off.

"Yes, my dear?" He pressed a little closer, his gaze never leaving my face, as his fingers lingered over the tips of my own.

I gave an apologetic little shrug. "I'm just . . . I've been alone for a while and there's no one to talk to . . ."

"You're one of the Fae, aren't you?" He still hadn't let go of my hand, and I seriously wanted it back, but I forced myself to let him hold it.

"Why, yes. I am . . . partially. My father was human; my mother was one of the wood spirits." I was fighting off the charm of the spirit seal, fighting to keep myself from falling into the swirl of joy and enthusiasm that danced around the room.

Halcon's brow narrowed. "My dear, you said 'was'?"

I let out a slow breath and tilted my head. "Yes, they're both dead. An accident. I'd rather not talk about it."

His fingers traced a pattern over mine, and again, the combination of love and disgust sent me reeling.

"As you wish, Morning Glory. So you are half-Fae . . . We welcome your mother's people in the Network, you know. The Fae are such a magical people. And you'd have many friends if you join us."

"Thank you. As I said, I've been lonely. I don't have many friends. Not really." And again I let loose with the winsome eyes.

Halcon patted my hand, then lifted it gently and kissed the top. It wasn't a sexual sensation, but he felt hungry, and I had a sudden vision that I was Little Red Riding Hood, facing the starving wolf.

I forced myself to keep a smile on my face as he let go of my hand and moved to the front of the room, making perfunctory greetings to the other women. He moved to the table with his bodyguards and enjoined us to take our seats. I slipped to the front row but took a seat on the side.

As Halcon launched into a lecture about the Aleksais Psychic Network, I tried to keep focused. The material felt as dry as cardboard, but the audience seemed rapt, caught up in his spiel, and I knew it was the spirit seal, doing its thing. I reined in my glamour, trying to fade out of the picture while I did some poking around. I couldn't close my eyes, in case they were watching, but I used a trick Morio had taught me early on—veiled sight.

Cats have a third membrane that covers their eyes, and while we—Fae or human—didn't, we could effect a magical version of it, allowing us to cut off distractions in the room. Basically, tuning out everything that didn't matter or that would disrupt the focus on energy. As I willed the veiled sight to wash over me, it was like putting on earmuffs and a milky sleep mask.

As the riffraff of sound and sight muted into the background, I could see the lines of energy emanating from Halcon to the audience. Or rather, from Halcon's pendant to the audience. The creeping vines of energy reminded me of . . . Fuck, they were almost like Vanzir's neon feelers. I sat very still, trying not to show any sign of physical reaction to what I was seeing.

The tendrils were wispy, not nearly as developed as Vanzir's, nor did they seem to be feeding tubes in terms of sucking energy off those they touched. No, instead they were transferring energy to the audience. And that was when I realized I might be in trouble. One was making an attempt to latch onto me and I had my wards up—it couldn't gain hold. If Halcon noticed, and I had no reason to think he *wouldn't* notice, then I was in trouble.

If I let the thing in, though . . . what would it find out? I struggled—I had to make a decision soon. I couldn't just let it continue until he realized he didn't have me swept up in his net like the others.

There was only one thing I could do. Let down my wards enough for him to attach, but then do my best to keep it at arm's length. I focused on my aura, looking for the spot least likely to cause me trouble if he managed to break through all the way. The second chakra—the sexual level. While it wasn't my ideal choice, it didn't deal with psychic matters as much as the other chakras. And I was pretty sure I could control any urges Mr. Halcon Davis might be inclined to try to stimulate.

As I opened up a narrow channel in the barricades I'd erected around my body and spirit, the feeler seemed to sense the vulnerability and dove for it. I braced myself, and sure enough, within seconds, a warm, viscous energy began to seep into my body. I felt like I was sitting in a puddle of warm pee—not anything I'd choose to experience. By the looks on their faces, the other women were experiencing something quite different.

I gritted my teeth, forcing the smile on my face to brighten, as the energy leaked into my system, drop by drop. Sure enough, within seconds, Halcon glanced at me again, and his smile, a crafty, artful one, made him look all too pleased with himself.

Beginning to doubt whether this was actually a good idea, I contemplated leaving, but then Halcon suddenly stood up.

"Ladies, we're going to bring in a group of our members for you to chat with. The leader is Jake Evans, and he'll take care of anything you need. Meanwhile, feel free to visit the refreshment table. If you're interested in joining our network, our society members will be carrying sign-up forms."

As I stood with the others, he motioned for me to come to the front of the room. I glanced around, then pointed to my chest, and he nodded. As I joined him, he reached out and wrapped his arm around my shoulders, walking me away from the crowd.

"I want to talk to you, Morning Glory. We have special need of people with a heritage such as yours. I think you could be a valuable asset to our organization, and I think you'd feel right at home here." His smile was wolfish now, and I was even more uncomfortable.

"You really think I have something to offer?" Again, I fluttered my lashes and affected a hopeful smile.

"Oh, my dear. I know it. We don't get many of the Fae— even half-Fae—here, and we are always looking to bridge the gap between the mortals and your mother's people. If you would come with me, please."

He started to lead me to the double doors leading into the back hallway when one of his Tregarts stopped him and whispered something to him that I couldn't quite catch. An influx of at least twenty other people seemed to fill the event hall, and sure enough, there was Jake Evans, leading the pack. Their vacant stares reminded me of something . . .

Stepford wives . . .

Oh hell yes . . . the members joining the new recruits reminded me exactly of the women in the movie. I hadn't seen the remake, but one night, on late TV, Delilah had pressed me into watching the original. It had creeped me out so much that I'd had a hard time going to sleep. I'd had the same reaction to *Invasion of the Body Snatchers.* And this . . . this meeting didn't seem far off from there.

I waited as Halcon finished talking to the Tregart. He turned back to me.

"Morning Glory, is anyone waiting at home for you? I wouldn't want to keep you if you have a prior engagement. But I do so want to talk over what I envision for you with our group." Personable and charming. If I didn't know better, if I couldn't sense energy the way I could, I would have thought he was just a really nice guy who cared a whole lot about the people in his organization.

Letting out another short sigh, I shook my head. "Not really. I told you my parents are dead, and I don't have any roommates. So I don't have to be home early." Playing right into his hands, I waited for him to pounce on the bait. Which he did, in spades.

"Well then, shall we go get some coffee? I know a Starbucks near here that's still open."

"Don't you want me to talk to your members, like the others?" I peeked over my shoulder, as he steered me back to the door.

"My associates can handle the job. Please, allow *me* to persuade you to join our little group? I sense a great deal of promise in you, and I like to welcome our most appealing newcomers personally."

Halcon aimed me for the doors, and as we approached

them, I realized the Tregarts had formed a semicircle behind me. There was no real way for me to get free. Halcon and his men had set up a spiderweb and I was caught smack in the middle, with them creeping in from all sides.

Remember, this is your trap, not his. You aren't in danger. Not yet. But you can't let on you're nervous or they'll become suspicious. This is supposed to be something you want.

As I gave myself a mental pep talk, we entered the hall, and Halcon turned me to the left. He kept up a steady patter of conversation as we moved swiftly down the hall, and I realized he was talking so fast there was no way I could get a word in edgewise. He was bulldozing me—or he thought he was—and I tried to control my nerves as he pushed open the side door and we exited the building.

We were on the side of the Community Center now, and I hoped that Shade was nearby and following. We were in the shadows, after all, so he might be. Praying that was the case, I feigned interest as Halcon continued to praise the Network for all the good it did its members and for its goals in the future, which sounded like a bunch of vague promises to me.

Meanwhile, I could feel the continuous probing from the spirit seal and I knew I was going to have to let down my shields some more or he'd be alerted.

"Where are you taking me?" I asked, breaking into the one-sided conversation.

"I want you to meet someone," Halcon said. "I want you to meet the founder of our organization. He's always in need of people who have a great deal of psychic power, and my dear, you have more than most anybody I've met, except for a few others of your heritage."

Gulakah. He was taking me to Gulakah.

"Your leader—he's not here tonight?" I deliberately stumbled over a crack in the sidewalk, giving Halcon a chance to rest his hand on my elbow. It also gave Shade a chance to catch up with us, if he was following.

"No, he keeps to himself. He's . . . he's not quite like the rest of the mortals."

"Oh, he's one of the Supe Community or Fae?" I forced

my voice lighter than I felt and also did my best to remain clueless, at least in Halcon's eyes.

"Not exactly. Wait till you meet him. He doesn't go out much—he's very . . . sensitive to the energy of others and of the city. He stays in seclusion. I hope you don't mind a little ride."

He was practically dancing. I wondered if he got brownie points for bringing in members who were psychically strong. Or did Gulakah just promise to let him live, providing he brought him enough fodder?

I still hadn't seen Faerman's wife . . . but as we headed into the parking lot, I wondered if she, too, had been the recipient of Halcon's unwavering attention. The seal could easily have charmed her, considering she wouldn't have recognized it for what it was.

At that moment, I noticed we were heading toward an SUV . . . and it was parked right near my Lexus.

I let out my breath in a long, slow stream. The others had to see us from here. Relaxing, I allowed Halcon to help me into the front passenger seat. He hopped into the driver's seat, the Tregarts slid into the back, and we were off. As we pulled onto the street, I sidled my gaze to the mirror on my side and was relieved to see Morio's SUV pull out on the street behind us. He was hanging back, but he definitely had us spotted. I focused on Halcon and listened as he continued to prattle on.

The Tregarts had remained silent throughout the entire evening. I decided that it would be only natural to say something to them. I turned around, breaking in when Halcon fell silent during a left turn.

"You're all members, too? How did you get involved?"

The three men looked startled, and one nervously glanced at the back of Halcon's head. Finally the second one cleared his throat.

"We've been friends of Halcon for quite a while. After a lot of hashing out things, he convinced us to come work for him. Best job security *ever*." He gave me a short nod.

"I see . . . so you've been in the network for a long time?"

Halcon broke in. "They've been with me since near the beginning, my dear. They watch my back." And with that, he began talking again, and I turned back around. Another side glance told me that Morio was still back there.

"Is there something outside that's catching your interest?" Halcon asked, turning right.

I shook my head. "No, just looking out the window. You said we were going to Starbucks?" We'd already passed two of the drive-through coffee shops. I knew it had been a ruse, but I needed to keep up appearances, and Morning Glory would have been concerned. My persona wasn't stupid, just naïve.

Halcon reached down and my door lock clicked. "I'm afraid that we don't have time to stop for coffee now, my dear. I promised our leader that I'd be back at a certain time, and when I called him from the Community Center to tell him about you, he was positively thrilled. He wants to meet you. He'll be especially interested in the fact that you somehow can resist my gentle . . . persuasion, Morning Glory." His voice shifted from friendly to cool. "If that is your name."

My stomach lurched. First, Halcon hadn't called anybody at the center. And second, he might not know who I was, but he knew something was up. I wanted to glance in the mirror again, reassure myself that Morio and the others were still behind me, but that wasn't a good idea. I forced myself to keep my eyes on the road in front of us.

"What do you mean? What are you talking about? I *am* Morning Glory. I hope you don't think I've been rude. I just . . . I don't know you, and riding with four strange men in a car—I thought we were just going to Starbucks." I allowed a tinge of hysteria to enter my voice. Maybe if he thought I was worried he was a pervert, he'd calm down.

Halcon peeked into the rearview mirror; he was looking at the Tregarts, but I couldn't see what was on their faces and I didn't want to turn around. After a moment, he let out a long sigh.

"I promise: I have no sexual interest in you. I just want you to meet the man who started the Aleksais Psychic Network because I think he'll have a great use for you." Once again, he glanced in the rear mirror at his bodyguards. "Neither are my men a danger to you. If you truly want coffee, we'll pull through the next Starbucks, but Morning Glory, once you meet Gulakah—our leader—I guarantee you, caffeine will be the last thing on your mind."

I let a beat go by, then another, before saying, "All right. I'm okay. I just . . . it's hard for me to trust. I've been hurt too many times in the past. I tend to get bristly . . ." I was hoping that he'd buy the explanation.

He didn't say anything for a few minutes, then gave me a short nod. "Yeah, I've met a number of women with that issue." For a moment, he almost sounded empathetic, but I reminded myself that not only was the man wearing a spirit seal, but he was working for one of Shadow Wing's henchmen, he was responsible for tearing people away from their homes, and most likely, he had been in on ordering them to turn themselves over to the eggs as demon fodder.

"I can wait on the coffee." I relaxed back into my seat.

Another ten minutes and we turned left onto a heavily wooded road. My internal compass told me we were in the vicinity of our stomping grounds—the Belles-Faire District.

The car slowed as we turned left yet again. A bright yellow DEAD END sign was posted at the corner. I sat up, looking around. There weren't any houses along the parklike spread of grass and trees. It was then that I noticed the entire street was fenced. This was one estate. One huge, freaking estate. And near the end, a gated drive opened up as Halcon held up his phone and said, "Open."

So the place was wired, and probably heavily. We pulled through the wide iron gates as they swung open and into a long circular drive, which curved around in front of a four-story mansion.

Cripes, this joint must have cost a fortune, even for as run-down and gothic as it looked. There were lights on inside, in a spotty pattern, and bodyguards at the door. By their size and bulk, I guessed they were also Tregarts.

Damn. Gulakah was living right inside the city, and somehow he'd managed to escape our prying eyes. My guess, by the humming ring of magic that permeated the place, was that this entire building and any other structures were under the protection of a cloaking spell, as well as whatever secrecy that technology could provide.

Halcon pulled up to the sidewalk, to where two of the bodyguards were waiting. One moved around to open his door, while another opened mine. I let the demon help me out of the car, again impressed that Tregarts could clean up so well to suit-and-tie standards.

Halcon hurried around to my side and took my arm. "Welcome to the home of the Aleksais Psychic Network. Come, let's hurry before it rains again."

It was only now that I noticed the weather—it had stopped raining and the moon was peeking out from behind a heavy cloud cover. I held on to the thought that tomorrow night, on Beltane, she would be full and I'd be out running with the Hunt.

As Halcon escorted me up the stairs, I caught a sound in a nearby bush. It was just a whisper—so faint that nobody else picked it up—but I knew that sound. I recognized it on an internal, gut level, and I could feel the connection through the Soul Symbiont ritual. It was Morio, in his fox form, slipping through the bushes.

Relieved, knowing that I wasn't alone, I focused on the steps as Halcon escorted me in to meet Gulakah.

The mansion was old, and unlike most of the mansions that I'd been in, the central staircase wasn't built of spacious marble, but instead of polished wood. The ceiling towered four flights above me. The main foyer was open to the very top of the building, and as I turned, I could see that the stairs continued on both sides from the second floor on up.

There was an odd scent in the air. Some sort of incense, but I couldn't quite place it. Halcon noticed me looking around, and he smiled.

"Beautiful, isn't it?"

I nodded. That, he had right. The place was a showstopper, and if this had been any other time, any other situation, I'd have gone over to the intricate wallpaper and studied it, and rubbed my hand over the burnished wood of the railing, wondering at the smoothness.

"Come. We need to go downstairs. My master awaits."

That was the first time Halcon had used the term *master*, and the way he said it told me that when he was out and about, Halcon was good at putting on a mask. But Gulakah scared the hell out of him, and here that fear showed.

We headed toward a door to the side of the stairs, and I realized we were going down to a basement. Just how freaking *huge* was this place?

"I'm . . . a little claustrophobic." I didn't want to go down there without knowing I had an exit close at hand. Basements weren't on my list of best places to escape from, and chances were it would be hard as hell to get out of there once that door closed behind me.

"Nonsense. Everything will be fine." Halcon opened the door just as a loud slam came from behind us. We whirled around to see that the front door had swung open, but there was no one in sight.

Halcon paled. "Hell. Not another one," he muttered under his breath.

"Another what?" I asked.

"Never mind. Wait here." He moved toward the door, cautiously, and I realized he really was afraid.

At that moment the lights flickered and died, plunging us into darkness. A lot of shouting went on, and I thought about trying to maneuver my way out the front door, but we had to make sure this was where Gulakah was. Indecision kept me frozen, and then a light touch on my shoulder made me jump. I kept my mouth shut as a low voice whispered in my ear.

"Go downstairs with him. You won't be alone. When you're there, I'll give you the word and you hit the Lord of Ghosts with that rune. We'll be right behind you. He's there, I scoped it out."

Shade! I let out a long breath and gave a short nod, and then the lights came back on. Halcon was examining the front door suspiciously, but then he shook his head and moved back to my side.

"I should warn you, we have a few ghosts around here. But they won't hurt you. Come on, let's go." He motioned for me to follow him, and, confident now that I knew Shade was around, I did.

We descended the stairs, winding down at least two floors' worth, to finally reach a large, spacious floor deep beneath the house. The ceilings were at least fifteen feet high, which accounted for the number of stairs, and the chamber into which we stepped was nearly as large as the entire first floor of the mansion.

Pillars and beams—no doubt load-bearing—were spaced evenly through the room. Toward the back, I spied a large throne, or perhaps it was just a massive chair, but it was huge, with a door beyond it. Four women were sitting around the base of the chair, and one I recognized from the picture that Faerman had given us. It was his wife, Syringa. They were harnessed, unable to go farther than their tethers, and they all looked afraid and exhausted.

As Halcon pushed me from behind, toward the throne, I realized that I'd just become Gulakah's fifth . . . wife? Hand-maiden? Whatever he was using them for. It took everything I had for me to force myself not to run. The sight of the tethers and harnesses were flashing me back to the chains Hyto had used to restrain me. Playful bondage with Smoky and his hair? Not a problem. The real thing with a megalomaniac who was also a god? No, thank you!

Halcon pressed on my shoulders once we neared the throne, pushing me to my knees. I swallowed the lump rising in my throat, but then, the door behind the throne opened, and I fell into a black hole of fear as Gulakah, the Lord of Ghosts, strode out in all of his reptilian glory.

Chapter 18

Fuck. It was him, in the flesh. Knowing Shade was around was no longer the panacea I needed to keep it together. I began to back up, the panic rising. I'd been in Gulakah's mind. I'd sensed him from the inside out, the anger and love of destruction and hunger for power . . . it was all there, wrapped up inside him.

Backing away, I bumped into Halcon, who was standing directly behind me. He laughed low, and now the charm was gone and a sadistic delight filled his voice. He caught hold of me and pushed me forward.

"I brought you another one," he said in a loud voice as he grasped my hands behind me to keep me pinned.

I struggled and he shoved me hard, knocking me to the floor. Something shifted inside, and as I began to stand up, I realized that the dress was skintight and shorter on me. *Fuck.* Apparently getting knocked to the floor was enough of an attack to break the charm.

As I scrambled up, Halcon let out a gasp. Gulakah hissed,

the snakes on his head waving like crazy. He turned to Halcon.

"You bring a spy into my lair? I have seen her before! She is the enemy."

"No—no, I brought you . . . I thought she . . ." Halcon looked confused, but he didn't have a chance to say anything else because right then Shade leaped into the room out of the shadows. The commotion was earsplitting as the women screamed. Gulakah was heading directly toward us, and Halcon was scrambling away, looking terrified.

"Now—do it, Camille. We'll be right behind you."

"The women—"

"Don't worry, there are reinforcements upstairs, making their way down here right now." And with that, Shade gave me a sharp nod.

Cringing, petrified, I held out my left arm, palm up, and as Gulakah came into reach, I clenched my teeth and slammed it against him. The world fell away in a flash of lightning and thunder.

The gate was faster than a portal and more abrupt. I cringed as the world spun, throwing me against the Lord of Ghosts. At least he seemed too surprised to do anything, and by the time he started to rouse himself, we were on the ground, in front of the gates to the Netherworld. The world was a mist of silver and gray, and spirits passed by, unaware of me, but whirling into a frenzy when they saw Gulakah. I gasped, choking on the stale air that filled the space. I didn't even know if I had to breathe here, but I didn't want to chance finding out.

Gulakah looked around, then swiveled to me and charged. I screamed, dodging. As I managed to evade him, there was a soft sound to my left, and Morio and Shade were standing there. Right behind them, Vanzir, Smoky, and Roz showed up.

Morio grabbed my hand and pulled me off to the side. "We have to prepare. We can do this. The Greater Asa Mordente spell."

I'd brushed up on the spell while waiting to leave for the meeting.

The Greater Asa Mordente was a soul-zapping spell that stripped away life like a torturer flayed away skin. It was gruesome and dark and painful, and it forever changed the person who used it too much.

"You think we're ready?"

"Never more so, babe, and we don't have time to argue." He nodded to Gulakah, who had engaged Shade, Smoky, Roz, and Vanzir. They were fighting him with their silver weapons, dancing just out of reach of the writhing snakes. Smoky looked pale and wan here, and I could see how being in the Netherworld didn't agree with him.

"Eat it, dirtbag." Vanzir let loose with his feelers, and the neon tentacles writhed toward Gulakah, seeking purchase. The Lord of Ghosts laughed and went to swat them away but then let out a snarl as one wrapped around his arm and dug in, slithering beneath the surface to suck at his energy.

Shivering, I turned back to take Morio's hands. "Yes. We do this."

As the others kept Gulakah occupied, Morio and I lowered ourselves into trance. The energy of the Netherworld was seductive, seeping through everything like the perpetual mists that filtered through the realm.

Deeper we went, deeper, seeking the purple fire that coiled through the Netherworld, the fire of death, the cleansing fire, the fire of destruction, the fire of the phoenix, the fire that charred to ashes but did not burn. My stomach lurched as the icy winds blew past. More and more often, the stronger our death magic, the winds would come and reverberate through me, chilling me to the core.

My fingers touched his, and a crackle sparked between us.

And then, one beat . . . two . . . and we were spiraling up together, my soul rising out of my body to merge with his. We were twin flames, two sides of the same coin, partners who made each other stronger. The flames danced around us, circling in a wheel of sparks, and we were the hub, around which the circle became a wheel, turning ever faster.

"There," Morio whispered, and his words shook the winds.

I looked in the direction he nodded and saw the tail end of the phoenix—the spirit of death. The spirit of rebirth. The cleansing force of the world. I cooed to it, coaxing it to join us, and it slowly moved in our direction.

"Come here, we have need of one of your feathers. Please, if you would find us worthy." I sang to it, charming it, enchanting it, bewitching it, supplicating myself. Morio buoyed me up with his strength, and together we wooed the creature.

It flew over us, then circled the entire scene. Bilocating, both in my body and outside myself, I could see that the guys were in a desperate fight with the Lord of Ghosts. Smoky was heaving his grandfather's sword, slashing at the snakes atop Gulakah's head. Roz was darting in with a serrated short sword. His face was bloody, and I caught sight of a gash along one cheek. *Cripes*, he'd been hurt.

Vanzir had managed to latch onto him with several of the feelers that spread out from his hands, and he was feeding—siphoning off the energy in massive waves. He threw back his head, laughing, and his eyes spun wildly.

Smoky landed another blow to the top of Gulakah's head, and the Lord of Ghosts let out a scream of anger and slapped my dragon, sending him sprawling across the ground, into the mists. But the moment Gulakah's back was turned, Shade came in, also carrying a silver sword, and stabbed at him from the back.

"We have to hurry. They can't hold him much longer." I turned back to the phoenix. "Please, we so need your help. We must right an imbalance. In the name of Pentangle, the Mistress of Magic, may we please have one of your feathers?"

The bird paused, hovered over us, and then zoomed off, but as it flew away, it shook its tail and one of the feathers drifted down to land on my shoulder. I whispered a *Thank you* as Morio grabbed it.

He let go of my hands and pulled a bottle out of his bag.

Opening it, he dropped the feather inside and shook it up, then handed it to me. I hesitated, but only a second, before taking a good-sized swig of the potion. I handed the bottle back to him and he capped it, putting it away before resting his hands on my shoulders as I stood in front of him.

"I'm ready, my love."

"So am I. We *must* do this. You understand?"

"Yes, I do." I raised my arms, so that my palms were facing front, as we matched our breathing to a pace. Once again, our energies merged, and there was no beginning, no end to where his fingers touched my shoulders.

> *Spirits of the soul, spirits of the night,*
> *Spirits of the dark, spirits of the light.*
> *Spirits of the mad, spirits of the sane,*
> *Spirits who were good, spirits of the bane.*
> *Spirits long ascended, spirits who long fell,*
> *Spirits who are fleeting, spirits who do dwell.*

The fight picked up as Gulakah once again slashed Roz on one of his passes. Roz let out a shout as a bloodstain blossomed across the back of his coat. Smoky echoed a thundering call and the Lord of Ghosts answered, rearing around to engage him.

Smoky's sword cut through one of the snakes on Gulakah's head and the serpent fell, slithering and hissing toward Vanzir, who stomped on its head. Shade darted in, landing another blow, but the god was just too strong for them to bring down with weapons, and none of them had the magic to entangle with him.

Shade drew back and began to transform into his natural form—the skeletal dragon, with darkened bones that creaked and moaned every time he moved. Gulakah let out another hiss and stumbled as Shade swept his wings toward the Lord of Ghosts, knocking him off balance.

Morio and I continued, building the energy, driving the spell forward, focusing on Gulakah as we wove the words, and the words wove the power flowing from Morio into me.

A lattice of energy, a skeleton of power, rose into the air in the shape of a flaming violet arrow.

> *Spirits of forever, spirits who are no more,*
> *Spirits of the world, we call you to death's door.*
> *The flames, they whirl 'round you,*
> *The dreams, they haunt your thoughts,*
> *Our summoning to abyss's edge,*
> *You will ignore it not.*

Gulakah must have sensed what we were doing, because he turned in our direction and for the first time seemed to hesitate. He wavered, and during that moment, Vanzir took the opportunity to latch onto him with another set of the neon tentacles that writhed out from the palms of his hands. Startled, Gulakah turned back to him, slashing through several of the waving fronds.

Vanzir stumbled back. "Motherfucker!" He darted out of the way as Shade swept in, again, disrupting the Lord of Ghosts to give Vanzir time to retreat. The dream-chaser demon's hands were bleeding profusely.

We turned back to our work, and I focused as the energy was beginning to reverberate in my palms. I knew what I had to do, and it scared the fuck out of me, but there was no other way.

> *Of all the spirits round us, one alone shall fall,*
> *Of all the spirits walking, one alone we call.*
> *We place this hex, we curse this spell,*
> *We send you to the gates of Hel,*
> *We seal your passage, never to break,*
> *We bid the earth to shift and quake,*
> *We bid the air to shake the trees,*
> *We bid the flames to swallow thee,*
> *We bid the ocean to open wide,*
> *To take you down with cresting tide.*

There were other creatures gathered round, but none attempted to interfere. They all seemed too afraid, and whispers ran rife through the area. Smoky was beginning to tire. Roz was bleeding and out of the picture, as was Vanzir. Shade kept distracting Gulakah so we could finish.

We began to move forward, toward the Lord of Ghosts, Morio's hands sure on my shoulders. *He believes we can do it . . . he trusts me to not screw this up. I can do this . . .* My thoughts were racing, but I corralled them and brought them back to the spell's end point.

> *We name you once, we name you twice.*
> *We name you here, we name you thrice.*
> *Hear our spell, answer our call,*
> *You who are about to fall.*

As I reached the end point, Morio's fingers began to lift off my shoulders as he propelled me forward. It was now or never. As I let out the last three lines of the spell, I rushed forward toward the Lord of Ghosts and planted my hands on his side. He didn't see me coming.

> *Gulakah . . . Gulakah . . . Gulakah . . .*
> *In the name of the Hags of Fate and the Harvestmen,*
> *Be you dead to these realms forever!*

The energy lashed through me like a fiery whip, whistling out of my hands, surrounding him with a purple nimbus of jagged bolts that forced their way through him, spiraling in through every pore, soaking in like water into a sponge.

I couldn't let go; my hands were fastened to his side, and I could feel the disruption starting in his body—all the way from his tail through his feet. A river of pain worked its way up his legs, into his thighs . . . great torturous cramps that spread through his stomach, up into his torso, racking his chest, washing through his arms and neck, up to his head, where the snakes began to writhe, their agonized death throes a graceful mockery of dance.

I wanted to pull away, but I couldn't, and as he dragged

me along with him, trying to shake off the pain, I began to see a field of empty space—a few dark stars glimmering against the backdrop. The field was growing bigger as it blotted out the mist and the gates of the Netherworld, and I blinked, trying to clear my vision, but it wouldn't go away. The darkness began to eat up the light, eat away at every thing that seemed familiar. I shuddered, trying to remember my name, trying to remember who I was, but the words would not come, and then there was no sense of what I was.

All I knew was that I existed—I had no clue of who or what I was. I couldn't sense anything except the blackness around me and the dark sparkling stars that stood out faintly from the void in which I was standing.

"You are here with me." The voice echoed through my thoughts, but I had no sense of who it belonged to. "You did this to me, and now you are here with me, bound to my side for eternity."

I had a vague sense that I should fear the voice, but the feeling passed through; I held it for a moment, and then let it go. "Who are you?"

"Who do you think I am? I cannot be killed. I'm a god."

"Even the gods can die."

"But if I die, who will guard over the night, and the dead?"

I felt myself turning. For all I knew, I could have been spinning and not realized it. The question made sense, and yet it did not. "There are many who guard the paths of the dead. No one is indispensable." I didn't know how I knew that, but it was truth, and truth reverberated through me like a shining thread. I clung to the sensation, and it warmed me up just a little in the bitter chill.

"They tried to tell me that, before they cast me out. But I know my worth, I know my power, and I kept hold of my roots."

I wasn't sure who I was communicating with, but I didn't like whoever it was. The ego was strong, so strong that it felt overpowering. "Until you let go of that power, until you surrender yourself to it and submit yourself to it, you'll never be strong enough to withstand it. Power over corrupts. Power from within compels and strengthens."

And again, a shimmer in the vast pool of darkness. I followed the spark, letting it lead me on.

"I do not submit! They told me that I was taking too much for my own. But I will not kneel to another, nor bow, nor supplicate myself."

I was getting bored of hanging out here. Was the voice right? Was this it? Had I been cast into an amnesiac state and dropped in some realm of limbo? And speaking of "I" . . . who *was* I?

"I may not know my name, but I know this. Until you learn to bow to greater power, you will never truly command." A flare caught my attention and I began to follow it. The voice was growing fainter.

"Come back—you put me here, you owe it to me to stay! Don't leave me here . . ." And then the voice vanished, as if snuffed out like a candle flame.

Without warning, a rushing sensation catapulted me out of the blackness.

"Camille? Camille? Wake up! Camille?" A sharp sting on my cheek brought me round as I struggled to sit up. I blinked, aching like a son of a bitch. As I looked around, I saw Gulakah's body lying there next to me, lifeless. With a groan, I let Smoky lift me into his arms.

Shade was helping hold up Morio, who looked like he'd been through a soot storm. As I glanced down at my hands and feet, I realized I looked just as bad. Roz and Vanzir were sprawled out on their backs on the ground. Scrambling, I pushed against Smoky's chest.

"Put me down—they're hurt!"

Smoky grumbled but let me down, and I raced over to them, every bone and muscle in my body aching. As I knelt between them, the smell of their blood filled my nose, and I realized that Vanzir was okay, but Roz looked bad.

"Smoky, you've got to get him back to the house. The rest

of us need to get into that compound and finish off the demons there. Halcon has one of the spirit seals!" I glanced over at the body of Gulakah. "Should we cut him to pieces or what? I don't want any of this resurrection or reanimation crap going on."

"Let me take Roz home, then I'll be back to fetch you and Morio. Shade, take care of the corpse." Smoky gently gathered up Roz and vanished.

I helped Vanzir sit up, and, after a moment's disorientation, he was able to stand on his own. His hands were covered with blood, his palms roughed up, but he looked relatively okay, although his clothing was splattered with gore and I had the feeling most of it was from Gulakah.

"Did we really defeat him?" Vanzir stared at the body in wonder. "I can't believe we killed a god."

"It was mostly Camille and Morio," Shade said. "Camille . . . at the end, took him out with the spell she and Morio were casting. We thought we'd lost her for a while there. Her body was okay, but her soul went wandering."

Went wandering . . . that was one way to put it. I closed my eyes, only to see the dizzying expanse of blackness again, and quickly opened them. The overpowering ego of the god stuck with me. Even at the end, he couldn't admit that he'd let himself get out of control.

Even the gods can die . . . Pentangle must have known that he wouldn't back down, that he wouldn't change his ways. If he had been able to admit his failings, the Hags of Fate might have let him live, but he'd upset the balance. The Ocean of Anger was too great and was feeding too many ghosts. I wondered how long it would take for the pendulum to swing back to the middle, for the spirits to realize they were free and depart.

And yet . . . and yet . . .

"Do you think we were right, to kill a god?" It still seemed overwhelming, and egotistical, even though we'd been charged with the task. Or rather, I had been charged with it.

"We were right to kill someone working for Shadow Wing, who destroyed a lot of innocent people in our city, and who was responsible for enslaving and impoverishing a number of others." Vanzir shook his head. "Don't let yourself dwell on it. You did the right thing."

I looked over at Morio but said nothing more. Something had changed with that spell, like Morio had said. I didn't know what, just yet; I couldn't pinpoint the feeling, but something had shifted inside. But Vanzir was correct—we had no choice. Gulakah was a nasty motherfucker, and we had to take him out, god or not. Maybe it was just the thought that we had actually been *able* to kill him that made me uneasy. Power was potent, and power could corrupt so easily if allowed to get out of hand.

Smoky appeared again, and he took hold of Morio and me, and—leaving Shade to deal with the corpse of the god—we vanished into the Ionyc Seas, back to the mansion, where Halcon Davis waited.

Halcon Davis was waiting for us, all right—or at least his body was. By the looks of things, Menolly had gotten to him, and he was very, very dead. I glanced around. Shamas was leading a group of officers and volunteers from the Supe Community to sort out the people who lived here now. The Fae women were huddled on a sofa, looking worn out but more alert than they had been when Gulakah and I had vanished for the Netherworld.

I walked up to Syringa. "Your husband is waiting for you. He misses you."

She blinked, looking confused. "How much time . . . what day . . ."

"What's the last thing you remember?" I took her hands in mine, sitting down beside her. She was lovely, ethereal, and her energy sparkled like a beckoning rainbow. I could see how Halcon had picked her out of the pack.

"Thursday? I went to a meeting for the . . ." She paused as someone wheeled Halcon's body past us. "Oh. Him . . ."

I jumped up. "I need to search his body before you take it—"

"No worries. I have it." Menolly came strolling up from behind. She patted the pocket of her jean jacket. "First thing I did when I took him down was strip it off his weasel-necked body."

"Why do you think that Shadow Wing didn't tell Gulakah to confiscate the spirit seal from Halcon?" It seemed to me that he'd want his demon general to have it.

"I think Shadow Wing might have been worried about Gulakah growing too powerful. He was, after all, a god. And Gulakah was using Shadow Wing for his own agenda, so he probably was playing along for a while." She shrugged. "We'll never know for sure, but . . ."

"You're probably right. So, anything else on Halcon's body we should know about?"

"No. Nothing else of value, but I'm sure when we search this mansion, we're going to be finding all sorts of useful information and items. Halcon Davis was the one storing the money. Gulakah didn't care about cash."

I nodded, thinking of how many people Halcon had had time to fleece. If he'd found the spirit seal around the date he disappeared, he'd had well over a hundred fifty years to con people out of their savings and goods.

"I dread going through here. It's going to take a long time."

"I'm asking Roman if I can set a group of vamps to do it—Erin can watch over them. They'll behave and not filch anything if Roman commands it." She gave me the once-over. "You okay? You seem strangely quiet."

I glanced over my shoulder at Syringa. Delilah was talking to her now. Looping my arm through Menolly's, I walked her away from where the others could hear and quietly told her about what had happened in the Netherworld, after I'd slammed into Gulakah with the Greater Asa Mordente spell.

She let out a low whistle. "The realm of the dead can't be easy to hang out in, not for someone with as much life in them as you have."

"That's just it . . . it wasn't easy, but it was . . . intoxicating. If what Morio said is right, and I'm to evolve into one of the Moon Mother's sorceresses, as well as her Dark Moon High Priestess . . . can I handle the power? Can I handle the responsibility? The thought of it frightens me. What if I lose myself?" My head throbbing, I looked for a chair.

Menolly bit her lip. "I doubt it. Not you. But all I can tell you is this . . . there's no going back. None of us can go back to the way things were. We have to go forward. Who knows what the future will bring. Maybe Shadow Wing will win, but for now, he's lost another battle, and we have another spirit seal, and that's what they call, I believe, having a good day."

Weary, aching through my entire body, and not sure what was going to happen next, I smiled and nodded. "Let's go home and find out how Roz is doing. I can't handle cleanup tonight. Let the others do it."

"That's my girl." Menolly leaned up and kissed my cheek. "You may be my big sister, but sometimes, it's okay to lean on others. I know you learned that lesson, but just . . . make sure you remember it."

We turned toward the stairs and, with Delilah joining us, headed on up to our cars. The night was dark, the sky misty, and we were standing on the eve of Beltane.

Chapter 19
֍

Beltane. I woke up early, along with Morio. Trenyth had made the journey over to our house when we'd called him up on the Whispering Mirror to take possession of the spirit seal, so it was safely back in Elqaneve, though how safe the Elfin City was, with the impending war, remained to be seen.

Morio and I headed out to Talamh Lonrach Oll after breakfast. Delilah was pouting because she had to stay home—but since she'd be transforming as the moon grew full later today, there was no way she could go with us.

And Aeval had specified that Morio and I would be undergoing some sort of ritual, so the others decided to stay home with Delilah. We'd hold our own celebration on the weekend. Even though Smoky and Trillian seemed a little miffed that they hadn't been invited, they'd agreed and just gave me long kisses as I headed out the door.

As we drove out, I tried to sort out what had happened. I gave Chase a call. "So, what did they find, as of this morning?"

He let out a long sigh. "A lot of broken people. They weren't the most stable to begin with, and being bewitched by the spirit seal made things a lot worse. I've asked Lindsey Cartridge if she and her group can help. Nerissa and Sharah will figure out the best way to counsel these women. It was mostly women, by the way, and before you ask, yes, some were assaulted. Most likely by the Tregarts."

"Oh great gods, I hope none of them get pregnant. We don't need any half-demon children running around the city."

"That's a possibility? I'll mention it to Sharah and Mallen. They're doing all the examinations." Chase paused. "We're also on a mad search to see if we can find any more spirit demon eggs—there are so many places where they could have been hidden, and it doesn't seem logical that Gulakah would only bring over two. For all we know, there may be spirit demons loose in Seattle right now."

"On that depressing thought, what did the vamps find in the mansion? I know a swarm of them were on the way over when we left."

"The list of assets is remarkable. Halcon Davis was a multimillionaire. We're going to have to figure out what to do with all that wealth. I'm thinking of dividing it up among the OIA, the Supe Community Council, and the Seattle Vampire Nexus, including a substantial grant for Vampires Anonymous." He took a drink of something, then let out a short breath.

"Speaking of which . . . Syringa? Your Fae lord's wife? She's not doing very well. Physically, she's fine, but when she realized what had happened, it . . . well, let's just say she's checked out. The body is here, but the spirit has fled, Sharah said. We're going to have to have a soul-catcher find her."

"You know about soul-catchers?" I had never heard Chase use that term. It rather surprised me.

"I do now, thanks to Sharah and Mallen. Anyway, I've got to go. We've still got a buttload of stuff to process, and I think it's going to take several weeks to work our way through the mansion and the paperwork. But at least Gulakah's dead . . . Thank you, by the way. What you and Morio did . . ."

"Hey, we do what we have to." Suddenly wanting to get away from the conversation, I said my good-byes and hung up.

"Getting too close for comfort?" Morio said, glancing at me.

I rubbed his arm. "Just overwhelmed, and not sure what tonight holds for us. I'm afraid. I don't know what reserves I have left."

"More than you know, babe. More than you know." And with that, he turned up the music as we sped along the freeway.

By evening, my spirits were back up. I was dressed in my priestess robes, and Morio was in his ceremonial kimono, and the drummers were gathered around the bale fire, their rhythms filling the air with anticipation and the summons to ritual. We'd spent the day eating and visiting. Morio had turned into a fox and let the Fae children pet him, and then we'd gone swimming in the hot springs and taken a much-needed nap. I was starting to relax and fall into the rhythm of the drums. My feet were tapping and I wanted to dance, so I moved to the edge of the fire and joined the other women who were letting the beat speak through their bodies.

The energy was on the rise—Beltane was the night of the rut, the night when the King Stag bugled for his mate. Beltane was the night when the gods fucked their brains out, when the Lord of the Forest impregnated the goddess incarnate. The Fae, usually rather reserved, let loose on this day, and all our wild, primal bloodlines came forth.

There were couples and groups fucking on the grass near the fire circle, women in the wild throes of orgasm, men rutting into them, growling, snuffling like Herne the Hunter, who lurked in the depths of the woods . . . like Pan—Old Shag of the meadows—who frolicked with the nymphs and celebrated the carnality of the body as it blended with the sublime musings of the soul.

Morio leaned up against my back, wrapping his arms

around me, moving with me as the drums led us deeper into the labyrinth of the sacred night. And then the horns trumpeted as Titania, Aeval, and Morgaine made their way down to the commons. They were followed by Bran, Mordred, and Arturo.

As they passed, their people bowed low, honoring the queens, honoring their power and lineage and strength. I knelt at Aeval's feet as she stopped before me.

"Rise, my child. You and your priest accompany me." And so I rose and took hold of my staff. We followed as they passed out of the common area, into the undergrowth. Tonight, the forest seemed to part for us as we walked through, and we made no noise, silently gliding through the woodland.

The echo of the drums followed us, and as we journeyed, animals joined in at our heels. A stag, pure white, followed Morio, and several stray cats cloistered at my feet. An owl flew down to land on Aeval's shoulder, and a raven perched on Morgaine's shoulder. Titania held out her hand and a mountain lion crept out of the bushes, padding softly by the Queen of Light and Morning.

As we continued deeper into the forest, the moon rose full and silver above us, and I caught my breath. I could feel the Moon Mother over my shoulder, calling me. Tonight was the Hunt. I'd never missed a Hunt since I'd been accepted into her order as a witch, and now she was riding me hard. The urge to let go and fly with her was almost too strong to bear.

I was fighting the pressure when we broke through into a clearing—a Faerie ring, with fly agarics the size of my fist encircling the meadow. In the center, a fire crackled, kindled from the nine sacred woods. The smell of yew was strong in my nose, and I felt so deeply at home that it scared me. My roots had grown in strongly during my time out here at Talamh Lonrach Oll, and I realized I could breathe here. I could let down my hair, let out my worries, and focus on my connection with my lady.

Aeval stepped into the Circle, and Titania joined her. Morgaine stayed outside with us, waiting. Mordred and

Arturo backed away. Bran came close but did not cross the line.

Aeval walked up to the fire and then turned. She tapped her staff three times on the ground, and a sound like thunder raced through the clearing. The next thing I knew, Derisa was standing there. High Priestess to the Moon Mother. The woman who had taken my oath when I first pledged as a witch, and the woman who had again taken my oath when I pledged into the Priesateshood. They kissed one another on the cheek, and then Derisa kissed Titania, who stood to one side, tall and regal, glowing like a memory of sunlight in the depths of the night.

A gust of wind blew through, the scents of violet and narcissus, of peach and musk and newly mown grass filling the air. I fell into the fragrance, letting it buoy me even further away from the events of the past days. It ran through me, a series of little explosions, like foreplay.

Aeval and Derisa motioned to Morgaine, and she entered the Circle. She slowly walked up to them and knelt at their feet. I wondered how much that cost her pride, but she said nothing, just kissed their hands as they extended them. Morgaine gave one glance back at me, and I saw the jealousy in her eyes, but she said nothing. She stepped over to the fire and waited.

And then Derisa turned to Morio and me and motioned us in. We both stepped forward, and when we reached her side, we knelt. I kissed her hand, then Aeval's, and Morio followed suit. As I stood, Derisa smiled and kissed me, long and deep, so that I was swirling in her passion.

"And so, once again we come to a turning point, my lovely Camille. You are priestess, yes, and doing well in your training, but there is another step you now must take. You will eventually become the High Priestess of the Dark Mother, even as I am High Priestess of the Bright Mother. Before you can begin to train toward that direction, you and your priest must show your courage and lead the Hunt."

Lead the Hunt?

I swallowed. I knew that running at the helm of the Hunt was reserved for the bravest warriors and those in the Moon Mother's favor, but that was about all I understood. I'd always run with the other witches, and then—the past few months—the other priestesses.

"What do I need to know?" I asked.

"The question is not what you need to know, but what you're willing to do and to face. Tonight will test you, both of you." Derisa stepped back as a distant baying echoed from the sky. "The Moon Mother, she comes."

Morgaine reached up, her eyes glassy, and I recognized that stare. "You run with the Hunt?"

"I am a daughter of the moon, even if it is over here, Earthside," she said, smiling softly.

I gazed up at the heavens. The baying of hounds was louder, and behind it the shrieks of night birds echoed, along with the thunder of running feet, the pounding of drums, and a cadence of song, in a language long forgotten, by women who could weave magic with their voices.

First came the Moon Mother, a silhouette in silver, with a bow and quiver slung over her back. She was beautiful and luminous, and her energy called to me, beckoning like a lover long lost. Behind her came the bears and panthers, the stag and wolf and all animals who raced under her open skies.

Morgaine was crying now, and I realized that I was, too. I reached up with one hand to the Moon Mother, my other hand firmly grasping Morio's. He said nothing, but his eyes were wide. As my lady passed, the song and drum growing louder, she reached out and caught hold of my hand, pulling both Morio and me onto the web, into her wake.

As we jumped, landing on the astral with her, I gazed up at my beloved Moon Mother. She had come to me when I was bruised and beaten in Hyto's lair, and while she could not free me, she'd taken me out, taken me off to tear up the world while he abused my body. She'd wrapped me in her arms, and kissed my tears, and offered me solace.

And now she bent down from her terrible height and

brushed my lips with her own, and then she kissed Morio, and her eyes were gleaming with silver light even as her body thrummed with a magnetic pull.

"Welcome to the Hunt," she whispered to Morio, and her words blew down a tree and swept across lakes, churning the waters. Turning to me, she cupped my chin in her hands and smiled. "So you join the dark paths of my order. Do not fear the word—fear only the misuse of it. But now, face the Hunt. For you will lead tonight, and *I will follow.*"

I stared at her. How the hell was I supposed to do that? I turned back to look at the stream of figures behind me, so vast it was hard to count, all of them waiting for my next move.

Skeletal riders astride skeletal mounts, with their eyes gleaming fire, waited. Hunters and warriors, priestesses—Morgaine among them—and witches. Wild feral spirits from the woodlands who came out to play in the night were poised, along with the animals over whom the Moon Mother watched. All of them watched me. If I wasn't confident, they would turn on me. They were loyal to their goddess. *I* had to earn their trust.

I stared at them. Would they listen to me? Would they laugh at me? Would I disgrace myself in front of my lady? And then I saw Derisa. She was standing behind the Moon Mother, to her right side. And I realized that she, too, had undergone this ritual. She, too, had led the Hunt in order to take her place as the Bright Mother's High Priestess. If she did it, then I could.

And that was when I noticed the staff in her hand. It matched my own, only instead of yew, it was made of oak. As I watched her holding it, I realized that her staff was awake and sentient.

I glanced at the staff in my own hand. "Wake up. I need you," I whispered.

It quivered.

"I command you, wake and help me lead the Hunt."

The crystal orb atop it glimmered and began to shine. A spark within the staff swirled, racing down through my hand, and I let my head drop back as it wove its way through my body, infusing me with a fiery strength. But it wasn't the fire of the open flame—no, it was the fire of the will-o'-the-wisps, the fire of the eye catchers, the fire of the sparkling lights at night. Dark Faerie fire, and it integrated itself into my nature, shifting me, changing me, transforming me.

I turned to Morio and pulled him close, kissing him deeply. "Happy Beltane, my priest. Are you ready to run at my side, to run with the Hunt?"

He nodded. "At your command, my priestess."

"Then let's get this show on the road."

I curtsied to the Moon Mother, and to Derisa, and then, turning to face the open sky, I leaped ahead into the void, thrusting my staff into the air, and we were off. With a shriek that echoed through the forests all over the world, I led the Hunt, deep into the Beltane night.

I raced through cloud and open sky, through the stars, under the glowing orb of the Moon, and behind me, the Hunt swept on, the Moon Mother at my side, as we tore up the night in mayhem and madness.

We rampaged through the country, sweeping through the astral and spirit planes, diving into the world of mortals as we passed over the deep, dark forests to catch up the valiant spirits of the dead who belonged to the Hunt—both animal and mortal. We ran on and on, breathless, mindless, caught in the chase as we terrified those who could hear our horns bugling through the night, until morning came, and once again, our feet touched the earth.

Chapter 20

A week later, Menolly, Delilah, and I were sitting on a blanket by the shore of Birchwater Pond with Maggie by our side. Everybody else was scattered around. Vanzir, Morio, and Roz—who had healed right up once we'd gotten him home and into the loving care of Hanna and Iris—were playing Frisbee.

Smoky was high in a tree, keeping a watch over the land, Bruce and Roman sitting beside him. Shade was helping Iris and Hanna grill the hamburgers. Trillian, Nerissa, and Shamas were setting the picnic tables with all the fixings for burgers and hot dogs. And over in a quiet glade, Chase was walking hand in hand with Sharah.

And in a strange quirk, we'd added to our guest list for the night. Wilbur, working his crutches and trying to get used to his artificial leg, was sitting on a stump next to Ivana Krask. The two were talking. I really didn't want to know what they were saying, especially since Rodney was there, along with Martin, and the gruesome quartet seemed deep in conversation. Well, Martin wasn't doing much talking, but he was behaving himself, at least.

I leaned back, staring at the stars that littered the twilight sky. We'd found three more spirit demon eggs and taken care of them. The Supe Community had taken over the mansion owned by Halcon Davis—it was cheaper than continuing to pour money into the hall they were trying to rebuild. Syringa, the wife of Lord Faerman, had come out of her stupor, and most of those who had fallen prey to Halcon Davis and the Aleksais Psychic Network were being treated on an outpatient basis at the FH-CSI.

Wrapping my arms around my knees, I looked over at Menolly and Delilah. "One spirit seal left to find."

"That's not going to win the war, though." Menolly was swigging out of a thermos. Morio had made her watermelon-flavored blood. "Let's face it, we just won a tremendous battle, but look how long it took, and how much it cost us. Do you really think Shadow Wing doesn't have anybody stronger than Gulakah? And do you think he's going to wait long before sending that person—demon—whatever, our way? Someone to pick up with Telazhar?"

"Or worse . . . we know they still have two of the spirit seals." I gazed out over the placid pond. Sometimes the depths of the most gentle-looking surface held demons. The memory of being in Gulakah's mind, and then locked with him there at the end, wouldn't leave me alone. I'd been having nightmares in which I was caught in the violent sea with him, and he kept pulling me down, below the surface.

Delilah reached out and took one of Menolly's hands, and one of mine.

"Whatever happens, we meet it together. We have a small army of our own, and it keeps growing. The Supe Community Militia have proven their worth."

I nodded. "Yeah, I know. But now that the general populace knows about zombies, how long before they begin finding out about some of the more nightmarish aspects of what they thought were myth and legend? They reacted pretty good-naturedly to us, because we aren't a big threat. Except to the hate groups. But what if they find out about the demons?"

"Panic, mayhem . . . but I guess we deal with that if—and when—it happens. Until then, we do our best, we tend to our loves, and we enjoy what we can. Because there's never any guarantee that tomorrow will come." Menolly leaned over and kissed my cheek. "Let it go for tonight?"

I nodded, pushing the worries out of my mind. Menolly was right. The demons might be hiding in the shadows, but right now we were alive, and we'd found another spirit seal, and we'd killed a god. We were surrounded by family and friends and loved ones. Considering what we were up against, it couldn't get much better than that.

"Who's that?" I asked, pointing to a figure who was walking out of the forest.

"I hope you don't mind, but I asked him if he'd like to come," Delilah said. She smiled. "I thought maybe it would be nice to have him here when we aren't worrying about some battle."

"Who . . ." But as I stood, I could see who it was. Sephreh—our father—and for once he wasn't wearing his uniform. He raised his hand to wave, and I realized he was really here. He'd come to join us. A smile broke over his face, and my heart warmed. My father was back. Maybe not the same as before—but perhaps it was for the best. We'd all learned a lot in the past six months.

An owl hooted softly in a tree as the waves lapped against the shore of the pond. Menolly, Delilah, and I joined hands and, carrying Maggie, hurried over to greet our father in the deepening night.

CAST OF MAJOR CHARACTERS

The D'Artigo Family
Sephreh ob Tanu: The D'Artigo Sisters' father. Full Fae.
Maria D'Artigo: The D'Artigo Sisters' mother. Human.
Camille Sepharial te Maria, aka Camille D'Artigo: The oldest sister; a Moon Witch and priestess. Half-Fae, half-human.
Delilah Maria te Maria, aka Delilah D'Artigo: The middle sister; a werecat.
Arial Lianan te Maria: Delilah's twin who died at birth. Half-Fae, half-human.
Menolly Rosabelle te Maria, aka Menolly D'Artigo: The youngest sister; a vampire and *jian-tu*: extraordinary acrobat. Half-Fae, half-human.
Shamas ob Olanda: The D'Artigo girls' cousin. Full Fae.

The D'Artigo Sisters' Lovers & Close Friends
Bruce O'Shea: Iris's husband. Leprechaun.
Carter: Leader of the Demonica Vacana Society, a group that watches and records the interactions of Demonkin and human through the ages. Carter is half demon and half Titan—his father was Hyperion, one of the Greek Titans.
Chase Garden Johnson: Detective, director of the Faerie-Human Crime Scene Investigation (FH-CSI) team. Human who has taken the Nectar of Life, which extends his life span beyond any ordinary mortal and has opened up his psychic abilities.
Chrysandra: Waitress at the Wayfarer Bar & Grill. Human.
Derrick Means: Bartender at the Wayfarer Bar & Grill. Werebadger.
Erin Mathews: Former president of the Faerie Watchers Club and former owner of the Scarlet Harlot Boutique. Turned into a vampire by Menolly, her sire, moments before her death. Human.

Greta: Leader of the Death Maidens; Delilah's tutor.

Iris (Kuusi) O'Shea: Friend and companion of the girls. Priestess of Undutar. Talon-haltija (Finnish house sprite).

Lindsey Katharine Cartridge: Director of the Green Goddess Women's Shelter. Pagan and witch. Human.

Luke: Former bartender at the Wayfarer Bar & Grill. Werewolf. One of the Keraastar Knights.

Marion Vespa: Coyote shifter; owner of the Supe-Urban Café.

Morio Kuroyama: One of Camille's lovers and husbands. Essentially the grandson of Grandmother Coyote. Youkai-kitsune (roughly translated: Japanese fox demon).

Neely Reed: Founding Member of the United Worlds Church. FBH.

Nerissa Shale: Menolly's wife. Worked for DSHS. Now working for Chase Johnson as a victims-rights counselor for the FH-CSI. Werepuma and member of the Rainier Puma Pride.

Roman: Ancient vampire; son of Blood Wyne, Queen of the Crimson Veil. Menolly's official consort in the Vampire Nation and her new sire.

Rozurial, aka Roz: Mercenary. Menolly's secondary lover. Incubus who used to be Fae before Zeus and Hera destroyed his marriage.

Shade: Delilah's fiancé. Part Stradolan, part black (shadow) dragon.

Sharah: Elfin medic; Chase's girlfriend.

Siobhan Morgan: One of the girls' friends. Selkie (wereseal); member of the Puget Sound Harbor Seal Pod.

Smoky: One of Camille's lovers and husbands. Half-white, half-silver dragon.

Tavah: Guardian of the portal at the Wayfarer Bar & Grill. Vampire (full Fae).

Tim Winthrop, aka Cleo Blanco: Computer student/genius, female impersonator. FBH. Now owns the Scarlet Harlot.

Trillian: Mercenary. Camille's alpha lover and one of her three husbands. Svartan (one of the Charming Fae).

Vanzir: Was indentured slave to the Sisters, by his own choice. Dream-chaser demon who lost his powers and now is regaining new ones.

Venus the Moon Child: Former shaman of the Rainier Puma Pride. Werepuma. One of the Keraastar Knights.

Wade Stevens: President of Vampires Anonymous. Vampire (human).

Zachary Lyonnesse: Former member of the Rainier Puma Pride Council of Elders. Werepuma living in Otherworld.

GLOSSARY

Black Unicorn/Black Beast: Father of the Dahns unicorns, a magical unicorn that is reborn like the phoenix and lives in Darkynwyrd and Thistlewyd Deep. Raven Mother is his consort, and he is more a force of nature than a unicorn.

Calouk: The rough, common dialect used by a number of Otherworld inhabitants.

Court and Crown: "Crown" refers to the Queen of Y'Elestrial. "Court" refers to the nobility and military personnel that surround the Queen. "Court and Crown" together refer to the entire government of Y'Elestrial.

Court of the Three Queens: The newly risen Court of the three Earthside Fae Queens: Titania, the Fae Queen of Light and Morning; Morgaine, the half-Fae Queen of Dusk and Twilight; and Aeval, the Fae Queen of Shadow and Night.

Crypto: One of the Cryptozoid races. Cryptos include creatures out of legend that are not technically of the Fae races: gargoyles, unicorns, gryphons, chimeras, and so on. Most primarily inhabit Otherworld, but some have Earthside cousins.

Demon Gate: A gate through which demons may be summoned by a powerful sorcerer or necromancer.

Dreyerie: A dragon lair.

Earthside: Everything that exists on the Earth side of the portals.

Elemental Lords: The elemental beings—both male and female—who, along with the Hags of Fate and the Harvestmen, are the only true Immortals. They are avatars of various elements and energies, and they inhabit all realms. They do as they will and seldom concern themselves with humankind or

Fae unless summoned. If asked for help, they often exact steep prices in return. The Elemental Lords are not concerned with balance like the Hags of Fate.

Elqaneve: The Elfin lands in Otherworld.

FBH: Full-Blooded Human (usually refers to Earthside humans).

FH-CSI: The Faerie-Human Crime Scene Investigation team. The brainchild of Detective Chase Johnson, it was first formed as a collaboration between the OIA and the Seattle police department. Other FH-CSI units have been created around the country, based on the Seattle prototype. The FH-CSI takes care of both medical and criminal emergencies involving visitors from Otherworld.

Great Divide: A time of immense turmoil when the Elemental Lords and some of the High Court of Fae decided to rip apart the worlds. Until then, the Fae existed primarily on Earth, their lives and worlds mingling with those of humans. The Great Divide tore everything asunder, splitting off another dimension, which became Otherworld. At that time, the Twin Courts of Fae were disbanded and their queens stripped of power. This was the time during which the Spirit Seal was formed and broken in order to seal off the realms from each other. Some Fae chose to stay Earthside, others moved to the realm of Otherworld, and the demons were—for the most part—sealed in the Subterranean Realms.

Guard Des'Estar: The military of Y'Elestrial.

Hags of Fates: The women of destiny who keep the balance righted. Neither good nor evil, they observe the flow of destiny. When events get too far out of balance, they step in and take action, usually using humans, Fae, Supes, and other creatures as pawns to bring the path of destiny back into line.

Harvestmen: The lords of death—a few cross over and are also Elemental Lords. The Harvestmen, along with their followers (the Valkyries and the Death Maidens, for example), reap the souls of the dead.

Haseofon: The abode of the Death Maidens—where they stay and where they train.

Ionyc Lands: The astral, etheric, and spirit realms, along with several other lesser-known noncorporeal dimensions, form the Ionyc Lands. These realms are separated by the Ionyc Seas, a current of energy that prevents the Ionyc Lands from colliding, thereby sparking off an explosion of universal proportions.

Ionyc Seas: The currents of energy that separate the Ionyc Lands. Certain creatures, especially those connected with the elemental energies of ice, snow, and wind, can travel through the Ionyc Seas without protection.

Koyanni: The coyote shifters who took an evil path away from the Great Coyote; followers of Nukpana.

Melosealfôr: A rare Crypto dialect learned by powerful Cryptos and all Moon Witches.

The Nectar of Life: An elixir that can extend the life span of humans to nearly the length of a Fae's years. Highly prized and cautiously used. Can drive someone insane if he or she doesn't have the emotional capacity to handle the changes incurred.

OIA: The Otherworld Intelligence Agency; the "brains" behind the Guard Des'Estar.

Otherworld/OW: The human term for the "United Nations" of Faerie Land. A dimension apart from ours that contains creatures from legend and lore, pathways to the gods, and various other places, such as Olympus. Otherworld's actual name varies among the differing dialects of the many races of Cryptos and Fae.

Portal, Portals: The interdimensional gates that connect the different realms. Some were created during the Great Divide; others open up randomly.

Seattle Vampire Nexus: The group now overseeing most of the vampire activities in Seattle and the surrounding areas. Run by Lord Roman, son of the vampire queen, Blood Wyne, the SVN now oversees Vampires Anonymous.

Seelie Court: The Earthside Fae Court of Light and Summer, disbanded during the Great Divide. Titania was the Seelie Queen.

Soul Statues: In Otherworld, small figurines created for the Fae of certain races and magically linked with the baby. These figurines reside in family shrines and when one of the Fae dies, their soul statue shatters. In Menolly's case, when she was reborn as a vampire, her soul statue re-formed, although twisted. If a family member disappears, his or her family can always tell if their loved one is alive or dead if they have access to the soul statue.

Spirit Seals: A magical crystal artifact, the Spirit Seal was created during the Great Divide. When the portals were sealed, the Spirit Seal was broken into nine gems and each piece was given to an Elemental Lord or Lady. These gems each have varying powers. Even possessing one of the spirit seals can allow the wielder to weaken the portals that divide Otherworld, Earthside, and the Subterranean Realms. If all of the seals are joined together again, then all of the portals will open.

Stradolan: A being who can walk between worlds, who can walk through the shadows, using them as a method of transportation.

Supe/Supes: Short for Supernaturals. Refers to Earthside supernatural beings who are not of Fae nature. Refers to Weres, especially.

Talamh Lonrach Oll: The name for the Earthside Sovereign Fae Nation.

Triple Threat: Camille's nickname for the newly risen three Earthside Queens of Fae.

Unseelie Court: The Earthside Fae Court of Shadow and Winter, disbanded during the Great Divide. Aeval was the Unseelie Queen.

VA/Vampires Anonymous: The Earthside group started by Wade Stevens, a vampire who was a psychiatrist during life. The group is focused on helping newly born vampires adjust to their new state of existence, and to encourage vampires to avoid harming the innocent as much as possible. The VA is vying for control. Their goal is to rule the vampires of the United States and to set up an internal policing agency.

Whispering Mirror: A magical communications device that links Otherworld and Earth. Think magical video phone.

Y'Eírialiastar: The Sidhe/Fae name for Otherworld.

Y'Elestrial: The city-state in Otherworld where the D'Artigo girls were born and raised. A Fae city, recently embroiled in a civil war between the drug-crazed tyrannical Queen Lethe-sanar and her more level-headed sister Tanaquar, who managed to claim the throne for herself. The civil war has ended and Tanaquar is restoring order to the land.

Youkai: Loosely (very loosely) translated as Japanese demon/nature spirit. For the purposes of this series, the youkai have three shapes: the animal, the human form, and the true demon form. Unlike the demons of the Subterranean Realms, youkai are not necessarily evil by nature.

PLAYLIST FOR *HAUNTED MOON*

I write to music a good share of the time, and so I always put my playlists in the back of each book so you can see which artists/songs I listened to during the writing. Here's the playlist for *Haunted Moon*:

Adele: "Rumour Has It"

Air: "The Word 'Hurricane,'" "Moon Fever"

AJ Roach: "Devil May Dance"

Amanda Blank: "Something Bigger, Something Better"

Android Lust: "Dragonfly," "Follow"

Audioslave: "Set It Off"

Avalon Rising: "Where the Sunset Is Golden"

AWOLNATION: "Sail"

Black Mountain: "Wucan," "Queens Will Play"

Black Rebel Motorcycle Club: "Fault Line"

Black Sabbath: "Paranoid"

The Bravery: "Believe"

Bret Michaels: "Love Sucks"

Chester Bennington: "System"

Cobra Verde: "Play with Fire"

Cynthia Smith & Ruth Barrett: "Faerie's Love Song"

David Draiman: "Forsaken"

Death Cab for Cutie: "I Will Possess Your Heart"

Dragon Ritual Drummers: "Black Queen"

Eels: "Souljacker Part I"

Fatboy Slim: "Praise You"

Faun: "Punagra," "Konigin"

Fleetwood Mac: "The Chain," "Gold Dust Woman"

Flight of the Hawk: "Bones"

Foster the People: "Pumped Up Kicks"

Gary Numan: "Dead Sun Rising," "When the Sky Bleeds, He Will Come," "The Fall," "The Angel Wars," "Hybrid," "Halo," "Walking With Shadows"

Godsmack: "Voodoo"

Gorillaz: "Demon Days"

Gypsy: "Spirit Nation," "Morgaine"

Hanni El Khatib: "Come Alive"

Heather Alexander: "The Garden," "March of Cambreadth"

Hedningarna: "Tuuli," "Ukkonen," "Raven," "Gorrlaus"

Hugo: "99 Problems"

In Strict Confidence: "Silver Bullets," "Forbidden Fruit"

Jay Gordon: "Slept So Long"

Julian Cope: "Charlotte Anne"

Kirsty MacColl: "In These Shoes"

Lady Gaga: "Paparazzi," "Born This Way," "I Like It Rough"

Loreena McKennitt: "Mummer's Dance"

Marc Lanegan: "The Gravedigger's Song," "Bleeding Muddy Water," "Judas Touch," "Riding the Nightingale," "Miracle," "Phantasmagoria Blues," "Because of This"

NIN: "Deep"

Orgy: "Blue Monday"

People in Planes: "Vampire"

Puddle of Mudd: "Psycho"

Róisín Murphy: "Ramalama (Bang Bang)"

Rolling Stones: "Sympathy for the Devil"

Stone Temple Pilots: "Sour Girl"

Sully Erna: "The Rise," "Avalon"

Thompson Twins: "The Gap"

Todd Alan: "Gently Johnny," "We Are the Walking Breath"

Transplants: "Diamonds & Guns"

The Verve: "Bittersweet Symphony"

Warchild: "Ash"

Woodland: "Rose Red," "First Melt," "I Remember," "The Dragon," "Morgana Moon"

Zero 7: "In the Waiting Line"

Dear Reader:

I truly hope you enjoyed Haunted Moon, *the thirteenth book in the Otherworld Series. I love writing this world; it expands and grows with each book, and I see so many possibilities ahead for the Sisters. The next book in this series will be* Autumn Whispers, *book fourteen, coming in October 2013. But before then,* Night Vision, *book four of the Indigo Court Series, will be released in July 2013.*

And so, I'm including the first chapter of Night Vision *here, to give you a taste of what's coming up in Cicely's world as she battles Queen Myst for control of the Golden Wood.*

For those of you new to my books, I hope you've enjoyed your first foray into my worlds. For those of you who have followed me for a while, I want to thank you for once again revisiting the world of Camille, Menolly, and Delilah.

Bright Blessings,
The Painted Panther
Yasmine Galenorn

As I stepped out from the forest, under the open stars, the dark silhouette of the Veil House warmed my heart, but it was a bittersweet moment. The house stood silent against the night sky, but signs abounded that it was slowly returning to life. The walls had been rebuilt, the roof repaired, and it was beginning to look like a house again rather than the bombed-out shelter that it had become. But it would never again be my home. After too many years on the road as a child, I'd returned to New Forest, Washington. I'd come home to my aunt Heather and the Veil House, only to lose both of them for good.

So much had changed over the past few weeks since I'd rolled into town. And so much was still in flux. Literally caught up by a whirlwind, I barely recognized myself now. Everything I'd ever thought about my childhood and heritage had been turned upside down.

A light flurry of snow fell softly, drifting flakes clinging to my shoulders like frozen butterflies. It was still cold, my breath a pale fog in front of me. Over the past weeks, I'd learned to hate the snow. Myst had destroyed my love for the icy months of the year.

"You'd better learn to love the cold," I whispered to myself. "Soon enough, winter will be your permanent home." I was standing on the precipice of a transformation, but for today, I was still Cicely Waters, Wind Witch and Owl Shifter. But soon, I'd be . . .

Who am I becoming, Ulean?

Are you afraid? Do not worry. The initiation will change you—make you stronger.

Again, I shivered. *That's exactly what frightens me. Will I still be me afterward?*

Ulean's laughter surrounded me, a gentle breeze that swept by, almost warm in its touch. The Wind Elemental had been with me since I was six years old. We were bound, and she guarded my back.

You will always be who you are. You'll just . . . know more about yourself—you'll learn to control your emerging powers better. You'll be you, but you'll also be a queen. And I will always be with you. Lainule bound me to your service before you ever knew who or what you were to become. Her visions guided her. I will not leave you.

And then she fell silent, leaving me with my thoughts again.

I kicked a pile of snow, wishing for spring. Wishing for any season that involved green growing things. Myst, Queen of the Indigo Court—the Vampiric Fae and upstart winter queen—had brought the eternal winter to town, determined to spread her ice and chill across the land. Her Shadow Hunters fed on bone and gristle and marrow and life force. Once we finally defeated Myst, the seasons would return to their normal ebb and flow, but until that day, we were caught in her unwavering grasp, even though we'd driven her into hiding.

"Any sign of Shadow Hunters?" Rhiannon, my cousin, emerged from the wood to stand beside me. "I'm sorry I'm late—the Summer Court has been keeping me busy." She sounded less than thrilled, but I knew that it was just her nerves acting up, the same as me.

I shook my head. "I don't see any. But they're out there, somewhere. I doubt if they'll show themselves until Myst regroups her forces. Who knows how many of them managed to escape? And there were plenty of others scattered around the country. And you know that they will come to her aid when she calls. She's just biding her time until she rebuilds her army."

"That's what I'm afraid of." Rhiannon glanced over her shoulders. "I wish I felt it was safe to go out alone. Do you think we should go back, bring a couple of the guards?"

I glanced back at the trees. They were back there, hiding in the woods, ready to join us if we required. But I'd managed to convince Lainule that—with Myst currently out of the picture—we really didn't need them, especially when we were headed to the Emissary's mansion. Myst couldn't get through their defenses—not when she was at the peak of her power, and not now.

"I think we'll be fine." I paused, then added, "But soon enough, they won't allow us to go out alone. Although, come to think of it, Lainule does. So, maybe . . . maybe . . . they won't be on our tail every place we go."

As the dusk fell across the snowbound evening, Ulean whipped around me. She seemed agitated.

Trouble. There is trouble in the Veil House.

Fuck. Maybe we *did* need the guards. *Shadow Hunters?*

No, not Shadow Hunters. Vampires, and they have Luna with them. She's afraid and she's hurt. I can feel her fear.

I turned to Rhiannon. "Luna's in the house and Ulean says she's hurt. There are vampires in there with her." I rushed forward, now hoping the guards would follow. I had no idea if they could see us from where they were in the forest.

Rhiannon plunged through the snow after me. "Damn it! Lannan promised allegiance—"

I raced through the snow, slipping on the icy crust a couple of times. "I don't think it's Lannan."

"Then who?"

"I don't know, but Lannan wouldn't do this, even as perverted as he is."

A sense of dread seeped through me. We'd gotten cocky and we'd gotten careless. Luna had gone to the market, assuring us she would be fine, and stupid us, we'd let her go.

As I bounded up the back porch of the Veil House, I saw that it had been fully repaired. I glanced over my shoulder. No sign of the guards.

Ulean, please warn Lainule we need help?

I will. Be cautious, Cicely. I do not know what's going on in there.

With Rhiannon right behind me, I slammed through the door and into the kitchen, skidding to a halt, but it was empty. Nothing but a silent room.

The kitchen had been entirely rebuilt. The new color was chiffon yellow, pale as the cool morning light in early spring, and it spread across the room, a gradient of apricot blushing toward the ceiling. The trim had been replaced, and all the cabinets and cupboards. The workmanship was meticulous.

I glanced around, trying to decide whether to go up the back staircase to the bedrooms or—

A noise from the living room caught my attention and I slowed, motioning for Rhiannon to keep behind me. I felt for the sheath hanging off my belt, gripping the hilt of my new dagger. Lainule herself had given it to me, and it was fit for a queen—wickedly sharp, made from a magical silver alloy, and deadly. Behind me, Rhiannon drew her matching blade.

We crept to the edge of the living room and peeked in. Here, where the smoke had damaged furniture and wallpaper but not the actual structure, the walls had been stripped, and now a pale green illuminated the room, and new furniture.

Standing in the middle of the room were two men— vampires by the looks of their eyes—wearing dark suits. Between them, they had hold of Luna, each holding one of her arms. They were ignoring her as they talked in soft whispers.

Luna was crying, softly, and I saw her shiver as one of the vamps reached down and tipped her chin up to stare him in the face. He said something and she let out a whimper, then fell silent.

"So, what the fuck are you doing with my friend?" I stepped out from around the wall. We needed more backup but we couldn't wait. What if they tried to kill her?

The vamps glanced over at me, then one snorted.

"Took you long enough, *witch*. We're here to deliver a message." He let go of Luna and shoved her forward with so much force that she went sprawling at my feet.

She landed hard on the floor, and I quickly bent to help her up. Struggling, she looked up at me, dazed. Her eyes were wide, and two ragged punctures marred her neck, dried blood from them coating her skin. I knew exactly what that meant.

"You fucking perverts, you fed from her." I whirled on them. "You'd better not be aligned with Lannan or I swear, I'll—"

The first vamp sneered. "Are you talking to us, little girl? Try being a little more respectful. You see, we don't give a fuck about your powers or your lineage or the fact that your oh-so-fragile neck is going to be used to hold up a pretty little diadem."

"Shut up," his partner said. He pointed to Luna. "The *girl* is your message." They turned to go, then glanced back. "Next time we meet, the warning will be harsher. You might caution your friends about being so carefree. We could have broken her neck without blinking an eye and left her on the street. We could have turned her and taken her with us."

"Who sent you? Who are you working for?"

They laughed. "You'll find out soon enough. We're just administering a not-so-gentle reminder that not all vampires in New Forest are as entranced with you as is that sycophant Altos, and his bitch whore sister."

I drew back my dagger, knowing it was a foolish move. But I had to do something. I couldn't take them down with it, but I could do my best to protect us—at least for a while. I moved in front of Luna.

"I don't care who hates me. Just don't take it out on my friends—" And then, I paused. Crap. I knew who had sent them. At least, I was pretty sure. "Geoffrey and Leo sent you, didn't they?" Behind me, Rhiannon gasped. "Get back, don't let them near you," I warned her, glancing over my shoulder to make sure nobody was behind us.

The larger vampire snorted. He cocked his head to the side, his obsidian eyes gleaming. "Don't worry. We're not out for the win. Yet. Just consider this visit a promise of things to come. Geoffrey likes the chase and the hunt. But you'd better prepare yourselves. Because when it's time to get real, little girl, you can be sure there won't be any place to hide."

And then, in a blur so fast I couldn't see them move, they were gone.

I stared at the front door. It was open, blowing in the wind.

"We're in deep shit, aren't we?" Rhiannon leaned close to me.

I nodded, staring at the snow that swirled in on the wind. "Yeah," I said softly. "And somehow, I don't think anything's going to get easier. Not for a long time."

Rhia and I managed to get Luna onto the sofa. I was attending to her wounds—the punctures were jagged and deep, and she'd lost a fair amount of blood—when Grieve burst through, followed by Kaylin and several guards.

Kaylin took one look at Luna, on whom he was crushing bad, and rushed over, sliding to the floor beside the couch. "Is she—" He glanced up at me.

"I'm not dead, if that's what you're asking." Luna groaned and sat up, pressing her hand gently to the bandage on her neck. "But damn, I hurt, and I'm dizzy."

"She's lost a lot of blood." I glanced around. "And there's no food in this place. We need to get her something to eat."

Kaylin pulled a candy bar out of his pocket and pressed it into her hands. "What happened? Did you cut yourself? Lainule said there were vampires up here . . ." He glanced around. The guards had already spread out through the house, making sure the coast was clear.

"The vamps are gone, for now." I let out a deep breath. "Geoffrey and Leo sent them. Luna . . . they . . ." My gaze went to the bandage on her neck.

Kaylin followed my look. "Those fuckers drank from her?"

His eyes grew dark. He was Chinese, and his long hair was pulled back in a ponytail. He looked our age—around his mid to late twenties—but in reality he was more than a hundred years old. With a night-veil demon wedded to his soul, Kaylin walked in shadows, in the dark.

"Yeah," I said slowly, standing so I could stop him if he tried to follow them. His eyes flashed dangerously, lighting with a fire I had only seen once or twice. "She'll be okay, Kaylin. They didn't feed enough to endanger her life."

I turned to Luna. "Can you tell us what happened?"

She shuddered. "I was on my way to the market—I wanted to make apple pie, but they don't have everything I need at the Barrow. I told the guards I'd be fine. If anybody had to worry about going out alone during the day, I thought it would be you and Rhiannon. I argued with them until they let me go alone."

"You left around four, right?"

"Yes. I wanted to stop in at the bookstore to see if a book I ordered last week had come in. It felt so good to walk down the sidewalk without being afraid that the Shadow Hunters would be hiding." She grimaced and stretched her neck, wincing from the pain of the bite. Vampires could make you come by drinking from you, but the aftermath? Not so fun. Kaylin and I helped her sit down again.

"I guess you should have taken a guard with you." I stopped, realizing I'd just spouted off advice Rhia and I had refused to take. With a sigh, I shrugged. "What happened next?"

"I stopped at a coffee shop after that, then the market. When I came out, it was just after sunset. I was waiting at a bus stop, to return here, when they came out of the alleyway. Before I knew what was happening, they grabbed me and we were standing in the alley. My packages were on the ground, and they had me pressed up against the wall. One of them turned to look at me, and that's when I realized they were vampires. I tried to look away but . . ."

Vampires could mesmerize with their gazes, and Luna, magical as she was, couldn't possibly hope to stand up against them.

"They both fed on me." Her voice was thick and she blushed. "I liked it. I hate saying that, but they made me like it. I feel . . . dirty. Used."

"Yeah, they have a way of making you feel like that. You didn't do anything wrong. This wasn't your fault." I flashed a look at Kaylin that said, *Don't say a word*, and then knelt beside her. "Did they do anything . . . else to you?"

She shook her head. "They dragged me into a limo. And then . . . we were here. I thought they were going to kill me, but the one—the bigger one—just told me that I was lucky this time. Then he grinned and said that next time, he'd finish me off himself. He said my blood was sweet." Another shudder, another look of horror. "That's right when you came in."

"Kaylin, take her back to the Barrows and make sure she's okay."

Kaylin said nothing, but wrapped his arms around her shoulders and, once again, helped her stand. It was obvious she was weak. Luna was short, plump, and pretty. The demon within Kaylin's soul gave him extra strength and speed, though, and he picked her up as if she was light as a feather, and carried her out the door, calling to one of the guards to accompany them.

As they left, I turned to Grieve and Rhiannon. "Want to make a bet this has something to do with our meeting with Regina?"

"You need to take guards with you, since I am not invited." Grieve glowered. He hated it when I went into Lannan's territory without him, but there wasn't much we could do about it. Having them in the same room together just wasn't conducive to keeping the peace.

I bit my lip. "Twenty minutes ago, I would have said no.

Now? Not so much. We'll take them, but they can't ride in the car. The iron would hurt them."

I pulled out my cell phone and dialed Regina's number.

Within seconds, the Emissary for the Crimson Court answered, her voice slick like honey and oil.

"Regina, Geoffrey and Leo just delivered a bloody message to us. I need to bring guards with us. You will allow them through the gate, tonight?"

Silence for a count of one . . . two . . . three. Then, she answered, in a voice that wavered only in the slightest. But that faint quiver told me there was cause for concern. "Of course. I'll tell my guards to be ready for them. How many are you bringing?"

"Five should do it. And Regina, thank you." Without waiting for an answer, I punched the End Call button. I knew Regina well enough to know that she wasn't going to say anything more over the phone. I notified the guards of the sudden change in plans, and they took off, heading for Lannan and Regina's mansion.

As Rhiannon and I prepared to leave, I held out my arms. Grieve, my Fae Prince, slid willingly into my embrace. "I wish you could go with me, but not a good idea." Softly, I kissed his lips, and he growled a little, causing the wolf tattoo on my stomach to respond. "I'll be careful, I promise."

"See that you are." His dark eyes were as black as the vampires', but their onyx core was filled with gleaming stars. Platinum hair cascaded down his shoulders, and he reached up, solemnly, to stroke my face, smelling of cinnamon and apples, bonfires and autumn leaves. "You are my everything. You are my queen. Do not let the darkness swallow you, my love."

Nodding, I turned to Rhiannon, who followed me out the door. The guards were already off and running toward Regina and Lannan's mansion. They would meet us there.

As we hurried to clamber into my Pontiac GTO, several armed guards waited beside it, making sure we were safely away. I turned the ignition, dreading what the rest of the night held. Because I knew in my heart the news was only going to get worse.

* * *

"They're never going to give up until they get even, are they?
Rhia leaned her head against the window, watching as the
dusky evening slid by.

I shook my head. "No, I don't think so. I wish I could say
yes and mean it, but . . . Leo and Geoffrey . . . they're dangerous. Not as dangerous as Myst, but we can't underestimate them. Regina sounded . . . almost . . . afraid."

Rhia jerked around. "Afraid? *Regina?*"

"Yeah, I know—an oxymoron. But she sounded . . .
cautious."

A brief flutter of fear raced through my stomach, knotting
it, but I pushed it away, focusing on the icy street as I navi-
gated through the silent neighborhoods. So many people had
fled New Forest, and though some were coming back, the
town seemed unnaturally quiet and subdued.

"We'll know what she knows soon enough." I turned onto
the street that led toward Lannan's mansion. The estate had
belonged to Geoffrey until he'd defied the Crimson Court
and been ousted from his position of regent. Now Lannan
Altos, the golden boy of the vampire nation and my personal
nemesis, had taken over the job.

The brilliant mansion lit up the night as we approached.
Gleaming white with gold trim, the behemoth rose three sto-
ries high, with who knew how many stories below ground.
Columns lined the wraparound porch, and urns sported rose
bushes that nestled beneath the snow. The tableau suggested a
Grecian temple more than a mansion belonging to New
Forest.

The entire estate sprawled across two acres, fully gated and
surrounded by snow-covered gardens and security guards in
dark suits. Vampires they might be, but they also carried guns
and stakes and whatever else they might need to defend
against enemies.

As we pulled in, one of the guards hurried up to open my
door. They knew my car by now and only gave us a cursory

pat-down. With their obsidian eyes cloaked behind dark glasses, and dressed in black suits, the vamps had an old-time gangster look going on. But there was no mistake—they were *vampires*, far deadlier than the yummanii mobsters.

Beside them stood our guards. I saluted them and they bowed, which felt weird as hell, but considering I was in line to become the Queen of Winter, and Rhiannon, the Queen of Summer, we'd have to get used to it.

I handed my keys to the valet. As we started up the steps, he carefully eased Favonis out of the way.

Rhia and I glanced at each other.

"I hate going in without backup," she said.

"I know, but Regina will keep us safe. Even though she's the Emissary to the Crimson Court, I trust her. She *has* to be diplomatic, and she knows that the Cambyra nation would come down on her head if either of us were hurt."

As soon as I rang the bell, the door swung open. The maid who answered was a bloodwhore, but she was perfectly made up, with her hair in a chignon, and wearing a stiffly pressed uniform and heels. She had to belong to Regina's stable.

"We're here to see Regina."

The woman curtsied, then led us through the spacious foyer, past the office that had once been Geoffrey's. But we didn't stop there. Instead, she led us to the next door down the hallway, where she tapped discreetly. After a moment, she opened the door, peeked inside, and whispered something. Then, standing back, she ushered us in.

As we entered the room, I was surprised to see that it was yet another office, but this was oh-so-official, with what I assumed was a print of the royal seal hanging over the cherrywood desk. The polished desk was a monster, filling a good one-third of the room. The top was clear except for an appointment book, a pen on a blotter, and a bronze statue that at first looked to be a woman kissing a man. As I drew closer, I saw that it was actually a vampire holding her victim.

Regina, behind the desk, stood as we entered.

She was blond like her brother; her hair was swept into an

intricate updo that must have taken an hour to fix. She wore a black linen pencil skirt that hugged her hips and a red corset, boosting her cleavage in an impressive display.

A large ruby teardrop flanked by two diamond baguettes hung around her neck from a gold chain. I knew they were ruby and diamond because Regina would never stoop to wearing costume jewelry. Matching earrings dangled from her ears, and her face was flawlessly made up.

Regina's eyes glowed with the soft, unbroken obsidian of all true vampires. She wore a neutral eye shadow, with thin, precise liner and heavy mascara that glittered with gold flecks. Her lips were crimson, moist and alluring, and her alabaster skin was like fine porcelain. When she smiled, the tips of her fangs showing, and motioned for us to sit, I felt a brief rush of hunger.

"Cicely, Rhiannon . . . please make yourselves comfortable." She waited until we were seated on the dusky mauve divan opposite her desk, then motioned for the maid to leave and close the door behind her. Sitting back, she studied us carefully, as if she were gauging what to say—or, perhaps, *how* to say it.

I leaned back against the velvet of the divan. I'd learned never to rush a vampire. The more you pushed, the more they pushed back. So we waited. Rhiannon nervously knotted her sweater sleeve in her hand, but after a moment, she let out a long breath and finally leaned back, waiting with me.

Regina stepped from behind her desk, crossing to the front, where she leaned her butt against the edge, her long legs stretched out in front, ending in five-inch stilettos. She glanced at the door.

"Lannan will be joining us shortly." She held up her hand as I shifted uncomfortably. "I know you'd prefer to deal with just me, but the fact is that he must hear what I have to say. Trust me, the news won't be pleasant for either of you."

"I have the feeling it will be just about as cheery as what we have to tell you."

On that happy note, we went back to staring at each other. Even though she didn't try to pull glamour on me, her gaze

unnerved me. I licked my lips and yawned, quickly trying to
cover my mouth. Were queens even supposed to yawn in
public? Flustered, I glanced up at the gorgeous vampire, and
to my surprise, Regina flashed me a little smile—probably as
genuine as she could manage.

"There are so many things changing. The old ways no
longer serve your people, nor mine. We must learn to adapt. I
think that our two nations have much to explore over the
coming decades, don't you think?"

Before I could answer, she straightened up. "But I'm
being remiss in my duties as hostess. Would you care for
something to drink? Some wine, or sparkling water, or a
café au lait?"

I was about to say no, when Rhiannon surprised me by
speaking up.

"Some sparkling water would be nice, with ice if you have
it." She cleared her throat and straightened her shoulders.

"And she can actually speak." Regina's laugh was throaty
and rich. I could never tell if she was making fun of us or
truly found us amusing. Either way, she rang a small bell and
a different maid immediately entered the room.

"Sparkling water for the Queen of Summer. Cicely—
what will you have?" Regina expected an answer, and so I
blurted out the first thing that came to mind.

"Mocha, please, with extra chocolate." A jolt of caffeine
would do me some good.

"Mocha, for the Queen of Winter. Extra chocolate and—I
think—an extra shot of espresso." Regina dismissed her
with the flick of a finger, and the woman scurried out of the
room.

It was still hard for me, watching the vampires treat their
servants like chattel, but even more disturbing, I realized I
was growing used to it.

After another awkward silence, the woman returned with
our drinks. Directly on her heels was Lannan Altos, who
swept over to Regina and kissed her hand and then her lips,
his tongue playing over them. After the maid had given us
our drinks, Lannan turned to face us.

Lannan Altos, Regina's brother and her lover. Originally from Sumer, they were two of the older vampires around. And Lannan Altos was my bane.

Lannan of the golden hair that flowed down his back, and the sleek, tight build. Lannan, the hedonist, whose obsession for me had become a dangerous game. Lannan, who longed to take me down and make me grovel willingly at his feet. Lannan, who enjoyed games of humiliation, at others' expense.

But Lannan—pervert though he was—had helped us when we needed it, though whether it was due to his own twisted agenda or not, I wasn't sure. And that meant I had to walk softly and try to keep out of his clutches and stay on his good side. He could do far more damage to me and our cause against Myst than I could do against him. *Yet.*

Rhiannon and I stood, giving him a cursory bow. As Regent, his position almost demanded it.

He moved in close, looming over me, and I was keenly aware of his presence. My body responded to him. It remembered him in a way I didn't want it to.

"A matter was brought to our attention just this evening, so I apologize for my tardiness. You will forgive me, won't you? Cicely?" And he fastened his gaze on me, holding me entranced with those eternally black orbs he called eyes.

I cleared my throat, mulling over the best response. After our last interaction—the day I'd left the mansion—I wanted nothing more than to kick him in the balls, but diplomacy won out for once.

"Of course." I turned to Regina. "But first, let me tell you what happened tonight." I told them about Luna and the vamps, and the message from Geoffrey and Leo. "We have to find them. We *have* to stop them."

Regina pressed her lips together before answering. Her voice was tight and brusque. "I have been in communication with the Crimson Queen. The situation is far more dire than you think."

Uh-oh. That couldn't be good. I glanced at Rhia and we waited for Regina to continue.

"When one of our esteemed Vein Lords went to visit the

Oracle yesterday, he discovered that . . . well . . . Crawl has gone missing."

"Missing?" At first I thought I'd heard her wrong, but one look at her face and I knew she was telling us the truth. Four little words. Enough to crumble the world.

Lannan stared at me, unblinking. "Yes, Crawl is missing and no one knows how he escaped from his prison." His voice echoed through the room, no longer smooth and elegant, but instead harsh and throaty. He was on his feet the next moment, pacing back and forth.

"Prison? Crawl's chamber is a *prison*?" That was the first I'd heard to that effect.

The Blood Oracle was esteemed, a seer among his people, revered as almost a god. I had no idea he was a prisoner, though it made sense. I knew they'd kept him tucked away between the worlds with good reason. The freak show was deadly, with no conscience whatsoever.

Lannan glanced at me. "Crawl was imprisoned by the Crimson Queen eons ago, when she first anointed him as the Blood Oracle. He's far too powerful and dangerous to be allowed among the populace, especially around breathers."

He paused by me, lifting my chin to stare into my face with those gleaming black eyes of his. "You, of all people, should know what he can be like, my sweet Cicely." And the Golden Boy was back.

Shivering—from both his touch and the memory of Crawl tearing into my neck with wanton thirst—I swallowed the lump rising in my throat and forced myself to remain steady.

Rhiannon looked ready to faint. "How did he get loose?"

Regina grimaced. "Not without help, I can tell you that."

The idea of someone helping Crawl escape was ludicrous. "Who the fuck would want to help him get free?"

She gave me a long look. "Think, Cicely. Who has everything to gain by causing mayhem?"

And then I knew. "Geoffrey . . ."

"Yes, Geoffrey and Leo found a way to set him free. Word on the street is that Geoffrey is planning a major coup against Lannan and me, while Leo's out for revenge against Cicely, and we also believe he means to kidnap Rhiannon."

"But why *Crawl*?" Rhia was so pale, she looked as bloodless as the vamps.

Lannan answered. "Crawl can wield dark magic. Ever since he tasted Cicely's blood, he's been talking about how sweet and rich and tender she was. The Oracle does not forget lightly."

"Leo means to turn me into a vampire," Rhia said.

Lannan nodded. "No doubt. And to exact his revenge on Cicely . . ."

Regina regarded him somberly. "To exact his revenge on the new Queen of Winter, he means to turn Cicely over to Crawl . . ." She paused, shuddering. "I wouldn't wish my worst enemy to be at the mercy of the Blood Oracle."

The room fell silent. I could barely think, let alone speak.

Lannan cleared his throat after a moment. "What are the Crimson Queen's orders?"

Regina held up what looked like an official decree. "Direct from the Queen: Our first order is to secure the safety of the newly arisen Fae Queens and New Forest. If Crawl is set free among the townspeople, the Vampire Nation will suffer irreversible damage to our reputation. *Then*—second—we find Crawl and return him to his prison. And third: We've been ordered to terminate Geoffrey and Leo."

"Do you know where they are?" I asked.

She let out a soft whisper. "No. We have no idea. I sent in guards to raid their last known hideaway earlier this evening. There was no trace of them or where they went. The owner of the club died under torture without revealing their whereabouts."

I crossed to the big bay windows. Every morning, they were covered with steel shutters. Now I stared outside, into the dim night.

The snow was piling up again. Myst was still out there, gunning for us. And now Leo and Geoffrey had freed a monster from his dark and fiery hell to claim the streets of the town for his own.

Myst was a holy terror, but she was somewhat predictable. Whereas Crawl . . . Crawl was beyond comprehension. He was as alien as an insect, and as dangerous as any predator who ruled the top of the food chain. Crawl wanted my blood, and Leo and Geoffrey were only too happy to serve me up on a platter.

Lannan was suddenly behind me, making no noise with his approach. He placed his hands on my shoulders and leaned down to whisper in my ear. "Are you afraid, Cicely?"

I turned to stare at him over my shoulder. He wasn't being sarcastic this time. His question seemed oddly genuine.

"Yes, I'm afraid."

"My offer stands, you know. Let me turn you. Renounce the Fae world and join me. It would be easy for you to fight back then. With your powers, combined with me as your sire, you could defeat Leo and Geoffrey."

His words entwined around me, and the wolf tattoo on my stomach growled a low warning note. Grieve could tell I was near to his rival.

I shook my head. "No. But, thank you. I think you really mean it—you really want to help."

"Don't be so quick to know what I want, girl." Lannan let out a low laugh. "I just don't want to lose you."

But the look on his face told me that Rhiannon and I weren't the only ones who were afraid. I turned to look at Regina. She, too, wore a look of concern on her face.

As I stared back into the night, too aware of Lannan's hands still on my shoulders, I thought I saw something dart past the window. As I wiped my eyes, whatever it was seemed to disappear.

Too much—there were too many enemies. Too much stress. I just wanted to go home and crawl under the covers, but even *home* now had a new meaning. Rhiannon joined me at the window, and I took her hand in mine. We stood there, linked, twin-cousins, fire and ice against the shadows outside, as they grew dark and long, and looming.

4980

Don't miss a word from the "erotic and darkly bewitching"[*] series featuring the D'Artigo sisters, half-human, half-Fae supernatural agents.

By *New York Times* Bestselling Author
Yasmine Galenorn

WITCHLING
CHANGELING
DARKLING
DRAGON WYTCH
NIGHT HUNTRESS
DEMON MISTRESS
BONE MAGIC
HARVEST HUNTING
BLOOD WYNE
COURTING DARKNESS
SHADED VISION
SHADOW RISING
HAUNTED MOON

Praise for the Otherworld series:

"Galenorn creates a world I never want to leave."
—*New York Times* bestselling author Sherrilyn Kenyon

"Thrilling, chilling, and deliciously dark."
—Alyssa Day, *New York Times* bestselling author

facebook.com/AuthorYasmineGalenorn
facebook.com/ProjectParanormalBooks
penguin.com

[*]Jeaniene Frost, *New York Times* bestselling author

M192AS0812